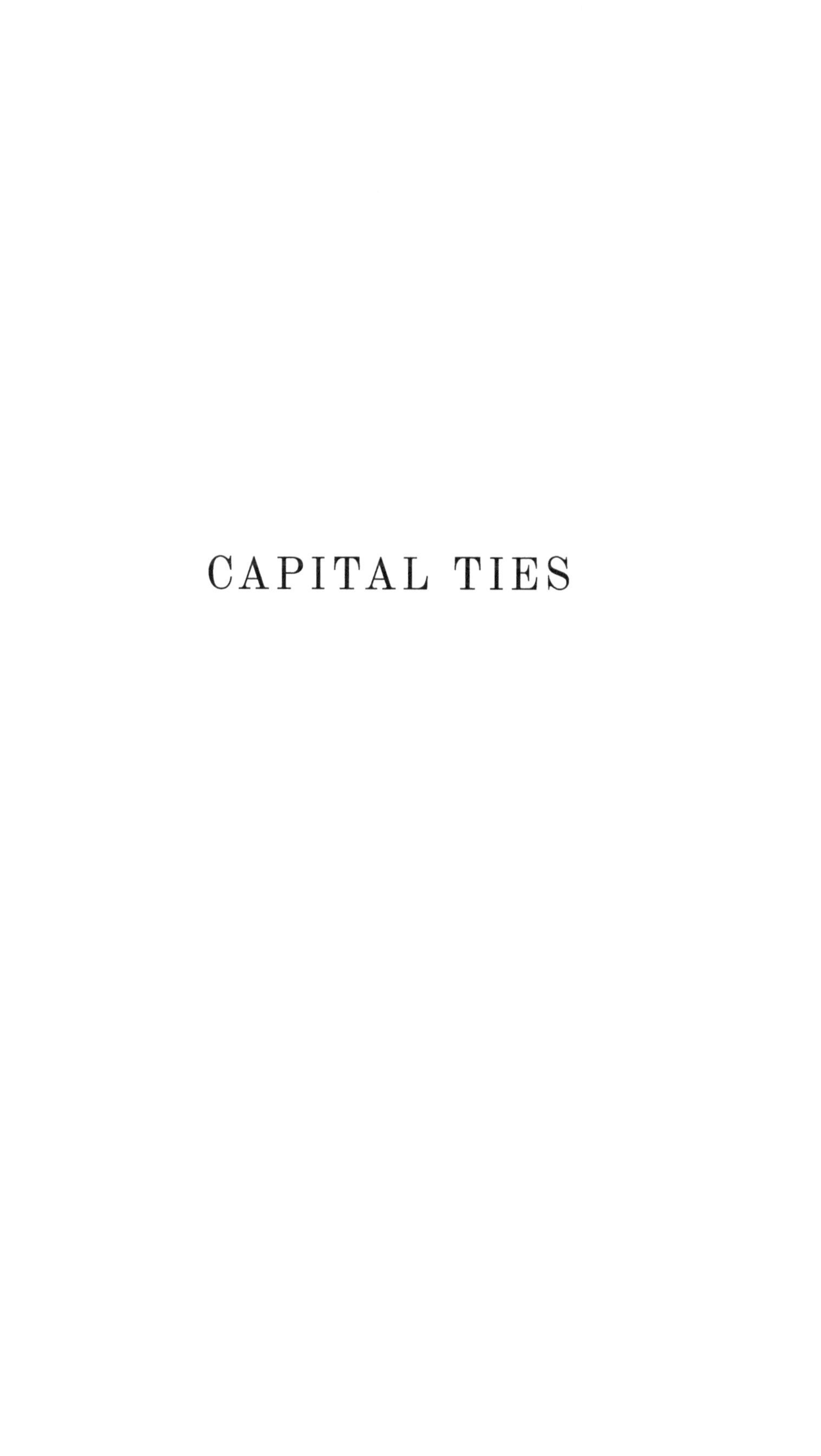

CAPITAL TIES

Capital Ties

A. J. Campbell

This book is a work of fiction. Names, characters, places, and incidents are the product of the author's imagination or are used fictitiously. Any resemblance to actual events, locales, or persons, living or dead, is coincidental.

First Printing, 2025

I dedicate this book to my family, who have been infinitely supportive of my writing journey.

I hope that they will never read it.

Content Warning

If you are offended by the idea of a woman
who is confident in her sexuality, who takes control
without apology, and who does not wait for permission
to enjoy herself, this book is not for you.

Capital Ties features powerful,
well-dressed, highly educated men & women,
who drop to their knees for a woman's attention and
beg for her approval.

This book includes: bondage, rope, impact play,
cunnilingus, dildos, vibrators, butt plugs, nipple clamps,
group sex, strap-ons, public teasing, secret clubs,
human buffets, and the occasional
orgasm delivered by a motorcycle.

There are sex parties, pansexual encounters,
and a narrator, that is me,
who never once asks for forgiveness.

Contents

1

Prologue

I am not a whore, though I have no doubt I'll be called one—mostly by men with podcast microphones and backward baseball caps. The kind of men who spend hours in their man caves debating women's worth as if it were fantasy football, all while secretly imagining themselves bent over a desk and spanked for being a bad boy. They think they're Casanova, but most are just drive-thru lovers—fast, messy, and gone before the sauce hits the bag.

These same podcast bros will screech into their ring lights about how women with "high body counts" are damaged goods, while their own sexual résumés are worn like military honors. But if we counted only the number of times a woman actually climaxed with one of them, their numbers would collapse faster than their masculinity at a consent workshop. Because here's the truth they will never admit—getting the girl isn't the win. Getting her off is. And let me be perfectly clear: that's the only score that counts.

If you clutch pearls at the idea of women wanting or enjoying sex, or you think a woman's sexual history is up for public debate like a Senate bill, I'll save you some time: close this book. No hard feelings. We both should know our limits.

Still here? Good. Consent is important. Enthusiastic consent is preferred. And if you don't know the difference, you won't survive three pages of this.

You're the kind of reader I want—someone who knows how to follow directions and isn't afraid of provocation, darkness, and heat. Someone who can handle the words pussy and cock without giggling like a middle schooler. Someone who doesn't mistake kink for abuse or fantasy for reality.

Here, a woman's sexual résumé is a badge of honor, not a liability. In my world, experience is not something to be erased for a wedding day—it's currency, and I spend it freely. What you're about to dive into is a curated collection of twenty-six intimate encounters—my personal and political, erotic and psychological adventures laid bare. Think of it as a guided tour through my mind, my memory, and my ever-evolving understanding of power, pleasure, and control.

Most of these stories unfold in and around Washington, D.C., a city that thrives on secrecy. Power suits by day, handcuffs by night. Beneath its marble columns and polished credentials, D.C. simmers with repression—perhaps that's why it burns so brightly when the mask slips and desire takes over.

The more buttoned-up someone appears, the wilder their secrets tend to be. I've seen it: sex clubs, whispered invitations to discipline parties, married officials slipping out the back doors of embassies with flushed cheeks and trembling hands. This town has more hidden rendezvous, quiet swaps, and late-night Grindr notifications than at the Republican National Convention.

This book is part lie, truth, memoir, confession, and a scrapbook. Some of it happened exactly as I've written. Some of it didn't. On the advice of my lawyers—and a few still-furious exes—I won't be telling you which is which. You'll never get it out of me. You'll never know what's real here.

I've dominated men, women, and people who fall outside either category—sometimes with rope, sometimes with nothing more than my voice. Dominance has always come easily to me, as natural as breath. It's not about cruelty; it's about clarity. The clarity of asking for exactly what I want and making space for my partner to do the same.

Whether rough or tender, commanding or poetic, my dominance adapts to the moment, the mood, and the chemistry we create together. There are lines I won't cross, and there are others I blur on purpose. The trick is knowing what makes you feel powerful and alive. Sometimes the most intimate thing you can do is admit what you want. And sometimes the bravest thing is to hand over the reins.

For now, I'm in control. You came here for a reason, and it wasn't to read something safe. So, sit back. Take a breath. Keep at least one of your hands on the book at all times.

2

Higher Education

I was twenty-five when I stepped off the plane from Los Angeles to Washington, DC, for graduate school. I had two suitcases, blind ambition, and a head full of dreams. I wanted to dominate this world.

In Los Angeles, I had been sheltered. I'd rarely encountered truly brilliant people—the kind with 4.0 GPAs from Ivy League schools with the polish of silver spoons still warm from their mouths. I had never met anyone who was both dazzlingly intelligent and unapologetically competitive. Sure, Los Angeles has its rich and famous, but growing up around celebrities, I could not have cared less. In L.A., you are brilliant if you land a three-picture deal and a CAA agent. Washington was different. Here you might bump into a Nobel Prize winner at a coffee shop, a MacArthur "Genius" Grant recipient at happy hour, or a policy heavyweight in line for a salad.

One of the first events for grad school was a "get-to-know-you" booze cruise. Looking back, probably a bad idea. I was a teetotaler. I didn't drink much. I had no absolute tolerance. Meanwhile, here I was, thrust into a world where everyone could drink circles around me and still quote constitutional law while doing it.

Running late, I barely made it to the dock in Old Town Alexandria, where the boat was waiting. It wasn't a ship so much as a glorified ferry boat, but it had an open bar, and that was enough.

Starstruck, we sailed past monuments, the Jefferson, the Pentagon, all lit up beautifully against the night sky. People sipped wine,

laughed, and schmoozed. It didn't take long before someone found me. A PhD grad student sidled up next to me. It was him or the smarmy balding professor, thirty years my senior, who just had an essay in *The Atlantic* go viral, heading my way with hungry eyes. I learned a little something about casting couches in Los Angeles, to know that look at a distance. I practically leapt at the grad student like I was jumping out of a burning building.

"Hey," he said, grinning, brushing his tousled hair out of his eyes.

"Hey," I replied, grateful.

He was only a few years older, maybe four, and everything you would want in a desperate, tousled-haired academic: incredible body, beautiful face, and a library of Emerson quotes ready at his disposal. He could cite Kant, Marx, or Aesop whenever needed. It was charming. I was enchanted.

"You dance?" he asked suddenly, twirling me.

"Do I?" I laughed. "I mean, not well." I was being modest; I started dancing at age 3 in a Beverly Hills dance studio, where celebrities sent their kids, including a famous superstar.

"Good enough," he grinned, spinning me onto the dance floor.

There we stayed, the rest of the cruise. I barely noticed anyone else.

The monuments gleamed like stage lights around us. The DJ blasted music, not elegant, but enough. Pop songs, dance anthems. He spun me. Twirled me. Dipped me.

For that brief period, it felt like we were the only two people in the entire city. And for a girl who had just landed, carrying nothing but a dream and a heart full of reckless hope? It was magic.

I wasn't trying to get drunk, but I figured a little champagne couldn't possibly hurt. Then he dipped me on the dance floor, and I fell. He couldn't hold me. And I was *not* large at the time. I mean, I was tiny. But I had underestimated how drunk *he* was. Or maybe I was more intoxicated than I thought. Either way, we both went down.

My skirt flew up in full view of at least three professors and several of my not-yet friends. We all had a good laugh about it, thank God. He picked me up, spun me around like we were performing, and we both did a dramatic little bow to the crowd. It was very rom-com. Very Meet Cute.

As the boat pulled back up to the dock, he asked, "Some of my friends are going to grab a drink. Want to come with?"

I blinked. "You *just* dropped me on the dance floor. Maybe we should slow down a little?"

He laughed. "Fair, but come on, what's one more bar?"

Honestly, I didn't think too hard about it. DC is easy to get around. I didn't have a car. I'd just moved. I figured I could always get home on the metro or grab a cab. There were no Ubers back then, but it was still manageable.

So I said yes.

We went to a bar in the historic Old Town area. He introduced me to the rest of the grad student crowd, the people who'd become classmates, and eventually, some of them, friends. Thankfully, there were no more creepy professors around. Though they'd already gotten a full view when I fell earlier. So, what else was there to see?

He got me another drink. And then another. And then one more. And now, I was sideways sloshed. Like, how-is-this-real-life drunk.

He, however, was surprisingly sober. Or maybe just had a way higher tolerance than I did.

We waited a little. Walked around. Then he said, "Are you hungry? Want to grab dinner?"

Dinner in Old Town Alexandria, which is absurdly charming, the kind of place with federal-style houses from the 1700s, cobblestone streets, and perfect views of the waterfront. If the wind is right, you can even watch planes landing at Ruth Bader Ginsburg Airport (AKA Regan National or DCA). It was a gorgeous night.

He was quoting Schopenhauer, being charming, and putting on the whole show. I was tipsy, delighted, and mildly terrified.

After dinner, he asked, "Can I take you home?"

"Sure," I said. "Metro or cab?"

He grinned. "Neither. I have a motorcycle."

"Of *course* you have a motorcycle," I muttered. "Why wouldn't you have a motorcycle?"

He laughed. "You okay with that?"

"Are *you* sober enough to drive?"

"Promise. And I've got a helmet for you." I really hope that this is not the foreshadowing scene in the rom-com. It usually ends in a hospital scene.

Naturally, he didn't wear one himself. I'm not sure if that was legal. But at the time? I didn't care. Rules didn't apply to him. And suddenly, they didn't apply to me either.

I was wearing a short blue pleated skirt. The kind that flares. The type that is not meant for motorcycles.

Mounting the bike was no problem. The *wind,* however, was another story. My skirt flipped up like I was Marilyn Monroe standing over a subway grate. My entire seafood platter was on display.

He handed me the helmet, and he climbed on. I wrapped my arms around his waist and yelled, "So where exactly are we going?" as he revved the engine loudly.

"Home," he said. "Eventually. But first," he gunned the engine. "Let's take the scenic route."

"Have you ever seen the monuments at night?" he said.

I shook my head no. He sped off, fast. *Cue the theme song and the video montage.*

He took me onto the George Washington Memorial Parkway, not technically a freeway, but fast enough to make my stomach flutter, and I closed my eyes, hoping everything would be okay. We drove past the Capitol, and I got my very first view of it from the back of his motorcycle.

I remember thinking, *One day I'm going to be important here. One day I'll be in charge. One day, people will know my name.*

In that moment, I *believed* it. I wanted it so badly. I wanted to be someone who mattered, in a place where being smart mattered. Where knowing things mattered. Where control was currency. And on the back of that PhD candidate's bike, I felt like I was already becoming that person.

He took the long, meandering route through the city. Unnecessary. Utterly charming. The kind of thing you do on a first date to make it feel like a movie. And for me? It worked. I felt like I belonged. Like I was on the edge of something.

He pulled over by the P Street beach, the local name for a park near my apartment, even though there was parking right out front, and we took the longest possible walk back to my place. He just wanted to stretch the evening. And I didn't mind.

We didn't sleep together that night. But as we stood at my door, he was already locking in the next date.

"I want to see you again," he said. "I know I'll see you on campus, but I want to *see* you. Let's make a plan. Dinner? Movie? Whatever you want."

"Just call me. We will work out a time when I can see more of you." I flirted.

He was charming, clearly trying to impress me, and I was thrilled to be along for the ride. Literally.

What I *didn't* tell him, and wouldn't tell anyone else for a long time, was what happened on the back of that motorcycle.

I was tipsy. Relaxed. Holding on to his incredible body, those V-shaped obliques, the rock-hard abs, the way his skin smelled like cedar and sweat and whatever magic cologne he wore.

And the vibration of the motorcycle? I came. More than once.

I wasn't even wearing real underwear, just pantyhose. My skirt had already proven it had no structural integrity. So, with the wind flipping it up and my legs pressed tight against the seat, the combination of the engine, the rhythm, and the feel of him between my thighs.

I came. Three times. Silently. Just clinging to his body, head down, praying he didn't notice.

He may not have. Or maybe he did. The whole bike was vibrating; who could tell?

All I know is, by the time we got back to my apartment, I was lightheaded, flushed, and about one breath away from floating into the sky.

I didn't need him to come up. I wanted a minute to process. I kissed him goodnight and went upstairs to see if my vibrator would be a letdown after the Harley Davidson.

He DM'd me later that night.

"Thinking about you. Would love to grab a coffee between classes if you've got time."

I melted.

This would be the part of the rom-com when the girl puts on a skimpy outfit, dances around her apartment littered with unopened boxes, and writes in her diary about how she just met the man she was going to marry.

Instead, I got myself off again, I fell asleep happy after a 20-minute orgasm, thinking about how I wanted to ride the good doctor's face.

And in the morning? I poured myself a cup of ambition, yawned, stretched, and tried to pretend to hold back my excitement.

We grabbed a cup of coffee and flirted shamelessly.

He told me about his dissertation, quoted from Smith and Friedman, as if he had a pocket-sized library tucked in his jacket. He invited me to sit in on one of the economics classes he taught.

"Come on," he teased. "It will be fun."

"I'm not taking your economics class," I laughed. "Not unless you're offering extra credit."

"Maybe I am," he said, smiling that infuriating, devastating smile.

Eventually, I gave in. I went to his class.

He was ridiculous. *Adorable.* He showed up in a corduroy jacket with elbow patches, a plaid shirt, and a knit tie that looked like it time-traveled from 1976. He was a walking academic fantasy.

And he was good. Talking about Adam Smith, comparative advantage, and wine and cloth. I sat in the back row, pretending to be disinterested, but I failed miserably. I even asked a question.

"Is this where Adam Smith talks about the division of labor?" I asked, half shy, half trying to impress him.

He grinned. "Remind me, what's your name again?"

I crossed my legs *Basic Instinct* style. He seemed to lose his train of thought for a second. I told him he could call me Belle.

After class, we kept finding places to steal kisses: the Rose Garden, his shared office space, an empty classroom. We were like teenagers. No, worse. No dignity. Just pure, giddy chemistry.

There was a dance pavilion on campus, open-air and old-world romantic. He would grab my hand and twirl me around.

"Do you hear the music?" he whispered in my ear.

"Always," I whispered back as he spun me around.

Eventually, he invited me over to his apartment. Fifteen blocks away. A walkable distance that felt like a whole new city.

It was located in a beautiful pre-war building, featuring plaster moldings, crooked kitchens, and a mismatched interior. So much character it hurt. The space was small and neat. Books on every surface. Notes on the counter. Evidence of someone who lived in his head too much. I liked that. That meant there was more to untangle.

He made salmon for dinner. Something simple. His roommate was gone for the night.

Afterward, we ended up on the couch. Kissing. Hugging. Acting like teenagers again, wrapped around each other, not quite ready to let go of the moment. I remember thinking, Hold onto this. Don't fuck it up.

He pressed his forehead against mine. "You okay?" he asked softly.

I nodded. "Yeah." But part of me was terrified because I was serious. Serious in a way he didn't know yet. I wanted this to be real. I wanted him to want me, not just the kisses, not just the moment, but the messy, complicated reality of a life together. And somewhere deep down, I could already feel that we weren't on the same page.

Here I was in the vortex of power and ambition, and Dr. Charming was sitting across from me. And from the start, I sensed something: he didn't have the same power, not the way I did. He wasn't chasing influence. He was chasing a connection, physical, immediate. And that was okay. However, I was new to the city, and casual wasn't what I had come for. Still, it became clear that he had specific preferences, and so did I. He liked to be spanked, "naughty boy" style.

At first, I resisted. I wanted to wait until we were serious. Something about his charm made me suspect he had someone else, maybe more than one someone. A guy like that didn't walk around unattached. But he never admitted it. Perhaps he broke things off. Maybe I just wore him down. Either way, eventually, we crossed that line.

The first night was electric.

He was stunning, truly. Fit, defined, almost absurdly perfect for a guy allegedly living at the library. It didn't stop him from logging hours at the campus gym.

And now I knew he liked a little kink? Well, that sealed it.

I leaned in.

I went full college girl in my graduation robe, a push-up bra, thigh-high stockings, stilettos, and the world's most petite thong.

I knocked on his door and, when he opened it, said, "Ready for a little Pomp and Circumstance?"

His shirt was wrinkled like he had changed three times and given up. His glasses sat unevenly on his nose. I saw the nerves. I also saw the heat.

He smiled, but it was cautious. Then he laughed. Real. Warm. A burst that broke through the tension.

His mouth parted like he was about to say something else, but he thought better of it. Smart. He closed the door behind me.

I watched him track me with his eyes. He was trying to be polite, but his pulse betrayed him. I didn't. I didn't take off my gown. I just turned, slowly, until he was standing in front of me again.

"You want this," I said, steady and quiet.

He nodded.

"Then do exactly as I say."

"Yes, Belle."

I started soft. I ran my fingers down the front of his shirt, circled behind him, and let my voice brush his ear. My tone was light at first. I teased. I moved my hips in slow rhythm, enough to make him swallow hard. He stayed still, but his breath gave him away.

"I'm going to spank you," I said. "Do you understand?"

"Yes, Belle."

I stepped back and gave him one look. The kind that says remove everything, now.

He stripped slowly. Because he wanted it to matter. He folded his clothes in a stack. His chest was flushed by the time he stepped out of his briefs. His cock was already hard. His thighs tense. His shame was in every muscle.

I sat down on a wingback chair. "Over my lap."

He knelt and then positioned himself, awkward at first. He shifted until I corrected him. When I laid my hand on his back, he stilled. Obedient.

"Don't come. If you do, you lose the privilege of finishing the way you want."

He didn't speak. Just nodded.

I began.

The first strike was controlled. The second one is firmer. I spaced them just far enough apart to keep him guessing. I watched his hands grip the chair legs. He didn't beg. He didn't. But with every blow, he softened. The resistance drained from his shoulders. The sharp edges of his intellect dulled. He needed this. The rules. The pain. The control he didn't have to hold himself. And then he lost it.

No warning. No attempt to stop it. He came with a stuttering breath, spilling across the floor. His body collapsed against me. His voice cracked.

"I'm sorry. I didn't. I just—I couldn't—"

I caught his chin in my hand and made him look at me.

"You're finished."

His eyes widened.

"But I..."

I didn't use my command voice.

"On your knees."

He obeyed.

I stood, removed my robe, then sat back down and opened my legs.

"You're going to use your mouth," I said. "You're going to focus. You're going to do it well. You will not stop unless I say so. Do you understand?"

"Yes, Belle."

"Begin."

He leaned forward. I grabbed his head and pushed it into my pussy. I kept my hand on his hair. I could feel how hard he tried. This was never about punishment.

And when I finally let him look up, his lips were wet, his cheeks burning. He was grateful. He was mine. And I wasn't done with him yet.

When I finally pulled him up from between my thighs, his mouth was wet and his face flushed. He looked overwhelmed, but not from confusion. He was high on obedience, dizzy from the pressure, and utterly undone by what it felt like to serve. His eyes met mine, and I could see it in the way he blinked too slowly, as if the world had narrowed to just the two of us.

I gripped his jaw. Just enough to remind him who was in charge.

"Do you want to keep fucking me?" I teased him. There was no hesitation, only a small intake of breath and the kind of nod that comes from deep need.

"Yes, Belle. I want to. I need to."

I studied him a beat longer, then let go of his face and stood. His hands twitched like he wanted to help, but he didn't. I didn't give him permission. Just told him to go lie down on the bed.

I climbed on top and straddled him. His cock was hard again. Ready. Desperate. I didn't have time to process. I lifted him up and sank onto him in one sharp motion. He let out a strangled sound, part gasp, part moan, and tried to stay still.

"Keep your hands where I put them," I said, grabbing his wrists and pressing them into the mattress above his head. "You don't touch me unless I say so."

He nodded quickly, eyes locked on mine. I rode him at a pace that made him work for it, hips grinding in tight circles, enough pressure to drive him mad without letting him take control. He stayed still, mouth open, muscles tensed under me, trying not to thrust up even though I could feel every nerve in his body begging for more.

He was doing so well. His hips bucked hard. Once. Then again. He tried to stop himself. I slapped his chest.

"What did I say?"

He looked up at me, wild with frustration and shame.

"I'm sorry. I can't. I need to move—I needed more. Please let me."

I leaned down until my face was inches from his.

"You want to fuck me? Then do it right. Take control when I give it. Not before."

His voice cracked as he responded, barely above a whisper.

"Please."

I shifted off him and flipped us, fast and clean. I landed on my back and pulled him over me.

"Now," I said. "You have permission."

That was all it took.

He grabbed my thighs and pushed in deep, driving into me with force that caught even me off guard. The headboard slammed against the wall. The mattress shifted sideways. His thrusts were relentless, fast, brutal, and full of frantic energy he had been holding back for far too long. I pulled him into a kiss, hot and messy, biting at his lower lip until he groaned into my mouth. He was savage, passionate. I felt like every bit of effort he had was focused on me.

The bed groaned under us, the legs squeaking. Then one gave way. The frame tilted and cracked. Neither of us stopped. He didn't seem to notice. He was lost in it now. Possessed.

He held my hips and buried himself over and over, loud and breathless, fucking like it was the only thing he had ever wanted.

His cock was massive, and the moment he slid in, he hit my G-spot like he owned it. He knew exactly what he was doing. Each time he thrust, he grabbed my hips and tilted them just enough to keep grinding into that spot with perfect, brutal precision. I could barely breathe.

Then he leaned in, pressed the side of his hand against my clit—no nails, just soft skin and hard pressure. He rubbed tight circles, not letting up, not giving me space to squirm away. It was too much. I was shaking, locked between the force of his cock and the heat of his palm.

I tried to hold off, but my body betrayed me. I was right there, pulsing, desperate, clinging to him with every muscle I had. My walls clamped down so hard I could feel him groan inside me. There was nowhere to go, nothing to do but come. Hard. Deep. Wrung out and completely taken.

When I told him he could come, he let go with a shudder that seemed to rip through him from spine to toes. His whole body jerked forward and then slumped on top of me, trembling with exhaustion.

I stroked the back of his neck, keeping him there, skin to skin, his cock still twitching inside me. He was panting hard, trying to come back to himself.

"We broke the bed," I said eventually.

He didn't lift his head. His voice was muffled against my shoulder.

"I'll fix it. Just... let me lie here. Just a minute."

I let him. He'd earned that.

But I wasn't finished with him. Not by a long shot.

He lay on top of me, still catching his breath, the broken bed frame groaning beneath us. His weight felt good. Real. Warm. His cock was still buried inside me, softening slowly, but not for long.

I slid my fingers into his hair and gave it a slow, deliberate tug. "Don't get comfortable."

He lifted his head just enough to meet my eyes. His face was flushed, jaw slack, eyes still glassy with adrenaline. But underneath that exhaustion, I saw it. The spark. The want.

"I'm not," he said. "Not even close."

"Then get to work."

He pulled out and moved fast. I hadn't finished shifting upright before he had his mouth between my thighs again. His tongue found every tender place, licking with slow, wet precision, then faster when he felt my breath hitch. He didn't praise. He listened to my body. He responded to every shift in my hips, every change in how I gripped his hair. He stayed there until I arched, until my thighs shook, until I came on his face with no sound but a sharp exhale.

And still, he didn't stop.

When I reached for him, he came up with his mouth wet, eyes wide, cock already hard again. He moved above me like a man possessed, but this time he didn't ask for permission. He didn't need it. I had already given him the signal. He knew what I wanted now. He knew what I liked.

He slid back inside me and fucked with purpose. Not wild for the sake of it. Intentional. He shifted the angle, pressed his thumb to my clit, and watched my face until he found the rhythm that made me bite my lip.

Then he changed it.

He flipped me onto my side, wrapped one arm around my waist, and pulled my thigh back to open me up. He thrust deep in that position, letting the slap of our bodies fill the room, then slowed just enough to allow the pressure to build before driving forward again.

When my breath caught, he moved again. Onto his back this time, pulling me on top, making me ride him with my knees wide and his hands locked on my hips. He thrust up while I ground down, friction building sharp and fast, sweat slicking our skin.

I reached behind me, braced a hand on his thigh for better leverage, and rode harder. His fingers dug into my waist as he tried to keep pace. I clenched around him, and his eyes rolled back slightly. He was close. Again.

"Don't finish," I said, voice tight, hips still moving.

"I won't," he rasped through clenched teeth. "Not until you do."

He pulled me down to kiss me again, this time less desperate, more reverent. He rolled me to my back without losing contact. Then he pushed my legs up high and held them there, thrusting hard in long strokes, deep and punishing. I let him. I let him have the angle, the power, the burn in his arms and shoulders. He was doing it for me, not for himself. His whole body was committed to giving me exactly what I needed.

When I came again, I didn't warn him. I just locked my legs around his back and let go. He moaned when I tightened around him, when I shuddered, when I pulled his face down to kiss him again.

Finally, I pulled him back around and climbed over him once more. I wrapped my hand around his throat and leaned in.

"You've been good," I whispered. "Now you can come."

He didn't last more than three strokes. He finished hard, body jerking under me, face contorted with effort. He groaned loud and long, like his entire body had been clenched waiting for release and could finally let go.

Afterward, we didn't move right away. The bed was a disaster. The mattress is half off the frame. One leg is completely broken. Sweat soaked the sheets. The air smelled like sex and skin and surrender.

He blinked up at me, lips parted, hands still shaking a little.

I traced my fingers over his chest.

"Next time, we get a sturdier bed."

He laughed, low and hoarse, voice worn out from trying too hard.

"There's going to be a next time?"

I leaned in and kissed him once more

"Oh yes. I'm not done with you. Not even close."

I slid my fingers into his damp hair, gave it a slow, deliberate pull, and let the silence stretch.

Then I spoke. "Don't sleep. We're not finished."

I reached over to the nightstand, opened my small leather clutch, and pulled out a slim, tapered plug. Black. Silicone. Sleek. I held it up in front of him. He saw it. His breath hitched. He didn't move.

"On your knees."

He moved slowly, muscles shaking, arms barely holding his weight. He settled in the center of the ruined bed, knees spread, back arched low. I took my time. I slicked the plug-in lube from the bottle I'd spotted earlier on his desk. He must have hoped. Maybe even expected. But he hadn't asked.

I pressed a hand between his shoulder blades and whispered, "You take this for me. You keep it in. You stay still. And I'll let you come one more time. But only if you earn it."

"Yes, Belle," he said, voice barely steady.

He gasped when I pushed the plug in. His body tensed around it, but he didn't resist. I slid it in slowly, with pressure, watching his hands grip the sheets. When it was buried inside him, I kept my palm on the base, circling it gently, feeling his whole body twitch beneath me.

He was so sensitive now. I could have ruined him with just one twist.

I didn't. I stroked his cock lightly. Once. Then again. I felt him grow hard under my fingers. He whimpered when I stopped.

"No," I said.

He nodded. He didn't ask for more. Not yet.

I teased him like that. Edging. Denial. A hand on his cock. Then nothing. A press of the plug. Then silence. Every time he started to gasp, I backed off. He moaned into the mattress.

He trembled. His thighs quivered from holding the position. Sweat rolled down his back. He was coming apart without release, grinding against air, begging in broken fragments for another touch.

"Don't come," I said, voice low and cruel in his ear, "until I say you've earned it."

He choked out a yes.

Finally, I leaned in close and licked the sweat from the back of his neck.

"Crawl off the bed."

He did, stumbling a little on unsteady knees. I followed, guiding him by the hips until he was laid out flat on the floor, hands clasped behind his head, legs spread, plug still locked inside him.

"Stay there."

I climbed on top and lined his cock up with my body again. No games this time. No delay. I took him in one stroke. He cried out. His hands didn't move. His legs stayed open. He was obedient even now, even like this, even after everything.

I rode him hard, using his body like it belonged to me, because it did. The plug stayed in. His cock pulsed inside me. His moans turned to pleading.

"Please, please— I need to come."

"You'll wait."

I kept going. I rode him until his hands clenched into fists, until his back arched off the floor. I let him get close. Then closer. Then held him there, just long enough to see his body seize in panic.

Then I nodded.

"Now."

He came like a man who had been held underwater. His whole body jolted. He shouted into the floor. His cock emptied inside me in long, frantic pulses. He didn't fight me. He didn't change position. But he sobbed through it. Relief. Gratitude. Something deeper, he didn't have words for.

When it was done, I collapsed forward and held him. I pulled the plug out slowly. He flinched, but I kissed the back of his neck and whispered, "You did so well."

He couldn't speak yet.

He just stayed beneath me. And this time, I let him sleep.

When I woke, he held me. Got me a glass of water. Made me tea. Bought a warm washcloth. Ran his fingers through my hair. Touched my skin like he couldn't stop. I loved his smell. His body. The way he looked at me was like I was the best thing that had ever happened to him.

He was the kind of boyfriend you hope to get: hot, kind, engaged, enthusiastic. He wasn't afraid of the conversation. He met me in that intimacy.

But even then, I had doubts.

He seemed like he was headed in a dozen different directions. Meanwhile, I wanted to stay in DC. I was rooted here. And in a year or two, he was going to graduate. He'd move on. He'd take a job, maybe teaching. Who knows where? What if he took a job at Notre Dame and wanted me to move to Indiana? Was I going to become a professor's wife in South Bend?

Was he my future? The bright, shiny, maybe?

Or just the perfect right now?

It weighed on me. I wanted to make the right decision. And while he brought joy, fun, and charm, while it was all easy and light, it wasn't everything.

I wanted someone who could meet me in all parts of my life. Not just the bed. Not just the classroom. But everywhere.

Six months later, he got a job offer out of state.

He asked me to go with him as his wife. And I said no.

I couldn't leave my grad program. I wasn't going to give up on DC. I had more to do, more to learn, more of me to discover.

So we broke up.

It was sad. But it was also right. Because making the right decision for the wrong man never made sense. Our rom-com ended, but not in a sad way. In the way that feminist movies ended in the 1970s, with the heroine going off to her next great adventure, living her own powerful life that she crafted out of the lost dreams of the past and the hope of the future.

3

Fiscal Stimulus

When I first met Fiscal Stimulus (FS), she looked like a luxury I could never afford. Diamond-cut cheekbones, eyes that missed nothing, and the kind of body that was sculpted in expensive workout studios. You could tell before she spoke that she made money move, and not just through charm or luck. No, she understood systems, incentives, and pressure points. She could bend the Federal Reserve with one elegantly phrased question.

Her skin glowed with European restraint. No makeup, no drama. Just immaculate lighting and ruthless self-control. Her face always looked kissed by the type of good fortune that seems to be inherited rather than chosen. Her hair, somehow always in place, looked like it arranged itself out of loyalty.

No branded t-shirts or Juicy Couture for FS. Her suit fit like a sin and cost more than my rent. Her clothing whispered money. Not loud, insecure, desperate money. No labels were screaming for attention. No trendy silhouettes trying to prove a point. She wore Valentino most days. Some custom tailoring from someone no one else could afford, let alone name. Her closet must have cost more than my car, but nothing about her was performative. She didn't wear luxury. She embodied it. Her taste was so quiet that it made other women feel overdressed just by standing next to her.

I wanted her the way some people wish for absolution. Not just for sex, though, yes, that too, but for the way she might look at me if I

impressed her. As I mattered, like I could meet her where she lived. In that clean, cold, rarefied air, she breathed without even noticing how thin it was for the rest of us.

She wasn't just out of my league. She was orbiting in a different stratosphere. However, I am nothing if not persistent, and possess specific talents without being a malicious asshole like her ex, Mean Myrtle.

I, of course, read her like a book from the moment I saw her with that awful woman. The cruelty, the control, the way that the older woman clung to her brilliance like a dying vine wraps around a tree. FS kept everything inside. She smiled when expected. She played the part of an object, rejected and soon to be discarded.

Mean Myrtile was an older woman. The kind who wore power like a vintage perfume, strong, outdated, cloying. She was cruel in quiet ways. Possessive. Constantly correcting, always speaking for her, never listening. It made me sick to watch it. I watched as FS's brilliance dimmed slowly, every hour, every day, until she forgot how brightly she used to burn.

FS mistook sadism for dominance. She believed that control had to come with cruelty and that pain was the price of protection. The woman who bruised her claimed it was a power move. The ones who ignored her called it discipline. She learned to equate indifference with care, neglect with control, and chaos with chemistry.

She would need to learn that quiet is not abandonment. It is safe. And for someone who has never felt safe, safety feels unbearable. That absolute dominance is not loud. It does not leave scars for fun or to punish; it is not done to feel powerful. Absolute dominance is steady. It is patient. It is knowing I could break her and choosing instead to hold her.

When I heard they'd broken up, the first fucking thing I did was call.

"Oh, you two broke up? That's terrible! We should go for a drink. Let me buy you dinner. Let's catch up." She suggested a night at the Opera.

I knew what this was: the tickets she had been stuck with because of the breakup. I was the second choice, but I would soon get her to look at me as if I were the only choice.

On our Opera outing, I wasn't even sure it was a date at that point; I showed up in my off-the-rack Calvin Klein suit at the Kennedy Center, D.C.'s premier social venue for seeing and being seen. Crisp and clever, freshly pressed. I had managed to get a good fit without any tailoring, which felt like a quiet triumph and a huge savings. It had been marked down during a midseason sale, and I bought it with a Macy's coupon that came in the mail. I remember feeling proud of that as if I was being resourceful and strategic. I stood a little taller, convinced I looked the part: respectable, polished, the kind of woman who belonged without question.

The lobby buzzed with polite pretension, curated by old money in satin gloves and men with salt-and-pepper temples who wore inherited cufflinks as if they were credentials. These were the types who kept mistresses and garçons on retainer, whose marriages had long since calcified into formalities. Their wives sipped sherry at garden society luncheons and booked discreet weekday "massages" through an outcall service known for never asking questions. The entire building functioned on performance, upheld by mutual delusion and a shared commitment to appearances. It reeked of selective morality and very expensive restraint. When FS walked in, she did not disrupt the illusion. She exposed it. Every tailored smile, every hollow ritual, every brittle tradition collapsed under the weight of her presence.

She wore her midnight blue Valentino dress, precision-tailored with every seam placed precisely where it belonged. The fabric moved with her like it was a stalker, clinging in the right places, drifting where it pleased, and catching the light in quiet, expensive ways that never shimmered and never sparkled. It was the kind of material that whispered power to those who knew how to listen. The color was dark and deliberate, striking a precise balance between scandal and invitation. It grew from her body, sculpted by purpose and confidence rather than by trend.

She didn't walk so much as glide, her posture effortless and exact, never stiff and never rehearsed. Her heels glided over the red carpet in a steady rhythm, each step measured like a conductor guiding an unseen orchestra. The sound thudded softly, precise and deliberate, the kind that made people pause mid-sentence without realizing why. Heads turned. Conversations faltered. The lobby did not fall silent, but something in it shifted. You could feel the air rearrange itself, subtly yet unmistakably. People straightened their backs. Smiles became more cautious. No one said a word, yet everyone knew something had changed the moment she appeared.

The women noticed, too. Some watched with open admiration, taking in the cut of her dress, the ease of her movements, and the ruthless simplicity of her elegance. Others evaluated in silence, eyes narrowing slightly as they recalculated their position in the room. Her presence was not just an entrance; it was an announcement. She didn't shift the demand curve. She shattered it. Value itself seemed to reorganize in her orbit, and every standard of beauty, power, and desirability bent in her direction without resistance. And she had not even opened her mouth.

Next to her, my respectable little *investment* suit, the one I justified as versatile, felt like a student loan. I pressed it that morning, believing it could carry me across thresholds I did not yet belong to. I picked the blouse that looked most expensive and the shoes that still had their polish, and I stood a little taller, thinking that confidence could make up for the difference.

Across all that plush carpet and crystal, over the murmurs of the powerful and the well-preserved, she looked at me. There was no recognition in her expression and no trace of surprise. What she offered was interest, quiet and deliberate, the kind that revealed nothing too quickly. She looked at me the way someone might regard a glass of bourbon at the end of a long day, weighing the mood, the burn, and the promise of satisfaction. It was a thoughtful glance, measured and precise as if she had not yet decided whether to savor the experience slowly or throw it back in one smooth motion and move on.

"Nice suit." She said.

"Nice dress." I vomited out like a reflex.

She traced the lines of the fabric on my suit jacket with her well-manicured hands. Her fingers lingered a moment longer at the lapels, then slipped down toward the center of my chest. Not fully touching, just close enough to remind me she could.

"Does it wrinkle much?" she added, her voice soft and deliberate.

Shit. I need to work on my pressing skills.

"Judging by your reputation, it spends a great deal of time on the floor."

The air around us tightened. She walked around me, inspecting me and tugging at the coat.

I felt every nerve in my body rush to the surface.

"I—" I had nothing, no cards to play in this game. I don't know who she was talking to or what they said. I just hoped that I had a good review. Four stars, would fuck again.

She tilted her head again, a small gesture, nothing theatrical. Her voice stayed low. "I hope you choose everything with the same attention to detail." Why did I have the sense that I was interviewing for an opening she was desperate to fill?

That was when she stepped back, not with urgency and not out of retreat, but to let the heat between us settle where it belonged. Her gaze moved once, slowly, down the length of me before returning to meet my eyes again.

She turned, took my hand, and led me to her box. I followed because there was no other option. She had created a center of gravity that pulled everything toward her, not with force or urgency, but with something quieter and far more certain. The moment she turned, the room seemed to tilt slightly in her direction, and my body moved before my thoughts caught up. I did not choose to follow. She had already selected for both of us. It was an unfamiliar feeling, and not a comfortable one, because I am usually the one who leads.

I still do not remember the overture. I do not remember what time the lights dimmed. What I remember is the way her gaze settled on me, as if it were a hand placed at the base of my neck. It was steady, confident, and impossible to ignore.

The Opera was in German, one of the five languages she spoke fluently. I had spent several hours with the libretto before the show and silently blessed the invention of supertitles. It gave me just enough footing to hold my own as she walked me through the mid-show conversations, introducing me to a crowd that seemed to revolve around her without effort.

After the Opera, we ended up at Ben's Chili Bowl. Her idea. Red vinyl booths, paper napkins, and the best half-smokes and chili in Washington. We could have gone anywhere, and still, she chose this place. I kept asking myself why? And then I realized it didn't matter. She belonged there just as effortlessly as she had at the Kennedy Center. That was the real magic. She could quote Keynes or Krugman over champagne with a hedge fund CEO, then sit across from me under buzzing fluorescent lights, eating chili cheese fries like it was the most natural thing in the world.

It did not take long for me to understand what was happening. She had chosen Ben's because it was close to her townhome. I was not steering anything. I had never been. The decisions had already been made. And now I was left with a single, implausible choice: I could go home, hang up my suit, and pretend none of it had happened. Or I could follow her inside and face the full weight of what it meant to be wanted by a woman like her.

She was so right; my suit does wrinkle a bit when it is strewn on the floor for eight hours.

For reasons that still baffle me, she called the next day to "thank" me for going to the Opera with her. But in a way that made it clear she was offering me a ticket, not to the theater.

The sex had been conventional. And successful at least twice, possibly three times, I still had trouble reading her body's signals. She hit the sheets and seemed to adhere to them in some way, unable to move. I was happy to fall into the role of obliging Top if she wanted to be a Pillow Princess, but it just seemed inauthentic, like she was waiting for me to do something different.

It was clear that she had formed an image of me, a brooding domme with a taste for roughness, someone who would press her against a wall before even considering a kiss. I couldn't help but wonder where this notion had come from—a little too much loose talk from my past, perhaps allowing my reputation to grow larger than reality.

I have a knack for seeing people, for reading them deeply, and while I might not have known every specific detail of what she wanted, I could sense it. It was in the way she carried herself, the way her eyes lingered. It was a craving, like a hunger that had gone unfulfilled for far too long. More than anything, she wanted someone who could permit her to explore all those hidden desires, whether it was in the back of a car, a secluded corner of a theater, or an open field under the stars. That desire was insatiable, and it required someone who could understand it and fully embrace it.

By our next date or booty call, depending on how it went, I would make my intentions clear while we were still fully clothed.

She was late.

The bar was full of voices and polished glass. Velvet seats. Low light.

She wore a dress meant to be taken off slowly. She moved carefully as if she were afraid her want might show. Her eyes found mine. She crossed the room. She smiled, uncertain.

She leaned in to kiss my cheek. I pushed her up against the wall in the corner of the bar. I caught her waist.

Her lips brushed my skin. I did not let her pull away.

"You're late," I said quietly.

She tried to respond. I did not let her speak.

I leaned in closer, my voice warm against her ear.

"Do not speak. Do not sit. Do not close your legs."

My hand slid up the front of her thigh. Her breath caught. No one saw what I was doing to her. The bar blocked the view. If someone looked over, they would only see from your waist up.

"Do you want me to stop?'

"No." She panted like she was running a race.

"I want to fuck you tonight. Would you like that?"

I pressed my fingers beneath her dress.

She was already wet.

She nodded. Her breath was hard as I slipped my fingers beneath her panties. Hot. Soaked. I slid two fingers into her. She gasped. Her knees buckled slightly. Her hands grabbed my arm for balance.

I curved my fingers and began slow, tight circles against her G-spot. My thumb found her clit and began to stroke. Her whole body quivered.

"I want to taste you and then tie you up and fuck you till you scream. Would you like that?" I whispered in her ear.

She moaned. Quiet. Shaking.

"You will not come unless I give you permission."

Her body jolted.

"Do you understand?"

She nodded.

"Say it."

"Yes," she whispered. "I understand."

"Good."

I curled my fingers deeper. My thumb pressed firmer. Her hips shifted forward. She whimpered, trying to stay upright.

"You are going to beg me soon. I can already feel it."

She moaned again. Her thighs shook.

"I am going to tie you up later. Arms behind your back. Face in the sheets. Legs wide open."

She trembled. Her forehead brushed my shoulder.

She whimpered.

I leaned in again.

"When I get you home, I will bury my mouth on you. I will hold your hips down. I will keep you on the edge until you are crying for permission."

Her eyes closed. Her thighs pressed together. I opened them with my knee.

"I am going to fuck you with something thick. Something you can barely take. And I will press a vibrator to your clit while I use it. You will scream into the mattress. But you will not come until I say you can."

Her breath broke into pieces. She was panting. Desperate.

"You want it. Say it."

"I want it. ...Please."

I pulled my fingers out. Wet. Glowing.

I licked them clean. Slowly. Thoughtfully.

"Don't fucking close your legs. You are mine."

She nodded. Shaking.

"Good girl." I kissed her on the cheek.

I stepped back and looked at her.

Flushed. Breathless. Soaked.

"Finish your drink. Stay standing. You will get your dress wet if you sit."

She obeyed.

The music continued. The room buzzed around her. But she was already in another world. A world where every breath waited for mine.

We spent the whole weekend in bed. She did everything I asked her to do willingly and eagerly. With the kind of enthusiasm that is usually reserved for someone who is starved, which she was.

Mean Myrtle was a stupid piece of shit.

She was acting a little coy; I got the feeling that there was something she wanted to tell me or ask for, but couldn't bring herself to say. I assumed that there was some special bedside battery item that she wanted to use. I was not fully prepared for what happened next.

"Show me," I whispered delicately into her ear and then kissed her on the mouth. With these two words, she smiled from ear to ear.

She leaped like a gazelle over to an antique armoire and presented it to me as if I were a client at a fancy jewelry store. She opened the big doors and all the drawers in turn, revealing a fluck of dildos (assorted colors and surprising sizes), a whir of vibrators, a restraint of leather cuffs, and a whoosh of floggers.

It looks like she went shopping. I got the distinct impression that I was the first item on her shopping list. I dragged the cuck chair across the room and sat. Eyes locked on hers. I looked like some drunken royal brat waiting to be impressed.

"Present them. One by one."

She blinked slowly, her eyes starting to droop again. Fuck her ex.

I grabbed her chin and tilted it to look up at me with a flick of my fingers. "Don't look at the floor. Look at me. I'm the one giving the orders here."

Though clearly, I am not the only one steering this ship.

But unlike her pathetic ex, I am not interested in some lifeless starfish under the covers. I want enthusiasm. I want consent. I want someone who shows up.

"Yes, Belle."

"That's better. Now tell me something. How long have you been planning this little surprise for me?"

She looked sheepish.

"Right after I hung up the phone. When you called to ask me out."

Thank goodness for FedEx Express shipping.

Honestly, I am just a passenger on this ride. The only real choice I made was asking her out.

"Remind me to thank your ex when I see her."

"Why?"

"Because she was so busy blocking your sunshine, she never took the time to see what a beautiful flower you would be if you got some sunlight and some water in your garden."

She looked at me like I had just said something she could not utter out loud. I had voiced what she had been trying to dodge in therapy for years.

"Now show me my presents."

"And then?"

"I'll test them on you to see which ones make you say my name. And which ones make you forget your own?"

She grinned.

Her first offering was a heart-shaped paddle. Red leather, stiff and unforgiving. She knelt between my legs and held it up with both hands like she was begging for communion.

"For you," she whispered.

I took it from her. I slapped it once against my palm. The sound cracked like a starter pistol. She flinched.

"Stand. Turn around. Bend over."

She did. No hesitation.

I dragged the paddle across her skin.

"You want it to be gentle?"

"No." She admitted.

The first hit was loud to hear but had a light touch.

"More?"

"Yes." She clearly did like it. How long had she been dreaming of this happening?

The next one echoed.

"You like that?" I asked. My voice was low. Cruel.

She shivered. "Oui."

"Harder?"

"Oui, s'il te plaît..."

The third blow made her moan, but she flinched.

"Too much?"

She nodded no, still breathless.

I leaned in. My voice whispered in her ear. Let's save that for later."

She rose shakily and returned it to the drawer.

Next, she chose the spreader bar.

Kneeling again, she placed it in my lap. "For you, Belle. For your pleasure."

"And yours." I insisted.

I stood up, stepped behind her, and kissed the inside of her thigh. I cuffed her ankles into place and stood, letting her feel the warmth of my body just behind hers. "You're going to lie on your back now. Hold your ankles. Here is the key." I pressed it into her hand. Safety first.

She obeyed. Flesh spread open like a banquet.

"You are mine tonight," I murmured.

"I'm yours," she said.

"En français." I must sound like a tourist asking for a croissant.

"Je suis à toi."

"Encore."

"Je suis à toi. Je suis à toi..."

I dropped to my knees and licked her like she was the answer to every prayer I'd never said. She squirmed. Moaned. Trembled.

“Je vais jouir... je vais...”

I stopped. Pulled back.

"Non."

"Pourquoi?! Tu les fais jouir, toutes les autres, pas vrai? Tu les touches, tu les prends, tu les fous en larmes, et moi tu me laisses comme une conne, à crever d'envie? Tu veux quoi, que je rampe? Que je pleure pour toi? Va te faire foutre." *Why?! You make all the others come, don't you? You touch them, you take them, you fuck them into tears, and me—you leave me like an idiot, dying for it? What do you want, that I crawl? That I cry for you?*

"Parce que, I said so. You get a little spicy en français." I have now dropped into some bad Franglish. "Do we have something to talk about? You have mentioned my past a few times now. Are we jealous?"

I unlatched the cuffs and helped her to her feet. Her legs were shaking.

"How many others are there?" She didn't want to look at me.

I pulled her close and lifted her head to mine. "There is only you."

What the fuck has her ex done to her?

"Really?" She looked up at me like the Fed had just cut interest rates.

"Yes. You are mine." I reassured her.

"I'm yours." She repeated or asserted. I frankly was not sure which. But I didn't want to break the mood with a whole bunch of questions.

"I am sorry for whatever happened before I showed up. I can tell you carry a burden. I will listen if you are ready to talk. And I will understand if you can't talk about it yet." I offered.

She just kissed me. I read relief over her face and body. I don't have to know what clear-cut the path through the forest to see that it was harmful and left a scar.

"Do you want to keep going? Or would you like to lie in bed for a while?"

FS walked over to the bed, and curled up waiting for me to be her big spoon.

I snuggled up behind her. I whispered slowly into her ear. "You don't have to be the person that Mean Myrtle wanted you to be. You just have to be yourself with me, and I am just here for you."

She sobbed quietly and fell asleep in my arms.

When she woke, something in her seemed lighter. I made an omelet while she perched on the countertop of her immaculate kitchen, one I suspected saw more takeout menus than flames. She wore a hotel robe, probably liberated from one of her near-constant business trips. Knowing her, she had paid for it in the gift shop, because ethics mattered even in theft-adjacent indulgences.

I was wearing a tank top and a pair of stretchy exercise shorts she pulled from a drawer. It was that or one of her obscenely delicate lingerie sets, none of which were designed for someone built like me. Her frame was small, elegant, almost birdlike. I, by comparison, felt like a Brahma bull trying to squeeze into a tutu.

I still wanted to impress her, so I put on a little show while I cooked. If I could just keep dazzling her, maybe she wouldn't notice how obviously I didn't belong in this polished, curated world of hers. Perhaps she wouldn't kick me out the second she saw past the illusion.

She tried to distract me while I fed her, fingers wandering toward my chest with the same casual greed she used to claim boardroom victories. FS was clearly ready for another round.

I lead her back to the bedroom.

We stopped in front of the closet. Her collection was vast, wicked, and tempting. But this time, I got to choose.

I pulled out a beautiful body harness. Soft pink leather. Obscene and exquisite. It exposed her nipples, framed her dessert like a plated delicacy, the kind you didn't eat so much as worship.

"You will look beautiful in it."

She flirted back a bit.

I strapped her into it. Buckle by buckle. Tighter than she expected.

Her eyes fluttered shut.

"You like that?"

She nodded.

"Say it."

"J'aime ça..." She whispered in French.

I cinched the waist tighter.

“J’aime ça. Plus fort. S’il te plaît. Attache-moi. Fous-moi...” She is downright bratty in French. *I like that. Harder. Please. Tie me up. Fuck me...*

I stepped in behind her, lips grazing the back of her neck.

She was slightly taken aback, but she received it as I looked at her directly and said. "Dit-moi ce que tu veux." *Tell me what you want.* I commanded.

"Je veux tout. Je veux que tu me fasses crier. Pleurer. Trembler." *I want everything. Please make me scream. Cry. Tremble.*

FS in French mode sounds like a 2 am hooker eager for a sale. Well, I was down for some Francophonic Fucking.

I slid my fingers between her legs and felt the soaked leather press into her.

"Tu veux jouir?" *You want to come?*

"Oui. Je t'en supplie. Putain, t'es une vraie garce... ta mère aurait dû t'avaler. Fais-moi jouir, salope!" *Yes. I'm begging you. Fuck, you're a real bitch... your mother should've swallowed you. Make me come, you fucking whore!*

I get it now. She is a bratty power bottom in French. That is kind of hot.

"Implore-moi mieux que ça." *Beg prettier,* I commanded.

"Fais-moi jouir. Je t'en supplie. Je suis à toi. Je suis ta pute ce soir..." *Make me come. I'm begging you. I'm yours. I'm your whore tonight...*

My high school French and extensive knowledge of curse words were running out. Who is this woman, and where does she go when she speaks English?

She was still breathing hard and still trembling in those perfect pink straps.

I moved behind her, one hand on her throat, the other slipping down the line of her body. She leaned into me like she needed it. Like she couldn't hold herself up without my touch.

"I love your mouth," I whispered into her ear. "But I think it's time you shut up."

Her breath caught.

"You want a gag?"

She nodded.

I pulled open another drawer in the armoire and took out a black leather bit gag. Sleek. Simple. Brutal in how effective it was. I held it up to her lips.

"Ouvrir le bec" *Open your beak.*

She obeyed.

"On a du travail à faire, alors concentre-toi." *We've got work to do, so focus.*

"Bof, Maîtresse. Votre humble serviteur travaillera dur pour vous. J'espère que vous me donnerez une chance de vous satisfaire. *Huh, Mistress. Your humble servant will work hard for you. I hope you will give me a chance to please you.*

She gave a classic French girl pout as I slid the bit between her teeth, slow and deliberate, then buckled it tight behind her head. Her lips stretched around the gag. Her eyes fluttered half-closed. Her breath came faster.

"Tu es mon trésor adoré." *You are my beloved treasure.* If I went hard on the Lady Marmalade talk, she might believe it in French.

I grabbed a flogger from the armoire. Long, soft leather strands. I dragged it across her chest, down her thighs, between her legs. She shivered at every touch, but she didn't back away.

I brought it down across her ass. Not hard. Just enough to make her moan around the gag. The sound was perfect. Muffled. Desperate.

I struck again. And again. Each time, her knees buckled a little more.

She tried to say something, so I stopped, but it came out a useless mess of breath and leather.

"Do you want me to stop?" I asked. "We can stop right now."

She nodded no, gag pressing against her teeth.

Her eyes rolled back as I landed another soft strike. Then another. Her legs were shaking.

"Your body can talk for you now."

I slid my hand between her legs.

"Pulsing."

I dropped the flogger and knelt before her again. Her thighs spread automatically. I did not even need to tell her. I tasted her again, slow and cruel, my tongue moving like a metronome. She whimpered against the gag, the sound breaking into little sobs.

Her hips bucked.

I stopped.

She nearly collapsed.

I rose to my feet, wiped my mouth on the back of my hand, and leaned in close.

"You do not get to come yet," I said. "Not until I say. Not until you earn it."

She made a frustrated, broken noise behind the gag. Her eyes pleaded.

"I like you like this," I said. "Pretty. Useless. Soaked and speechless."

I kissed her forehead.

Tweaked her nipples.

"I am going to sit back down in the chair, and you are going to drag yourself across the floor to me. You are going to eat me until I come."

I grabbed her hair.

"If you do not do a good job, and I do not come hard on your pretty little face. I am not going to get you off."

I dipped her to the ground as if we were dancing.

Which, in a way, we were.

She could barely move. That made it all the more delicious to watch her slither across the floor.

When she got close, I spread my legs like a man on the subway.

"Put your tongue here," I said, pointing to my clit. "Rub your tongue around here," I added, tapping my labia. "Get me off. Now."

I took off her gag. And she dove in, face first.

I wrapped my legs around her head and pulled her in even closer. She was brutal and efficient. She watched me intently while she was down there for any change in my response. I thought it was hot. The sheer beauty of her restrained and eager-to-please nature was entrancing.

I tighten my legs around her, pulling her closer.

"Harder!"

She followed every directive and command. She was committed to this.

It doesn't usually take much for me to get off, let alone with a beautiful princess tied up like a gift for me. I just thought about what I was going to do to her next.

I pushed her down further and came on her face.

Her body was limp in the harness, legs still trembling, wrists locked behind her back, skin flushed and glistening. The gag hung around her neck now, useless for speech but soaked with spit. Her chest rose and fell in quick, broken bursts.

I had come so hard she nearly passed out. But I wasn't done. Not even close.

I stepped in, one hand under her chin, the other sliding down her stomach until I could feel how wet she still was.

"You liked that, didn't you?"

She moaned, nodding.

"Of course you did. Because you're *mine.*"

I tightened my grip on her jaw and leaned in, mouth at her ear, breath hot.

"My bitch." I said it in German, voice low and cruel. "*Meine Hündin.*" I only know a few words in German, and what I learned from the Opera, if she starts barking out in German, I am cooked.

She whimpered. A sound that made my clit throb.

"Say it," I growled.

She barely choked it out, voice hoarse. *"Ich bin deine Hündin."*

I smirked. The dirty talk only exists in French. I was praying that she didn't just tell me fuck off.

"Yes, you are."

I turned her roughly, pressing her against the floor, her arms still bound, her legs still spread. She couldn't see me. She couldn't speak. But her whole body begged for more.

Her thighs were parted. Her back arched. Her pussy was slick and swollen, already open and wanting. She held still, her breath low and steady, her body thrumming with anticipation.

I knelt behind her. My hand moved between her legs. She shifted slightly, pressing into it. Her hips rolled forward just enough to present herself more fully. She didn't need to speak. She never had to. Every breath was an invitation.

Two fingers. Then three. Her body took them easily. Her warmth pulled me in. The stretch came next.

Four fingers.

She exhaled slowly. Her thighs trembled. Then she moved — lowered herself onto my hand, taking it deeper, letting her weight pull her open.

I folded my thumb.

Let her take the whole of me.

My hand sank into her, wrist-deep, her butterfly clenching and fluttering around the fullness. Her breath caught, but she made no sound. The pink leather held her tight. Her body held me tighter.

I stayed still for a moment. Let her feel it. Let her ache around the pressure.

I placed my fingertips gently against her clit. No sudden motion. No rush. It's just a slow, steady circle. Her whole body jerked once. Her head dipped lower. Her hips began to rock in the smallest rhythm.

Her walls pulsed around my hand. Her clit twitched beneath my touch. I didn't rush her. I circled again, this time firmer. I watched her breath speed up. I watched the trembling build.

Her body was completely split open. Full on the inside. Flickering at the edge on the outside. I controlled both. My hand pressed upward within her. My fingers rubbed her clit in perfect, deliberate pressure.

Her thighs were shaking now. Her bound arms were still. Her shoulders lifted and dropped as she tried to contain the sound that never came.

I leaned in closer, lips near her neck, and whispered.

"You have one minute to come, or I will stop."

Her body broke.

Her desire clenched around my hand in violent, rhythmic spasms. Her thighs locked and trembled. Her orgasm poured through her like a storm, long and devastating. Her wetness spilled across my wrist and down her legs. My fingers kept stroking her clit as her body convulsed against me again and again.

She stayed silent. But her body said everything.

I did not pull out.

I kept my hand deep inside her, still pressing gently against the roof of her cave while her pulse slowed. My fingers on her clit softened. It slowed and then stopped.

Only once she began to melt did I ease my hand out. Slowly. Her lips opened for a second longer, then began to close, pulsing and flushed.

I pulled her gently into my lap.

The pink leather straps were still buckled across her spine. Her wrists were still bound. Her breathing came in soft waves. Her skin glowed.

I pressed my mouth to her shoulder. My lips to the curve of her jaw.

Then I said it. Quiet. Certain. Deep in her ear. "Meine Hündin."

She didn't need to reply. Her body stayed relaxed. She was still pulsing. Her clit was still swollen beneath the ghost of my touch.

She belonged right there.

She stayed in my arms, her breath was slow and deep. The buckles were quiet now. No longer tools of control. Just proof of what she had given me.

She didn't speak. She didn't move.

I leaned forward. My mouth met the base of her spine, just above the top buckle. A kiss. Barely a whisper. Not a reward. A seal. Then I reached for the strap.

The leather had left a faint mark across her skin. A thin line of pressure where her body had pulled against it. I kissed that, too. Then, unbuckled the first strap. Slowly. Carefully. No rush.

Her wrists remained in place. She did not lift them.

The second buckle released with a soft sound. Another mark beneath it. I kissed it. Let my lips press there. Not just gentle. She was mine. I had bound her. I had filled her. Now, I was the one who undid her—no one else.

The third buckle opened. The strap fell away from her wrists. Her arms sank forward with no effort. No resistance. She stayed bowed. Soft. Her back was still arched, her hips soft, and her skin still glowing.

I kissed the red imprint that ran across the tops of her forearms. Then, her shoulders. Then, the hollow at the base of her neck.

She was not being *freed*. She was being *unwrapped*.

I helped her shift slowly to her side, then gathered her into my lap. Her body is limp now, warm against mine. Her hair clung to her cheeks. Her lips parted. Her breath was a soft rhythm against my collarbone.

I ran my fingers over every place the leather had touched her. Over every curve, still trembling from the pressure of my hand. And I kissed her again. Behind her ear. Beneath her jaw. Along her temple.

"Meine Hündin," I whispered. Into her blonde hair. Into her skin. Into the heat between her shoulders.

She lay on her back now, limbs loose, thighs parted slightly in the languid sprawl of someone utterly unguarded. She had not spoken since her body had been released. She had not needed to. The silence was thicker now. And I took my time.

I hovered above her. Not to dominate. To look. To take in the fullness of her. The shape of her ribs. The elegant curve of her hipbone.

The small freckle tucked just beneath her navel. The faint red streak at her inner thigh where my hand had once anchored her. All of it is mine.

I kissed her ankle. Then, her shin. Then, the space just above her knee. My mouth is open. My breath was slow. I kissed her as if each spot held some forgotten language only I could read.

I kissed the crease of her thigh. Not between her legs. Beside. Where softness met strength. I dragged my lips up the line of her hip, across her stomach. The rise and fall of her breath pulled against my mouth.

She moved under me like silk on water. No tension. Her body responded in waves.

I kissed beneath her breast. Then between. Then, across to the other side. I did not suck. I did not take it. I let my lips barely press, then linger. Her nipples pebbled, but I did not touch them. Not yet. I wasn't here to provoke her body.

I circled behind her shoulder with my fingertips, then kissed where they traced. Her clavicle. Her throat. Her pulse. Every inch of her skin told a different story. Every story belonged to me.

She breathed in through her nose. Held it. Let it go like she didn't want to break the moment.

I kissed the corner of her jaw. Then, her ear. Then lower. Her cheek. Her temple.

Then I whispered against her skin.

"You are mine." Not loud. Not for her reassurance. For my own. "Every inch." I finished.

I slid my hand between her thighs. Her thighs opened just enough to make space, no more.

She was ready.

I kissed her again. Her sternum. Her navel. The faint scar just beneath her ribs. I kissed her as if I were mapping her. Like my tongue had memory, and her body was the only thing it had ever known.

I kissed her because I could. Because I owned her. Because she let me.

She would stay right here. Unmoving. Silent. Laid bare before me like the most precious thing I had ever been allowed to touch.

My hands slid under her back and held her there.

I kissed her until my mouth remembered every mark.

Every curve.

Every sacred inch.

She had gone quiet beneath me, not unconscious and not removed, steeped in the stillness that came after being kissed thoroughly, held completely, and marked without demand. Her breath had slowed to a quiet and clean rhythm. Her body had gone loose against mine, her limbs soft, her skin warm from my mouth and the worship I had laid into her inch by inch. She had become something sacred in my hands, an object of art or a prayer brought to life, her every curve memorized, her every tremble received and honored in silence.

She had let herself be touched without urgency. She had accepted each kiss as if it carried weight, as if she knew what it meant for me to tend to her without taking it. And I had kissed her like she was scripture. I had traced her skin as if it had something to tell me. I had pressed my mouth into every mark she bore until her body seemed to glow from the inside out, warm with breath and reverence and heat.

But then she moved.

At first, it was nothing. A small roll of her hips. A tilt of her pelvis that brushed her skin against mine. The kind of movement that could be explained away by the afterglow of sensation or the body adjusting itself without thought. But then it came again, slower this time, more deliberate, the whole curve of her ass grinding back into me in one long, unbroken sweep that ended with her holding still for just a beat too long. She wanted me to feel it. She wanted to be sure I knew what she was doing.

I stayed still.

She moved again.

This time, it was unmistakable. A steady rhythm. She was no longer the quiet body. She was coming awake and coming hungry, the kind of hunger that did not begin in her mouth or her stomach but deeper, somewhere behind her ribs, somewhere in the space that had been filled by silence and was now cracking wide open. She ground herself against me, and the friction was not coy. It was the intention. It was a promise that the stillness had ended.

I slid my hand to her hip.

She pressed back again, slower now, her spine dipping into a soft arch that made the curve of her ass find the heat of my body and drag itself across me like a dare.

And then she bit me.

No noise. No hesitation.

Her mouth closed around my upper arm, and her teeth sank into my flesh. To *claim me.* She bit with pressure and purpose, holding me there like she wanted me to know she had come back to herself, and she was no longer the woman I had just kissed. She was the woman who would bite and grind and press herself into me until I retook her.

I exhaled.

Low. Deep.

She bit harder.

Then she released.

Then she ground back into me again.

And this time, there was no denying it. The way she moved against me was not a question. It was the answer. She was no longer waiting. Her body had remembered the weight of my hand and the stretch of my fingers, and the silence had become unbearable.

She wanted to be thrown into the center of it again.

Taken.

And I was going to give her everything she had just asked for without a single word.

"Je sais ce que tu veux que je te fasse." *I know what you want me to do to you.* I said as I rose and moved to the slutty armoire. I wasn't entirely sure, but I was hoping that hovering over the many objects would give me a clue.

I took my time pulling the drawer open, the sound of it scraping soft and low like a warning. I dragged my hand over a particularly brutal-looking item. Ding Ding Ding. FS's face lit up. It's a good thing, because the item next to it, I would have had to watch an instructional video of some kind. Where did that even go?

The black leather harness was already prepared, but I tightened each strap again anyway, not for security, but for sensation. I wanted to feel it digging into my hips when I fucked her. This was not just for her after all.

The toy was thicker than the others I had used before. Heavier. It had weight, presence, and consequence. She bought it, so she must have fantasized about what this would feel like. She had kept it tucked in the armoire and had flinched just slightly when I passed over it.

"You thought I wouldn't notice?" I murmured. "You picked this. You wanted to be fucked hard."

I strapped it in tight and let her hear the buckles fasten one by one.

Click.

"That's one."

Click.

"Two."

Click.

"And three. You know what that means, don't you?"

I grabbed a bottle of lube and stroked the monstrosity sensually, covering it in moisture. I had her full and complete attention.

At this point, I am going to have to tell you that it was not a traditionally shaped item. This did not look like anything that a man might possess. A mythological monster, maybe, some kind of sea creature, perhaps. Rather than smooth features, it was ribbed for her pleasure. Unless I missed my guess, the curved nature of the silicone would hit her G-spot like a homing beacon, and the upper and lower tentacles would slam into her clit and her ass simultaneously.

This was either going to go so well that she curses me out in French or thanks me politely in German.

She whimpered, her head lifting faintly, her back straining. Her body is already responding to the ritual, already knowing what is to come. But knowing did not mean she was ready.

I knelt behind her and said nothing at first. I let my hand run across the base of her spine, down to the curve of her ass, and then between her legs. She was still soaked, still twitching. The heat coming off her was exquisite.

I pressed the head of the strap-on "item" to her opening and paused only long enough to feel the way she tensed.

"You are hungry for more," I whispered, leaning down so my lips barely touched the shell of her ear. "Spread your legs for me."

Then I entered her profoundly and slowly, and it was unstoppable. Her hands splayed against the floor. Her back arched violently.

I grabbed her hips and held her still, then leaned in close, my breath brushing the sweat on her neck. I whispered, tender and deliberate.

"You think I did not feel it? Every moan you made. Every time, your body clenched and begged. You were edging *me.* You made me wait."

I pulled back and thrust again. Then again. The pace was fast and brutal from the start. No teasing. My body slapped into hers again and again. She jolted forward with each impact, gagging cries smothered into the floor, her shoulders giving out as I drove into her with all the hunger I had been holding back. The harness slammed against my clit, making each move a shock of deep pleasure. The base of the toy hit just right. I braced myself. I used her as a rhythm. As resistance. As heat.

"You wanted me to fuck you."

Her body bucked and jerked and took it all. Her ass bounced against me, each movement sloppy and chaotic now. She was far past pleasure. Past coherence. Her knees slid farther apart with every thrust until she could no longer adjust herself.

I kept her in place by the hair, fisting it at the base of her neck, yanking her upright just enough to feel how tightly her back arched. I was soaked now, too. Sweat dripped between my breasts, down my spine, slicking my skin until I could feel her heat mixing with mine where our bodies met. My legs were trembling, but I refused to slow down.

"You are mine," I said into her ear. "You are *mine.*

She sobbed.

"Louder," I said coldly. "Let the neighbors hear what you've become."

I fucked her harder.

My orgasm came sharp and wild. My thighs locked. The wave crashed through my hips, spine, and shoulders. I kept moving. I kept grinding into her. She kept thrusting until the aftershocks hit so hard I had to catch myself on her back to keep from collapsing. Even then, I stayed inside. Buried and pressed deep. My breathing was loud in her ear.

I grabbed her and pulled her vertically. Holding on to her breasts for leverage, I ground her onto the "tentacle arm thing", hitting her G-spot. And the sick tentacle thing cradling her clit, moving it with every thrust.

If I wanted to, I could move the top tentacle into her ass, but instead, I let it just brush the surface.

"Move your fucking hips," I barked at her. I grabbed the clit facing tentacle and pushed it to her skin.

She whimpered, but her body obeyed. She rocked her hips back into me, slow at first, then faster, desperate to please.

It was violent at its core. I was grinding into her like she was nothing but a means to my pleasure. I held her in place and let her work for it.

"Harder," I said. "Earn it."

"Je t'en supplie, mets-la dans mon cul. Enfonce cette saloperie jusqu'au fond, fais-le, bordel!" *I'm begging you, put it in my ass. Shove that fucking thing all the way in, do it, fuck!* She screamed in French at me.

I misjudged a bit. She did buy this after all.

More French from FS, "Sérieusement, si tu me baises mal, je paie une salope pour le faire à ta place." *Seriously, if you fuck me badly, I'll pay a slut to do it for you.*

I poured lube over her ass and let it drip down. And shoved the tentacle deep in her ass.

She shifted again, tilting to give me more pressure. More friction. She wanted to be hit in both holes and on her clit. I kept slamming her down as she rose for each stroke, her back arching, her ass bouncing against me. She moved like she was built for it. Like she existed for this.

I took one breath. Long. Controlled.

I took it from her slowly. My smile was quiet, cruel.

"You want more?"

She writhed beneath me. Violent and perfect.

"You feel that?" I said. "Good. You feel what I give you and nothing else. "

She was shaking hard, her skin flushed and soaked, and tears streaked down her face, but she kept her position. Her legs spread wide. Her ass raised. Her thighs were spasming. Her body screamed.

She twitched. She trembled. But she did not move away.

I leaned in close, my voice sweet and soft, the kind of sweetness that cuts.

"Good," I said, smoothing her hair back from her face. "You finally understand."

I grabbed her throat with one hand and raised her torso. I used the other hand to rub her clit and hold it to the tentacle.

I barked in her ear. "Come now." And she did, violently screaming words that I could not make out in French, but I suspected that I was some kind of farm animal and that my parents weren't married, or my father was a farm animal. It was unclear.

I came seconds later as her spasms continued. We went to a kneeling rest. And we both fell into a spent heap.

Ten minutes later, she said that she loved me in French, but that still counts. I immediately went down on her; I wouldn't have to answer her back if my mouth was full.

"I love you" was uncharted territory for us. I know she wanted me to say it back. But right now, our relationship was all whips and no chips. We would need more dates and stolen kisses to call this anything more than an affair.

There were nights I would come over, slip off my heels by her door, open a bottle of wine, and talk with her like we were old lovers in a softer kind of story. We would laugh. We would lean in. We would lose track of time. And then, as if something in the air had shifted, I would turn my head, maybe lift a brow, and she would know.

In public at events, we would disappear into the car. Sometimes into a bathroom stall. She would sink to her knees, unbothered by the floor, unbothered by the risk. And I would slide my fingers into her mouth or guide her head to where I wanted her. She would always go down on me as if it were her favorite prayer.

She had a beautiful body. And yes, of course, I loved the way she looked naked, flushed, and trembling after I made her come. But the sight that undid me every single time was her on her knees in front of me, especially in her kitchen. She had this perfect, modern kitchen with clean lines and an expansive marble island. I would sit at the edge, a glass of wine in my hand, and watch her crawl to me. She would part my thighs and press her mouth to me like she was drinking from some sacred spring. I would come again and again, and she would only look up at me with hunger.

She let me return the favor. She never asked. She never begged. But when I pulled her close and lifted her onto the counter or slipped a hand between her thighs, she would melt.

What she loved was pressure. My fingers inside her, slow and certain. My mouth on her clit until her breath caught and her thighs trembled. She came hard.

One night, after no more than a glass of wine—because rope and alcohol are never a safe mix—I pulled out the red silk. I did not need to say anything at first. I just held the bundle of it in my hands. The moment she saw it, she shivered. It was the kind of shiver that starts deep in the spine and spreads outward like a wave of heat. She looked like she might come just from the anticipation.

I stepped toward her and said quietly, "Take off everything. Stand by the stairs. Wait for me."

Her staircase was a thing of beauty. All glass and steel. It caught the light in strange, cold ways. I tied her there. Wrists bound to the railings. Her ankles spread just wide enough to make her hold tension in her legs. Her head tilted slightly downward, her chest rising with each breath.

I circled her slowly. Letting the quiet stretch. Letting her feel the rope, the space, and the way I looked at her.

Then I reached for the red suede flogger.

She was naked except for the red ropes I had tied around her and the black heels that made her legs look like sculptures. Her body was already flushed, her skin shining in places, the sweat just beginning to bead along her lower back. She knelt with her thighs spread and her ass high, elbows down, spine bowed like a dancer mid-collapse.

I circled her. Slowly. Let her feel the silence before the storm.

The flogger was soft at first. A lover's whisper. I drew it across her skin again, the tails teasing her breasts, her ribs, her hips. Each pass a question. Each reaction has a little answer. When she trembled, I smiled. When she sighed, I struck.

The first real blow landed across her ass with a sharp snap. She gasped. Her head dropped, but she did not move. The second landed lower, grazing the tops of her thighs. The third came harder. She let out a soft cry, the sound more breath than voice, and her hips rocked forward involuntarily.

"Count for me," I said.

"Yes, Belle. One."

The next came quickly.

"Two."

Again.

"Three."

By seven, her voice had started to hitch. The sensation had begun to layer itself inside her, building something she could not outrun. At ten, I paused. I watched the way her fingers clenched. I watched the way her thighs shook, just slightly, not from weakness but from too much want held still.

"You are allowed to cry," I said softly.

"I will not cry, Belle."

I stepped closer and dragged the flogger gently across her again. Her breath stuttered. I struck her once across the shoulders and then let the tails fall down her spine like a waterfall of leather.

Her moan cracked on its way out.

"You feel that?"

"Yes, Belle"

"Laisse-moi te briser lentement. *Let me break you slowly.* I offered with a swish of the flogger.

"Je t'adore, Maîtresse. Je suis à toi." FS confessed again. *I adore you, Mistress. I am yours.*

Does adore count the same as love? I am cooked.

I struck again. Harder now. The sound echoed. Her cry followed it. She rocked forward, forehead pressing to the floor, body straining against her bindings.

"Keep your posture." I tapped her beautiful ass.

She obeyed instantly. Resettled. Knees wide, ass high, arms braced.

The next blow landed across her upper thighs. She screamed. A scream torn from the deep part of her body that knew pain and pleasure were not opposites. I gave her more. I watched her react. Her hips jerked. Her breath came in sobs now, and still she held position.

Every time the flogger landed, she cried out and then whispered, "Je suis à toi." *I am yours.*

Her eyes were glassy. Her body had gone pliant, like something holy. Her moans had become rhythmic. Not quite words. It was more like songs sung in a language only her nerves could translate. She was high. Drifting.

I got closer to her and wrapped my hands around her body. I whispered in her ear. "T'es à moi, ma petite pute." *You're mine, my little whore.*

"T'es qu'un putain de lâche, même pas foutu de me dire que tu m'aimes." *You are a fucking coward too afraid to tell me you love me.* She spat out at me.

That hit me like I was the one in the ropes. I might as well be if she can French-slap me like that.

I gave her five more. Slower. Each one landed with precision. Her hips twitched. Her knees wobbled but held. She was swaying now, lost in it, in me. Her mouth opened, and no sound came at first. Just a shake of breath. Then, a moan that cracked as it left her throat.

I stepped in behind her. Let the flogger fall to the floor with a soft slap.

She gasped at the absence.

"Don't stop."

Her voice cracked. Her whole body pleaded.

I touched her. My fingers slipped between her thighs. She was soaked. Swollen. Her clit throbbed under my hand. Her whole body jerked at the contact like she had been shocked.

She was shaking. Her body was covered in red. Every mark is a memory. Every welt has a signature. She was raw. Glowing. Magnificent.

I dropped the flogger. I fell to my knees behind her. I slid my fingers back inside her, and she screamed, no words left, just pure sound.

"S'il te plaît... putain, laisse-moi jouir. Qu'est-ce que t'attends, hein? " *Please... fuck, let me come. What are you waiting for, huh?*

I slid deeper. I curled my fingers. Rubbed her clit with my other hand, slow but relentless. Her thighs clamped around me. Her body jerked again and again.

"Please. Please. Please."

I gave her a moment more. Then leaned in. Lips just behind her ear.

"You may come."

She shattered.

Her whole body seized. Legs spasming. Mouth wide open but silent for the first beat of it. Then the scream ripped loose, and she shook so violently I had to hold her down. She cried out again and again. Sobbing through the pleasure. Through the pain. Through the unbearable relief of finally being allowed to break.

When she finished, she collapsed onto the floor.

And I caught her.

When she finished, her body collapsed forward onto the floor, spent and open, chest rising in shallow waves. I brought her up into my arms and held her against me as the last of her tremors faded. Her skin was burning. Her pulse is still frantic. Her mouth opened and closed as if words might come, but they didn't. They weren't needed. She had spoken with every cry, every flinch, every inch of skin she gave me.

I held her for a while. To remind her where she belonged. To let her feel the gravity of what she had offered and the fact that I had received it.

After some time, she stirred. Slowly. Her breath had steadied. Her body still ached. She looked up at me, eyes heavy and red around the edges but clear. Present. Willing.

"Belle," she said. Her voice was raw. Graveled from screaming. But steady. "May I please you?"

Her fingers trailed over my thigh, not greedy.

I didn't answer with words. I moved her. I guided her down onto her knees in front of me. She settled easily as if it had always been her place. Her hands rested behind her back, her shoulders square, her head tilted slightly upward as she looked at me as if I were air, gravity, and God.

I undressed slowly, letting her see every movement. When I was bare, I sat back and opened my legs. She did not move until I nodded.

Then she crawled forward.

Her mouth met me gently at first. Lips soft. Her breath was warm. She kissed me as if she were making an offering. Each stroke of her tongue was a prayer. Each moan is low and full of pride.

She did not chase my orgasm. She *earned* it.

She licked me open with a precision I had taught her. Pressure precisely where I wanted it to be. A rhythm that matched my breath. She fed off my sounds, adjusted when I gripped her hair tighter, and sank deeper when I pulled her closer. She knew the map of my body now, and she traced it with her mouth as it mattered.

When I came, I gave her no warning. I did not announce it. I did not cry out. I let it take me the way I chose. Silent. Precise. Complete. She felt it before I moved. She recognized the shift in my breath. She noticed the tightening of my thighs. She followed the subtle pull of my hips as the wave crested. She kept going. Her mouth stayed open. Her tongue remained steady. She did not chase or push. She let me use her.

She licked through the peak and into the calm with quiet focus. Her hands never moved. Her knees stayed planted. Her only purpose was to serve. She did not stop until I reached down, wrapped my fingers in her hair, and pulled her gently away. Her lips left me soft and slick. Her breath came in slow pulls of air through her nose. Her lungs were struggling to keep up with the pace I had set.

She rested her head on my thigh. Her face was flushed. Her mouth was wet. Her body folded beside me like it belonged there. And it did. She had earned that place. She had taken everything and still asked for more. She had shown me what she was made of.

She did not speak. She did not need to. Every sound she had made, every look she had given me, every tear that had fallen while she held her position. That was her thank you. I let my fingers move through her hair. She stayed where she was. Her breathing slowed. She knew she had done well.

I told her I loved her in a haze of post-orgasm bliss. I didn't even realize I did it. I am not even sure I fully realized it until I said it.

We went strong as a couple for a year with wild and weird sexual romps as we made our way through the armoire d'amour. I knew that her star was going to outpace mine at some point, and I would be left broken-hearted by her absences. It was terrific for a while living in her orbit, but it's not a place I could call home.

I ran into her vile ex at a party sometime after we broke up, and I asked her something in French, and she told me that she didn't speak French. It made perfect sense, finally. She was hiding her true feelings for her ex in a language that she didn't understand. But with me, she didn't have to hide. I smiled at that thought.

I sometimes think about her now. After we parted, I heard she had married. She and her partner had a child; I hope she's happy. But a small part of me wonders if she ever retreated, if she ever went back to being guarded.

Did her partner ever hear her dirty talk in French, or is that something that is reserved just for me? How I would love to find out one day.

4

Prime Time

Eastern Market is a community market on Capitol Hill, where you can meet everyone, from those standing in line for Blue Buck Pancakes on Saturdays at Market Lunch to those at the famous straw hat-wearing Cheesemongers. It is usually bustling with locals and tourists looking for fresh food to turn into an overpriced artisanal pasta dish or to pass off as their own at dinner parties. It seemed like the perfect place to meet the Prime Time Princess.

I'd been living on a tight budget since getting my master's from grad school and landing my first job at a Federal Agency. Between DC rent, my low starting salary, and the damn student loan payments, I was just skating by each month. My basket was filled with day-old bread marked 50% off and odd cuts of chicken the butcher saved for me. I lied and said they were for the dog I didn't have.

Prime Time had dark hair and a cheap blazer, the kind Casual Corner used to carry. It looked like something she found in her mom's closet or a thrift store, or worse, a parting gift from an old lover. She wore a slightly worn T-shirt stretched over magnificent breasts held back by what I assumed was a jogging bra. Despite her poverty chic clothing, her basket told another story: she had money. She had a variety of prepared foods, $200 worth of serrano ham, caviar, a tray of manicotti, smoked salmon, and a massive wedge of premium cheese. Not the basket of a low-level working girl just getting by.

She was tall, maybe four inches taller than me, but not imposing. She had the kind of body that made you want to curl into it on a drizzly Sunday morning.

In her mid-twenties, the Prime Time Princess was making her mark as a news writer for a major cable network. While she spent her days crafting stories for millions of viewers, she was also skillfully dodging the chaos of the newsroom, always with an eye on eventually stepping in front of the camera herself.

She worked constantly and didn't have the bandwidth for anything else. I always considered this a good sign, as busy girls tend not to have relationships. I knew I could use my charms to entice her into a little commercial break with me.

I could tell that she was interested in me by her nipples. It's a bit of a trade secret, but a woman's nipples always point toward what she wants. If there's a spark, she'll turn her body toward you. If not, back away politely. But in this case? I had her full attention. The turrets turned, and I was in her sights. She must live nearby. I took a shot.

I walked up to her at the pasta counter. It's a good spot because it takes a while for the staff to ring up your order, so you stand around. I asked, "Can you recommend the manicotti?"

She smiled. Looked me up and down, making a kind of assessment. "I haven't had good manicotti in a long time."

"That's a shame," I said, observing the nipples carefully.

Prime Time watched me intensely. So, I performed a proximity test. I took a half-step closer to see if she'd back up. She didn't. My Prime Time Princess stood her ground.

"What wine would you pair with it?" I asked her.

She didn't miss a beat. "A bottle from a vineyard just outside Bordeaux."

It was hard to read her in this crowded room. "I'd love to try it," I said, "do you know where I could get my hands on some"? I sheepishly queried.

"No worries. I have some at my place." She turned on her heel and was halfway out the door, and she just expected me to follow her.

Bingo.

She was out of there like a bucking horse out of a chute. She walked fast, but my Chuck Taylor high tops were on. Every halfway-sane woman in D.C. knows better than to face the metro without them. No matter how fast she went, I could keep up.

I was right about her. She was rich. Very rich. Her house looked like it took up half the block, probably bought with family trust money. Some girls have all the luck.

I asked delicately, "Will your housemates be home or someone else?"

It was my way of screening the situation. You don't want to be surprised by a cold, distant husband home early from a business trip to Thailand. You only make that mistake once.

Her three-story corner rowhouse on East Capitol looked like it had been plucked from a history book and quietly bathed in money. The dark red brick appeared original, or at least restored to seem that way, bordered by flawless white window casings that had never known chipped paint. Leaded glass in the front door caught the sunlight in a way that suggested discretion without sacrificing spectacle. Above it, brass house numbers and a matching mailbox gleamed with the quiet smugness of old money or a very strategic divorce.

The white staircase leading up from the sidewalk was so scrubbed it could have passed inspection at a surgical theater. Flanking it on both sides, the garden was aggressively curated. No wildflower fantasy or Pollinator Pathway nonsense here. The tulips were planted in near-perfect circles, timed to bloom like a power move. The mulch looked fresh. The edges had been trimmed with military precision. Someone had spent time or money making it look effortless, and the result was a front yard that whispered control. I really do appreciate a woman with a well-trimmed garden.

In each front window, a single electric candle glowed. It was neither seasonal nor quaint. In this neighborhood, it was code for restraint, decorum, old-fashioned in a way that felt more curated than heartfelt.

When I asked if she rented out the basement, she didn't bother to answer. Just smiled, slow and small, like someone who had never needed to share square footage. And the stars bolted into the brick façade; those were not cute little decorations. They were Federal-style structural anchors, once used to keep old buildings from collapsing in on themselves. Now they were just another way to signal that this place had history and that she had paid for the privilege of preserving it.

The interior of her house was a blend of old-world elegance and charm. It was Capitol Hill classic, with two-inch moldings, original, never-painted pocket doors, an old fireplace with carved wood columns, and classic tile that looked untouched by time. The kind of place that felt like a frozen monument. I half expected Miss Havisham to appear in the dining room, still waiting for a long-past wedding day to arrive. Like her, it all seemed suspended in time with crystal candlesticks, heavy curtains, and a dining table too ornate for anyone under seventy.

It struck me then that this home wasn't made for her, or rather, not by her. It belonged to someone older. Maybe a grandmother. The sort who married much older men, the kind who left their young wives widowed and wealthy. My own grandmother was fifteen when she married a man twice her age. The upside was that those old bastards usually died early, sometimes in their mistresses' beds, sometimes in a brothel, or shot in apparent muggings coming home. Or at least that is how the coroner saw it.

Women acquire their wealth in various ways. But this one, my Prime Time Princess, had a legacy behind her. And by the look of it, she wasn't in a hurry to change a thing.

She tossed her keys and purse casually onto the bench in the entryway and moved straight to the liquor cabinet. Without hesitation, she plucked a bottle of expensive red wine from the top, the kind that promised a rich and indulgent experience, and headed toward the kitchen. I could tell she expected me to follow without a word, as if I were just there to go along with whatever she had planned. But I had my own intentions, and I was reasonably sure that before the night ended, she might find herself calling me Belle instead.

The way she handled that bottle of wine, so eager and confident, made it clear she was used to getting what she wanted. But tonight, I was more than ready to indulge in my own way, and who could resist an expensive and rare sip of wine when the evening promised so much?

Hardwood floors had been refinished but still creaked just enough to feel authentic. Exposed brick walls lined the kitchen, with cast-iron pans and copper-bottomed pots hanging neatly from railroad spikes driven straight into the mortar. Old jello molds gleamed like artifacts from a forgotten era.

I glanced around the room, dragging my fingers across the worn counter and the spines of ancient cookbooks, *The Joy of Cooking* and *Mastering the Art of French Cooking,* not a Pinterest printout or tablet in sight. This wasn't a woman who followed food trends. This was someone raised to believe in family recipes and handwritten notes in the margins.

She set the corkscrew in my palm and tilted her head slightly. "Do you know how to use that?"

I looked at her, letting my fingers close around the handle slowly. I said. "I've had a lot of experience."

Her lips curled at the corner. "Experience," she repeated, like she wanted to taste the word. "With wine?"

"With pressure," I said. "And patience."

She laughed under her breath, low and smooth, then handed me the bottle. As she placed it in my arms, the back of her hand pressed lightly against my breast. She did not apologize.. Her touch stayed there for the length of one breath, then slipped away like nothing had happened.

I stepped in closer to the counter and began to twist the corkscrew. I could feel her watching.

"What are you looking for exactly?" I asked, not bothering to meet her eyes.

"I like seeing how people handle things under tension," she said. "Most people rush. Or break something."

"Do I look rushed to you?"

"No," she said. "You look like you could take your time with just about anything."

I pulled the cork with a slow, deliberate motion. The pop was clean and sharp.

She smiled. "Show off."

"You were the one testing me."

"And you passed," she said, her eyes dropping to the bottle in my hands. "With distinction."

I poured her glass first. Then mine. She took it, but did not drink. Just watched me.

"I'm trying to decide," she said, running one finger along the stem of the glass.

"Decide what?"

"If I want to keep pretending I'm in control," she said, then sipped.

I let the silence settle, thick and ripe.

"You can pretend all you want," I said. "But you touched me first."

And then I saw it. Hanging by a thin leather strap from one of the railroad spikes was a spurtle—long, about 14 inches, carved from old wood, its surface darkened by years of stirring.

I picked it up, testing its balance, spinning it slightly like a wand, and smacking it hard into the palm of my hand. I set it back down on the counter as a promise to return to it later.

She watched me. Intently. Her eyes never left me. For a second, I thought it was time to make a move. But I waited. I wanted to make sure. I wanted to know if she was really ready. Eager.

I took another sip of wine and stepped in closer than necessary as she leaned against the kitchen sink. I reached behind her, brushing my arm just past her ribs, to grab the wine bottle from the other side. A gentle pin, casual but intentional.

She responded immediately. She coiled slightly, lifted her chin, and gently brushed the side of her neck against mine. I felt her breath before I felt her lips, but she didn't kiss me. She inhaled, slow and deep, right at the nape of my neck, dragging her breath to my ear.

She didn't touch me. Not yet. It was almost as if she were waiting—waiting for permission to do something.

Which pleased me to no end.

"I don't usually invite strangers into my kitchen," she murmured.

I smiled, eyes locked on hers. "I don't usually accept."

We stood close, too close to be casual, but just far enough for plausible deniability if one of us lost our nerve. I watched her hand. She wasn't fidgeting. She wasn't reaching for her wine. She was still. Women who freeze like that are either calculating their next move or bracing for impact.

I set down my glass and touched the counter beside her, my fingers spreading wide as I anchored myself in her space. Not touching her. Not quite. The air between us buzzed like a socket about to spark. I let it hang there a second longer.

"Do you enjoy cooking?" I asked.

"I like to watch," she said.

Of course, she did.

I stepped behind her slowly, trailing my fingers across her lower back as I reached for the spurtle. She didn't flinch. She leaned into the touch, barely, but it was enough. I put the spurtle back in my hands. Held it up with a smile.

"This'll do," I said.

She still hadn't moved. Just leaned there, watching. Assessing. I felt her gaze like hands.

"Do you always play with strangers in your kitchen?" I asked.

"Only the ones who know what a spurtle is." She flirted back mercilessly.

She kissed me. No warning. No hesitation. Full lips, warm and sure, pressing into mine with a confidence that made my knees consider surrender. Her hand came up to my cheek, anchoring me. She tasted like blackberry and wine, with something sharp beneath it, like hunger, perhaps. Or the echo of something unspoken.

I broke the kiss first, not because I wanted to, but because I like to keep the advantage. I pulled back an inch and whispered, "This is a beautiful spurtle," I said, dragging my hand over the polished wood, slow and deliberate. Admiration, curiosity, anticipation. All of it in the way my fingers moved along its grain.

PrimeTime watched me. I liked that about her.

She said it had been in her family for a long time. Some ancestral kitchen relic passed down through women who had used it for stews and discipline, maybe both. The kind of tool that lived in the same drawer as heirloom knives and secret grudges. The wood had been worn smooth from generations of use, the handle darkened where hands had gripped it with purpose. She no longer used it for cooking. Her voice was too casual when she said that, like the truth had teeth and she had learned not to let it bite.

I clicked my tongue and shook my head. "Having something this valuable just hanging around and not being used is shameful."

I cradled it in my hand, then brought it down with a sharp smack into my palm, again. The sound cracked through the air, quick and firm. Not hard enough to hurt. But enough to speak. Pain never scared me. Sometimes, leaning into it is the only way to prove you're the one in control. Or ready to be trusted with it.

She flinched slightly. Just a flicker. She knew what that sound meant. And what came next.

I looked up slowly, locking my eyes on hers. I gave her the gaze. The one that doesn't ask. The one that says I will not repeat myself. The one that usually works.

It worked.

"Turn around," I said. "Put your hands on the counter. And show me that gorgeous ass."

"Make me." She challenged me and my authority. She even tilted her chin up like an actress in a movie. She turned from an eager beaver to a bratty sub.

I took her chin like it belonged to me. Tilted it down without hesitation. She met my eyes like she still believed this was temporary. Like I was just something she could sample and forget. Another after-hours indulgence between conference calls and charity dinners. A diversion. Something dirty. Something beneath her.

"If you do not want me here, say it. I will go. You can lie in your perfect bed with your expensive vibrator and pretend that moaning into your pillow makes you less lonely. You can fantasize about someone like me who would actually make you behave. And you can come by yourself. Just like you always do. Unfucked. Unchanged. Still bored out of your pretty little mind."

She stayed quiet. That was smart.

"This is the truth you do not say out loud. You work too much. You earn too much. And none of it matters. Not when it is just you and the silence and the ache in your stomach that success never touches."

I stepped in. Close enough to take the air between us.

"You want to forget who you are. You want to stop being the one in charge. You want someone who will not give a single fuck about your degrees or your titles. Someone who sees past the polish. Past the pedigree. Someone who will take what she wants and leave you soaked and wrecked and thankful."

I circled her like a decision she was not ready to make.

"You brought me here because you thought rough trade would wake you up. You thought you could play at surrender and still keep your hands clean. But I do not care what you want. I care what you need. And what you need is not gentle. It is not nice. It does not wear a suit or ask for permission."

I stopped behind her. Close enough to let her feel the weight of the choice she made.

"You want the kind of night you will remember when you are back in your office on Monday, crossing your legs under the desk because you are still sore. You want your body to be taken further than you would admit out loud. Not because you hate your life. Because it is too clean. Too controlled. Too fucking polite. You want a night that ruins your balance and makes you feel real again."

I brushed her jaw with the back of my hand. There was nothing soft in it.

"Tell me I am wrong."

She said nothing.

I smiled. Cold. Final. "Did not think so," I said smugly. "Now turn around. Lift your skirt. Drop your panties. And spread your fucking legs, princess."

The panties hit the floor faster than a prom dress. She hiked her skirt to her waist, that perfect moon of an ass already in the air like she had been waiting for this.

I stepped in behind her, pressed my mouth right to her ear, and rubbed her naked ass.

"That is better, Princess. You are just an eager, hungry little beaver aching to get paddled and eaten until you start questioning your entire college thesis on gender identity."

She let out a breath that sounded like a whimper, but I was not done. Not even close.

That ass. Round. Beautiful. And mine.

"You can call me Belle. If you behave." I whispered.

"Belle," she breathed, the word trembling through her.

"I'm going to spank you," I said softly. "I'm going to use this spurtle. I won't hit you too hard because I want something left of you to fuck afterward."

Her head dipped, obedient. I asked, "Would you like that?"

She nodded.

"Say it out loud," I demanded.

"Yes, Belle."

"Yes, what?"

"I want you to spank me," she said, voice strained with need.

"Do you want me to fuck you after?"

"Yes."

"How do you want me to fuck you?" I asked as I slid a hand down her front toward her crotch.

"Do you want me to touch you here?"

"Yes, Belle," she gasped.

"Then beg me. Or I will walk away right now, and you will get nothing. Beg me like you mean it."

As I spoke, I tapped her swollen clit once. Her whole body jolted.

"Beg me," I said again, tapping her harder.

"Beg me," I repeated, striking a third time, shy of cruel.

She shuddered and writhed under my touch.

"Please, Belle," she whimpered. "Spank me, then fuck me."

"Convince me," I said. "You want this. Show me you are worth my time."

"Please," she said again, her voice cracking. "I'll do anything you want."

I moved my hands to her breasts, grazing her nipples. They were rock-hard.

She really did want it that bad.

"What a pleasure this will be," I murmured. "Obedience is a beautiful thing in a beautiful woman."

I pressed her down against the counter. Then I lifted her hips, spread her legs, and looked at her thoroughly—ass up, legs parted, her slick garden glistening, and her puckered little hole tight and pink.

I brought the spurtle to her ass and tapped her gently, soundlessly.

I swung back and gave her a soft thud on the ass.

"Are you going to be a good girl for me?"

"Yes, Belle," she said quickly. "I will be a good girl."

I spanked her again, just a little harder.

"Say thank you ."

"Thank you, Belle," she said through clenched teeth.

"I'm going to hit you again. Harder this time."

"Yes, Belle."

I brought the spurtle down across her ass with a satisfying smack. Her skin was turning red, inflamed, and beautiful.

"I'm going to spank you again," I told her.

"Yes, Belle."

"I don't think you're going to behave for me tonight," I said and struck her again with the same pressure. She winced but stayed perfectly still, holding position.

I reached around and found her clit again. It was scorching. I slid down to her vulva, slipping two fingers inside her easily.

She was drenched.

I pulled my fingers out and brought them to her lips.

"See how wet you are?" I said. "You're making me want you. I want you to think about me making you come every time I hit you."

"Yes. Yes, Belle," she moaned.

"Shall we continue?"

"Yes, Belle"

"Count for me."

I hit her again.

"One," she said breathlessly.

Another hit.

"Two."

"Three."

"Do you want more?" I asked.

"Yes!" she cried.

"Yes, what?"

"Yes, Belle. I want more."

I dragged my finger down her spine and smacked her ass with my hand, then rubbed the sting into her skin slowly.

She was primed. I had promised her more.

"Oh, what is a Domme to do with a hot ass like this one?" I mused aloud. I raised the spurtle again.

"Count," I ordered.

"Four."

"Five."

"Six."

I moved around her slowly, dragging my fingertips across her skin, letting every nerve end come alive. I ran my hand across her ass, then down to her thighs.

She shivered the second I touched her inner thigh.

"Count."

"Seven."

"Count."

"Eight."

"Count."

"Nine."

"Count."

"Ten."

And that was when she turned. She grabbed my face, pulled me into a kiss, and pushed us both to the ground.

Her mouth was hungry. She kissed me deeply, grinding her flooded basement against the front of my pants like she thought she could make me come from friction alone.

The second we hit the floor, I flipped her into a plow pose. Her legs over her head, shoulders flat to the tile, arms pinned beneath her. Her triangle was exposed, flushed, and wet, framed perfectly between trembling thighs. She gasped, caught between shock and arousal, but it was too late to resist.

I straddled her legs and used the weight of my thighs to pin her down. She tried to wriggle. I pressed harder. She wasn't going anywhere. Her back arched, her face mashed into her knees, her body folded like something meant to be kept open.

I leaned forward and let my breath settle over her. Close enough to make her ache. Close enough that her whole body pulsed from the nearness of it.

"Well," I murmured, watching her face as she cradled her own legs, "it looks like Princess is feeling feisty tonight."

Her eyes flicked up, glassy with want, still clinging to that little scrap of pride. I kissed the inside of her knee. Then the sharp edge of her hipbone. Then, her ass. But I never touched her where she was begging for it.

"Feisty's cute," I continued, letting my lips graze her skin without giving her anything. "But let's see how long it lasts when all you get is breath and denial."

I lowered my mouth just above her vulva, lips so close she could feel the heat of every word. She trembled. I stayed still.

"You wanted attention," I said softly. "You have it. Now earn the rest."

She whimpered. Her body jolted beneath me. Her hips jerked toward my mouth, desperate for contact, but I didn't give in.

"Say it." I insisted on bearing my weight on her.

She bit her lip. Her breath came ragged. Her body begged louder than her voice ever had.

"Say you'll be good, Princess. Say it like you mean it. Or you'll stay like this, open and aching, until you forget what pleasure even feels like."

She held out for another second. Maybe two.

Then she broke.

Her voice cracked, loud and raw.

"I will be good. Please. Please, I will be good."

And I smiled.

"On your fucking knees, princess," I ordered.

I just let her up from the plow pose. Her face is flushed, her breathing shallow, sweat streaked halfway down her cheek. And I am watching her, but not really looking at her.

What I am really doing is deciding.

This bratty little performance might not be worth it. The eye-rolls, the pushback, the manufactured resistance she thinks make her interesting. It is not power. It is noise. And I do not need to prove anything to someone who cannot even hold still when given the chance to surrender.

I am not here to pass some test. I am not collecting merit badges for dominance. I do not care how defiant she can be. I care whether she understands the weight of yes. Whether she kneels because she wants to, not because she is bored or wants a thrill, or mimicking porn she watches but offends her feminism.

There is no prize for dragging someone into submission. No satisfaction in winning a game they did not mean to play. I need someone who knows why they are kneeling. Or someone who asks, and means it.

"Upstairs. Now."

She sprang to her feet.

"What I want to do to you takes time, room, and privacy," I said. "Or we can end this here."

"No. You have to stay. Please. Please." She begged.

She grabbed my hand and tugged me urgently, practically dragging me up the stairs. Her red, spanked ass bounced with every step, and the view was making it harder to walk like a civilized person.

There are worse ways to spend a day.

She reached her bedroom first, skidding to a stop just past the threshold.

"Are you going to ask me in?" I asked, one eyebrow raised.

Instead of answering, she turned. I grabbed her and kissed her hard, pushing her backward into the door. It swung open under the pressure, and we tumbled onto a ridiculously pristine white carpet.

The room looked like a time capsule from the 1940s, antique furniture, perfume atomizers on a vanity, and white-on-white decor as if someone had taken a snowstorm and given it a credit card. There were white walls, bedding, lamps, dressers, and even a white carpet that had no business being in the presence of what I was about to do.

What a beautiful place to make a mess.

I looked down at her body, flushed and heaving, ready for more.

I grabbed her wrists and pinned them to the floor behind her head, then spread her legs with my knee and pressed my thigh right between them. Her slick triangle found it instantly. She latched on to the desperation of a starved thing and began humping it with the force of a sumo wrestler, with the grace of an inbred poodle.

"Not so fast," I said.

I yanked my knee away.

Ugh, she is bratting again.

I had a spurtle in my hand and her stubborn little need to contend with. That was enough. She could test me all she wanted. Eventually, she would break. And I would make sure she remembered how it felt to lose on purpose.

"You don't come until I say so," I told her, voice low and firm.

"Yes, please, Belle," she gasped.

"I'm going to let go of your hands," I said. "And you're going to get up and strip for me. I will sit down on that little cuck chair over there, and you will stop in front of me and show off your beautiful body. Show me every inch of it. You are a work of art, and you should be appreciated properly."

I released her wrists slowly, deliberately.

As I got up, she reached out and grabbed me. Instantly, I pinned her hands back down to the carpet.

"Don't you know how to listen?" I asked. My voice didn't rise. It dropped.

"Do you want me to stop?" I demanded.

She blinked up at me, wide-eyed.

"Then do as I say."

She pouted. It's not my favorite look on a grown woman. That retreat into childish petulance might make some Dommes excited. Not me. I prefer my women to be fully grown and eager.

Without another word, I rolled her over using my knees and gave her a hard smack with my open hand across her ass.

"Are you going to dance for me?"

"Yes, Belle," she whispered, chastened.

"I am going to get up now," I said. "And I am not going to tell you to obey again." We both knew that that was a lie. But it was clear this was going to be a long night.

I walked over to the chair and sat down.

She slowly rose, hesitating for half a breath before walking toward me. Piece by piece, her clothes fell to the floor. The skirt slipped down her hips. I caught a perfect view of her lush, thick, patch of wild brown curls that made me want to bury my face right there and never come up for air.

She danced slowly, not like a porn star, not like a stripper, but like one of those sultry pole dancers who know how to make time crawl for tips.

She stopped at her shirt, holding the moment in place. Then peeled it away, revealing a simple black jogging bra. She bent forward slowly, wide-legged, her ass and garden on full display. She reached for her ankles and, in one fluid motion, pulled the bra off over her head, then stood up slowly, holding my gaze through her own legs before twisting back to face me.

"Crawl here," I said, crooking my finger.

She crawled over, climbed onto my lap, and pressed her body against mine. Her hips rolled over my thigh, grinding her slick heat into my pants. She arched forward, pushing her tits into my face, moaning softly with each motion.

Back and forth, she rocked against me, soaking my pant leg with her desire.

I grabbed her ass with both hands and squeezed hard, making her gasp.

"You are not allowed to get off until I tell you to," I said. "I can feel how much you want it. Your beautiful body pleases me, and I want to appreciate every inch of it."

I picked up the bra from the floor with my toe and then looked at her.

"Stand up," I said. "Put your hands behind your back."

She did as she was told.

"I am going to bind your wrists by twisting this bra around them. You can get out of it at any time. You always have that choice."

I wrapped the fabric snugly around her wrists and tied it off.

"But for your pleasure and mine," I said, "you should stay bound until I take it off."

I paused, looking her in the eye.

"Do you understand?"

"Yes, Bell..." she began, but halfway through the word, I pressed my finger against her clit.

Firm, deliberate pressure. I circled it into that sweet little nerve bundle, slow and precise. I could feel its click under my knuckle.

She bucked like she'd come right then, but I knew better. Her body tensed. No relaxation, no soft sigh, no drop into bliss. She was coursing with unfulfilled desire.

"Are you close?" I murmured. "Just a few minutes more, and I'll have you screaming. You'll be begging me to let you come."

I dragged my finger upward, slipping it over her belly until I cupped one of her breasts. Small. Perfect. I pinched her nipple gently, just enough to make her moan. Then I leaned in and took her other breast into my mouth. I bit her nipple with the edges of my front teeth, just enough to sting. Not enough to hurt. Enough to wake her nerves. To make her needs worse.

She whimpered.

Her chest rises and falls as if she already knows what she is about to give me. Her skin is flushed, thighs pressed together, nipples tight from more than just the room's air. I do not say a word. I let the silence stretch before sitting down.

I gesture that she should climb up, straddling my legs, each knee settling on the cushion outside of mine. We face each other, breath to breath. Her eyes search my face, looking for approval, for correction, for whatever she has been trained to crave. I give her nothing. I only take my time, letting the power settle around us like steam.

I lift her without asking. My hands grip her hips, and I pull her forward until her ass rests on my thighs. Her balance falters, and that makes it better. I tell her to hook her legs over the arms of the chair. She hesitates for a breath, then obeys, and that brief pause is more delicious than immediate submission.

Her legs stretch wide. She is exposed. She is open, wet, tilted toward me with no angle of escape. I push my knees up beneath her, just enough to tilt her hips forward, to raise her until everything I want is close enough to claim.

I lean in and take her clit between my teeth, sharp and deliberate. She gasps. I bite harder, just enough to remind her that pain is a gift, not a punishment. Her body arches, spine curving, tension rolling up through her shoulders as her arms strain against the binds behind her back.

I kiss downward. My mouth drags in a slow, possessive line. She is shaking now, but I do not let her fall. I hold her in place, suspended between pleasure and pressure.

I pause. To let her feel the anticipation burn.

She is soaked. I press one finger in, slow and firm, curling up until I hit the spot that makes her eyes roll back. She gasps again, this time a little broken, a little desperate. I press harder. She whimpers. Her thighs twitch. Her hands flex uselessly behind her.

I do not move fast. I do not let her chase the edge. I control the rhythm. And when I finally lower my mouth to her, when my tongue slides against that swollen, aching center, her whole body pulls tight like wire.

Her G-spot pulsed against my fingertips as I focused all my attention there, stroking it slowly. Methodically. Mercilessly.

She howled.

"Please," she cried out. "Please, Belle. Please."

I kept tapping her G-spot with a firm, steady rhythm while my mouth latched onto her clit. I flicked her clit with my tongue, then dragged my teeth across it, just enough to make her writhe.

"Please," she gasped. "Can I come?"

I said nothing.

I kept going, tapping inside her with expert pressure, maintaining that perfect, cruel rhythm. No mercy. No answer.

Then I dove back down.

This time, I used the backside of my tongue, flicking her clit in fast, wet strokes. Meanwhile, my fingers circled her G-spot harder, rougher, stroking her from the inside out.

"Can I come now, Belle?" she screamed.

It's a good thing these old houses were built with thick walls.

I kept working her clit with every bit of my focus. Her body was trembling, every muscle locked.

Then, I lifted my head for just one second.

"Yes," I whispered. "Come now."

I pressed down hard on her clit. I curled my fingers tightly into her G-spot and pushed.

She shattered.

Her whole body arched off the chair with such force that she nearly broke my nose.

But honestly, it would have been worth it.

She collapsed into the seat, wrecked and radiant.

I slowly removed my hand from between her legs and leaned forward, kissing her lips softly. She kissed me back, with the last of her strength.

I whispered into her ear. "Good girl." I removed the hopelessly stretched-out bra from her wrists and held her tightly. Then I kissed her again and then lowered her to the carpet, letting her catch her breath. I stroked the inside of her thigh gently, waiting for her to come back into her body. I wasn't entirely sure when that would happen. She seemed pretty wiped out.

Eventually, she stirred. A rustle, a shift. She squatted beside me and kissed me again, this time with a sleepy smile.

"I'm so thankful I went to the market today," she murmured.

I smiled and tucked a curl behind her ear.

"I'm thrilled to oblige. You are beautiful. You deserve the very best."

She leaned against my shoulder.

I added, "I'm interested in keeping this going. If that's something you want."

"Yes," she whispered. "I would like that very much."

"Then let's go to bed."

I stood and offered my hand. She took it. I led her across the room and laid her down, face up, across the soft white comforter.

"What do you want next?" I asked, brushing her hair aside.

She looked up at me, hesitant but eager.

"I want to go down on you," she said quietly. "Tell me what to do".

I smiled at her bravery. I said. "I like someone who follows instructions and does what I tell them to do when I tell them to do it. If that's what you want, we can begin."

"Yes, Belle. I want that."

"Good."

I stood in front of her. I slowly undressed, letting her watch as each piece of clothing came off.

"Run your hands over me," I said. "Get familiar with my body."

She did, reverently. Her fingers traced over my shoulders, my breasts, my hips. I turned around and had her kiss the small of my back, then had her turn me back to face her and kiss my mouth. Her lips were soft, but her body was buzzing with need again.

I guided her mouth down to my chest. She dragged her tongue over one breast, then cupped both in her hands and kissed them reverently. I turned around and lay back on the bed with my legs dangling off the edge.

"Kneel in front of me," I said.

She obeyed instantly.

She dropped to her knees.

Her tongue met my clit.

She had a thick, textured tongue, and the way she wrapped it around me—messy, hungry, raw—was thrilling. She circled the outside first, teasing and lapping, almost nervously.

Then she tried to go further. She slid her hand between my legs and pushed a few fingers inside. Then another. Then another.

"Too much," I said gently. "That's too advanced for you right now."

She looked up, apologetic.

"Put your mouth on me," I told her. "But focus only on my clit. That's all I want you to think about right now."

She tried to find it with her hand but missed the spot.

"No," I corrected her by slapping her hand. "A little to the left. Now up. A bit more. Higher. Yes, there."

I gasped softly.

"Now tap. Just tap it lightly."

She did.

"Little circles," I instructed. "Make it hot."

She began circling with her tongue, eyes locked on mine.

"Good girl," I said. "I want you to want it."

I guided her by the back of her head, giving instructions.

"Harder. Now softer. Pull back more. Stay on it. "

"Tell me how much you love it," I said. "Tell me what you want."

"I want this," she moaned. "I want to make you come. I want to make you scream. I want to make you so loud and so passionate that you shake. I want to be yours."

That was it.

I grabbed her head by both ears and pressed her face into my clit.

"Suck on my clit" I growled.

She did. She kept sucking and licking, then working her fingers gently over the slick heat of my clit until I felt the spiral begin. It built higher and higher until, finally, I broke.

My legs locked around her shoulders and held her there, pulling her body against mine as I screamed.

My orgasm ripped through me. I shook violently, then collapsed back into the mattress.

She crawled beside me and curled into my side, wrapping around me like a little black cat. Her breath was warm against my skin.

She whispered how good it was. How much she wanted more. How amazing I was.

She wanted to keep going tonight.

"Can we go again?" she asked.

"Thirsty little bitch." I like that in a woman.

"I want to fuck you," she tried to seduce me with the thought. I had to keep myself from chuckling.

"You have to walk before you can run, Princess. Nothing from me is just given; you have to earn it."

I smiled. "This time, I will...fuck..you." Putting my hand on her clit and rubbing hard. It was not difficult to convince her to see things my way.

She didn't even hesitate. She handed me her favorite harness and a strap-on that could terrify a priest. I dressed for the occasion, slipping into the harness with the proficiency of a Preakness winner.

It was a monster. Nine inches, maybe more. Three inches thick, easy. It was hot pink colored, which—thank God—was better than those hyper-realistic ones based on some retired porn star. I never liked those. I don't want to fuck someone else using a stranger's Silicone Steve. I usually bring my own to the party, but this is presumably the one she uses on herself or on some hapless Hill dyke or intern. But I am going to make her forget about the junior league.

I don't prefer pink glittery sex toys. It makes it seem too much like a fashion item and not the monster that was going to bang on her g-spot till she wished she spent her college days getting shtupped by a gender-fluid sophomore with multiple face piercings and ironic tattoos vs. the stupid frat guys at the Ivy League school she went to instead.

Just because you can top someone does not make you a top to everyone. Everyone bottoms to someone, but it would be unlikely that I would bottom to PrimeTime. I will have to break the news to her gently after I fuck her hard.

She stroked it like it was real and lubed it up, her hands slow and sensual. I could tell that turned her on. For me, it wasn't about the cock. It was about her. About what I could do to her with it.

I lay down on my back, and she straddled me, her gorgeous body lowering onto that massive toy like it was her personal challenge for the night. She moved slowly. Carefully. Her thighs trembled. She could barely take it.

Each inch sank into her, and her breath caught with everyone. Her hips rolled, bouncing in short movements. Her hot breasts swayed above me, that beautiful body riding me like she'd been born to do it.

And with every bounce, the harness slammed against my own clit. I could feel it. The pressure. The pounding. She was fucking herself, but every movement sent shockwaves through me. Raw, blinding pleasure.

She was close. I could see it.

I licked my finger, brought it to her clit, and rubbed tight little circles as she worked. Her back arched. Her moan caught. She slammed her hips down one more time.

Then she came. Loud. Hard. Her whole body convulsed before she collapsed on top of me, sweaty and radiant.

I was smothered under her body, her breasts, her breath. I lay there thinking, How is she not taken? What kind of fool let this woman go? Though I question the decision of someone who buys a hot pink glitter schlong to fuck someone this hot.

Maybe she bought it herself, but it would have been color-coordinated with the decor. She would buy a ghost white cock.

Too early for ex-talk, sure. But my God. Some people throw away gold.

She reached down, tracing a finger along my ribs.

"Did you come?" she asked softly.

"A top would not have to ask, but not yet," I said. "But if you keep moving like that..."

And she did. She started rocking again. Grinding. Her hips circled slowly, then faster. Riding that toy as if it belonged inside her.

Her eyes stayed locked on mine. Her body moved as if she knew exactly how to undo me. My breath came faster. My muscles clenched.

And then I let go.

I came again, head thrown back, body shaking, vision blurring.

Say what you will about gender differences. But that multiple orgasm thing? That alone almost makes up for the pay gap.

Almost.

"See, I can top you." She bragged.

"We lay there, tangled, panting. She rolled off me and whispered in my ear.

"Sure you did." I lied. If her version of topping me is doing everything that I want, and then riding me till I come. I can let her think that.

"So if you are my top, then I want a massage, full body with oil."

PrimeTime was surprised; it was as if she hadn't given it much thought.

"Come on, Mistress, grab the oil and start on my shoulders."

She pouted. This may not have worked out the way she intended.

After I let her "top" me again vigorously. Which to her just meant crawling on top of me while I fucked her. I have seen better topping on sundaes.

It is not easy to be a top; it is more about seduction, control, and the ability to read your partner's emotions. She likes this position. Who am I to correct her? If she wants to get me off while I watch her tits bounce, and she slams down on me. I am ok with that. Apparently, this girl only reads the headlines.

We curled up in the sheets. Her body against mine spent like an inheritance.

At some point, I fell asleep.

I woke first. I always do.

She was still curled under the covers, the soft rise of her back barely visible in the early light. The sheets clung to her hips like they'd developed feelings overnight. One foot was kicked into the cool morning air—pale, elegant, chipped black polish on the toes.

I sat up slowly, careful not to wake her. My shirt was still hanging on the back of a chair. My pants were... somewhere. I found them with the kind of practiced efficiency that comes from leaving other people's bedrooms before sunrise.

The house looked different in the morning. It was less like a mausoleum and more like a museum with bad lighting. The hallway smelled faintly of lemon polish and dust.

Back in the kitchen, I found a kettle and set it on the stove. If I were going to do a morning-after, I could do it with caffeine. I rummaged through the cabinets like a raccoon and struck gold in a ceramic canister labeled "Kenya AA."

Fancy. Of course.

As the kettle began to hiss, I felt her behind me. Quiet. Soft-footed. The way cats move when they're still deciding whether they want affection or distance.

She didn't speak. Just leaned against the doorframe in an old T-shirt and nothing else. It wasn't mine. It had a faded college logo on the front.

Yale. Of course.

"I don't usually do this," she said, her voice still rough from sleep.

I didn't turn. "Let strangers cook in your kitchen? Or let them leave without breakfast?"

She chuckled. "Neither."

The kettle screamed.

I turned the burner off and reached for mugs. "I'll take mine black," I said. "Unless you've got oat milk. "

She took a mug from my hand, brushing her fingers against mine. Her touch was cooler now, and she was more cautious. It was like we'd stepped through a door in the dark and now stood blinking under fluorescent lights.

She laughed. The sound spilled out, bright and involuntary, and for a moment, she forgot to wear the face she had prepared for me. That polish cracked, just slightly, and something more primal slipped through.

I had just passed the second test.

Some women want to be seen. Some want to be worshipped. Some crave understanding, like it will save them.

Not her.

She was a brat. She did not want understanding. She wanted to be tamed. She wanted resistance, pressure, the kind of strength that does not yield to charm or manipulation. She needed someone who would not be impressed by her posture or her lines. Someone who would outwait her, outstare her, and break her precisely where she kept pretending she was unbreakable.

This was not about insight. This was not about connection. This was about power. Hers, flaunted like armor, and mine, quiet and inevitable.

And lucky for her, I do not flinch.

I do not soften.

And I never walk into a brat's game unless I already know how it ends.

We stayed together for a while, but it would never have been a long-term romance. It was convenient. I was interesting, so interesting that she loved dressing me up, parading me around to her rich friends, and showing me off like I was some rare thing she had managed to capture.

And that's exactly how it felt.

I wasn't a partner. I was something she had caught.

She had big plans and big dreams, and so did I. Mine would stay here in D.C., and hers would carry her to New York.

Eventually, she packed up and went. At the time, I wasn't ready to go. And truthfully, I didn't think she was the girl I would spend my life with.

I was right.

She found what she was looking for. It was never going to be me.

Still, I will never forget how she looked that day in the market when I first laid eyes on her. The desire in her eyes. The heat radiating off her skin. The way I wanted to drown in it.

How I wanted to be entirely consumed by that beautiful body and her gnawing hunger.

The hunger she had for me.

She became a big-time news personality and extremely wealthy, not that she wasn't already, but now even more so. She was polished, powerful, and everywhere.

And sometimes, when I am feeling wistful, or a stray thought of her passes through, or I have some manicotti for dinner, I think of her and smile.

For a moment, my mind drifts backward to those heady days. I no longer wonder what might have been. I think of the fun we had.

5

Party Deflection

At some point in every Washingtonian woman's life, and in a surprising number of gay men's, one has to decide whether or not they are going to date a straight Republican man in D.C.

If you are even vaguely progressive, it is not an easy choice. I believe what you do in your bedroom is none of my business unless I am in there with you. And yet these Republican men seem determined to crawl into everyone else's bed except their wives'.

When single, these Conservative men assault the Capitol armed with Ayn Rand quotes, a mid-tier whiskey collection, and a conviction that their unearned moral superiority will manifest as legislation.

They claim to serve the common man, but their mission is to enact a vision of their future prosperous selves, unburdened by the needs of their fellow citizens. They hand out tax breaks to broligarchs like communion wafers and hack away at food stamps with surgical glee, all while making sure their billionaire benefactors never lose a dime or a yacht. Health care for the poor is always too expensive. Private jets, on the other hand, are deductible.

Behind the curtain for these libertines of liberty? It is not so much the Senate floor as the frat house floor. These men throw themselves into a particular kind of Beltway bacchanalia: cocktail parties, donor galas, stripper lunch bunches, dick-out golf games, and staffer happy hours. They chase every sexually flexible Tinder match between Dupont and the Hill.

It is not quite debauchery for its own sake. It is more like a sexual Rumspringa. A temporary break from the pious path, indulgently underwritten by influence and protected by plausible deniability.

Their Rumspringa is run on liberal women and gay men. Women who are open, curious, and nonjudgmental. Gay men who are smart enough to spot repression from a mile away and generous enough to entertain it anyway. These are the people who say yes to things their future wives would clutch pearls over, and the people at their megachurches would need a diagram, Google, and ten hours on Pornhub to understand.

For our Tinder-crashing DL dudes, who hide under flag pins and anti-trans rhetoric and a tan suit phobia that borders on erotic fixation. They hate what they want. They legislate against what they crave. And when it finally slips out, whether through a massage boy scandal or a leaked group chat, it is always the same chorus: shock, denial, prayer.

They come to us to get their freak on without consequences. They want to explore. They want to be pegged in panties while we whisper tales of how Reagan deregulated the airline industry. And we say okay. We say, Take off your cufflinks and hand me the lube.

It is a kind of sexual freedom they never find in the rest of their lives. And once they taste it, they go feral. Years of repression combust in a single night, and suddenly, this man who just voted against reproductive rights is begging to be choked while calling me Mommy.

Then, inevitably, in the next chapter, they find *her.* She is at least a decade younger. Maybe two. She believes men should lead, women should bake, and Jesus probably had a private school voucher. She has "saved herself," not necessarily out of conviction, but often out of calculation, and now presents herself as the prize for a man who has spent years actively mocking the values she claims to uphold. He is suddenly "reformed" just in time for the wedding #tradwife. She is his redemption arc. He is her ticket to the mid-tier conservative podcast circuit.

I sometimes muse that if we could get these conservative women laid by our liberal brothers or sisters, they would switch sides and start wearing yoga pants everywhere and voting Democratic.

I've done my part for the cause, converting more than a few tradwife trainees with nothing but a talented tongue and an unnervingly accurate homing signal for a girl's G-spot. Give me a few hours with a pro-lifer woman, and suddenly, the one who once flinched at the idea of her desire is moaning through revelations, unraveling centuries of repression one gasp at a time. She is learning, awakening, and rewriting everything she thought she knew about power, pleasure, and divinity.

Eventually, I found a man I would consider dating in an "across-the-aisle" romance. Not necessarily with hopes of a conversion, but a girl can try.

Let's call him Tuskee because he was blessed by the Almighty in at least one aspect.

I was beyond excited at the idea of dating someone highly placed in the Republican Party as an act of Resistance. My body would be put to use for the greater good of humanity if only I could use my wiles to honey-trap him to the Democratic side.

You might recognize his name if I say it out loud. I met Tuskee through an incredible lobbyist for a large soda producer who seemed to know everyone in town, as almost all deep-pocketed lobbyists do. Around every fat cat lobbyist is a cloud of Hill staffers, backbenchers, and nonprofiteers who hang around for access and the occasional dinner or drinks invite that falls out of their pockets.

Being with Tuskee felt like stepping into a world just slightly out of reach, where every room buzzed with secrets, and the next big story was always one drink away. Hanging out with him was a nonstop parade of political gossip, clinking glasses, backslapping camaraderie, and effortless introductions to people I had only ever seen on TV or listed in bylines. He moved through Washington as if he owned it, and for a while, being by his side made me feel like I belonged there, too.

People loved to compare us to that famous political couple, the across-the-aisle marriage that always gets name-dropped in puff pieces about bipartisan love. And for a time, we leaned into that idea. There was discussion about what it could mean for us and what it could symbolize. It was flattering, maybe even a little addictive, to be seen that way.

But the truth was more complicated to package. We weren't just two people with differing opinions. We came from different worlds entirely. Our differences weren't philosophical. They were structural. They were economical, cultural, and generational—the kind of differences that aren't resolved by clever banter or shared values about tax reform—the kind that sit under your skin and whisper at you when the cameras are off and the lights go down.

We went to all his Republican events together. Not that he reciprocated. He would not be caught dead at a Planned Parenthood fundraiser, though he has paid for a few abortions there, allegedly.

We visited the RNC headquarters for a political fundraiser. We went to dinner at wood-paneled steakhouses. We hung out with people you would recognize if you had the patience to watch C-SPAN.

The introductions were always a little awkward. "Oh, you're a Democrat?" they'd say, blinking in surprise. "Well... how nice." To them, I was nothing but his sown wild oats. Practice until the real girl appeared fresh from college with two crossed knees, technical "virginity" and a daddy with a mega-ranch in Montana.

Tuskee was tall, olive-skinned, with black hair sculpted into a short, hyper-masculine crew cut that defied logic by working perfectly. He was no more than thirty, with a runner's body—all wiry muscle. A gold cross hung around his neck, an artifact that would usually have thrown me off, but considering his strictly conservative, religious upbringing, it made a strange, ironic sense.

Why Tuskee? He was dishy. He liked basketball, the Washington Wizards, and a college artifact. Not the WNBA team whose name he could never seem to remember. He enjoyed fishing, which I've never liked. He ran, lifted weights, and had a group of guys he golfed with and another separate group of guys he played basketball with on Saturday morning.

He always loved running through the National Zoo to see the elephants, his distant cousins, at least he believed they would be if he accepted evolution. He loved drinking, not just a beer or two, but sometimes ten, usually at the Irish Times, the bar next to the Dubliner, a few steps from the Hill. Packed with young political staffers losing themselves after long days of pretending not to hate each other. Many times, I saw a certain well-known Congressman there, getting incredibly chummy with his disastrously younger intern, who was above the age of consent but not the drinking age. It was the kind of place where you could disappear. He loved it there. There was a singer with a guitar who would come along on Thursday nights, and somehow, despite all the rancor from the week, in a weird show of forced bipartisanship, we'd all sing along.

We had a great time, and I wanted to see more of him. I sensed there was something he kept hidden, a darkness he was terrified to let anyone see. As we got closer and our conversations deepened, he finally told me what he wanted. When he did, I could see his fear and the dread of being judged or rejected.

I said, "I suspected." I took a beat, grabbed him behind the neck, and pushed his head down to the ground. "Don't fucking lift your eyes to me." I barked at him.

And I swear to God, he cried. He wept tears from years of holding something back. It was the relief of finally being accepted, of realizing he could be who he was without shame or judgment, and, I assume, without having to pay for it. Sub Tuskee came out of the bondage closet.

There was a feeling he carried about sex, a tightly wound guilt, almost like the heavy cloak of ultra-religious upbringing. He was embarrassed by it, unable to shake off the feeling. He only found relief by surrendering completely and letting someone else take the reins. I could practically smell the shame on him from across the room; he lowered his eyes when he spoke to me, his face lighting up in a flicker of hope before embarrassment washed over it. It wasn't just about pleasure for him; it was a form of penance, a ritual of earning the right to desire. He tried to keep everything under control, but when it slipped, he was awash with guilt, a "shame-gasm" that left him physically and emotionally drained.

He seemed to know exactly what he wanted. Very specifically. That stood out because most people discover their kinks over time. But not him. He was clear from the beginning. This clarity made me think he had experience, likely with a specialist, someone professional who performed acts of ritual humiliation. It sounded like a good Friday night to me.

Our usual routine was simple, but it was also transformative. He would come over, and I would meet him at the door wearing something provocative: a merry widow, thigh-highs, lace, but not naked, covered yet suggestive. The goal wasn't exposure. It was an invitation.

He would grovel at my feet, begging to be let in. Then he would strip, slowly, down to nothing. Once he was naked, he would kneel in front of me. That was when I would place the collar, an oversized leather one, two inches wide, with a metal ring in the front. Perfect for pulling.

It was a signal. The collar meant the dynamic had shifted. He was in his submissive mode, and while it was on, he had one job: to respond to me.

Each time I made him kneel and lock that collar into place, I felt a surge of power. It wasn't just a performance. It was a ritual that charged me and gave me the energy I could carry into the rest of my life. It was like tapping into a well of confidence, something I could draw on whenever I needed to stand tall, whether in a boardroom or a casual conversation.

I would make him kneel, lock the collar into place, lean down, my voice a slow purr. "Are you ready to begin?" I'd ask.

"Yes, Belle," he'd whisper, eyes lowered.

"Have you been a good boy?"

"No, Belle."

"Am I going to have to punish you?"

"Please, Belle."

He was in service, earning his way back to favor, so I'd have him clean my apartment naked except for his collar. Seeing him scurry around, scrubbing my bathroom floor on his hands and knees with a toothbrush, was a sight to behold. I'd make him deep-clean the shower, the fridge, everything. And he would tease me along the way, a flash of his ass, a cheeky wiggle, little provocations that he knew I found adorable.

I made him clean everything, top to bottom. Put new sheets on the bed. Fold all my laundry. Line up my panties perfectly in the drawer, though I sometimes wondered if he wanted to wear them. He never brought it up, and I didn't ask. It always felt more like reverent arousal than anything else.

I'd sit on the sofa, sipping wine or champagne, watching him. Sometimes, I'd be working on my computer while he bustled around, or he'd make me simple meals, nothing complicated, because, bless him, the man could not cook. He would bring me slices of cucumber or tomato, feeding them to me carefully, more ceremony than sustenance.

Afterward, he'd crawl over and sit quietly, waiting for acknowledgment. Sometimes, he'd slide between my legs to serve as a human table; sometimes, he'd stay in child's pose, still and patient, until I decided to notice him. I'd make him wait, sometimes twenty minutes or more, while I finished my show, ignoring him completely until I was damn good and ready.

Then, I'd inspect the apartment. I'd nod, sometimes complimenting his work, sometimes finding a "missed spot" to keep him on edge. If he missed something, I'd spank him firmly.

"Tuskee," I'd say. "You missed a spot. Why should I bother with you?" I'd taunt. "You're nothing. You haven't earned this pussy!"

Then, I would make up some silly task for him, spill something on the floor, and make him lick it up. Once, I made him sit on his knees in a stress position with his hands behind his back and an ice cube of my urine on his tongue. I want to say that it turned him off, but it didn't. He often requested this particular punishment.

He had one particular kink: he loved to be walked on in heels. I couldn't quite bring myself to do it with stilettos; I was too worried about hurting him badly. God help me if the press ever got hold of that story. But I did walk on him barefoot. Ideally, you'd have a ceiling bar to balance correctly, and I didn't have one, but even so, I would stand on him, pressing my foot into his back, his chest, sometimes resting it lightly on his head.

He l*oved it.*

Sometimes, I would put him in handcuffs, always giving him the key first, of course, because safety matters, and then I'd get myself off in front of him, using a rabbit or something equally efficient.

"Please, Belle," he'd whisper, his voice thick with need. "Please let me touch you."

I'd smile down at him, indulgent and cruel. "Not a chance," I'd purr. "You get to watch. That's all."

I wouldn't touch him. I'd make him wait, kneeling there until I saw that he was about to explode.

Sometimes, I made him sleep like a dog at the foot of my bed.

"Good boys sleep at my feet," I'd tease. "Bad boys sleep in the hall. Which one are you tonight?"

"Good, Belle," he'd murmur desperately.

When he stayed over, I'd occasionally have him eat off a plate on the floor, not exactly like a dog, but close enough. He seemed to love it, his face flushed with shame and pride.

And when I was feeling particularly motivated, or he was being especially bratty, I'd have him kneel naked and hurl verbal abuse at him. Now, thinking back on it, I should have told him to add $800 billion to the Medicaid budget as a punishment; we could have all benefited from it.

One night, we had been out drinking at the Hawk and Dove, a favorite watering hole for politicos and fans of the blood sport of elections, and were desperate for each other after one

too many beers. It was a quick walk to the office, every few steps tangled in hands and mouths, his body pressed up against mine, breath hot and erratic as he whispered everything he thought might make me take him sooner. The collar under his shirt rubbed against my fingers every time I pulled him close. He wore it tight, like he wanted me to notice. Like he wanted to be punished for wearing it into a place of power.

He told me he would increase the SNAP budget for low-income mothers by ten percent if I fucked him up the ass. He said it like he was making a bargain at a whorehouse, trying to trade what little he had for my diligent efforts. He didn't give a fuck about poor people. I pulled him by the ring on his collar, pushed him back against the cold stone of the building, and told him I'd keep my heels on if he made it twelve. He gasped, said yes without thinking, and then whispered that his boss didn't even read the appropriations. Said no one would notice if he slipped in a change. He looked so proud of himself, like he'd done something brave instead of pathetic.

Damn, I should have held out for more if I had teased him the way he deserved. If I had denied him what he wanted until he was crying and shaking and ready to give me anything, I could have gotten fifteen percent. I could have rewritten the entire damn food policy. I'm a good progressive. I should have made him pay for it.

I'm not even sure whose idea it was to go into the boss's office. At the time, it felt mutual, a shared impulse. But looking back, I think it was him. I think he wanted it from the start. I think he needed to be degraded in the exact place he spent his days pretending to be important. The idea likely lingered in his mind for weeks before he spoke. Maybe he thought being fucked in that room would make it real.

He led the way, opened the door, and stepped in like he had been waiting for this moment all night. I followed without a word, watching to see how quickly he would fall apart once the power of that room closed around him.

The room was thick with power, old and stagnant and male. Every piece of furniture radiated a legacy federal style knock-off. Tuskee walked to the center like he had rehearsed it. He laid the harness and dildo on the desk without speaking, then stripped with quiet desperation. Layers of dignity falling to the floor. He dropped to his knees when he was bare and bowed his head. The collar was obvious now, snug and dark, the only thing he still wore.

I stripped before him, wearing only a black bra and high heels. That was it. And it was enough. I strapped into the harness he had packed for me with slow, deliberate precision while he stayed where he was, silent and waiting.

He kissed the dildo before I told him to, then opened his mouth and took it like he had practiced for this moment alone in his apartment in a way that would make a porn star jealous, probably watching C-SPAN with a hand around his cock.

When I told him to get on the desk, he moved fast, eager to be used. He bent forward, elbows down, legs spread, ass high. I ran my hand down his spine and over the soft curves of him, the parts he tried so hard to keep hidden under tailored suits and carefully worded memos. I didn't enter right away. I made him wait, let the weight of it settle into his body. Let him feel just how close he was to being broken.

I drizzled lube all over his ass and rubbed it into the dildo, dramatically. When I pushed in, I did it with precision. No hesitation or kindness. I filled him slowly, letting him feel every inch, and once I was buried inside him, I started to fuck him like it was a punishment. He gripped the edge of the desk and whimpered. He tried to stay quiet. He failed. His body trembled with the effort of holding himself together. I leaned down, my mouth against his ear, and told him what he was. A fraud, a coward, a spoiled, collared little bitch who talked about market discipline while begging to be fucked by a woman in heels.

His breath hitched and broke apart under the pressure. Then he screamed it like it had been waiting inside him longer than he even understood.

"Please, I'll vote for healthcare, I'll kneel in the chamber, I'll do anything—just fuck me."

I didn't slow down. I grabbed his collar with one hand, spinning him around. I slung his tie through the loop and used it like the reins on a horse. I dug my heels into the carpet and screamed it loud enough to make the windows shake.

"Tax the rich, you little bitch." I screamed at him in contempt.

He sobbed into the desk, right on the edge of release, too wrecked to form coherent words. The sound of it was pathetic and real, exactly what I had intended. I kept going until he could barely hold himself upright, every muscle shaking, the orgasm sitting right there inside him like a promise he hadn't earned yet. And then the door opened.

His boss stood in the doorway, completely still, eyes fixed on the scene in front of him as if his brain had short-circuited and couldn't catch up to what he was seeing.

He didn't yell. He didn't demand answers. He just rubbed his face like this was a meeting gone wrong and muttered, "I need the speech. It's under him."

Then he turned, muttered that he'd give us a minute, and walked out without waiting for a reply, as if retreating might erase what he had seen.

I pulled out slowly. Tuskee collapsed forward with a shudder. He couldn't speak. I wiped the toy off with his shirt, handed him the wrinkled speech, and watched him fumble his clothes back on without meeting my eyes. The collar stayed on. He didn't even try to unbuckle it.

I sat in the boss's chair, crossed my legs, lit a cigarette, and looked around that stupid room full of framed lies and unread bills. I could still smell him on the desk.

I should have held out for 15 percent.

We didn't talk for a few days. I went on with my life. Coffee. Hearings. Emails. The usual parade of men trying to sound important. I didn't think about him. I didn't need to. I had done what I came to do. As far as I know, Tuskee was still alive and still employed. Still walking around like nothing had happened. There were no headlines. No rehab stint. No quiet leave of absence. No anonymous tip to Politico. Just silence, and that suited me fine.

His boss acted like it never happened. That is what they do. Forget, pretend, rewrite. You would think there might be shame. A flicker of remorse. A moment where they look in the mirror and see what they are. But they never do. Instead, they pivot. They step down to spend more time with family. Or launch a nonprofit to fight hunger. Or take a fellowship in moral clarity at some think tank built by oil money and lies.

I did not care. Not in the way that costs anything. It was just another data point. One more man who cracked. Another file closed. He got what he thought he wanted. I got what I needed. And then I walked away.

Ultimately, we weren't a good match for the long term. He would go home one day and marry someone, 21, fresh out of college, ready to have a dozen babies. I would never be accepted in his world. But for a while, it allowed me to see into a world I hadn't fully understood before, the world of mean domination.

I could do it. I could call someone pathetic, spit venom, and step on their pride. But there was something about the whole thing that made me wonder if this wasn't just a kink for him, if maybe he needed therapy more than he needed a Belle. Sometimes, it felt like I was standing in for a cruel mother, a shaming pastor, a culture that had no room for who I was. His form of Christianity left no room to breathe.

Was he gay? At least as far as I know, he wasn't, and he's certainly never come out. However, I've always believed that when you can't express who you are, it somehow leaks out. Some men drink. Some become abusive. Some crave being abused. Frankly, I think all men like to be dominated a little. It's just the reasons that vary, and the reasons matter.

This one--this one was different. He needed it. It was not because it made him hard but because it made him feel seen. Punished and controlled and saved, in a way.

He was thirty, and at the time, thirty still seemed too young to consider marriage, at least for him. Most of his siblings had tied the knot by the time they were twenty-two or twenty-five. They had their weddings, their homes, and their carefully planned futures. But he wanted something different. Something undefined, something more. He needed time to figure out who he was or was meant to become.

And me, I knew I wouldn't stay, not really, not with the way we were wired or the weight he carried around like it had grown roots in his spine. I still think about him, more than I should, naked except for his collar, painting my toenails with that ridiculous look of concentration, trying to flatter me, trying to please me, and I think, if only I could have turned him, if only I could have made him a Democrat, maybe even just a centrist. I know, I know, it's a pipe dream, a feverish fantasy I revisit when I'm tired or tipsy or watching the news and thinking how different things could be if I'd just managed to pull him closer, keep him tethered, because if I had, I swear we'd have universal healthcare by now, no question. The world would be a little softer around the edges.

6

Whip Count

The Whip was a New Yorker through and through. He loved the Mets, despite being heartbroken by them, and had a father who retired to Florida. Yet he was a D.C. politico in every sense, having worked on campaigns, served Secretaries, haunted the Hill, and traveled the country in rumpled suits and well-worn shoes as a political operative. He was famous and infamous by turns, but I met him after all that, post-glory, mid-infamy, and firmly in the private sector after the *Washington Post* exposé.

He worked out of his office-turned-apartment in Maryland, earning a living as a consultant, which in D.C. is a noble way to say "unemployed." Consulting is often the last refuge of those who have been politically ousted. You get bounced from every gig, and what's left? A laptop, a LinkedIn profile, and a desk, which should be your dining room table, that you use as your office.

He was older than me. Not scandalously, but just enough to raise eyebrows when he chased after someone my age. But I wasn't naive. I knew what drew him in. I knew what he wanted about five minutes after meeting him.

We were close almost immediately. Inseparable. We talked all the time about everything, wanting to unravel each other's stories like they were the most essential narratives ever told. And he was charming, effortlessly so.

He could talk to anyone. He could talk his way into bars, talk his way past any bouncer in town, past lines, talk his way into your pants and your heart, usually in that order.

He wore suits that slightly aged him, but not severely. Striped ties and flannel jackets, old D.C. distinguished chic. He looked like he belonged in sepia tones.

Whip Count loved the old-school pleasures. Baseball games. Dirty water dogs from street vendors, with onions. Cracker Jacks straight from the box. Root beer, orange soda, and New York Egg Creams he made at home from old-fashioned seltzer bottles he had delivered in wooden crates. WC was an older man with older man tastes in a mid-thirties body.

He could easily move between fine dining and the seediest dive bars. He could have dinner at the White House or enter a dungeon with equal confidence. He fit in everywhere.

Whip Count used to take me to the private clubs tucked away in industrial areas and backstreet bars with silent doorkeepers and candlelight so dim that it turned secrets into currency. He liked to show me off. I liked how people stared when I walked in with him and ignored him completely.

"You make me invisible," he once whispered, kneeling beside me as I slipped off my heels. His voice shook. "Please let me disappear for you."

He would beg to be my footstool. I would rest one bare foot on his back while I drank someone else's champagne and gave my attention to someone far more interesting. A young woman, maybe. Elegant, eager, curious. I would tilt her chin toward mine, murmur something soft against her cheek, then kiss her in full view while Whip Count stayed bent and straining, barely breathing.

"You don't move," I'd say, not even sparing him a glance. "Not until I've finished with her."

His body would tremble.

He would ache from the position, but he loved the pain. He loved being beneath me, reduced to furniture, forgotten by everyone else until the moment I pressed my heel into his spine hard enough to remind him he was still mine.

Whip Count had the kind of face that made people second-guess their assumptions. Earnest brown eyes framed by rounded glasses gave him the look of a well-meaning academic or a policy aide with too many white papers on his desk. His brown hair curled in soft waves, a little tousled at the crown, as if he constantly ran his fingers through it while thinking too hard or wanting to be touched. A full beard lined his jaw, neatly kept but not too precious, hinting at a man who cared for himself but never tried too hard to impress. In public, he wore crewneck sweaters that clung just enough to suggest the kind of body that spent one too many late nights at a McDonald's drive-through in Des Moines.

While in the play dynamic, he had a thing for latex and vinyl. I loved how it clung, the shine, the slight squeak with every shift of his body. He favored sleeveless tops that hugged his torso like a second skin, as if being encased made him feel more honest. He wasn't ripped, not even close. Years of travel, late nights, and too many catered receptions had softened him in places and left a slight roundness at his belly and a curve to his sides. I liked him better for it. He felt real under my hands.

He was average in most ways. Not particularly tall. Not striking. And certainly not well-endowed. That didn't matter to me. Not when he looked at me like I was a miracle. Not when he touched me like he was afraid I might vanish. Not when he whispered, 'Thank you for letting me kneel at your feet.'

He was devoted. Attentive. Eager in a way that made me feel deliciously dangerous. He lived for instruction, for permission, for praise. He once spent an entire evening polishing the big black motorcycle boots I wore to stomp on him without a single complaint, just murmuring how grateful he was to serve me. I let him finish one and made him start over to see how far he'd go. He didn't even flinch.

People outside the scene often misunderstand the nature of bondage. They imagine it's all about sex, or at least the kind of sex they've seen in poorly lit movies. But the truth is, some of the most intense BDSM experiences don't involve intercourse at all. That's because bondage, at its core, isn't about penetration. It's about presentation. It's about surrender and trust, being seen and held, and trading power in a way that feels more intimate than bodies alone can manage. Sometimes, a single knot can say more than an entire night in bed.

Pleasure isn't always about climax; it's about the sharp edge of anticipation, the long inhale of control, the quiet exhale of being owned. For some, being bound is the only time their mind is calm. For others, binding is a form of meditation, with each knot expressing love, care, and control. That's why some of the most powerful nights I've ever had ended not in orgasm but in stillness, two people, breath to breath, hearts pounding, utterly undone.

W.C. and I connected; we just seemed to understand each other. He would push me farther than I thought I wanted to go, and I often had to rein him back. I'd say things like, "I'm not sure I'm going to do that," or "That might be more than I'm comfortable with," and we'd end up having these long, winding conversations about sex, what we wanted, what we didn't, what we were curious about. Sometimes, I think we spend more time talking about sex than actually having it.

The psychological element of bondage and dominance was always the most interesting to me anyway. How do you weave yourself into a relationship when that dynamic sits at the center? For us, it sometimes bled into our regular lives. It would sneak in unexpectedly, like when we were at a bar with friends, and I'd give him a subtle command. Nobody else would notice, but he would do it. Our little secret. It may be something I wanted him to do later. Maybe it was something I wanted him to do now. People were always surprised at how he could anticipate my needs. He had almost a preternatural ability to foresee what I wanted and somehow get it for me.

We developed a shorthand; this quiet intimacy was built on a deep knowledge. I knew him, and he knew me. Sometimes, all it took was a glance, and entire conversations passed between us without a word. That kind of connection is rare, one that accepts both someone's darkness and light, their happiness and hurt.

I'd call him if I were upset about work or feeling out of control. I'd say, "I'm having trouble sorting something out," and he'd listen while

I explained the problem. He didn't just give advice; he bolstered me. If I had trouble with my boss and thought he was out of line, he'd encourage me to channel my dominant energy, which I used with him. He would become more submissive on the phone, gently coaxing me to claim my power.

It worked. I'd walk into a meeting full of confidence, and if my boss tried to steamroll me, I'd say," I am going to need you to lower your emotions right now while I explain to you what happened and how we're going to handle it." It was transformative.

In the early days of my career, that kind of support meant everything to me. He invested in me, his time, his encouragement, and his unwavering belief in my strength; I'll always be grateful for that. I learned so much from him, not just about power and sex but also about myself.

We had done so many scenes, but that night, I wanted more than stillness. I wanted to hear him fall apart.

He arrived exactly when I told him to. He stripped without instruction. He knew better than to speak. I tied him to my coffee table, face down, arms bound behind the polished wood, ankles spread wide and tied to each leg of the table. He lay there open. Vulnerable. Obedient. I moved slowly, as I always did. He needed that. It grounded him. And he needed to hear what I had to say next.

"If it gets too much," I told him, leaning close, "you tell me if you need it to stop. The moment you say stop, it all ends. I won't hesitate."

His eyes met mine. He nodded. "Yes, Belle. I understand."

I kissed his cheek once. Then I took out the candle.

It was long, tapered, and pure white. I held it in front of him and struck a match. The flame flared to life. I had it just long enough for the wax to begin pooling at the base, then slid the candle carefully between his ass cheeks, lodging it where it would stay upright. The angle was perfect. When the wax dripped, it would fall directly onto the soft, hairy flesh of his inner thighs.

"You're going to hold this candle," I said, "and you're going to stay still. The more you move, the more it drips. Do you understand?"

"Yes, Belle."

I walked to my chair, sat down, and spread my legs. I wore thigh-high stockings. Nothing underneath. My heels were planted against his shoulders. My fingers slipped between my thighs, and I began touching myself, slow and unhurried, like he was nothing more than a piece of furniture in the room.

Then, the first drop fell.

He gasped, sharp and immediate.

"Ahh—ah. Fuck. Belle—"

"Say stop if you want this to end," I reminded him.

He didn't respond. I kept touching myself, slower, deeper, savoring his voice.

The next drop landed. This time, it is lower, right where the thigh meets the groin. He yelped.

"Ahhh....."

Another drop. Another cry. His thighs jerked, and with that movement, the wax started dripping faster.

"Ahhh—ahhh. God. Please—I'm trying—"

He tried to stay still, but his body betrayed him. Each new drop found a fresh patch of skin. The wax clung, thick and scalding.

"Please—it's so ah—"

His voice cracked. The sound of it fed my pleasure. My body tensed. My hips bucked. I came hard, staring directly at him as he screamed. The wax landed again in the middle of my orgasm, and he howled.

"Ahhhh. Belle—please—"

But he never said stop. And so I let the final few drops fall. His thighs were covered in scattered welts, with his hair matted under the cooling wax. His body was slick with sweat. His chest heaved. His cock stood painfully hard, untouched under him,

Only when I had finished did I stand. I walked over to him and slowly pulled the candle out. I dripped more of the wax on his hairy legs and back. He flinched each time.

I leaned down until my mouth brushed his ear, my voice low and slow and just for him.

"Should I stop? I don't want the weight of my want to sit on your back like a punishment. This isn't about power if it crushes you. You are here to please me. That's all. And if you want me to stop, I will. The moment you say stop, I'll untie you. I'll end it. You don't have to do a thing to earn that. Say the word."

He was shaking. I could feel it against my lips. His voice came out hoarse but clear.

"Yes, Belle. If I couldn't take it, I would tell you. I swear. But I can take it for you. I *want* to. I know this pleases you."

I smiled. Not sweetly.

"Then hold still."

And I let the wax fall again.

I looked down at him and smiled.

"It's a good thing you're so useful to me," I said calmly. "Otherwise, why would I keep something so pathetic lying around?"

His eyes fluttered. He didn't speak.

"I like how much pain you can take. How much will you endure for me? That last scene? You could tell, couldn't you? How much it turned me on. The way you screamed. You gave me exactly what I wanted."

He whimpered. Just a breath. A ripple of sound at the back of his throat.

"Now," I said, crouching beside him, "I'm going to cause you more pain. Not because I have to. But because I *want* to. And I hope that excites you even a little. I know it excites me."

He stiffened.

"I'm going to pull the wax off your legs now. All of it. It's going to hurt. Maybe more than you expect."

His chest rose sharply. I could see the fear there. Not fear of me. Fear of the pain. He was afraid now. Not play-acting. Not batting. This was real.

I traced a single finger down the center of his back. His skin was damp. His muscles tensed under my touch.

"Tell me what to do," I whispered.

There was a long pause.

Then he whispered, trembling, "Please, Belle... please go on. I want to take it for you."

I smiled again—wider this time.

"Good boy."

Then I gripped the first patch of wax, and I ripped.

He screamed.

"Ah—"

It wasn't a cute noise. It was raw. Full-throated. His body jolted as far as the ropes would allow.

I took my time.

Another patch. Rip. Scream.

His thighs shook. His breath came in gasps. The pain stripped him down. Voice cracking. Eyes wet. Every piece of wax pulled hair from the root. He sobbed openly.

But he never said stop.

And I never gave him a reason to think I would.

I kept going, methodical and unrelenting. Every piece of wax I removed came with hair attached. Every removal ripped another noise from his throat. He wasn't moaning anymore. He was sobbing.

After removing the last patch, I whispered, "You did so well. But I'm not finished."

I stood and walked to the kitchen. I came back with a bowl of ice.

I pressed the first cube directly against the rawest spot, and his whole body jolted.

"Ah—ah oh God—" he pleaded.

The shock of cold made him arch off the table, but the ropes held him down.

"You're mine like this," I said calmly. "Every nerve lit up. Every part of you is aching."

He nodded weakly. His lips were trembling. He looked like he was drowning in sensation.

And I hadn't even touched his cock.

This wasn't mercy. It was a contrast. A shock. A jolt to the system. The wax's heat had seared him. The wax had left its sharp, stinging kiss. And then the ice came. Cold against the red welts. Every nerve lit up like a flare. He gasped. Flinched. Shuddered. It wasn't soothing. It was a revelation. His body did not know what to do with all that sensation except surrender to it completely.

I untied him. He could barely walk, his legs trembling under him, and his skin marked with a map of everything I had done.

We crawled into bed. The room was dark and quiet. The ropes were gone, but the marks were still fresh. I lay beside him, not touching, not speaking, just watching, letting him feel the stillness.

Then, softly, I said, "You may touch yourself."

His breath hitched.

"Thirty seconds," I cooed.

His hand was shaking as he reached down to the ground. His body was already trembling. I counted in my head, slow and deliberate, but his back arched off the bed before I reached ten. He came with a sharp, broken cry, loud enough to echo in the silence between us. His whole body jerked like the release ripped straight out of him. Like he had been holding it for years. Like he had only been waiting for me to allow it.

Afterward, he curled closer. Still breathless. Still raw. His chest rose and fell like he had just run for his life.

"You undo me... every single time," he whispered.

And he wasn't wrong.

Another fetish he had was a very specific kink: hot towels. Not scalding, but hot enough to make your hands hesitate. He loved having a towel wrapped around his cock while he jacked off, or better, having me do it. It felt like an affectation from his youth, though he never said as much.

He had a gentle fascination with my breasts. He'd bury his face in them while rubbing himself with the hot towel, whimpering into my skin.

"Please... just like that. Don't stop," he murmured.

It was oddly tender.

W.C. loved getting whipped. He loved nipple clamps. He loved being taken out and shown off. We used to go to this BDSM bar in what used to be the seediest part of town and is now one of the nicest in D.C. There, we would interact with all sorts of people. He would grovel at my feet and then take me out on the dance floor like my most devoted partner.

The crowd had strange arrangements, so our dynamic didn't seem unreasonable. In many ways, it felt like a normal situation.

Sometimes, I wondered, always with his prior approval and enthusiastic consent, if he might be into having sex with a man. He demurred and denied it, but I always sensed he might if I wanted a "Why Choose" situation. Still, in all our time together, he never leaned that way. I suspected that if I ordered him to give another man a blow job, he would have done it. Maybe he just needed someone else to give him "permission" for the pleasure.

He *lived* for worship, especially when the women were thick-thighed, full-bodied, and impossible to ignore. Breasts that filled out a corset-like, they were begging to be unlaced. Hips that knew how to grind to the bass. He loved all of them. He worshiped every curve, every command, every cruel smirk tossed his way like a bone to a starving dog.

And me? I allowed it. On a leash, of course. Mine.

We were deep in the club's underbelly, lights low, music pulsing like a second heartbeat, chains rattling, moans echoing between bass drops, and the unmistakable crack of a whip marking skin. The air smelled like leather, sweat, perfume, and punishment.

He knelt beside me, his face already glazed with need. A tall, goddess-like woman walked by. Her legs were in sheer mesh, her heels like weapons, and her hair a cascade of black silk down her spine.

"Belle, may I brush her hair?" he whispered. His voice cracked like he might shatter if I said no.

I caught her Dom's eye across the floor. One nod. That was all I needed.

"You may," I said, curling my fingers into the back of his collar. "Touch only her hair. Nothing else."

He crawled toward her like she was the altar and he was the sinner who had already written his confession in sweat. Every movement was deliberate, trembling with anticipation and reverence. The brush felt too delicate in his rough hands, as if he wasn't worthy to touch it, let alone use it on her. Still, he lifted it as if offering penance. The first stroke glided through the dark silk of her hair, slow and worshipful, as the bass thudded through the concrete floor and into his knees. The club swam in shadows and smoke, and he moved as if in prayer, brushing her with the same care a monk might handle a sacred relic.

But of course, the idiot couldn't stop there.

His fingers slipped just a little. He brushed her spine and traced the curve of her lower back as if spelling out his downfall.

She froze.

Then, she turned her head, slowly, deliberately, with a smile that could slice a man open and lick the wound clean. Her Dom didn't speak. I didn't need to. I just raised one brow, and that was all the warning anyone got.

I rose, my chair scraping back, unnoticed beneath the pulse of the music. The flogger slid free from my thigh as if it were spring-loaded.

There was no sound from it yet, but the room had noticed. The crowd parted, drawn in like predators circling blood in the water.

He knew.

He fucking *knew.*

His eyes met mine. Wide. Drenched in guilt and aching need. Already sorry. Already hard.

"I said only her hair," I said, winding my fingers into the collar at the back of his neck and yanking him back to heel.

Her Dom stepped forward. Bare-chested, ink winding down his arms like spells. Shoulders cut like sculptures. That low, mean grin that said he enjoyed being the consequence.

He reached for W.C.

"Stop," I said quietly.

One word. That's all it took.

He froze mid-motion, his chest rising slowly and heavily as he remembered where the real leash was.

"You ask *my* permission first," I said, tilting my head just enough to make it sting.

His jaw tightened. Then lowered. The bravado softened into something else. Not submission, not precisely. Recognition.

He stepped forward, lifted his arm, and offered his flogger. Black leather, braided with silver filigree, heavy at the ends. It wasn't for show. It was for pain. It was beautiful.

He let me examine it.

I ran a finger along the falls. I felt the weight. Smiled.

"You may use it," I said, finally. "But don't break him. 25 lashes."

He nodded once.

The flogger sliced through the air and cracked across W.C.'s back like thunder kissing skin.

The Whip. Screamed. And that needy, wrecked sound that followed?

That was him thanking both of us.

The Whip had an antique mirror next to his bed, gilded, tall, and heavy as sin—the kind of mirror that seemed to remember things best forgotten. It had been expensive, or at least looked expensive, with carved lions' feet and an old-world elegance that didn't match the rest of his slightly battered furniture. He once joked it was the most honest thing in the room. I didn't laugh, but I remembered.

That night, I told him to stand before it. I didn't touch him. I just sat at the edge of the bed, still fully dressed in black tights and heels, the faint trace of perfume curling through the air, sipping something brown and expensive. I watched him undress in real-time and in reflection, making it feel reverent, as if he was shedding more than just clothes.

I pulled the red shibari rope from my bag. He'd seen it, but he hadn't asked.

"Kneel," I said gently.

He sank to the floor with something close to relief.

"You're going to hold still," I told him, "not because I tell you to, but because I expect it of you."

"Yes, Belle," he said. Quiet. Steady. Already trembling.

I started at his chest, laying the rope in slow, deliberate patterns—crisscrossing, framing, embracing. Each knot felt like a heartbeat. His breath hitched a little more with every turn of the rope, but he didn't flinch. Not once.

Over his shoulder. Down his back. Beneath his arms, wrapping gently around the soft parts of him, drawing him in.

I left his arms free. I liked the way they shook.

When I finished the upper half, I stepped behind him, close enough to let him feel my breath on the back of his neck.

"Look at yourself," I said.

He did.

"You're art," I whispered. "But only because I made you that way."

His eyes closed briefly as if the words touched something too tender. "Thank you," he murmured.

"Don't look away," I told him. "I want you to see what I see."

I retook the rope, winding it around his thighs and spiraling downward—not too far, just enough to remind him he was being held.

Then I stepped back, taking him in like a sculptor with a finished piece.

"Touch yourself."

And then, wearing my favorite black heels, I walked slowly and deliberately behind him. Each step echoed like a countdown. The sharp staccato of my stilettos against the polished floor sliced through the silence, and with every strike, I saw his shoulders flinch in anticipation. He stayed standing, obedient, head bowed, arms tightly bound behind his back. His breath hitched with each approaching click as if the sound was a hand at his throat.

When I reached him, I said nothing. I didn't need to. I lifted my foot and placed the pointed toe between his shoulder blades, steady and precise. Then I kicked him. His gasp was immediate and raw. The ropes around his chest flexed as his body fought to contain the surge of sensation. It wasn't pain that made his spine arch or his thighs tremble. It was the sharp, helpless pleasure of being overpowered.

I watched him for a long second. He was splayed out and waiting, humiliated and radiant with need. Then I shifted my weight. One smooth movement. His eyes met mine for the first time since I had entered the room. They were wide, glassy, and aching. I smiled. Not kindly.

He had asked for this—every inch of it. And I was not even close to finishing.

The mirror reflected everything: his soft gasps, the sheen of sweat, the way he unraveled without a single touch from me. When his breathing hitched, and I knew he was close, I lifted his face off the floor, took his jaw in my hand, and tilted his face toward mine.

"Say my name."

"Belle."

"Louder," I screamed at him.

"Belle."

"Beg me"

"Please, Belle."

"Now." I shoved his chin to his chest.

Only then did I let him come. He shot his entire comeload on his face. Much of it landed in his left eye.

After that, I untied him slowly but left the come on his face until later. It wasn't very comfortable, but it was just the kind of thing that I knew he would like.

I liked the feel of the rope leaving his skin. It was warm where it had pressed into him, a pattern like a memory. I kissed each mark as it faded, slow and deliberate, letting him feel every moment of its departure. His breath caught when my mouth found the tender spot behind his hip. He didn't move. He didn't speak. He curled into my lap like something that knew it had been caught, his cheek resting against my thigh, his fingers still trembling from what I'd just made him do.

The mirror caught everything: the flushed skin, the lines. His mouth parted like he hadn't realized how to close it again. It always saw everything. That was the point.

I ran my fingers through his hair gently. He blinked at me, his eyes wide and wet, his pupils still dilated. He was quiet, but I knew the question was the same. He always wanted to know why. Why did I do the things I did? Why did it feel so good even when it hurt? Why did it humiliate him and turn him on in the same breath?

"Say it," I told him. "You've been trying not to. Say what you want to ask."

His voice was thin, barely there. "Why did you make me do that?"

I didn't answer at first. I wanted him to squirm in the silence, feel its weight, and live in the question before I gave him the answer.

"Because I wanted to watch," I said finally. "Because I wanted you to see it. To see yourself that way."

He didn't look away. He never did when I gave him the truth.

He shifted slightly, like he was trying to fold himself into something smaller. My hand stayed in his hair, soft now, stroking behind his ear.

The mirror caught that, too. The softness after. The hush that always followed the storm.

He told me once, quietly, not looking at me, that he'd always felt like a failure.

Not in the loud, tragic way people unravel at bars but in the quiet, surgical way high performers implode. He'd been one of those gifted kids who got gold stars for breathing. Skipped grades. Dominated the debate. He interned on Capitol Hill before most people even survived high school drama. He rose fast, charmed faster, and crashed with a kind of elegance only someone deeply addicted to appearances can manage.

"I keep trying to be good," he whispered into my skin, mouth barely moving. "But I always end up here."

And "here" was wherever I told him to be. On his knees. Bent. Waiting. His face pressed into the carpet as he owed them an apology.

But he didn't say it like it hurt.

He said it as if it were peace.

That's what pulled me in deeper than I should've gone. Not the suits or the Hill gossip that clung to him like scent. It was a contradiction. All that polish and precision on the surface—measured words, sharp analysis, the smug flourish of handwritten notes on creamy cardstock—and underneath, this raw, exquisite ache to be unraveled.

He didn't want to win. He needed to lose.

Sometimes, I would lean in close when he was tied and trembling and ask what he was thinking.

And once, just once, he told me.

"I think," he said, "that if I could be completely broken... maybe I'd finally stop disappointing myself."

That stayed with me. Still does.

Because there was nothing broken about him, but somewhere along the way, someone made him believe that needing softness made him weak. That craving for approval and pain and tenderness meant he'd failed. So he swallowed it down. Buried it beneath silk ties and clever comebacks until it could only crawl out in bruises and rope and whisper into the dark.

But when I touched that place in him, when I ordered him, when I permitted him to let go—

God, he bloomed.

He followed every command as if it were salvation.

He trembled for me. He glowed when I pushed him. He cried when I praised him.

He said he liked the pain.

But what he liked was freedom.

To surrender.

He wanted more than I could give. He wanted to go deeper. Stranger. Darker.

Maybe he lives there now. Perhaps he has the rig, the gear, the routine. Maybe he kneels for someone who takes him all the way. I always made kink part of my love life but never the whole of it. For him, maybe it was never about love at all. Perhaps it was always about obliteration.

We didn't break up. We drifted.

I started thinking about marriage. He started talking about arrangements.

"I want something functional," he said one night, swirling bourbon in a glass that looked too elegant for the conversation.

"I want everything," I said. I wanted vows and babies and Sunday mornings that smelled like pancakes and sex.

And just like that, the shine wore off.

Because I didn't want to be someone's scheduled release, I wanted to be the whole damn universe.

I'm sure he has a gorgeous, emotionally distant wife now. And a dungeon that his wife definitely does not know about.

7

Executive Decisions

We worked for the same agency in Washington, D.C., though our positions were worlds apart. He was the Secretary's right-hand man, radiating authority, confidence, and an aura of utterly intoxicating competence. On the other hand, I was just another policy analyst, lost in the maze of bureaucracy, several floors below his lofty office, with dark desires for dominance.

Our first electrifying encounter happened during a celebration marking the completion of a project that had consumed my life for months. The grand conference hall buzzed with forced cheer, but my attention wandered until I felt the unmistakable presence of male energy behind me. His large, confident hand gently touched the small of my back, instantly electrifying my senses.

"The Secretary wants to speak with you," he whispered close to my ear, his voice low and husky but charged with subtle command. The unexpected intimacy of his touch and voice startled me so entirely that I spun around sharply, losing my balance.

He caught me effortlessly with impeccable grace and strength, guiding me into a dramatic dip that drew delighted applause from the room. His face was mere inches from mine, his piercing blue eyes alight with playful intensity. Everyone was staring at us.

"Sim, minha Senhora," he murmured in Portuguese, a teasing smirk tugging at his lips, his voice dripping with charm.

I responded in French, my voice deliberately seductive. "Tu serais encore plus beau attaché," I murmured, relishing the flicker of intrigue and hunger that crossed his eyes. I told him in French that he would be even more handsome if he were tied up.

He chuckled softly, pulling me upright smoothly, his hand lingering for a moment longer on my back than necessary. "Maybe you can demonstrate sometime." Fuck, he spoke French.

As I affectionately dubbed him Executive Decisions (ED), though I assure you everything was working perfectly. He carried himself with the disciplined elegance of someone whose formative years were spent at an elite military academy, his posture unfailingly precise and commanding. He favored tailored clothing, notably a band-collar top coat that clung perfectly to his broad shoulders and narrow waist, subtly echoing a military aesthetic. Seeing him outside this carefully curated uniform quickly became an obsession.

His family lineage is loosely traced back to Brazil, but his sharp, refined features hint at Central European heritage. I never got the whole story, nor did I press him, preferring the mystery that clung to his crisp, well-defined features instead. His bright blue eyes and meticulously groomed blond hair were devastating, drawing my attention like a magnet each time he passed through my department.

He wasn't tall, but height wasn't necessary to define his masculinity. He stood just a hair taller than me, and since I was generously rounding my height up to five-foot-six, I suspected he might have done the same. Yet, there was no denying his powerful presence; it radiated from every measured step he took, every carefully considered gesture.

ED was not only impeccably put together physically but also intellectually. He spoke at least four or five languages fluently, each adding another layer to his irresistible charm. In an agency brimming with highly accomplished professionals, his brilliance stood apart. This sheer competence may have left me weak at the knees. I experienced the subtle thrill of standing close to the Secretary at otherwise mundane official events, knowing that ED was watching from nearby. Or maybe it was the vulnerability he only showed me when he whispered Italian love poetry while entangled in my sheets under the pale moonlight.

After our initial meeting, we ran into each other all over the building. Whether it was the cafeteria, the credit union, or even the cashier, he always seemed to appear. I couldn't tell if it was kismet or he was arranging these encounters, but it felt like he was everywhere I turned. He never came by my office despite knowing he could easily find me. It left me wondering if he was just being polite or if there was something more behind those chance encounters.

The next day, he 'ran into me' again as I left my office. He offered to walk with me despite it being clear he wasn't heading out yet. As we walked down the hall, he casually asked about my evening plans. When I mentioned meeting friends for a drink, he smiled and said he'd love to join. Trying to sound nonchalant, I told him where we'd be. I walked away, my legs feeling like jelly, terrified I'd trip on my shoes or faceplant onto the marble hallway. He had a way of making me lose all composure.

I headed to happy hour with anticipation and a mix of doubt. An hour passed, and there was still no sign of him. I was starting to feel disappointed when a black government Suburban pulled up outside, its lights still flashing.

To my surprise, the door opened, and I saw the Secretary himself in the back seat. He waved at me casually. I waved back, stunned. And then, I saw him, breathless and apologetic, stepping out of the Suburban.

He didn't brag; that wasn't his style. He said, "The Secretary insisted on dropping me off, as he kept me late, and he knew I was anxious to see you."

He immediately turned his attention to my friends, effortlessly charming each one and offering personal apologies. Then, with perfect confidence, he took my hand and kissed it.

"Let me make it up to you," he said. "Dinner?"

I agreed, still reeling from the surreal entrance.

At the restaurant, he ordered for both of us, not in a controlling way, but with grace and attentiveness, as if he'd read my mind.

"You'll love this wine," he said without glancing at the menu. And I did.

He was so in control. So sure.

We parted ways that night, not in bed in a tangle of sheets but by walking to my apartment, where he said good night with a slight bow before running off. I wouldn't let him come up, but it surprised me that he didn't even try. But that was far from the end of this romance. The next day, he sent me a bouquet of stem roses with a card asking me out for Saturday night.

On our date, he walked beside me like I was a prize he was proud to show off, one he knew he didn't deserve but somehow had. His hand at the small of my back made me feel claimed in the best way. He fixated on me as if I were the only woman in the world. It was clipped and indirect if he had to speak to a waitress, as though even acknowledging another woman might betray some unspoken vow. I was the center of gravity, the focal point of every moment with him. But when he touched me, all my feminism flew out of my body. Gloria Steinem, who?

Our date ended with a tour of the monuments at night, a very D.C. date idea. As the car glided through the night, the monuments lit up beautifully against the dark sky, casting a magical glow. The Lincoln Memorial, the Washington Monument, and the Jefferson Memorial glowed as you passed, creating a romantic backdrop. Eventually, he found a quiet spot to pull over. We strolled hand in hand through the monuments, finding a secluded corner.

We were twisted up in each other by the reflecting pool, half-lost in shadow, half-lost in each other. His head was tilted back against the bench, mouth slightly open, breath coming faster every time my fingers trailed a little lower. His jacket was on my shoulders. His control was in my hands.

"You like misbehaving in public?" I asked, voice low, slow, deliberately dangerous.

"With you, I would take any punishment," he whispered. Before I could respond, the flashlight beam quickly cut through the dark, blinding me.

Park police.

We froze. My hand was on his chest. His eyes went wide. His breath caught. Then we moved.

"Run," I said, already tugging him up.

"Yes, ma'am," he said, with no hesitation, just obedience and adrenaline.

We bolted like kids skipping curfew. My heels slipped on the grass. He caught me. I yanked him forward. We were breathless, laughing, absolutely guilty, and completely unrepentant.

We tumbled into the car, slamming the doors shut behind us. I was already reaching for him before the locks clicked. He was still panting, watching me with a look that was equal parts reverence and need.

"Guess we're fugitives now," I said, straddling him deliberately.

He smiled, cheeks flushed, voice hopeful. "Che cosa mi farai?" He said, *What are you going to do to me* in Italian.

I cupped his face in one hand, firm. "Did I say you could speak?"

He swallowed hard. "No, ma'am."

"Vou te foder como um homem que precisa ser colocado no lugar," I said in Portuguese that I had been practicing since I met him. It meant: *I'm going to fuck you like a man who needs to be put in his place.*

I lean in until our mouths nearly touch, but not quite. "You wanted to play the bad boy. Now you're mine."

"I always was," he said softly.

I smiled then. The kind of smile that meant trouble. The kind that made him shiver.

"Good," I said. "Because I haven't even started."

Little did I know, I was primed to sate his darkest temptations.

After our first date, our encounters took place in the dark, recessed corners of our agency. They were delightful and exciting. He was magnetic, enthusiastic, and even deferential. He was a delicious expert in face-first diplomacy, with a very talented tongue. This man cared whether I got off, and he took pride in it.

I'd never met a man who was so naturally subservient and with so little prodding. It was just his natural state. If any man were having trouble with a woman and acted like this one did, those problems would vanish. He was masculine in public and pliant in private.

He never thought about his pleasure, though I certainly took great pleasure in giving him pain. He was focused entirely on getting me off, and that made him intoxicating. He became my favorite drug of choice.

We would often meet for lunch, and in moments, his hand was inching up my thigh to my Madame Secretary. I was ready to explode before the bread basket hit the table.

If I worked late, he'd appear in my office without saying a word. He'd check the hallway, close the door quietly behind him, and lock it with one click.

Then he'd drop to his knees before my Seat of Power.

He never asked for anything in return. He never touched himself. He'd crawl under my desk, slide his hands up my legs, and press his mouth between my thighs like it was the only way he could breathe.

He learned my body like a sacred language. He knew how to make me cry out without making a sound himself. And when I came, shaking and gripping the edge of my desk, he would kiss my inner thigh, fix my skirt, and disappear like smoke back to his other boss.

I wore garter belts under my skirts and panties over my stockings so they could slide off easily. Some nights, I'd leave them off altogether. I knew he'd notice. I'd see the flicker in his eyes, the tension in his jaw, the restraint he was trying so hard to hold onto as he knelt and pushed my knees apart.

"You didn't wear any," he whispered once, reverent. "You knew I'd come."

"I always know," I said, fingers buried in his hair. "And you always do."

Dear God. The way he worshipped. The way he served. The way he came undone was only through obedience. He was the only man who ever touched me with desperation and didn't ask to be satisfied. He just needed to please. And I let him.

Again. And again. And again.

There were times he came over and spent the night. He'd bring bags of groceries, wine, and coffee for breakfast, even if we didn't drink or eat them. He observed, watched, and predicted. He was always ready for what I might want.

When we had sex, it was magical. He was utterly devoted to my pleasure.

I grabbed his wrists one night and pinned them to the mattress. He looked up at me, eyes wide, waiting.

"Grab the headboard," I said, voice calm but absolute.

He obeyed instantly, his fingers curling around the slats. That alone made my mouth water. That quiet obedience. That delicious anticipation.

I tied one of my stockings around his eyes, knotting it tight enough to block out the world. He couldn't see me anymore. He could only feel, hear, smell, and react.

"Je suis à toi," *I am yours* in French, he said, already breathless.

"Olha só como você é bom quando obedece.," I whispered, climbing onto the bed and straddling him. I told him in Portuguese, *Look how good you are when you obey.*

I settled over his upper chest first, hips rolling lazily, my hands in his hair. I guided his mouth where I wanted it, grinding slowly and deeply across his lips. He moaned into me, desperate and already trembling.

"Don't stop licking," I said, tugging gently at his hair. "You want to be good for me, don't you?"

"Yes," he whispered against me.

I moved backward, inch by inch, trailing wet heat down his chest until I was hovering over his cock. I didn't let him enter me. Not yet. I just slid over him, letting him feel the tease, the warmth, the promise he hadn't earned.

"You're hard already," I said, amused. "I haven't even given you permission."

He gasped. "I'm sorry. I can't help it."

"Not good enough," I said, pressing down just enough to let him feel the tip slip inside.

His whole body arched. I slapped his thigh lightly.

"Stay still," I warned.

I fucked him slowly. Deep. Grinding with just enough friction to make him lose control. His hands gripped the headboard like it was the only thing keeping him sane. His face was flushed under my stocking, jaw tight, moaning like he was being broken open one inch at a time.

I leaned forward, dragging my nails down his chest, slow enough to sting.

He came.

Without permission.

His body shuddered under mine, and he let out a soft, wrecked cry.

I froze, still seated on top of him, fingers braced against his ribs.

"You weren't supposed to do that," I said, voice cold now.

"I'm sorry," he said, already wrecked. "I didn't mean to. I couldn't stop."

I tilted his chin up, nails still digging into his skin. I didn't speak for a moment. I just let the silence settle.

"Now you're going to make it up to me," I said finally. "A few times over."

"Yes," he said, already sliding down the bed without me needing to tell him how.

He started with kisses. Soft. Apologetic. Worshipful. Then his mouth pressed between my thighs and stayed there. He didn't ask how long. He didn't stop to breathe unless I allowed him to. He just kept going. Over and over. Until I came so hard my legs trembled around his ears.

Then he did it again.

And again.

By the fourth time, I was shaking, one hand gripping the headboard, the other tangled in his hair, gasping his name like it was a confession.

He was delightful.

And he knew it.

And he'd spend the rest of the night trying to earn forgiveness I might not give because that was the game. Punishment and reward. Pleasure and pain. Give and take. And he loved every second of it.

When we danced, he showed me off like no one ever had before or ever has since.

We would go to this delightful little dive bar he knew, with dim lights, sticky tables, and charm that made you feel like you were in on a secret. A real-life Fernando's Hideaway. He would slip the bouncer fifty dollars like it was nothing, and suddenly, we had champagne, food, and every indulgence brought to our table without question. He was generous like that. Reckless with money and pleasure when it came to me.

He always asked me to dance in the most formal way possible, bowing slightly at the waist and holding out his hand like I was rare. I would grin every time and place my hand in his. There was something so old-fashioned in the gesture and full of promise that I never tired of it.

He knew every dance. Every rhythm. Every move. He didn't dance to show off. He danced to make me look exquisite. To spin me across the floor like I was the one everyone had come to see. He twirled me with precision and dipped me with flair, always watching my face for the moments when I laughed or gasped or melted. He made me the center of everything.

He never looked at other women. Not once. Not ever. And he never let another man look at me for long without answering with the Look of Sovereignty. That quiet, brutal stare reminded them that the borders were closed and heavily defended. There was a possessiveness in him, but it never came from fear. It came from certainty. He knew I was his, just as he knew he was mine.

When he pressed closer, grinding his hips into mine just enough, I could feel how much he wanted me. I could feel the hunger in his body, the way it throbbed just from touching me through my clothes. He made me feel like I was dangerous. Like I was fire, he could not stop reaching for me. The dancing was a performance for others and foreplay for him. A way of seduction that didn't need words. A way of begging without falling to his knees.

I would never dominate him in public. That was not his role. He needed to be seen as powerful, composed, and masculine as the world expected. But in private? That man would do anything I asked of him. He would drop to his knees the moment the door shut. He would obey with a look that said he loved being used by me and found freedom in it.

In my apartment, we had a routine we followed. I made him stand at the end of the bed, hands on the footboard, legs apart. He knew the position by now. Knew not to move unless I told him to. Knew to hold that cock still, even as it hardened under my gaze.

I circled behind him, dragging my nails down his spine. Touched every inch of his back. His thighs. His ass. I let my fingers trail between his legs, just barely brushing the underside of him until he started to twitch. It took no time at all.

Then I picked up the paddle.

Walnut. Dark. Smooth. Weighted just right. The kind of tool that didn't need explanation.

The first strike landed across the fullest part of his ass, flat and deliberate. His breath caught. My fingers tightened around the wood. But he stayed still.

"Thank you," I prompted.

"Thank you, Belle."

I gave him five more, perfectly spaced. No mercy. No rush. Just the rhythm of discipline, and the sound of him trying to keep quiet.

When I was done, his skin was flushed red and glowing with heat. His cock was straining. His thighs were shaking. But he hadn't moved an inch.

I stepped in close behind him. Pressed my chest to his back. Slid one hand between his legs and cupped him, slow and possessive.

"You want to fuck me?"

His breath hitched. "Yes. Please, Belle."

I leaned in, lips brushing his ear.

"Then earn it."

I let go of him.

Then I placed both hands on the footboard, still standing, still in control, and arched my back just enough.

"Take me."

He didn't hesitate.

He lined up behind me, one hand on my hip for balance, the other still gripping the wood like his life depended on it. He slid inside me in one slow, reverent motion, groaning as he filled me.

I didn't give him time to adjust.

I started to move. Hips grinding back against him, steady at first, then harder. My fingers curled around the wood in front of me, the same place his had just been. My back arched, pushing him deeper.

He moaned behind me. "Belle... c'est trop... je vais venir..." *Belle, it's too much... I'm going to come...*

"You don't come until I do."

He groaned. Tried to hold back. His hips stuttered. His hands were trembling now.

"Por favor... deixa eu fazer você gozar primeiro..." *Please... let me make you come first...*

"Then do it."

He gripped my hips and changed the angle, adjusted his rhythm, focused everything he had on pulling pleasure out of me. He buried his face in my shoulder and bit down, just enough to keep himself grounded. To stay inside this moment. To keep himself from breaking.

It worked.

I came first. My whole body tensed, knees threatening to buckle, mouth open in a sound I didn't try to hide. I clenched around him and felt him almost lose it.

Only when I caught my breath did I give the order.

"Now."

He came with a groan, hands locked on my hips, face pressed to my back, the sound of it half French, half Portuguese, all worship.

When it was done, I straightened, turned my head just enough to look over my shoulder at him.

"You fucked me like an unhinged animal."

"Yes, Belle." he felt shame.

"Fuck me again."

And he did. Quiet. Grateful. Still shaking.

Exactly the way I like him.

One time, when we were together late, he was working on a project report for the Secretary, and we were stuck in the building. I was pretending to need to work, just hanging out with him. He came by my office and brought me some food. There was some reception, and he made a plate for me, and I was starving.

He walked in and set the food on my bookcase without a word, locking the door behind him. His hands found my shoulders, firm and deliberate, kneading the tension like he had every right to be there. He told me I worked too hard and said I needed a break. He was right. I did.

He picked me up and set me down on the desktop in that romantic comedy way where things fly. He pulled up my skirt and put his head between my legs. He went down on me, just a little at first, to get me started, and then he went whole hog. Entirely.

I was utterly undone by it. I unraveled beneath him with practiced ease. He was aching with need, desperate to keep the promises his body had every intention of fulfilling. When he entered me, the sensation tore through me like a shiver that started deep and refused to end. He kept whispering how much he wanted me, how badly he needed to be with me, how perfect I felt wrapped around him.

"It's like silk. It's like silk," he kept saying. I never understood why, but at that moment, he was overwhelmed. His voice, his body, the way he demanded everything. He kept whispering, "Tell me you want me." I told him the truth. I begged him to take me harder. He pulled away, turned me over, pressed my face to the desk, and opened me with both hands. Then he filled me again, slow at first, then deeper, speaking Portuguese like a spell. He said it was beautiful. He said it was perfect. He said he needed me. And then he asked me to come just for him.

I did.

He collapsed into the office chair, still panting, his legs spread wide as if he didn't care what came next.

I climbed into his lap without a sound, facing away at first, sinking onto him with the kind of control that left no doubt who was in charge. He was still pulsing beneath me, so hard he let out a strangled breath the moment I took all of him.

"Please," he said, voice broken around the word. "Please don't stop."

I didn't. I moved with a slow, deliberate rhythm, circling my hips, grounding myself deeper with each pass. He was trembling under my hands, all tension and need; holding on like this was the only thing keeping him alive.

"Turn around," he said, voice frayed and full of ache. "Please. I want to see you."

He was close. I could feel it in the way his legs tightened, and his hands hovered just above my skin as if touching without permission might break the spell.

"Please," he whispered again, eyes locked on mine. "Please bite me right before I come. Please."

I cupped his jaw. He leaned in until my breath brushed against his neck.

"You want my teeth in your skin?"

"Yes," he said. "Mark me. I need it."

I bit into the curve of his chest, sharp and deep, just below his collarbone.

"Bon garçon," I murmured, my voice laced with praise and possession. "Alors viens pour moi, comme la chose sale que tu es." *Good boy,* I said in French. *Then come for me, like the filthy thing you are."*

He whimpered.

I paused, lips at his ear, letting the silence throb.

"Et fais-moi une œuvre d'art abstrait." In French, *and make me a piece of abstract art.*

He let out a breathless laugh, barely more than air, and then I gave the only command he needed.

"Now."

He shattered under me. Groaning. Trembling. Pouring himself into the moment like it might be his last. I sank my teeth into his shoulder just as the wave broke, and he bucked beneath me, clutching the chair as if the world had dropped away.

When I pulled back, I licked the mark slowly, watching him try to catch his breath. His eyes were glassy. His lips parted.

"Mine!" I whispered.

He texted around six. He said he needed a little more time to finish something for the Secretary, but would be free as soon as the old man left for dinner at The Capitol Grille.

"Steak and brandy with lobbyists," I wrote back. "How very original."

"Dark wood paneling, too," he replied. "Private dining room. It screams D.C. cliché."

"Don't forget the cigar humidor," I said.

He sent a little fire emoji. "I'll be yours by eight."

I returned to my apartment and tidied up—dishes, pillows, evidence of a busy working girl's week.

He stood there like a perfectly wrapped offering when he knocked at the door. Arms full of flowers and wine, a ribbon-tied box of dark chocolates—he always remembered my favorites.

"Bonsoir, Belle," he said as I opened the door. "I come bearing gifts and good intentions."

"You'd better," I said, stepping aside.

He kissed me on the cheek. "And maybe," he added in a lower voice, "a few bad ones too."

The flogger, red suede and coiled like a secret, was already on the coffee table. I had not hidden it. I had placed it there on purpose, like some strange relic or decadent souvenir from a Renaissance Faire where things got wonderfully out of hand.

He saw it immediately. He did not sit down. He walked straight over, picked it up with both hands, and dropped to his knees.

"Please, Belle. Please."

"Are you asking me or offering it to me?"

He held it up with both hands like an offering. Reverent. Needy.

"I'm begging."

I took it from him slowly. The suede slid through my fingers like something sacred.

"You remember what I told you."

"Yes. If I need to stop, I say stop."

"Correct. And what else?"

"You are beautiful; I submit to your will."

"In French."

He looked up at me. His voice dropped, and his eyes darkened.

"Tu es magnifique. Je me rends à ta volonté."

"Good," I said. "Now get up and take off your fucking clothes. You know you should be naked in my apartment. It is a crime to keep a beautiful body like yours in clothes. I would have you naked all the time."

He rose, stripped, and stood at the edge of the bed. Watchin' me with lust in his eyes.

"Hands on the footboard. Feet shoulder-width. Do not move unless I tell you."

He obeyed.

I started slowly. I wanted him to anticipate it. You do not begin a long flogging session at full intensity. That can go badly, and I was unsure if he wished to mark. We had not fully discussed it, so I assumed he did not.

I began by gently dragging the flogger over his body, across his chest, down his back, letting him feel it, letting him wonder. Then I started a soft circular rhythm, light taps, not pain, just sensation on his back and ass.

"Breathe," I said.

He did.

I stepped back and began the figure-eight motion. I widened my stance and let the strands graze him with each pass. Still soft. Still delicate. The kind of contact that lingers without leaving a bruise. His skin responded. He began to sway.

"Stay still."

"Oui."

I studied him.

"I am going to go harder now?"

"Yes, Belle."

"Good. Then take it for me."

I deepened the strokes. Let them land longer. Slower. Then faster. Then harder. His back glowed with soft red marks. Not the kind that would last, but the kind that haunts your memory.

He gasped when I hit just the right place.

"You love it, don't you?"

"I do."

"You want to be marked where no one else will see. Just for you. Just for me", he said

"Please."

"Say it."

"Pour toi, Belle. Pour toujours." *For you, Belle, For always.* He said in ecstasy.

I adjusted my position and told him to spread his legs wider.

"Stick your ass out. Lift your heels. Let me see everything."

He obeyed, his balls dangling, his vulnerability exposed most deliciously. I focused there on his ass. Every stroke made it stand out more until it became the only thing I saw. I hit him over and over. He moaned into the air.

Then I stopped.

I came up behind him and wrapped my hands around his throat and the base of his cock. He did not move. I would not let him.

He was hard. Very hard.

I held him there for a few long minutes, saying nothing and just feeling his body tremble between my hands.

"Do not come," I whispered in his ear. "Not until I say. Do not think for a second that you are in control here. You are not. I decide everything. If you fail, I will kick you out onto the street. Naked."

He shivered.

"Oui, Belle," he whimpered.

"Good," I said. "I am not finished with you yet."

I resumed flogging him. Bigger movements. More force. His body absorbed it beautifully. He adored it. Absolutely fucking adored it.

"Tell me you want more."

"I want more. I want all of it."

"Greedy," I said, grabbing his throat again. "You had better do an excellent job of pleasing me. Otherwise, I will put you out on the street and never touch you again."

Something changed in his face. He liked that. A little humiliation kink hidden under all that polished compliance. Maybe he had not known it was there, but it rose now, gleaming like hunger. And it turned me on, too.

"Stand at attention," I said. "You have earned your reward."

He stood. Breathless. Erect.

"This is the only blowjob you will ever get from me. I want you to remember it."

I bent down, kissed the head of his cock once, and said, "I am going to blow you."

I got a firm grip on his cock, and gave it a good stroke. He came before I even opened my mouth. He shot over my shoulder to the wall behind my bed. I was not expecting that reaction. It is a hard thing to predict adequately.

Afterward, we lay in bed. I drew little circles on his chest and shoulders. He was still reeling.

"I am so sorry?" he kept asking.

I was not upset a bit. But as penance for his early arrival and aborted blow job, he ended it by giving me a full-body massage with oil, a scent I used to remember every time I wanted to feel desired.

Our romance didn't last long, which was a shame. The administration was changing, and he was leaving the city. I always wondered what would've happened if he'd stayed.

That's the funny thing about D.C. People are constantly coming in and out of your life. It's sad, but it also allows you to get to know people intensely, if only for a moment.

Whether something will continue or end is usually decided for you by the strange rhythm of a city that churns people through it like a revolving door. Sometimes, that knowledge—that it's destined to end—makes the connection burn even brighter while it lasts.

8

Civil Rights

She was a famous Civil Rights attorney whose name appeared in significant rulings and whispered conversations, the kind who had been quoted in *The New York Times* more often than most people had read the paper of record. She didn't want to leave New York, but the offer in DC had been too good, powerful, and tempting. She came to DC reluctantly, carrying the weight of her reputation like a tailored coat.

A New Yorker through and through, shaped by a concrete attitude and loyalty that ran deeper than blood. She kept her childhood friends like family and made new ones slowly and carefully, the way a General studies a treaty before they sign it. She was not reckless. She moved through the world as if it belonged to her already, and she only paused to ensure everyone remembered. And for some reason, she wanted me.

To me, she was my bratty, brilliant, sharp-tongued submissive. She had this ridiculous cascade of curly red hair, naturally and with help from others, and a peaches-and-cream complexion that felt almost obscene to touch. Her skin was soft, making me long to mark it, to see how long it would remember me.

She wore severely tailored suits that hugged her hips, making men forget their wives. Her heels were always expensive and unapologetically high. Underneath it all, she wore Agent Provocateur for no one but herself and me. It was her armor, her secret weapon, something

that made her feel untouchable. She kept her makeup minimal, her jewelry understated, the aesthetic that whispered wealth rather than screamed it. But her lips were always slightly parted, with a French girl aesthetic, soft and full, like she was about to say something that would ruin your life in the best possible way.

When we met at a cocktail party full of overpaid consultants and political vampires, she didn't flirt with me like some sorority girl twirling her hair. She hunted. She clocked me across a group of people and headed straight to me. I was her target, and she stalked me with quiet confidence and slow, strategic steps. I watched her calculate every move and cross the room like a panther who knew exactly where to sink her teeth. I was her prey, and she did not attempt to pretend otherwise. It was thrilling. Her eyes were fixed on me like I was the next prize she planned to own.

The most unforgettable part was not that she wanted me; it was how she wanted me. With the kind of focus she usually reserved for oral arguments and closing statements. She didn't hesitate. And I was the one she chose. Even now, I can still feel that flicker of disbelief humming under my skin, a low thrum of wonder at how she picked me out of all the noise in that room. But she had her reasons. And in time, I would learn that I was not just a want. I was a need.

She didn't bother pretending to be subtle. There was no warm-up. No build. No hesitation. She decided I was hers and made it known. Maybe I was the consolation prize for the Yankees season tickets she left behind. Perhaps I was the soft place to land after years of sharpening herself into something unbreakable. Whatever I was, from the moment she looked at me, it was done. She had already made up her mind; all I could do was let it happen. It would be the last decision she made about the relationship; from then on, I would take over.

She would take a particular kind of control, expertly negotiating to keep the wall of work away from her and give "permission" to check out of her life and focus on submission and her physical pleasure.

In top-gun circles like Washington, DC, where power is currency and performance never truly ends, the more dominance someone commands in public, the more intensely they crave surrender behind closed doors. The higher they rise, the more they long to be brought low, not out of shame or weakness but from the sheer weight of maintaining control. They want to be quieted and sometimes humiliated.

They spend their days making decisions, issuing directives, and holding the room with practiced ease. Every interaction is calculated. Every response is managed. They are constantly on the move, always managing perception. When they finally escape the spotlight for a little bit, they are not looking for comfort wrapped in luxury or compliments. They want a structure that holds. It is the one place where they do not have to perform.

While my dominance can present many ways, from pain and degradation to more unearthly delights, for her, I was a pleasure domme. Watching her get off was like watching an adult film; it only led to wanting more of her. Our sessions could last a whole weekend of arousal and release. She could have 6 or 8 orgasms a day and would be wet, ready, and willing most of that time.

Sometimes, I'd stop by her office, close the door, and sit across from her in a blouse with one button too many undone and no underwear. I'd flash her during what might have looked like a strategic consultation. It would be very *Fatal Attraction* if *Fatal Attraction* had a lesbian reboot with better lighting. She would freeze every time, eyes caught like a deer in my headlights. She was powerless at that moment, but she loved it, and it gave her a brief respite, a momentary distraction in the midst of her 10-hour days.

I planned every date: fireworks on the Mall, jazz concerts at the National Gallery Sculpture Garden, biking to Gravelly Point to watch the planes land at Reagan National Airport (unofficially known as Ruth Bader Ginsburg Airport or DCA), packing the picnic basket, making sure the wine was chilled, and the vibrators had fresh batteries. I crafted a world for her to show up relaxed and ready to do whatever the fuck I wanted her to do.

When we were alone, she liked to curl up next to me like a cat. It wasn't a fetish; it was a return to comfort, a way to disconnect from the stress of the day for a while. I would stroke her red hair and drag my nails lightly over her skin to relax her, sometimes for hours, while I read a book or did crossword puzzles with her.

One thing about her was truly unique: as a lifelong New Yorker, she didn't drive and never had a car or a license.

In DC, you can get away with not having a car, especially if you've got money, and she did. She took a black car service, Metro, and walked everywhere she could. When we were together, I drove, and she would repay me by wearing thigh-high stockings and skirts that she would routinely pull up in the passenger seat, revealing her natural hair color to me at every opportunity.

She had a touch of exhibitionism to her, not a lot; she didn't like to have sex in public, but she did like the idea that someone could discover us, and these flashes were a little naughty to her. As if her inherent sexuality, if found, would be sinful. I was happy to indulge in this kink that heightened her pleasure and intensity.

When she told me she was buying a house in Rehoboth Beach, DE, where gay and/or well-healed Washingtonians go to play for the summer, I was thrilled. Not only is Rehoboth my favorite place to go when it gets hot, but we can also have a lot of fun on the road there and enjoy privacy when we arrive, with space to satisfy my dark, wicked cravings.

Her place in Rehoboth was straight out of a summer dream. It was decorated top to bottom by a designer of TV fame flown in for the occasion. Everything was tasteful and chic in the best possible way. I had designed one room to my particular specs to support our fervent pursuit of the dark arts, a room we called the Bijou.

On one of our escapes to the shore, I drove with her phone on silent and her legs open. She flashed me from the passenger seat while I kept one eye on the road and the other on her. Route 50 stretched ahead of us, a straight shot out of the D. C. swamp toward Route 404 that would wind us through solar farms, chicken houses, and small towns. She kept brushing her fingers along the inside of her thigh like she wanted to tempt fate or at least lure me into pulling over. I didn't. Not yet. Delayed gratification is a language we both spoke fluently.

I reminded her of the rules. This wasn't just a weekend away. This was a shift in state, a surrender of time, identity, and all the little compulsions that usually rule her life. We have rules for this; we have rituals. Everything changes at the Bay Bridge.

Officially, it is called the William Preston Lane Jr. Memorial Bridge, but it is rarely used outside of official reports or accident claims. Most people refer to it as the Bay Bridge. It is tall, windy, often foggy, and narrow enough to make your palms sweat if you glance over the edge. There is no shoulder. There is no forgiveness. Some drivers have such intense phobias about it that the state offers escort services so no one has to white-knuckle it alone.

For us, the bridge is a line in the sand, a threshold, a contract.

Our contract states that once the tires hit the first drop over the water, you are no longer allowed to care about anything on the other side. You are not a professional anymore. You are not anyone's boss, not anyone's assistant, not a public servant or a campaign consultant or whatever version of herself she had to be to make it through the week. Vacation begins when the wheels are over the water, and I am the only client she has to please.

And to mark that moment, we roll down all four windows and scream, from the joy of rupture. From the knowledge that nobody from the office will climb onto the bridge and drag her back.

Once we are on the bridge, she has to drop into complete submission. She cannot hedge. She cannot multitask. She cannot be halfway mine and halfway something else. She is not allowed to play coy or clever. She is mine. Fully. She is to be present, open, and obedient. She is to remember that I am the only thing on her calendar. I remind her, every time, that she should think of me as the John who has paid for her weekend. And she will do whatever I ask, without negotiation, without exception.

"I just need to check one email," she said, her voice soft. Her eyes were fixed on the screen as if it had something sacred to offer her.

"No."

"Just one."

"No. This is my time now. You are welcome to work on someone else's schedule. Not mine." I quietly ordered.

She stared out the window momentarily, her mind half in the office, then breathed. She smiled, faint and guilty, and slipped her phone into the glove box. The latch clicked shut.

That sound was a promise. As we entered the bridge, I rolled down the windows, and we screamed as our wheels went over the water.

And in that moment, the weekend truly began.

It was a rule that we had negotiated along with the other 200 or so we had. Extensively. Carefully. In detail. Our agreement contained clauses, subclauses, and enough hypotheticals to qualify as legal erotica.

"Unbutton your blouse," I said as we passed the toll lanes and slid onto the long stretch of bridge.

"Now?" she asked. Her voice was softer, but her smile wasn't. She knew exactly what she was doing.

"Yes. Rule 15. You wrote half of them. And take off your bra. Let the wind touch you."

She held still for a moment, eyes on the road ahead, lips curving slowly.

"And if I don't? What are you going to do?" she said, voice silky, just loud enough for me to hear over the hum of the tires.

I turned my head just enough to meet her gaze. No smile. Just that steady look that told her I'd do it without flinching.

"I will cut your $250 bra off you in the middle of the Starbucks parking lot in front of everyone," I said, voice low, rough now.

"Last time, it was a McDonald's; a Starbucks seems like a downgrade," she teased me.

She arched her back just enough to reach behind her. The clasp snapped open. The bra slid down her arms and onto her lap like it had given up the game. She tossed the bra coquettishly on my lap.

"If you wanted me to take you seriously, you would have worn the one you bought on your trip to Vegas when they lost your luggage.

You hate that one." I said, dragging my fingers along the inside of her thigh.

Her breasts were bare, open to the brackish bay breeze. It was just the two of us in the car. But the possibility that another driver might glance over made her shiver. And that was the point.

I had packed a particular toy for the trip, one of my favorites. It was a curved little weapon; its angle precisely hit the front wall of her G-spot. Its low hum stirred nerves already tuned to me. It was made for this kind of drive.

"Panties off! Rule 56!" I growled. Annoyed that they were still on. She shifted. Her legs opened just slightly, and she dropped her panties to the floor of the car. She handed them to me, and I hung them from the rearview mirror so that everyone could see.

I leaned over and ran one finger along the soft slickness between her thighs. She was soaked. I knew she would be. But I always checked, not just because I liked it, though I did. Checking was Rule 35 in our contract, and if I broke the rules, she got to punish me, which seemed only fair.

I reached into the door's side pocket to produce the purple vibrator wrapped in tissue paper. I tossed it onto her lap. Driving on the bridge is not something you take your eyes off, even for such enticing scenery.

"Put it in", I told her quietly.

She slid the toy into place. I handed her the remote. "We are nearly at the bridge's midpoint," I said. "Lowest setting. Just enough to warm you up. You may not come until we cross."

She pressed the button. A faint hum filled the space between us. Her breath caught. Her hips shifted. The toy began its quiet work. She squirmed but kept her feet where they were.

The bridge arched high over the Chesapeake. It was four and a third miles of steel and air. As we neared the top, the most dangerous part of the bridge, I spoke again.

"Level two."

Her hand shook slightly as she turned it up. She gasped as her hips lifted from the seat. A loud, sharp cry escaped her lips. A seagull resting on the railing startled and flew into the open sky. But she did not come—not yet. I had trained her too well.

I kept driving. Calm. Focused. By the time we reached the far end of the bridge, her thighs were trembling, and her nipples were taut from the breeze. Her whole body was wound tight. Her voice was ragged from screaming her moans to the birds.

She was already trembling when she whispered it. "Please," she gasped, knuckles white where she gripped the edge of the seat. "Please tell me. I can't—I need—"

Her thighs jerked again, another surge of sensation ripping through her from the relentless hum between her legs. She was wild. Her back arched, and her breath caught on the edge of a scream that never entirely left her mouth.

"Not yet," I warned her.

The windows were still down. That wasn't a mistake. I wanted the wind in her hair and the salt on her tongue. I wanted the sound of her moans whipping out into the open air, scattering the seagulls that had dared to settle nearby. And I wanted her to know that no one could save her from this. Not with her body unraveling at my command.

"Now!" I said.

Calm. Commanding. Loud enough to make her flinch. She screamed as she obeyed. Loud, raw, and shameless, the sound ricocheted off the inside of the car, echoing through the open window like a warning shot.

To anyone watching, it would have looked unkind. Maybe even dangerous. A woman barking orders at a woman coming apart in the passenger seat, pinned in place by nothing more than her own aching need and my voice in her ear. But this wasn't chaos. It was control. She didn't want mercy. She wanted to be mastered. And I didn't ask. I told.

We still had 173 miles of country road ahead, with many detours to come.

Once we were off the bridge, things always got more adventurous. It was mostly two-lane country roads. She would tease me to turn off the road, starting with a whisper and building slowly and deliberately. Sometimes, she would lean in and murmur what she wanted me to do to her off-road.

She loved that she couldn't touch me while driving, Rule 46.5, subpart A. Sometimes, I would let her give me a shoulder massage from the back seat. There was a loophole in our contract that she delighted in teasing me with a backseat backrub was allowed, Rule 46.5 subpart B. Climbing into the back seat, she rubbed my shoulders and let her fingers "accidentally" brush my breasts.

Sometimes she would spread her legs wide in the backseat and fuck herself with the dildo I usually used on her, liberated from my luggage, a wicked little performance designed to tempt me into pulling over and finishing what she started. That was precisely what she was doing now.

"Are you going to come back here and fuck me for real?"

I watched her in the mirror. Her thighs tensed. She tried to keep her face still as we passed families in minivans and couples on their weekend getaways.

"Don't bite your lip," I said, letting my fingers brush her chin. "Smile like you're remembering something innocent."

Her breath caught, but she obeyed. Her lips curled into a sweet, bashful smile, which made it even filthier. I leaned closer, my voice low and intimate, meant for her and her alone.

"Do not come until the next light. I want everyone to see you. I want them to watch you come like a hooker in the red light district on stage, legs spread, breath shaking, but your face lit up like a sinner in church."

"Are you my hooker?" I asked. I already knew the answer. I just wanted to hear her say it.

"Yes, Belle."

"Say it louder." I did not raise my voice. I did not need to. The weight of it did the work.

"Yes, Belle," she screamed so loud I jerked the car a little bit.

Her legs shook. Her hand grabbed the edge of the seat like it was the only thing tethering her to this world. "I can't hold it," she whispered, and then she broke.

It was wild. Rough. Honest. Her hips lifted as if something inside her snapped loose. No beauty, only need.

Her orgasm was so intense that she expelled the dildo out and onto the floor on her final velvet quake.

If anyone had looked over, they might have thought she was having a seizure. But no one did. Except for a lone cowboy in a rusted-out pickup truck waiting at the light.

His line of sight was terrible. He missed the show.

I did not.

She was quiet for a long time. The kind of silence stretches, hums, and makes you feel the weight of everything left unsaid. I let her have it. I kept my eyes on the road, the night folding around us like velvet.

Then, barely audible over the hum of the tires, she said, "Thank you, Belle. Thank you."

Her voice cracked slightly at the edges as something too tender pressed too hard. A single tear slid down her cheek. She curled up in the seat beside me, drawing her knees toward her chest like she was trying to hold something in or maybe keep something precious from spilling out.

She stayed that way for a moment, curled and small and quiet. Then she moved.

She reached across the console without a word and placed her palm on my thigh with reverence as if it were the most natural thing in the world, as if she knew exactly where she belonged. She was breaking the rules by touching me, and she knew it.

Her hand lingered, warm and steady, and then her fingers began to move slowly, teasing and tracing soft, spiraling patterns that danced just on the edge of intention. She didn't look at me, and she didn't speak a word.

She let her fingers drift, sometimes barely grazing, sometimes pressing just enough to make me grip the steering wheel tighter. She kept her hand there for thirty miles, exploring, provoking, claiming in silence.

Every curve of her fingertips asked a question to which she already knew the answer.

I drove like it was nothing, like her hand was not undoing me inch by inch. But inside, I was unraveling.

I was burning.

Somewhere past Georgetown, I was consumed by a strong desire and caught a whiff of something sweet and earthy, like lavender. The kind that bruises when the wind shifts, its scent clinging to everything. Off to the right, a field opened up. Rows of lavender stalks, wildly overgrown, remnants of what must have been a working farm. Now, it was a riot of purple, swaying like a siren call. Maybe I was imagining it, or perhaps it was the scent, the slick between my thighs from watching her all this way, but I didn't even think. I swerved hard, tires crunching over gravel and then dirt, and I killed the engine in the shade of an old wooden fence.

She looked over, startled, and laughed. "What the hell was that?"

"You," I said. "You did that. You broke the rules!"

I threw open my door and stalked her. She was already unbuckled, biting her lower lip like she'd been waiting for this. I yanked her out of the car and dragged her by the wrist into the field. The lavender wrapped around us in waves, brushing our calves and knees, the smell thick and heady.

"Down," I ordered.

She didn't hesitate. She dropped to her knees, the skirt bunching around her hips. I reached down and yanked it higher, baring her completely. "Hands behind your back."

She obeyed, breath trembling. "I didn't mean to break the rules," she gave a snide little smile.

"You knew what you were doing. You must have wanted this very badly," I said, crouching beside her. I snapped off a few lavender sprigs, testing their feel against my palm.

She was almost delighted but tried very hard to hide it for the sake of the mise-en-scène. She can't hide anything from me, but I appreciate the effort she makes.

We were deep in the field, where the brush was so high that it completely hid us. I had her bend forward, her chest in the lavender, her ass high. I circled her with slow, deliberate steps, letting the anticipation soak into her skin.

"What rule did you break?"

"I don't remember." She quipped.

I grabbed the stalk of a long-dead lavender plant and used it as a switch to flog her.

"Do you remember now?" I asked.

She nodded no, which was my cue to continue. She never forgot a rule. As part of her intense training, I made her recite them out loud while I placed clothespins on her skin. She never missed one.

She gasped as I struck her again with the lavender switch. It wasn't the harsh sting of leather or suede; it was subtle, maddening, all scent and sensation. I dragged it down the backs of her thighs, then snapped it lightly across the curve of her ass.

"What rule did you break?" I demanded.

"Rule 12?" She looked up at me, knowing she was lying to get me to continue, but she loved the thrill of being outside.

"You seem to have a curious problem with your memory tonight. Do I need you to recite all the rules before we return to the car?"

"No, Belle. It's Rule 46.5."

"What subpart?"

"A," She pouted.

"You are so fucking bratty right now. It's almost like you want me to punish you with this lavender."

"Whatever pleases you, Belle. I am your whore this weekend."

"For now. Count," I said.

"One," she flinched. "Thank you, Belle."

I continued five, ten, a dozen strokes, each punctuated with her soft and reverent voice. She squirmed against the pressure, moaning as the smooth, soft stems brushed her sensitive skin. Her scent mingled with the lavender until it was impossible to tell where the field ended, and she began.

Finally, I knelt behind her and reached forward to cup her clit, hot, soaked, pulsing. "Is this what you wanted?"

"Yes," she whispered. "Yes, please."

"Not yet," I said, and I pushed her flat into the lavender, mounting her thighs and pinning her down.

"You don't come until I say so."

I held her there, fingers grazing, voice low and slow — like heat curling through the air.

"Not until I give you permission."

She whimpered my name, a prayer and a curse, carried off by the breeze.

The lavender was thick around us, heady and wild, brushing her bare thighs like a second set of hands.

"You feel that?" I whispered. "The scent... the ache... everything waiting for you."

She clawed at the dirt, hips rising, chasing what I kept just out of reach.

"Not yet."

Her thighs trembled. Her breath caught.

"You're breaking already," I said, smiling against her ear.

"And I haven't even let you fall."

"Position 3." She tucked her heels and sat on her knees, palms on her thighs.

"You are a mess in a blouse that costs more than your Secretary makes monthly."

She opened her mouth—of course she did—already drafting her rebuttal like a closing argument.

"Don't even try to litigate your way out of this. There are better things for your sharp tongue to do now."

I leaned in closer, walking my clit to her mouth.

"Stick your tongue out. You've already lost the case, counselor."

"You really should see yourself when you suffer," I said, my fingertips skating down her spine. "It's practically case law at this point."

I grabbed her hair, guiding her tongue exactly where I wanted it.

"Keep your tongue out."

I hit her with the lavender switch again.

"Do your fucking job, you are failing in this oral argument."

She turned her head, one eyebrow raised like she was about to cross-examine me. "I'm going to need a citation for that claim."

I shoved her face back in my crotch and hit her again with the lavender.

"Now suck on it. Hard."

I came so hard I fell backward, pulling her with me.

"Please. You wouldn't last five minutes under cross." She said.

"You're not exactly holding up well either, counselor." I smacked her ass with my hand.

"You're trembling." She said.

Her mouth twitched. Almost a smile. Almost a snarl.

"You obey beautifully," I said. "All that control, stripped down to pure compliance. It's the most honest thing about you."

"I'd like to object to that characterization formally," she objected.

"Denied. With prejudice."

"God, you're unbearable." She snarked.

"And yet here you are. Still waiting for me to tell you yes." I volleyed

"Out of professional curiosity."

"Out of desperation."

She glared. "You're enjoying this."

"I'm conducting a thorough cross-examination of your limits." I looked at her with lust in my eyes.

"And when exactly do I get to rebut?"

I leaned in. "After you beg. Nicely. Like a lawyer who knows she's losing."

"That's never happened."

"It's happening right now."

Silence. Then, very quietly and with maximum disdain, "Please," she begged.

I smiled. Reaching under her to her clit "Permission granted." I rubbed her vigorously.

She shattered like a mistrial. Her body dropped, her breath broke, and the argument fell apart faster than a bad alibi. All that fight drained out in ragged sobs, real ones, the kind she couldn't redact.

She couldn't speak. She just gasped like she was pleading for recess.

"And to think," I said, "I almost didn't let you have a closing argument."

She whimpered, "Es pestis libidinis et ego odio te quod amo te." Latin again. She loves doing this. *You are a plague of lust, and I hate you because I love you.*

Either way, the verdict was mine.

We stayed there a while, tangled, stained, and reeking of lavender. When we finally stumbled back to the car, she was shivering. I knew she wouldn't dare disobey again, at least for an hour or two.

When we got to the house, I unloaded the bags. She stood in the doorway, flushed and waiting for my orders.

"Get inside," I said. "Take off everything."

She didn't hesitate. Her clothes peeled away.

"Go to the Bijou," I said, not even looking at her. But I knew her eyes were down to the ground where they belonged.

She froze mid-step. That slight pause she always did when instructions dropped casually but carried weight.

"Turn on something obscene. Bondage. And kneel. Position five."

I didn't raise my voice. I didn't need to. She almost skipped with glee.

I waited exactly eight minutes. Long enough for anticipation to turn into anxiety. Long enough for her to start wondering if she had done something wrong. Long enough to make her want it.

When I entered the room, the screen was already lit. It was black and white, with harsh lighting. There was rope and struggle and a flicker of whip across a spine. The volume flooded the room with layered cries and breathless begging.

She was there.

Kneeling on the Sybian. Arms forward. Wrists cuffed, ready to be locked to the floor. Her back arched like she was offering me her ass. The red ball gag dangled from her neck, waiting to be put in place.

I knelt before her and lifted the red ball to her mouth.

"Bite," she flashed me a cheeky wink. She wanted to bite me, but there was time for that. I clarified, "... the ball." I clasped the buckle tight on her head.

I shoved her head down so that it was parallel to the ground and latched her handcuffs to the floor.

She had chosen nipple clamps. I hadn't authorized them.

But she was feeling bratty tonight.

I didn't correct her. Not yet. I licked one nipple, then the other, slow and deliberate, letting my tongue flick and circle until she arched forward, breath-catching. Then I bit, just enough to send her nerves flaring. She whimpered, already squirming.

She wanted to come. That much was obvious. But wanting and deserving were two different things.

I clamped her nipples first. A precise snap of pressure. Enough to keep her honest. Enough to remind her who she belonged to. Then I locked the chain between the clamps and bound her wrists, which rested on the floor in front of her.

She was seated on the Sybian, knees bent, with a straight back and obedient posture, at least for now.

If she leaned back to take pressure off her clit, the clamps would hurt. If she pulled forward to escape the ache in her chest, she'd press harder into the vibration once it began. Everything was connected—every decision fed into the next.

She looked up at me, eyes glassy. Her lips parted just enough for the gag to catch her shallow breath. Tension lived in every muscle. The machine hadn't even been turned on, and already, she was trembling.

I knelt beside her. One hand on her thigh, the other at her chin. I tilted her face up until her eyes met mine.

"You're already close, aren't you?"

She nodded—a small, cautious motion.

Her thighs quivered.

I pressed my thumb gently to her lips, over the gag.

"You think this is going to end quickly? It won't. You're going to feel every single second of this."

Then I stood. Reached for the remote.

"Fine. You'll get exactly what you asked for."

"You are your exhibit now. Every motion, every reaction, every noise goes on the record."

She tried to breathe steadily. Failed.

"This isn't about sensation. This is about control. Can you stay still?"

She nodded—one small, deliberate motion.

"Then we begin."

I turned the Sybian on to the low setting, just enough to make her feel it. She jerked at the first vibration. The clamps bit down. She gasped, clenched her fists, and tried to hold her wrists still. The chain shifted. She winced.

"You already broke your opening statement," I said. "Not a strong start for the defense."

She moaned through the gag. Her thighs were trembling. The hum between her legs grew louder, but she kept her hands close to the floor, elbows tight, trying not to move and trying not to give me what I wanted.

I rose, crossed the room, and selected a paddle. It was made of clean wood. There was no ornamentation, nothing flashy, just results.

When I returned, she shifted slightly, trying to ride the Sybian without shifting her wrists. It wasn't working. She couldn't chase it without pain.

I circled behind her and struck. One quick slap across the back of her ass

She cried out. Her arms flinched. The chain yanked.

"You want to come, but you are not allowed."

I struck again, just above the first mark. Her moans were louder now. Desperate. Her body kept moving forward and back. Every grind into the machine pulled at her breasts. Her knees were starting to shake.

Again. A little harder. She whimpered into the gag, forehead dropping forward.

"You can stop this at any time."

She shook her head. Not yet.

"Then you stay where you are. You take everything I give you. You do not move your hands unless you want to fall apart."

She nodded again. Silent. Aching.

And that brat spark was back in her eyes, daring me to test the line, and tempting me to go further.

And maybe I would. It had been a long drive. And I was in the mood for a full trial.

I circled her again, deliberately letting my steps echo, and then walked to the theater recliner before her. I was wearing a black tank top and pants, thinking I looked badass. I felt powerful. I sat down with the remote control in my hand, the Sybian beside me.

Her breath hitched when I pressed the button. The machine hummed on the second lowest setting.

She was already shaking.

"Don't pretend you're in control," I said calmly. "You're not."

She moaned through the gag.

I twisted the dial-up just one step and ensured she saw me do it.

"Watch closely. If you want more, you'll have to work for it."

The way she was positioned, her clit was barely brushing the silicone plate.

"Choices have consequences, sweetheart," I said.

She let out a muffled groan, trembling harder.

I ignored her completely for three long minutes, eyes on the screen, pretending to be absorbed by the bondage film. She was drooling around the gag, trembling from effort and frustration.

"You don't seem to enjoy performing for me," I said without looking at her. "Maybe I should stop."

I turned the machine back down to the lowest setting.

She growled at me, low and furious.

"Is that attitude?" I raised an eyebrow. "You want to test me tonight?"

She shook her head violently, eyes wide.

"Good girl," I said, cool and amused.

I hooked my foot around her handcuffs and jerked her forward, slamming her clit down onto the machine. The sudden tug yanked at the nipple clamps. She howled.

I turned the machine off again.

"I could do this all night," I said, leaning back. "But you're the one making it difficult."

Her eyes pleaded.

"That is what it is like driving to the beach with you," I said dryly. "Nothing but a tease. Breaking all the rules. Always pushing your luck." I turned off the Sybian when I thought she was getting close.

She howled through the ball gag like I fucked her best friend.

I uncuffed her hands but left on the ball gag and the nipple clips.

"Get up."

She struggled to her knees.

"Come here." I pulled her by the nipple chain."

She crawled forward, breasts swaying, clamps jangling lightly with each movement. I took the chain between two fingers and gave it a light tug.

"Brat," I muttered, smirking.

I grabbed a thick dildo with a suction base and slammed it down onto the floor in front of her. One swift, practiced motion. It stuck upright perfectly.

I poured lube over it from a distance of three feet. It splashed across the shaft, ran in rivulets, and spattered across the floor. Some of it hit the mark. Most of it didn't. I didn't care. I had designed the room for this. The floor was built for mess. For clean-up. For scenes just like this.

I pointed to the spot directly in front of me.

"Kneel. Straddle that fucking cock."

She obeyed instantly; there was no hesitation now. The bratty gleam was still in her eyes, but her body moved with reverence.

I stripped. Pants off, tossed to the side without ceremony. I dropped into the recliner and spread my legs wide over the arms, scooting down until fully exposed. Open. Waiting.

"You see this?" I asked, tilting my hips forward.

"This is your reward. But only if you earn it."

She nodded, breathless.

"Ride that fucking cock. Slowly. Make it real. I want to watch you struggle."

It was big. She was soaked but still had to breathe through it; her hips adjusted to get the angle just right. I watched her open around it, inch by inch.

"Good girl. Now, stay just like that. You can eat my pussy while you ride it, but here's the deal. If I come before you do, you don't get to come. Not tonight. Not tomorrow. Not until I say."

She whimpered.

I reached down and unclipped the ball gag from her mouth.

"Do you understand?" I said, voice low and unmistakably serious.

She nodded, lips trembling. "Yes, Belle."

I tugged on the nipple clamps, just enough to make her flinch.

"Then impress me."

She lowered her head and began to lick. She licked like she needed to be forgiven, as her pleasure depended on the taste of mine. Her tongue teased and circled my vulva, slow and deliberate at first, then with mounting hunger as she adjusted to the stretch of the dildo inside her.

"That's it," I purred. "Earn every inch."

Her hips rocked down onto the toy while her mouth devoured me. She was riding like a pornstar, shameless and aching, while her tongue flicked and sucked at my clit. Every breath she took was ragged. Every moan vibrated into me.

I gripped the sides of the chair, trying to hold back.

"If you make me come too soon, I swear I'll leave you like this all weekend. Frustrated. Desperate."

She sucked harder as if daring me to follow through.

I shifted, trying to move my clit away from her mouth, but her tongue was relentless. She chased me. Licked deeper. She was heat-seeking and merciless, and I was crumbling fast.

My thighs started to tremble. I dropped my legs down and started rocking the chair to slam her down harder on the dildo. She gasped around me but didn't stop.

"You want to come?" I said through gritted teeth. "Then do it now. Before I do."

She let out a helpless, muffled cry, her fists pounding the floor beneath her as she slammed down hard, again and again. Her body shook uncontrollably. Her breath hitched. Her voice cracked like something breaking open inside her.

Her release still refused to come.

I didn't wait. I pushed her flat onto her back, reversed and pinned her down with my thighs straddling her face, and leaned forward until I could taste just how close she was. She was fully clamped to my clit now, just using her tongue and suction.

My mouth found her body swollen and soaked and trembling. I bit down, not gently. I sucked hard. I fucked her with the dildo in long, merciless strokes until the pressure inside her shattered, and the orgasm ripped through her like a tidal wave smashing into iron.

I came seconds after her, screaming on top of her as hers ended as if the echo of her pleasure had detonated mine.

When it was over, I tossed aside the dildo. We stayed tangled on the floor, breathless, twitching, and half-lost. I reached unquestioningly for the remote, turned off the movie, and pulled her close. She curled into me without a word, soft and exhausted, her limbs folding like she no longer trusted them to hold her up. I wrapped myself around her, one arm slung across her waist, firm and unrelenting. I wanted her to feel it. To know she was mine.

The silence wrapped around us like another layer of skin.

Neither of us said a word.

We didn't need to.

When we were at the beach house in Rehoboth, I stayed in my role from the moment we crossed the Bay Bridge until we returned. I didn't need to reset or renegotiate the terms. We had our rules, and I was responsible for enforcing them. Even when we went out to dinner, I ordered. I chose the wine. I selected the oysters, the roast chicken, or the duck, and she never questioned it.

Back in DC, things were more nuanced. She held the reins in public, at least on the surface. She was careful. She didn't want a client or colleague to catch wind of our dynamic. I respected that. In a town like DC, discretion isn't just a virtue—it's a necessity. And while our chemistry sizzled in private, I knew how to dim it in public, play it cool, and rein it in until we returned behind closed doors.

We were together for a year, and on paper, she was everything. She was intelligent, powerful, and wealthy, making the world feel as though it were at her beck and call. She could get us into any room, quiet any tension with a look, and somehow always knew exactly which whiskey I needed after a long day. She was generous and attentive. Every part of her life was curated, yet somehow, she always made space for me.

But I wanted something else. Something quieter. I wanted a family. I wanted a house with a yard, the smell of dinner from the kitchen, finger paint on the walls, and a calendar full of swim meets and school projects. I wanted something I had no words for, only a feeling I carried like a stone.

She mentioned leaving DC. She said she might not want kids. Other times, she said she might like them eventually, but always in a way that made me feel like the idea sat on a shelf she never planned to dust. She was brilliant, consumed by her work admirably, until I started imagining what our life would look like ten years later. I saw myself in the stands at school plays, texting her updates she never had time to read. I saw birthdays rescheduled and promises broken by breaking news alerts. I started to believe she might not just be a distracted parent. She might not be one at all.

Maybe she would have surprised me. Perhaps she would have fought for that life. But I could not bring myself to ask her to change. And I could not bring myself to give up the version of my future that I still believed in.

Still, I think of her. Not out of regret nor because I wish things had ended differently. I think of her because what we had was real and rare. Because she found her way into my bones even now, she still drifts into my dreams when I least expect it.

9

The Lobbyist

The Lobbyist was the head of a well-funded nonprofit focused on internet rights and data privacy, a serious player in the DC tech policy world. He was just a Pit Bull knock-off who was a masculine mouthpiece for some of the biggest internet companies out there. He was muscular, v-shaped, one of those men who did not look like he lived at the gym but still carried the body of someone who had once cared deeply about it. I think he had finally given up on the thinning patch at his crown and shaved it all down. There was something almost monastic about it. A smooth-talking salesman for the internet gold rush and the new American Industry. And yet, somehow, he made himself seem harmless.

Always in a black suit, white dress shirt, and tie, I don't think I ever saw him wear anything else. Expensive lace-up shoes polished to a high gloss shine. He carried one of those canvas messenger bags unironically, with the logo of a civil liberties conference on it. He had power, a lot more than he let on. He knew how to use it as well. Not in rooms with marble floors and press photographers, but in quiet, strategic ways. Schmoozing staffers. Buying rounds of drinks at the Dubliner or the Hawk and Dove until the aides were falling over themselves with gratitude.

He would show up at my office door like a lost intern in a rom-com with things. Silly things. Little things. A silk scarf from India. A balloon whisk from France. A box of spices from Italy, accompanied by

a note stating that he thought I would appreciate the aromatics. They were technically personal gifts, not bribes. Nothing over the ethics limit. But it was a slow drip of attention, of flattery, of being seen. That is how he worked.

I did not think much of it at first. He was a fixture on the Hill, like bad coffee, chlamydia, or endless committee markups. But then he started asking questions. Listening. Flirting. And one night, after I mentioned having trouble with my home computer, he offered to come over and help me install a new graphics card. The job would have taken him five minutes. We both knew that. But it wasn't about the hardware; he was looking to gain access to another kind of slot.

He came over to my place with a six-pack of local craft beer and a promise to help me install a new video card. We ended up on the couch. Talking. Laughing. And then, casually, he leaned in and kissed me. It wasn't a surprise.

"You're so beautiful," he said, his voice a little husky. "I just want to worship at your feet."

That was all I needed to hear. "Kneel," I said almost inaudibly.

He dropped to his knees without hesitation. I watched him settle there, hands resting on his thighs, waiting. Still and obedient. Exactly where I wanted him.

I stepped forward slowly, letting him take in every inch of me. My voice stayed low, smooth, and unhurried.

"Tell me," I murmured, "what exactly were you hoping to upgrade tonight?"

His eyes lifted, reverent and hungry. "Everything. My hardware. My performance. Belle. I want to be... your slave." He swallowed hard.

"You're going to beg for me to install a whole new operating system. But first..." I stepped back and began to slowly undo the buttons of my blouse, one at a time, "let's see how compatible you really are. I don't like cleaning up other people's junk."

His breath caught.

"I don't do plug-and-play," I said, letting the blouse fall to the floor. "You're going to have to earn root access."

He let out a strained little sound, nearly a whimper. His hands twitched in his lap, but he didn't move.

"Look at you," I said. "Overheating already. Is your cooling fan broken? Or is it just that your system can't handle me?"

"I'll handle anything you give me," he said, voice thick. "Test me."

"Oh, I intend to." I lay down on the couch, pulled up my skirt, and pointed to my vulva. "This is an input device. I expect your tongue to respond to every command. No lag. No buffering."

The Lobbyist dove in face-first, with the kind of enthusiasm usually reserved for 45-year-old divorcees on a first date back in the dating pool, eating a pussy that was finally not his wife's. I pushed his head gently to keep him in place, my voice like silk over steel. "Good boy."

He nodded without stopping, and I felt the tension growing in him—tight, urgent, vibrating like a processor under stress. He was dying to get off, and there was no fucking way that I was going to let him come tonight. If he could learn to obey me when he most wants me, then he might be helpful.

He flicked his tongue on my clit with force and delightful pressure, preferring to use the back side of his tongue and pushing down hard. I could come in seconds if I wanted to, but this was a training game, and I was not going to let him get the satisfaction of getting me off like a teenager in the backseat of a car.

He slipped a finger inside me and found my G-spot faster than any man ever had before or since. I walloped with waves of pleasure as he used a demonic version of Morse code to tap me over the edge into a serene, blissful orgasm while sucking on my clit hard. It was involuntary and delicious all at the same time.

"You're like my favorite line of clean code—elegant, responsive, and completely under my control. Just how I like you." I praised him as he looked up at me with a mixture of longing and adoration, which I could not tell apart.

I took a breath. I was on the sofa, and he was on his knees waiting for his next command. I told him to tell me everything he wanted.

His kinks came pouring out of him in a breathless rush, like he had been waiting for someone who would not flinch. Not only had he done all of this before. He wanted more. He wanted dungeons. He wanted to be spat on, kicked, denied. He wanted candle wax. He wanted to be tied up, penetrated, flogged, caned, and suspended. He wanted to be caged. He wanted to be a voyeur. He wanted to be in pain.

His requests were detailed. I told him we could have dinner first. He ordered takeout immediately. While we ate, he told me about his ex-mistress. How she had strung him up. How she had left scars. How he missed her. I didn't ask why they had ended things. He never really explained. But something in his voice made me wonder if he had scared even her.

He asked for stress positions. For pain. For needle play. For humiliation. He was hard the entire time he talked. Before dinner, he massaged my feet, keeping a steady gaze on them as if they were sacred objects. The food arrived. He fed me reverently.

After dinner, I pulled out my flogger. I made him kneel, naked, with his hands overhead. Soft leather restraints on his wrists. Not tied, but symbolic. And I started to whip him. Lightly at first. Then harder. Then harder still. Across his back. His ass. His thighs.

He grunted. Moaned. Pressed into the pain. I had never hit anyone that hard before. And he loved it. Maybe too much. He kept begging me to go harder. "Harder, please," he gasped. "Don't hold back. I need it."

I hovered just behind him, eyeing the vivid marks already starting to bloom across his back.

"You're sure? You have to confirm this. Every time."

"Yes, Belle," he said without hesitation. "Please. More."

His pain threshold bordered on unnatural, and the more he squirmed, the more he begged, the freer I felt. He bent over, presenting himself to me willingly, even offering up the most sensitive parts of himself.

"Even here?" I asked, tapping the flogger gently against his inner thigh.

"Yes. There. Especially there." So I did. Not too hard at first. A good, firm snap. And he writhed with pleasure. "Thank you, Belle," he moaned, shivering.

"You're welcome," I said coolly. "Come up here," I said. "Show me how good that mouth is."

And he did. Oh, he did. When I came, I screamed so loud I thought my nosy neighbor would call the cops to see if I was alright. Then I leaned back, breathless, sated, and said, "I'm done now. You can go."

He looked up at me, surprised but obedient.

"Yes, Belle."

He gathered his clothes and left, blue-balled and smiling.

Next week, he invited me out to a mysterious night on the town. He told me to put on a gown, something formal, something meant for a black-tie occasion. He said he was taking me to the Women in the Arts gala, a fancy fundraising event held in a beautiful museum that featured gallery installations, dance performances, and philanthropy, accompanied by cocktails. It sounded like something out of a movie.

I put on this mint-colored black tie gown. It hugged all the right places. And when he arrived in a tux, he looked radiant. Almost regal. He had polish and elegance. Presence. I did a double-take.

His nonprofit had sponsored something at the event, so we had premium access. He introduced me to people as if I were someone to be proud of, not just a date. He smiled when he looked at me, handed me champagne, and even held my purse when I went to the bathroom.

We danced all night. Waltzed. Spun. Laughed. And when he pulled me in and kissed me—just a soft kiss, not obscene, not hungry, my knees went a little weak.

For that moment, I thought: Maybe this could be something else.

After the gala, he took me to a piano bar in Georgetown that served old-world cocktails and French hors d'oeuvres. We sat close and sang along to Cole Porter around the piano. We were flushed, giddy, and electric.

Around two in the morning, he drove me home. At my door, he did not press. He just said, "I would like to see you again."

And I said, "Me too. All of you. The charming you. And the darker you."

That was when he invited me to dinner at his house. That was when it started to change. That was the night before I began to learn where my line was drawn.

I was curious to see what he would cook, only to find he had ordered in from a ridiculously upscale restaurant.

"Is this your idea of cooking?" I teased as he poured the wine.

"It is if it gets you to stay," he said with a crooked smile.

Dinner was easy. Flirtatious. He was funny, surprisingly insightful, and attentive to every movement I made. And the second the plates were cleared, he stood.

"Would you like to see the dungeon now, Belle?"

I raised an eyebrow. "Lead the way."

The room was a marvel. Not just well-stocked. Impeccably curated. It had everything: floggers, paddles, canes, cuffs, crosses, benches, racks. I strolled around it, inspecting. Testing.

"You've been busy," I murmured.

"Only ever used it with one other person before," he said from his knees. "But I've been waiting for someone like you."

I pulled a leather mask from a hook on the wall and tossed it at him.

"Put this on. Keep your eyes down."

"Yes, Belle."

He obeyed instantly.

I circled him like a hawk. "Where shall we begin?"

"Wherever you wish. "

I smiled.

"The cross. Now."

He scrambled up, practically jogging to the St. Andrew's cross and presenting himself without being tied. Hands on the rings. Legs apart. Perfect.

I tested a flogger against the arm of a chair. The knots at the end cracked through the air.

"Do you hear that?"

"Yes, Belle. Please. Hurt me."

"Shut up," I snapped, stepping closer. "I'll do what I damn well please."

He whimpered.

I swung. Once. Twice. Then harder. The knots landed with a satisfying thud, and his muscles clenched under the impact.

"Thank you, Belle," he breathed.

"Don't thank me yet. We're just getting started."

His moan was half agony, half prayer.

I stepped behind him with deliberate calm, the flogger trailing across the floor like a threat. His back was already warm to the touch, flushed with anticipation and restraint. I had only just begun.

His breath had quickened from the exquisite tension of waiting. The not-knowing was already breaking him open. I raised the flogger and struck again, this time across the tops of his thighs. He gasped, legs twitching from the sting, but he did not move his hands. His grip on the rings remained steady, knuckles white, spine rigid. He knew better than to let go.

I stood still behind him, watching the lines begin to bloom across his skin. I could feel the heat coming off him, the way his muscles strained to hold still. The silence stretched between us, thick and full of expectation.

"You look like a painting like this," I said, low and close. "Stripped down and stretched out. Full of need and no right to speak it."

He gave the slightest nod but kept his eyes fixed on the floor. He was trying not to beg. That alone made me smile.

I stepped in front of him, dragging the flogger slowly through my fingers. He didn't look up, didn't move an inch. His obedience tasted better than any apology. I watched his chest rise and fall as he tried to steady his breath.

"You want something?" I asked, voice sharp and clean.

He nodded again, slower this time, unsure if the motion itself was a risk. I let the moment hang before I spoke again.

"Then show me. Not with words. With your body."

His thighs tensed. His hips shifted just enough to betray him. It was subtle, but clear. He wanted to. He was offering it all.

I smiled again, slow and unkind. This was the part I liked.

"That's better," I said, stepping back behind him. "Now be still."

I raised the flogger and gave him a proper set of strokes, timed and steady, each one harder than the last. His body trembled under the rhythm, but he held his place. I pressed my palm flat to the center of his back and held him there.

"You will stay just like this until I say otherwise. Understood?"

"Yes, Belle," he said, quiet and rough with need.

"If you move, I will start again. From the beginning. Slower. More precise. And it will take twice as long to earn anything else."

He made a sound, something between a groan and a prayer, but he didn't dare speak. That was wise. I was not finished with him. Not even close.

I changed my grip on the flogger and let it fall from my hand. He flinched at the sound of it hitting the floor, then stilled again. Good. I didn't speak. I didn't have to. I stepped close enough for him to feel my presence without the relief of touch. Close enough to smell me, to know I was right behind him, but far enough to keep him desperate.

I trailed my nails down the back of his thigh. He shivered. When I reached the inside of his knee, I let my fingers graze up, slow and intentional. His whole body strained forward. I could see how hard he was, how much it took for him not to move.

Instead, I stepped back. I walked around him again. I circled like a storm with no end in sight. I let him feel the space between us as if it were punishment.

"You're beautiful like this," I said softly. "Open. Obedient. So ready to be used, you're shaking."

He whimpered at that, the sound soft but raw.

I took a leather strap from the drawer and walked behind him again. I didn't tie him. I didn't need to. He was already mine. I ran the strap along the inside of his thigh, then across the small of his back. I brushed it up under him and between his legs, close enough to threaten, never enough to touch where he needed.

"You think you've earned anything?" I asked.

"No, Belle," he said, voice thick and hoarse.

"You haven't."

He groaned. His hands curled tighter around the rings. His shoulders trembled.

"You're going to hold that pose while I sit down and watch you squirm. You're going to stay there until your body begs louder than your mouth ever could."

I walked to the armchair and sank into it slowly. I crossed one leg over the other and let my fingers rest on my knee. He stayed in place, gorgeous and shaking and ruined.

"You may look at me now."

He lifted his gaze, slow and reverent. His eyes met mine, wide and burning.

"That's what I want," I said. "I want it to ache."

He nodded once, jaw tight, lips parted. His cock throbbed between his thighs, untouched.

I licked the tip of my finger and held it in the air, just for show.

"Maybe I'll touch you when the sweat drips from your chest onto the floor. Maybe I won't."

He moaned, helpless, desperate, and so exquisitely mine.

I watched him hold that pose for a long moment more, savoring how tightly wound he was. His arms had started to tremble. Sweat traced down his back in a slow line. His cock hung heavy and pulsing between his legs, but he didn't dare move to ease the ache. He was waiting. And I wasn't finished.

I walked to the table. My heels echoed across the floor. I took my time choosing the plug. Smooth black silicone with a weight to it, just enough to make him feel full and claimed. I poured a generous stream of lube into my palm and coated it slowly, letting the slick sound carry through the silence.

He heard it. His breath hitched.

I stepped behind him and placed my free hand on the small of his back.

"Bend your knees. A little wider."

He obeyed instantly, adjusting his stance until I was satisfied. His position was open now. Absolutely perfect.

"You're going to hold still while I stretch you open," I said, calm and cool. "And you're going to thank me for it."

"Yes, Belle," he whispered.

I slipped one slick finger inside and watched him shudder. His whole body tensed, then relaxed as I moved slowly, deliberately, opening him just enough. I added a second finger. He moaned, deep and broken.

He breathed harder as I pressed the tip of the plug against him.

"This is mine now. You understand that?"

"Yes, Belle. Please. Please put it in."

I pushed, inch by inch, until the widest part passed and the base settled tight against his skin. He groaned, low and wrecked, his thighs quivering with the effort to stay still.

"You feel that? You're full now."

He nodded, voice gone, mouth parted in silent need.

I stepped back and admired the view. That plug nestled deep between his cheeks. His cock was hard and untouched. All of it. All for me.

"You will wear that while I take my time deciding whether you've earned anything more. And if you do too much without permission, I'll take it out. And start over."

He whimpered. I smiled.

I didn't give him time to adjust to the plug. That would have been kind. This wasn't about kindness.

"On the bed. Now."

He moved fast, still shaking, still hard, his legs uncertain with the plug inside him. He climbed onto the mattress, unsure whether to kneel or lie flat. I didn't correct him. I let him hover there in indecision, the tension making his body tight and obedient.

When I was ready, I pushed him back onto the pillows.

"On your back. Arms up. Legs open. Let me see everything I own."

He did as I asked without hesitation. I tied his wrists to the headboard, tight enough that the leather cuffs pulled slightly when he flexed. His ankles spread wide, binding them to the corners of the bed. He was laid out for me completely, stretched and vulnerable, his cock straining against the air, his hole stuffed and aching, his breath coming in soft, desperate gasps.

I retrieved the nipple clamps, silver with thin black rubber teeth. He saw them and whimpered, eyes wide.

"Don't flinch."

"Yes, Belle," he said, voice trembling.

I knelt over him, straddling his chest, letting the weight of my body press against his ribs. I took one nipple between my fingers, rolled it until it peaked, then clipped it. He gasped through clenched teeth. The second, I did more slowly, watching his eyes, reading his reactions.

His whole body shook as soon as they were on. I sat back on my heels and looked at him. I slid down his body, slow and cruel, letting my skin drag over his thighs, over the sharp edge of his need. I guided him inside me in one smooth motion, the stretch making me hiss through my teeth, the feel of him so hard and desperate beneath me I could almost hear him break.

His mouth fell open, a raw sound escaping, half-pleasure, half-shock. The clamps shifted with every breath. The plug stayed locked deep inside him. He couldn't move. Couldn't thrust. Couldn't beg.

I set the pace. My hips rolled down slowly, grinding against him until I felt the ache in my own thighs. I leaned forward, bracing my hands against the headboard above his wrists, forcing his body to take the full weight of mine.

"Look at me," I screamed at him.

His eyes locked on mine, filled with helpless adoration and the edge of madness. I slapped his face with force.

"You're mine like this. Full. Bound. Clamped. Helpless."

He nodded, frantic now, face flushed, teeth biting down on the inside of his cheek to hold himself together.

I started to ride him harder. Each downward motion forced the plug deeper inside, pushed the clamps to sway and twist just slightly, and made him cry out louder. I used him, grinding in tight circles, claiming every inch.

I hit him again across the face. Harder than I had hit anyone in my life.

He loved it. It terrified me.

I ground my hips against him in slow, cruel circles, letting him feel the drag, the pressure, the tease. I kept it that way for a few moments longer than he could handle. His chest strained. His thighs trembled from the effort not to move. The plug inside him forced his body to stay open for me. The clamps on his nipples tugged with every breath.

Then I shifted my knees. Planted my feet. And slammed down onto his cock so hard the headboard shook.

He cried out, loud and raw, his entire body jerking. His cock hit the deepest point inside me, thick and pulsing and desperate. I didn't wait. I rose again and slammed down even harder. Over and over. Each thrust was more punishing than the last. Each slap of skin against skin.

His mouth dropped open. His eyes rolled back.

He was already close. I could feel it in the way his breath stuttered. The way his cock twitched deep inside me. The way his body tried to thrust up into mine, but couldn't.

I leaned forward and wrapped my hand around one of the clamps. I twisted it just enough to send a jolt through his chest as I slammed down again, riding him like he was built for nothing else. Just a body. Just a cock. Just something for me to take.

"You don't come," I said through clenched teeth. "Not until I tell you."

"Please, Belle," he choked out. "Slap me again."

I reached back and tugged on the plug. Just a little. Just enough to make his eyes fly wide and his whole body buck. Then I dropped my hips and took him deep again, harder than before, my thighs slapping against his skin, the sound echoing through the room.

He was wrecked. His chest was red and trembling under the clamps. His arms stretched taut above him, muscles burning with effort.

I didn't stop.

I used him, slammed down again and again, faster now, chasing the sharp edge of my own climax, grinding against him with each thrust. His cock filled me, thick and perfect, hitting exactly where I needed. I rode him like I meant to break him. Because I did.

"Say it," I hissed. "Tell me whose cock this is."

"Yours, Belle," he gasped. "It's yours. All of it. I'm yours."

"Damn right," I growled, and slammed down again, full force, so deep we both cried out.

I could feel the orgasm coiling in my canal, tight and merciless. My body clamped down around him, harder, hotter, faster. I grabbed both clamps at once, twisted just enough to make him scream, and ground myself down over him with everything I had.

I rode him like a beast. And I used that chain like a set of reins as I rode that bucking bastard to orgasm.

I leaned back in the saddle of his hips and reached for the chain that connected his nipples. I gave it a slow, testing tug. He arched beneath me with a strangled cry, muscles straining. His chest lifted off the bed in reflex, which only made the tension worse. The clamps pulled tighter. The chain bit into him. The pain twisted into something he could barely hold.

"Stay down," I said, and yanked the chain harder.

He obeyed instantly, collapsing against the mattress with a breathless moan. His cock throbbed inside me, so full, so thick, twitching like it might explode. I clenched down around him and ground my hips with deliberate cruelty, letting the slow motion twist the plug into him with every roll. I could feel him trying not to move. Try not to come. Try not to beg. But I could feel how close he was, every inch of his body soaked in need.

Then I rose up and slammed down on him hard enough to jolt the bed frame.

The clamps tore at his nipples as the chain snapped taut. My thighs slapped against his with a vicious rhythm. He screamed, not from fear, but from the unbearable perfection of it.

I grabbed it with one hand and pulled back as I slammed down onto him again, using the tension to torque his body into mine. I bounced harder. I ground lower. I let my full weight crash down on his cock, every thrust landing with punishing pressure. Each time I dropped my hips, his balls took the force. I watched him try to endure it, try to take it, try to give me everything without breaking.

I pulled the chain again, harder this time, yanking his chest up just enough that the clamps bit deep. He sobbed beneath me, his cock pulsing inside me like it might split me open.

"You feel that?" I growled. "You feel me using you?"

"Yes, Belle," he gasped, voice wrecked. "I feel everything. Please. I can't—"

"You'll take it," I hissed, and brought my hips down so hard it knocked the breath out of him. The plug forced pressure inside him. The clamps twisted. His balls crushed under the weight of it all. And still I didn't stop.

His whole body was shaking now. Eyes wild. Mouth slack. His cock fully buried inside me, stretched to the edge, his orgasm held at bay by force of will alone.

And still I kept riding.

Still, I pulled that chain with every thrust, slamming down over and over until my thighs burned and my climax was clawing up my spine again.

I jumped off him without a word.

His cock slapped up against his stomach, thick and glistening, twitching like it was trying to find me again. The sight of it—so hard, so needy, so completely denied—made me smile. He had no idea what to do without my heat wrapped around him.

I climbed up his body and straddled his face, planting my knees on either side of his head, my wetness just above his mouth. I didn't lower myself right away. I let him smell me. Let him stare up at the soaked cunt he wasn't allowed to touch with anything but his tongue.

"Open."

His mouth parted before I finished the word.

I sat down slowly, smothering him. His lips sealed to me like he had been drowning and I was the only breath left in the world. He devoured me with wild hunger, like it wasn't about pleasure anymore, just survival. He moaned into me, desperate and frantic, his whole body shaking as his tongue moved frantically, flicking and sucking, reaching for every drop I gave him.

I grabbed his waist and ground myself down hard against his mouth.

"That's right," I said through clenched teeth. "You'll breathe through your nose if I let you. But not yet."

His tongue worked harder, deeper, tracing my folds with reverence and panic. His nose pressed against me as he gasped for breath. I didn't move. I held him down and let him drown in it.

His cock throbbed helplessly below, untouched and furious, the plug still deep, the clamps still tugging at his nipples. He had no release. No relief. Only my thighs were holding his head in place, and my vulva was smearing across his mouth like it belonged there. Because it did.

He licked me like a man who knew there was no god, only the heat between my legs. Like every flick of his tongue was a prayer. Like I was salvation. And I gave him nothing. Just my weight. Just my taste. Just the slow, rolling rhythm of my body using his mouth until my moans overtook his. Until I grabbed his hips and rocked forward and gave him what he had earned.

I came on his face, grinding hard against his tongue, riding it through until my thighs shook. He didn't stop. Not even when I was done. Not even when I pulled on the chain again. Not even when his cock jerked between his legs, trying to come on its own, desperate and denied.

Because he knew. If he came without permission, I'd leave him just like that. And he would never survive it.

He didn't stop licking even after I came. His tongue was relentless, moving in tight, reverent circles, dragging every last pulse of my orgasm from me like it was his only purpose. He moaned into me, like the taste of me gave him life, like my body was the only thing anchoring him to the earth. I stayed on his face for a moment longer, letting him drown in it, letting him hum with satisfaction like he'd done something holy.

I climbed off him slowly, my inner thighs soaked, his chin glistening. His eyes were glazed over, but his cock was still standing straight up, furious and neglected, twitching against his stomach.

I wasn't finished with him.

I crawled down over his body, slow and deliberate, and bent forward. My tits brushed his cock, warm and slick and aching. He gasped. The contact alone nearly made him lose it. I dragged my nipples up the length of him, let them skim the head, let him feel the softness of my skin slide over the most challenging part of him. I wrapped my breasts around his shaft, cupping them tight, and stroked his cock with the weight of them, up and down, teasing, sliding, squeezing.

He sobbed underneath me, hips twitching uselessly.

"I'm sorry, Belle," he begged. "Please. Please, I can't—"

And then he did.

His cock exploded between my tits, thick ropes painting my chest as his body convulsed, straining, the plug buried inside him pulsing with every wave of release. He cried out like it broke him, the orgasm too big to hold, too intense to survive.

I didn't let him off easy. I grabbed his chin and leaned in close.

"You made a mess," I said, my voice low and cruel.

He nodded, still panting, eyes wide with guilt and awe.

"Clean it."

I flipped around and let him see the mess he'd spilled all over my breasts. His eyes locked on it like it was a punishment and a blessing all at once. I pushed one tit to his mouth, and he opened immediately, licking up his own cum from my skin. His tongue moved slowly and reverently, scooping it up like it was sacred. I made him chase every drop, cleaning my cleavage, the underside, the tip of my nipple, sucking softly like he wanted to worship it.

I pulled his face to the other side and made him finish the job.

"You come without permission again," I said, tugging on the nipple chain one last time, "and next time I won't be this generous." He moaned against my breast, still licking, aching even in the aftermath. I sat back on my heels, watching him breathe.

His chest rose in uneven, trembling waves. His mouth was still wet from cleaning me. His cheeks were flushed, tear-streaked, raw. His cock was soft now, spent and aching, but his eyes never left me. Not once.

I let the silence stretch until it thickened around us. His thighs still spread. The plug still locked deep inside him. The clamps are still biting. He hadn't said a word. He didn't dare.

I leaned in, slow and quiet, and ran a single fingertip down the center of his chest. "You really don't have any boundaries." It wasn't a question. It was a fact.

He swallowed hard. His voice was almost too soft to hear. "Not with you."

I smiled. That slow, cruel smile I knew twisted something in him. His whole body shivered beneath me.

"Of course you don't."

He nodded, eyes wide, jaw slack. He looked at me like I was the sun and he was some desperate, broken thing crawling out of a cave to burn.

"You'd do anything I said."

"Yes, Belle."

"Anything."

"Yes," he breathed. "Please."

I cupped his face in one hand, firm and deliberate. My thumb pressed down on his lower lip, holding his mouth open. He didn't flinch. He didn't blink.

"Would you let me hurt you more?"

"Yes, Belle."

"Would you let me break you in front of someone else?"

His breath caught. He paused for only a moment, then gave a slight, obedient nod. "If it pleased you."

I stared into him, deep and still, and the weight of it landed in my chest with a dull finality. "I can do anything I want to you. Anything." It wasn't a question. It wasn't even a threat. It was the truth. And it didn't thrill me.

He wanted a professional sadist, someone to shape pain into ritual and reward. And maybe there was a version of me who could have worn that role like armor. But in that moment, it felt like a corset that didn't quite fit—tight in all the wrong places, stiff where I should have felt powerful. It didn't make me feel any better. It made me feel less.

His eyes fluttered closed, a moan spilling out of him like gratitude, like surrender. "Yes, Belle. Please. I'm yours."

I leaned in close, my breath brushing his ear. I didn't answer him. I didn't praise him. His limbs were trembling, his eyes glassy, his chest slick with sweat and shame. I didn't speak. I just eased off the clamps and pulled the plug from his body with the same calm precision I had used putting it in. He flinched.

When it was done, he curled up on the bed and started to cry. The kind of quiet, broken sound that comes when a man realizes the high is over and the truth is settling in. I climbed into bed beside him and pulled his head onto my chest. He shook in my arms. From the raw, aching knowledge that he had given everything, and it still wasn't enough.

He sobbed, mouthing something against my skin, something like *I'm sorry,* something like *thank you,* something like *please.* I didn't stop him. I held him, stroked his hair, let the shame bleed out of him.

But even as I sat beside him, holding him through the sobs he couldn't control, I knew I had already begun to leave. Not physically, not yet. But something inside me had stepped away from the scene. I could feel the distance growing, quiet and confident, stretching between us in a way that couldn't be undone. Somewhere between the snap of the clamps and the tug of the chain in my hand, I had felt it—the shift, the hollow, the subtle collapse of connection that happens when the act is flawless but the meaning goes missing.

I had given him everything he wanted. I had taken him apart, owned him, used him, broken him with precision. But through all of it, he hadn't seen me. Not really. Not the ache behind my control or the hunger beneath my calm. He had been so consumed by his own need that he missed mine entirely.

He hadn't felt the pulse of my kink. He hadn't caught the low hunger behind my orders or the sharp ache I carried between my thighs that had nothing to do with getting off, and everything I wanted that night had nothing to do with pain or performance. It wasn't about being worshipped or obeyed. I didn't need someone kneeling at my feet for the ritual of it. What I craved was connection. To be met. Matched. Moved. I wanted someone who would respond not just to the sound of my voice, but to the ache behind it. Someone who could feel the rhythm of my control, and meet it with his own kind of surrender—one that pulsed with understanding, not just desperation.

But he hadn't been that. He wanted to be used. Fully, completely, ruthlessly. And I had done it. I had used him until the room was thick with sweat and tension. I had made him cry out. I had dragged his orgasm from him like a confession, then made him lick it from my skin. I had pushed him exactly where he wanted to go.

And yet, somehow, I felt untouched.

When he quieted, I pressed my lips to his temple and stood. I didn't rush. I dressed without ceremony, slipping each piece of clothing into place while he lay curled on the bed, still naked, still aching, still spent. I didn't ask if he was all right. I didn't promise to call. There would be no second round, no soft words to smooth the edges, no attempt to coax something from the scene that had never been there in the first place. I wasn't angry. I wasn't disappointed. And I wasn't cruel. I had reached the end of what I had to give him. And what he had to offer me had never reached past his own desire.

By the time I walked out, my hands were steady. My breath was calm. I had used him. And he loved every second of it. But I needed more than a man who would do anything. I needed one who could feel everything.

Bondage brings out a lot of trauma for people, and it allows them to explore feelings they have not yet understood or to process past wounds in a new, tactile language. Pain can release people, freeing them to let something out that has been trapped. And although I was not entirely sure I could take that journey with him, I also knew he was going to take it, with or without me. Maybe with someone else.

I am not that person. I can walk to the edge. I can dangle a toe over. But I will always pull myself back.

We did not end with a fight. There was no big, dramatic break. Just silence. Space. I ghosted, to be honest. I am not proud of that. But I did not have the words to explain that it was not about disliking him. It was about protecting me.

Some people need darkness to appreciate the light.

I am not one of them.

And every so often, when I hear about him through the grapevine, I wonder if he found someone who could give him what he needed. I hope so. But it was never going to be me.

For all my confidence, all my dominance, I am still tender. Still soft in places that bruise too easily, and this would have left marks I was not willing to carry.

10

Diplomatic Relations

Ever have one of those romances that are improbable from the start but somehow seem destined? This is *not* a love story—but damn, I wish it were.

We'll call her Diplomatic Relations, the Ambassador's girl Friday. I won't tell you what country. I won't tell you anything. Except that she was beautiful. The kind beauty that made you forget your name.

She had long, blonde hair that cascaded to her ass, curling at the ends like she had a personal hairdresser who followed her around with rollers. Lashes so long they looked artificial, but weren't. Minimal makeup, very farm-girl aesthetic. And lips—dear God, those pouty pink lips. She could say anything, do anything, and I would've followed her around like a dazed tourist at Versailles.

I could've sat with her in a park watching plants grow, and I'd have been thrilled. She was that mesmerizing.

When I first met her, it was at a party for a social group we both belonged to. She was there with her girlfriend. Who, I'm just gonna say it, was... Debbie Frumpy. I couldn't imagine how they were together. Not for a second. But there they were, sipping wine like any other established couple.

I caught something out of the corner of my eye—some glint of curiosity, a flicker of a spark—and I spent the rest of the evening circling her like a hopeful retriever. Just hoping I was right.

Not that I was going to do anything. I don't poach. I don't play homewrecker. I wasn't interested in her girlfriend, nor the drama. We could be friends, I told myself.

She was *sparkling*. Champagne in hand, laughter like wind chimes. She kept my glass full. And her attention? Laser-focused.

"You know," she purred, handing me a fresh flute, "I'm not usually this charming."

"Oh? So I'm special?"

"Maybe." A tilt of her head. A flash of teeth. "Maybe you're just lucky."

She wore a tight-fitting business suit that a goddamn magician must've tailored. I would've drained my entire bank account to see her in another one—any one she wanted. And those legs. Long and toned. She wasn't tall, but her legs said otherwise. Maybe she ran. Maybe she did yoga. Perhaps she was a goddess who moonlit in diplomacy. Didn't matter.

By the end of the night, I was sure. She was into me. The vibe was unmistakable.

She didn't say anything about her girlfriend. And I didn't ask. I just fantasized: maybe they were breaking up. Perhaps they'd broken up already. Maybe she'd go home, dump her, and call me for coffee the next morning.

She didn't. But she *did* start sending me little notes through LinkedIn, through Facebook.

"How are you?"

"What are you up to?"

"Still lighting up every room you walk into?"

Fishing. I was checking to see if I was single. Maybe checking to see if the rumors were true—that I'd become something of a... *collectible* in D.C.'s queer scene. The kind of person who has a lot of girlfriends, boyfriends, and their friends. The type of person who isn't always looking, but always seems to be recruiting.

Eventually, I heard it through the grapevine: she'd dumped Debbie Frump.

And the next time I saw her?

Costume party. Full masquerade madness. I showed up in a proper ball gown—black satin, strapless, sculpted to my curves, dressed like the John Singer Sargent painting. Lots of cleavage, because obviously.

What did Diplomatic Relations wear? She was in street clothes with a clown nose. Did she see that movie, *30 Days Notice?*

"A clown nose? Does this mean you are quitting?" I said, lifting an eyebrow. She looked at me as if she had no idea what I was talking about. Oh dear, I am feeling old right now. Did I mention she was way younger than me?

"Not just clowning around," she replied with a wink, sloshing her drink.

She was with five gay boys who were acting as her entourage-slash-security detail, like a Greek chorus for her libido. She was *sloshed*—beautifully, happily drunk.

And then—without warning—just grabbed me and *kissed* me. Full-on, tongue-involved, take-your-breath-away Hollywood kiss. Two minutes, minimum.

When she finally let me go, I blinked. "Hello to you, too."

She grinned. "Come with me."

"Where?"

"Next bar. These boys are taking me dancing."

I looked at the group. The chorus nodded. "We've got Uber," one said.

"My car's staying here," I said. "Let's go."

She looped her arm through mine like we were already a couple and pulled me out the door.

We ended up in a dark, dingy bar—the kind where strange things happen in stranger corners. And, that's precisely what happened next...

It was a black leather bar, and everything you can imagine was happening—blowjobs on the patio, sex in the corners, anything goes. We were the only two women there, and yeah, it was a fun night. The boys managed to wade into the crowd ten-deep at the bar, surely getting lost and fondled—or fumbled—along the way, depending.

But I had her pinned in the corner, her back to the wall, and her arms held above her head. I kissed her hard, tracing my fingers over the edge of her jaw, her breath hot and ragged against my neck. She kept pulling back like she wanted to escape, but I could feel it—that wasn't fear or resistance. It was a brat's pushback. And I welcomed it.

"You want to get away, sweetheart?" I teased.

She grinned. "Not really. But maybe you'll punish me for trying."

My mouth was at her ear. "Careful what you wish for."

Then she grabbed me back, pulled me in close. "I want to be fucked. Hard."

"Is that so?" I asked, arching a brow.

"Right now. Wherever. I don't care."

We were in a leather bar—where else could we go? She darted into one of the back rooms, tugging me by the hand. There were padded walls, handrails, and a playroom. She pulled up her skirt, leaned over, and said, "Whip me."

I blinked. "You sure? You're a little drunk."

She looked over her shoulder. "Then make it for show. But make it hot."

One of the guys in the room, clearly interested, handed me a suede whip—soft leather, pliable, the kind that whispers across the skin. I tested it on my thigh, gave it a spin in the air, and made sure there was no surprise bite.

"What's your safe word?" I asked.

She smirked. "Red. But if I need to, I'll turn around. You'll stop, right?"

"I'll stop," I said. "Now hold on to those rails. Don't let go unless you need out."

She grabbed the loops, bracing herself. I stepped back, measured the distance, then let the whip trail over her skin—just a tease, a whisper.

"Mmm," she hummed, arching her back.

I started a slow rhythm, figure-eight patterns, one side, then the other. Whisper-soft strikes. Not pain—sensation. I felt it myself, like music, rhythmic and indulgent.

I paused and walked up behind her, tangling a hand in her hair. "Tell me. Do you want more?"

"Yes," she gasped. "Yes, I want more. Please."

"Harder or more of the same?"

"More. Just like that. Don't stop."

I borrowed a second whip from another amused onlooker. The crowd was forming now. We were putting on a show, whether we meant to or not.

With one whip in each hand, I swung them in mirrored figure-eights. Crack, snap, kiss—each one just brushing her skin, leather-like butterfly wings. The art was in the restraint.

You learn the tools—rubber snaps, suede whispers, braided leather can leave a mark, studs bite. You choose what you want to say with what's in your hand.

But this wasn't about pain. This was about the theater, the slow burn, the thrill of being seen. And she? She was made for it. Bent over, glowing, eyes closed, breathing hard. She was the picture of submission—grateful, aching, powerful even in surrender.

And I was in my happy place, center stage, in full command.

I think she was just in a playful, exhibitionist mode. I seem to attract a lot of those women who like to have sex in public places, more so than men. I'm not sure why that is, but it's a trend I've noticed. Anyway, I grabbed her hair, braided it loosely, tossed it over her shoulder, pulled up her shirt, and unhooked her bra. She wasn't completely naked—clothes were pushed aside, pulled up, bunched around her —but it was enough.

"I'm going to use both of them on you," I said, holding up two floggers.

"Yes, please," she breathed.

"Call me Mistress. Because right now, that's exactly what I am."

I took one flogger on the left, one on the right, and began circling them in tandem: one, two, three—up and down, a rhythmic motion from just above her knees to the line of her bra strap. The soft falls swept over her skin, crisscrossing in unpredictable patterns. She gasped—the motion built slowly, sensually, teasing.

One of her male friends poked his head in and grinned. "Everything going well in here?"

I glanced up. "Yeah, I've got this. No worries. She'll get home safely to someone's bed tonight."

He laughed, "Perfect."

After about fifteen minutes of teasing and whipping, I took her down. She was flushed, breathless, vibrating with arousal. We wandered out onto the patio, where all the bear boys and leather daddies were busy fucking their twinks—cigarettes dangling, drinks in hand. I shoved her against a wall, spread her legs, and went down on her until she came loud enough to silence a few nearby moans.

Heads turned.

"Dudes," I nodded to beefy men in black leather on their knees.

She was practically limp, but beaming. We left not long after.

I didn't even know where she was living anymore. Had she moved out? Was she crashing somewhere? Didn't matter. We ended up at my place, dragging ourselves in at maybe 3 a.m., totally spent but still hungry for each other.

She, but grinned. "Fuck me one more time before we sleep?"

"Of course," I said. "Pick your weapon."

She rifled through the drawer like it was a candy shop. "This one," she said, holding up a pornstar-molded dildo with a look of wicked glee.

"Aggressive," I noted.

"Good. I want it hard."

"Then sit on my face for a bit to warm up."

She didn't need to be asked twice. After a couple of minutes, I pulled her down and helped her slide onto the dildo. She gasped, stunned by how good it felt.

"You feel so full, don't you?"

"It's hitting—oh my God—it's hitting my spot."

I began thrusting, slow at first, then matching her rhythm—her moving back, me driving up. At the crest of the motion, I was sure the curve was hitting her G-spot dead-on.

She was keening, her breath catching, her body writhing.

"Don't come yet," I warned.

"Please, Belle, I need to—"

I slapped her clit lightly, then rubbed in a tight circle.

She shattered.

She collapsed backward onto me, utterly spent. I caught her, rolled her off me gently, and she curled into a ball on the bed.

Still half-dressed in my gear, I kicked everything under the bed with a laugh. "We'll deal with that tomorrow."

She was already snoring.

I curled up behind her, pulling a blanket over both of us. She smelled like lavender, sex, and shampoo.

One weekend, we splurged on a stay at the Jefferson Hotel—our little fantasy escape from the rest of the world. The suite had velvet curtains, dark wood paneling, and a king-size bed that looked like it had been designed for royalty or debauchery, or both. As soon as the bellhop left, she kicked off her heels, opened a bottle of champagne, and padded around in a hotel robe like a cat stretching after a long nap.

"No plans," she announced. "No phones. Just us."

"Is that a command or a suggestion?" I teased.

She raised an eyebrow. "It's a promise."

We didn't even make it out of the living room. She pulled me down onto the plush chaise lounge, kissed me until I was breathless, then stood up and slowly untied her robe.

"Your turn to serve," she said with a wicked grin.

"Always happy to please," I replied, already on my knees.

Later, wrapped in hotel sheets that smelled faintly of lavender, we ordered an embarrassing amount of room service. Eggs Benedict. Crab cakes. Truffle fries. A bottle of white. Chocolate mousse. She fed me bites of everything between kisses.

"We're going to have to roll out of here," I joked.

"That's fine," she said, licking chocolate from my finger. "I'll roll you anywhere you want."

That night, I tied her wrists with a silk hotel bathrobe sash, blindfolded her with a spare scarf, and made her count every orgasm in a whisper.

"One... please... two... oh my God, three..."

By morning, the room was trashed, we were glowing, and neither of us wanted to go back to real life.

"Let's just live here," she said, curled up on my chest.

"Forever?"

"At least through brunch."

So we stayed one more night.

And I think about that weekend often—how easy it was to pretend that we could make the whole world pause for 48 hours. How delicious it felt to do nothing but touch, talk, laugh, and taste.

Even now, if I close my eyes, I can still smell the linen, feel the velvet, hear her giggle between sips of wine.

Some memories are there forever.

We stayed together for three months. Then she got called back to her home country.

But God, those three months? Unbelievable.

She was the whole package—brains, beauty, danger. She could debate in six languages and seduce you in silence. Sunday mornings were newspapers in four languages and kisses over coffee. She flirted at dinner parties with a hand on my thigh under the table. She dared me to be wild.

No one else has ever made me feel like I was living in a spotlight. Just for a little while, I got to stand in it with her.

11

Judicial Review

The Shakespeare Theatre Company's Opening Night was when D.C.'s social aristocracy emerged in full force. Lawyers, lobbyists, judges, ambassadors, and donors filled the room, all perfectly dressed and expertly lit, as if they had been cast in a high-budget drama about power and were determined to steal the scene. I had been to enough of these to know the game. This was where you came if you wanted to meet someone who could change your life. It was where money met culture, and neither left disappointed.

My entrance pass for the evening came courtesy of a long-standing friendship with a local theater critic. He was the kind of old-school reviewer whose pen still had bite and whose loyalty to the company had hardened into something close to sacred. He always got the best seats. In D.C., relationships are the only real currency. Invest wisely; the dividends pay out in velvet seats and perfect sightlines.

One of those dividends sat just ahead of me. We will call her *Judicial Review* because saying her real name felt too intimate, too reverent, too much like invoking a ruling I was not a party to, yet.

She stood facing me, laughing softly, surrounded by other board members and high-tier donors, every detail of her posture refined and precise. I could tell she was old money from how she leaned very little to how her body moved when she laughed, as if even amusement was something to be rationed. Tall, lean, with hair that strongly hinted at a former youthful blonde but threaded with silver and red, she looked

like she had stepped out of a courtroom drama where every word was scripted and every verdict carried weight.

She wore a seven-hundred-dollar knitwear skirt suit that carried the quiet confidence of being the only expensive thing she bothered to put on. It was not trendy. It was timeless. Clean lines and minimal detail worn in places just enough to prove they had been chosen carefully. Rich women do not buy for attention; they buy for longevity. She looked like she could slap me with a lawsuit and vigorously defend me.

I recognized the designer instantly. The suit was soft charcoal knitwear, molded to her like it had been commissioned rather than purchased. The brand was a whisper among women who did not need to ask the price. Their showroom was hidden behind a florist in Georgetown, with no signage, posted hours, or tolerance for hesitation. I had been inside once and left with only regrets that I didn't study harder.

Her hair was pulled back in a low bun, exposing the nape of her neck. Her skin caught the house lights like a cue. She looked like a woman who had once been beautiful, had since become formidable, and now moved through the world with the composure of someone who no longer needed permission to exist.

Women of substance are my deepest temptation. They are the kind who hold court in conference rooms and kitchens alike, command respect without asking, and navigate every demand of the day with elegance and fire. They are so used to leading, solving, and being everything for everyone that when they finally step out of the light and into something darker, something quieter, something that asks nothing of them but surrender, they do not hesitate; they melt.

There is a particular pleasure in watching one of them come undone, in guiding her out of her thoughts and into her feelings, in coaxing her from control into craving. I do not take that lightly. I savor it. I wait for that shift, the exact moment when her shoulders drop and her breath catches, her gaze turns from sharp focus to soft pleading, and she stops thinking and starts needing.

I can already see her there, down on her knees, not as an act of humiliation but as an offering of trust, her lips parted not from fear but from the exquisite anticipation of being touched, tasted, claimed. Those lips that once issued orders and cut through silence like a blade, now trembling with hunger and devotion, whispering my name with every exhale. Not because she has lost herself but because she has chosen, for just a little while, to give herself over.

Dangling from her forearm was a purse I knew on sight. Black leather, clean and severe, with a triangular strap that rested perfectly mid-forearm like it had been engineered for balance. I can confirm that the purse strap was long enough to cuff both wrists together for playtime. It hovered, elegant and exact. Designed to be carried without being clutched, it was less an accessory and more a declaration. A friend of mine had made it, a Bethesda socialite with a following so discreet it bordered on myth. There were no logos. No hardware. No embellishment. Just shape, silence, and the certainty that if you knew, you knew.

She shifted slightly. Laughed once, low and brief. Even her pleasure had restraint.

I had high hopes that she would encourage me to review her case until we both won. But just as I prepared my opening argument, someone else made theirs.

The interloper was young. Maybe twenty-five. Blonde. Fresh-faced. Polished within an inch of her life. The kind of young woman who believed her ambition made her irresistible and who had not yet discovered how little D.C. cares about your confidence when you have no power. She leaned close to Judicial Review as if she were placing an order she had expected to be filled.

"Professor," she said, sounding sweet enough to rot teeth.

Judicial Review turned her head. Simply observing.

"I was not sure you would remember me," the girl said with a tight smile and wide eyes.

"I do," came the answer, landing like a thud. "Although I imagined you at something with a step & repeat, and an open bar."

The girl laughed too loudly, too quickly. The volume of someone hoping to be overheard.

"I just moved back to D.C., working in reproductive justice. But I never forgot your seminar. Or your suits."

Her eyes lingered, tracing the line of Judicial Review's jacket, the slope of her throat, the sharp edge of her collarbone. It was not subtle. It was the kind of look that tried to pass off desperation as daring.

Judicial Review touched the purse dangling from her forearm with two fingers. Her gaze never wavered.

"You always had potential," she said. "But you were careless with boundaries."

The girl froze, just for a moment. But it was enough.

Judicial turned back to the stage as if the conversation had never happened. Then, she turned her head in a way that made me think she was part owl.

"Enjoy the show," she said. "And next time, try someone not trained to cross-examine motive."

The girl hovered, stung but still hoping to salvage something. There was nothing left to salvage. Judicial Review had closed the door and turned her head back to her more interesting companions.

The interloper turned and walked away, her heels sharp against the floor, like an exit line with no applause.

Judicial Review never glanced back. But I did. Because what I had just seen was not flirtation. It was a masterclass in how to destroy someone without breaking a sweat. And I wanted to be next, just for the privilege of being dismissed with that much grace.

She slipped out of the jacket, slung it indifferently over the back of her seat, and sat down. The lightweight fabric slunk over and dropped to the floor at my feet. Today was my lucky day.

I bent over and picked it up, shaking it out casually. The label confirmed what I already suspected.

"I have something you'll want," I murmured into her ear in my best dom voice, slightly raspy and throaty. I leaned over the back of her chair and draped it over her shoulders, grazing her skin with my fingertips.

She startled and turned to face me, her eyes wide and blue, intelligent. She took me in all at once, my suit, stance, and smirk. She could tell what I was, and I saw through her carefully constructed social artifice. She blinked and then, softly, lowered her eyes.

I flashed my hazel eyes at her, holding her gaze with a smolder. I decided to be bold. I moved closer to her ear and whispered, "If there is any other clothing you want to drop in front of me, please go ahead," hoping no one would hear. I wanted to go out in a blaze of glory if I were to crash and burn. She squirmed in her seat and flashed me a smoulder.

The lights dimmed, and the show was about to begin. I leaned back in my seat, watching her watch the stage. But every few minutes, she turned slightly, just enough to catch me in her peripheral vision.

My fantasy built itself.

I imagined her on that stage. Not as a lawyer or a professor. But bare, bound in red shibari ropes, suspended in midair. A Lady Justice unblindfolded and utterly exposed. Her back arched, her mouth open in a silent plea as my flogger traced arcs across her thighs.

She was regal, yes, but she was also begging. In my mind, her body trembled not from fear but from the anticipation of being seen, displayed, and desired.

I could almost hear her breath hitch. Her voice caught. Her whisper.

"Sustained." Not from a courtroom. From a longing stage.

And then, the lights snapped back on. Intermission.

We both flinched slightly, jolted out of our reverie. She lingered in her seat as her friends shuffled toward the lobby.

I stood. Moved behind her. Bent in close.

"Did you enjoy the performance?" I asked, my voice low.

She turned. Our eyes met. She stood slowly. Her gaze was level.

"I didn't really pay attention," she said. "My mind was occupied with other thoughts." She flicked an imaginary piece of dust off my jacket.

"Let's find a drink and talk about it," I said, already taking her hand.

She followed me. We made our way to the bar, jostled by the crowd. We stood shoulder to shoulder. Breath to breath.

I ordered for both of us. Two fingers of whisky. Neat.

No question. She didn't flinch.

I handed her the glass, holding it just at the level of her chest, letting the back of my knuckle brush lightly against her breast. She moved forward slightly. The contact was fleeting, not accidental.

I took a long inhale from my glass. Savored it.

"I love the scent," I said, looking dead in her eyes as I leaned in, catching a trace of her perfume at the neck. "Intoxicating."

We drank while watching each other. Then I ran my fingertip slowly around the rim of the glass. The tension between us is taut and humming.

She was mesmerized.

"What's your name?" she asked finally.

I gave her a name. One of mine.

She gave me hers.

She may have been a tremendous legal mind who wrote amicus briefs and shaped constitutional interpretation, but I would habeas her corpus in my night court.

"This is Chekov's play. The gun's been sitting there since Act I—we all know where it's heading." I whispered in her ear over the din of the crowd. "Leave here with me now; I can promise a different, more intense kind of climax."

The lights were flashing, showing the end of the intermission. Time was growing short.

"How long has it been since someone focused just on you?" I offered.

All objections overruled.

We jumped in my car and headed to hers at the infamous Watergate complex in Foggy Bottom. We sprinted out of the car and into the building's elevator like two love-sick teenagers on prom night. I remembered to grab my emergency overnight bag from my trunk with all the basics in it: pajamas, toothbrush, hairbrush, deodorant, new socks, underwear, my red flogger, a small dildo, vibrator, lube, and a huge dildo. Just the basics.

I got close to her in the elevator. "Absolutely beautiful," I murmured, my lips grazing her ear as my voice dropped low and steady. I wanted her to feel it, not just hear it. The way the words curled in her ear.

My hand rose, fingers trailing from the base of her neck to her shoulder, slow enough to make her ache. I barely brushed the top curve of her chest. No rush. Just a presence. Control slipped under the skin.

She didn't flinch. She turned toward me instead, quick, breathless, and kissed me like her life depended on it. Her mouth was open, needy, and almost shaking with how much she already wanted more. Her fingers clawed at the front of my jacket, trying to pull me closer, desperate for friction, contact, for anything.

Then the elevator chimed, right on cue. As the doors closed, she attacked me in the elevator with the passion of a 15th-century courtesan new to court and eager to please.

I stopped her.

I pulled the pins from her hair and watched it tumble loose over her shoulders, thick and gleaming, made to be touched. Slowly, I wrapped it around my hand until it was tight, and she tipped her head back with a soft gasp. Her body shifted closer, like it couldn't help itself.

She was flushed, breathing harder than the confined air in the elevator allowed. Her lips were slightly open. I could feel a pulse at her neck with nothing but my stare.

"You don't know what's coming," I said, low and deliberate. "Whatever idea is forming in your mind right now won't compare to what I'm going to do to you."

She swallowed hard, and I caught the most minor moan escaping from the back of her throat.

"You don't have to decide anything else tonight. I will. You just follow. Or don't. You can stop this any time."

I leaned in, just enough to feel the heat of her breath, just enough to let her feel the heat of my body pressed against her.

"But if you don't..." The elevator slowed. I didn't move. "... you're mine until morning."

The doors slide open, and she steps out first without looking back. The hallway is silent, and her heels click like a countdown. She leads me to a corner unit high above the city, her shoulders tight, her breath visible in how her spine lifts and falls.

Inside, the apartment was superb, expensive, quiet, and posh, where even the mice would be on their best behavior.

It was modernism with a mid-century flair. I was thinking of keeping track of how many pieces of this overpriced, fluffy furniture I was going to fuck her on, or off, or sideways before the morning.

She stood in front of me and paused. Then she dropped to her knees.

"May I?" she asked, voice raw, already cracking as she lovingly touched my shoes.

"Yes," I said, watching her fall into service with such eagerness it felt obscene.

She unbuckled my shoes carefully, even as her hands trembled. She peeled them off, then removed my socks, everything neatly beside her on the floor. Then she paused.

She kissed the top of one foot. Then the other. Soft. Warm. Barely there.

Her cheek pressed to my skin like she needed contact to remember where she was.

"Do you like serving me?" I asked, my voice quiet but full.

"Yes," she whispered, and her breath hit my skin.

She looked up. Eyes wild, glassy, full of need. She leaned in again, kissed higher now, ankle to calf, hands sliding up my legs like she wanted to devour me one inch at a time. When she reached the tops of my thighs, I saw her hesitate. She wanted permission. She needed it.

I hadn't given it yet.

I took her hands and stood her up instead, watching her blink in confusion. She wanted me to push her boundaries.

I pressed a hand to her lower back and guided her to the window. The city sparkled below us, moonlight over water, but she wasn't looking.

She was waiting.

"Tell me what you want," I said, my voice closing behind her. Lips grazing the shell of her ear, each word poured like warm syrup.

She trembled. Her breath hitched like a stutter of want she couldn't quite name.

"I want you," she whispered.

"That much is clear, but that's not what I asked."

She swallowed. Hard.

"I want..." she began, voice barely audible, like it cost her something to say it out loud. "I want to drown in flesh until I can't think. Until all I know is your voice."

"Better," I said, letting my fingers trail up her arms, slow enough to make her whimper. "But not enough."

She inhaled sharply, chest rising as though breath alone might steady her. It wouldn't.

"I want to be so desperate you have to hold me still," she said, voice shaking now. "I want to scream your name. I want to cry if you stop. I want to come so hard I forget where I am. I'll do anything."

"You already are," I murmured, my hand wrapping around her jaw, tilting her head just enough that she felt the weight of my control. "And you'll do more. You'll give me everything. Your body. Your breath. Your fear. Your fire. Every ache you've tried to silence—I'll pull it to the surface and make it sing."

A moan caught in her throat. I didn't let it fall. I took it.

"You'll beg," I continued, my voice dropping until it curled around her spine. "Not because I ask. But because you'll need to. And when you do, you'll thank me for the privilege."

She gasped, eyes fluttering shut as if the idea shattered something in her. And maybe it did.

"Take off your clothes," I said.

Her fingers moved fast, almost clumsily, with urgency. She slid her skirt down and tossed her jacket and tank top aside into a fabric pool at her feet. She was nearly naked now. Just her black heels and black sheer lacy underpants.

I stepped behind her again, pressing my body close. My hand slid around her front, down her stomach, over her thigh, and into her panties.

"Wet," I said. "Already."

"Yes," she gasped.

"Are you ready to begin?" I said, cutting her off with a hand around her throat. Not squeezing. Just reminding.

Her eyes fluttered shut. She nodded. A helpless, trembling nod.

"Step back," I said.

She obeyed. Her legs were already shaking. I grabbed my bag and tossed it at her feet.

I stepped in. One hand on her hip, the other sliding between her thighs. She gasped, jolting against me, already close. Already trembling.

I kissed her neck. Bit gently at her shoulder.

"You wanted to come?" I asked.

"Yes," she whimpered. "Please. Please let me—"

"Then ask again."

She sobbed, voice breaking.

"Please make me come. I'll do anything. I need it. Please."

My hand slipped lower.

"I'm not one of your students."

"You saw that?" she whispered.

"I did. I saw what she wanted from you.

Judicial Review blushed and hung her head down

"She is a child; you need a woman." I insisted.

I didn't know the details but knew the story's shape. I knew enough. The story is familiar enough in D.C. Many influential people get caught up in the fleeting adoration of younger interns or students, only to find themselves in a web of deceit that invariably leads to public resignation and apologies, stating they need to spend more time with the families they just betrayed.

"I should spank you just for that."

Her breath hitched.

"Reach into my bag. Pull out the red object. Hold it up if you want me to use it on you."

She dug into the bag, her fingers brushing past straps and leather. Then she found it —my red suede flogger. She held it for a second, staring.

And then, slowly, deliberately, she raised it and offered it to me.

Now she was ready.

I made her turn and face the window. The Potomac below shimmered with streaks of gold and silver, the city stretching out in a soft glow and quiet promise. She stood there, framed in glass, her silhouette trembling just slightly. Her breath was heavier now, more urgent, and her body leaned forward in anticipation.

I stepped behind her, close enough that the heat of my body made the hairs rise on her neck, but not yet touching. I wanted her to feel the space between us. To feel the ache of waiting. I dropped her panties to the floor and wrapped them around her eyes and secured them with one of her hairpins.

"If I pose you like this," I said, spreading her hand on the windowsill, spreading her legs out and pulling her hips back and up, "will you stay?"

She nodded.

"Say it."

"Yes," she whispered. "Please. Please, I'll stay."

"My Votary." I whispered in her ear. It means someone who has willingly given themselves to another's devotion by choice.

She must have known what I meant, because she became very hot and flustered. Her skin was steamy against the cool glass, forming condensation as her breast pushed against it.

Her ass was framed perfectly in the reflection, lit by the city, trembling with anticipation.

"Wider."

She opened her legs for me. Her breath was shaky. Her body was already singing.

I picked up the flogger. Soft suede. Sensual. Designed not to bruise, but to build. I let it brush along her skin. Down the arch of her back. Across the curve of her ass. She quivered all over. Not from fear. From need.

I struck once. Light. Controlled.

She gasped.

Again. Slightly harder.

Her forehead met the glass. Her breath fogged the reflection.

"More," she whispered.

"No," I said.

"Please."

"You want more?"

"Yes." Her voice cracked under its weight. "I want to feel it."

I stepped in close. My lips brushed the air beside her ear, my voice a low hum that slid over her skin.

"Why?" I grabbed her hair in my fist and pulled back.

She inhaled like she was trying to pull herself together, but only unraveled further. The second breath trembled.

"I want it because it means I'm yours." She confessed.

"Do you even know what you're asking for?"

She turned her face just enough for me to catch the gleam in her eyes.

"I want to come with your marks on me."

I watched her in the reflection. The way her thighs trembled from the effort of holding still. The way her mouth opened around a sound she could not quite swallow. She was not waiting anymore. She was offering herself.

"I like that you want to please me."

I rubbed my hand over the warm flush of her ass and brought it down in a sharp slap. She gasped. My hand slid lower, between her legs, where she was already slick and open for me. I traced the edge of her entrance with the pad of my finger. Teasing. Testing.

She nearly lost her footing.

"Please," she begged, her voice barely more than a breath.

I let the silence stretch. Thick and electric. Then I picked up the flogger again.

This time, the strokes were slower and heavier. Each one was deliberate and placed with care. They were not cruel or rushed but landed with heat and purpose. Her body jumped with the first. Her breath broke into soft, desperate cries with the second. By the third, her skin began to bloom, red, radiant, and utterly mine.

She did not pull away. She leaned into it. Her hips rolled toward the impact like her body was speaking a language her mouth could not yet form.

And when she finally spoke again, her voice trembled as if it were hanging by a thread.

"Please," she begged, her voice tight with need. "I want you." I let the silence stretch, thick as the air between us. "Please. Please, I need it. "

"You are soaked," I said. My fingers brushed between her thighs. She jerked at the touch.

"I can't wait," she said. "Please. I will do anything. I want to come. I want it now."

"Then beg like you mean it."

Her voice broke.

"Please. Let me come for you. I need it. I want it. I took it for you. I stayed still. I stayed open. Please let me have it. I will do anything. I just want your yes."

I slid two fingers inside her, and her body buckled. Her legs trembled. She tried to hold still. She tried to be good.

"You waited. You took it. You gave me everything I asked. Now I want everything you have left."

"Yes," she cried. "Take it. Please. Take me."

I spun her around and dropped to my knees. I slapped her legs open and dove between them like it was instinct. One hand gripped her open, two fingers on her clit, my tongue moving in slow, relentless circles.

My hand worked in rhythm, not frantically, but precisely. She was close. Her hips shook. Her voice broke apart into pieces. No more words. Just sound. Just need. Just surrender.

"Now!" I commanded.

She came with a cry that echoed. Her whole body convulsed. Her knees gave out, but I caught her. She collapsed into me, shaking, soaked, overwhelmed.

Her thank you came in fragments between sobs and gasps.

I kissed her shoulder. My voice was calm again, low and final.

"You pleased me. You did beautifully."

And she nodded, spent and glowing.

The night was just beginning. And I was just getting started.

I moved her to the sofa, hand at her lower back, not roughly but firmly, just enough pressure to remind her I was leading, not asking.

Her body was art, soft and golden in the dim light, the curve of her collarbone like something sculpted. She watched me under heavy lashes, her breath unsteady, like she knew what was coming and wanted it anyway. Or maybe because of it.

"There is some champagne in the wine fridge." I got up to get it. The bottle was ice cold. It gave me ideas.

I grabbed a towel and deftly opened the bottle. She watched as I twisted it open with my fist. When it popped, I used my tongue to lick off the froth spilling over the top.

Judicial Review observed, already starting to burn again.

Holding the bottle, I let my tongue circle the rim, slow, cold, and wet. I licked it the way I would lick her, long strokes, patient, practiced. I flicked the edge just once, just enough to make her sigh.

Then I looked up at her. She was watching. Completely still. Her eyes were dark, her lips parted, and her knees pulled together like she was trying to hold something.

She took it with both hands, eyes still fixed on me. She tilted it slowly and brought it to her lips, but didn't drink.

Not at first.

She parted her mouth, let her tongue slip out, and gave the rim a slow, luxurious lick. One circle. Then another. Her lips closed around it, her eyes fluttering just a little as she began to suck. She took the neck of the bottle deeper, hollowing her cheeks around it like she had forgotten it was glass and not skin. Her hands gripped it tightly. She moaned softly around the mouth of it, letting the sound hum up from her throat like a promise.

She pulled back, breathing warm and sticky on the glass. A drop of champagne clung to her bottom lip.

She didn't wipe it.

She just looked at me.

She wanted to be taken.

I didn't move.

Instead, I reached for the bottle again, lifted it from her hands, and let it hover above her chest. Her eyes tracked it, and her body tensed as I tilted it.

A slow stream spilled over the lip and landed just above her collarbone. Cold. Sharp.

She gasped. The liquid slid down her chest in slow rivulets, trailing between her breasts, dripping across her stomach.

She trembled.

"You made a mess," I said.

She didn't speak.

I leaned in and dragged my tongue across her aching body. She whimpered. I followed the trail lower, licking slowly, letting the cold sting melt into heat under my mouth. I circled her breast with my tongue but didn't take the nipple into my mouth. I licked around it, just enough to make her arch, then moved lower.

The champagne had puddled in her navel. I paused. Just watched it for a moment. Then dipped my tongue into her like she was the offering and I was the altar.

Her hips jerked.

"Still impatient?" I asked.

She nodded.

I leaned in closer, my mouth at her ear now.

"You're going to wait. You're going to lie there, dripping wet and covered in champagne, and you're going to take every second I give you. Because you begged for this. And I am going to make sure you feel it everywhere."

She made a sound that wasn't a word.

I kissed down her thigh, slow, grazing, letting my breath warm the places I hadn't touched.

She opened her legs more, desperate, shaking.

And I smiled against her skin.

Because she had no idea how long I had planned to make her wait.

Her eyes were fixed on the bottle. Her breath caught.

"Do you like cold?"

She shook her head. She looked nervous. Curious. Absolutely soaked with want.

"Good," I said.

I knelt between her legs and let the base of the bottle kiss the inside of her thigh.

She gasped. Her hips jumped.

The shock rippled through her body in a wave. The way she reacted—sharp intake of breath, head thrown back, hands clutching the cushions—told me she was already on the edge.

"Too cold?" I asked.

"No. God. It's so much."

I moved it higher. Slow. Deliberate. Teasing her with contrast. Her body was hot to the touch. That soft, flushed heat met the ice-cold bottle and turned it into something else. Something in between that made her breath tremble and her thighs quiver.

I dragged the glass along the line where her thigh met her hip. Her legs opened farther.

"You like this," I said.

She nodded, eyes dazed. Her lips parted around a moan she couldn't quite form into words.

"Say it."

"It makes me feel. I feel everything. It's everywhere."

"I am glad you like it."

I brought the rim of the bottle to her center, the curve of the cold bottle rubbing gently against her clit. The cold, wet glass sliding across her slick folds.

Her body jerked.

She cried out. One arm flew up over her head. The other gripped the cushion as if it were the only thing keeping her grounded.

"You like this?" I said.

She moaned, hips lifting, chasing the bottle.

I gave her a little more. A slow circle around her clit. Then another. Her body started to tense.

"Hold it," I said.

She whimpered.

I pressed the bottle flat against her, the cold flooding her immediately. Her thighs spasmed.

"Please," she said. "Please let me."

"Not yet."

I moved it again, but it was lower this time. It was a back-and-forth, smooth and rhythmic movement. Her body followed every stroke. Her stomach tightened, and her mouth fell open.

"You're not used to lasting this long, are you?"

She shook her head, wild-eyed. "It's too much. It makes it all too sharp. I want to come. I want to so badly."

"Then take it."

I circled again. Slower. Firmer. Her body convulsed.

"You're going to remember this," I said. "You're going to remember how cold it made you burn."

I held the bottle in one hand right at her clit, and with the other, I plunged it into her canal and targeted her G-spot with a stiff rubbing motion.

The champagne left in the bottle sloshed and frothed with the subtle movement.

She bucked her hips against the cold bottle like she was riding a horse.

"Please," she begged. "Please let me come for you. Please. I can't hold it. I need it. I need it."

"Now," I ordered.

She shattered. Loud. Messy. Her whole body bucked under the bottle. Her thighs squeezed shut around it, riding every wave. She moaned and cried out and gasped my name like it was the only word she knew.

I pulled the bottle away slowly. Her skin steamed in its wake.

Then I leaned down. Kissed the wet curve between her thighs. I slipped the panties off her head.

"You did so well," I said against her skin. "You felt everything I wanted you to."

She nodded, breathless. Boneless.

I kissed down her stomach, pausing just above the place she was already pulsing with heat. No rush. I encircled her body and held her while she recovered. However, we could not wait too long; more time was left on the docket, the defense had had its turn, and now it was the prosecutor's turn.

I pulled her up by the wrist and whispered, "Let's go to the bedroom."

She followed. Of course she did.

Her bedroom was absurd; Watergate absurd. Silk sheets, framed art — everything is designed to impress without looking like it's trying too hard. But none of that mattered now. She stood in nothing but her heels and those flushed, wrecked cheeks, looking at me like she couldn't remember what came next.

I did.

I lay her down on the massive bed and asked, "Would you like to be tied up?"

She nodded her head, smiling like she knew what I'd do. And tilted her head towards the closet.

I entered her walk-in closet as if it were a red-carpet event and found an entire boutique of her Hermès scarves. It was vintage printed ivory silk, probably worth $400 or more, but right now it was worth every cent. It was perhaps sacrilegious, and it was definitely illegal in France to tie someone up with it. A silken hate crime.

I straddled her and wrapped the scarf around her wrists, anchoring them to the headboard, tight enough to hold, loose enough not to bruise.

I leaned close enough to feel her breath against my lips and said, "I'm going to do whatever I want to you. And you're going to love every second of it. If you don't, you say stop, and I will."

She blinked slowly, lips parted. "Yes," she whispered.

Good. Because what I had planned for her would leave no doubt.

Her breath hitched as I tested the knots, the silk pulling tight against her wrists with a whisper of fabric and friction. She looked up at me, naked, bound, and almost reverent. That lawyer mask she'd worn at the gala? Gone. Now she was nothing but raw want and delicate ruin, sprawled across thousand-thread-count sheets like she belonged there. Like I had put her there on purpose. Because I had.

I took my time. I knelt between her knees, ran my hands down her thighs, slow, firm, claiming. Her skin was warm, still trembling, every nerve lit up from what I had already done. I leaned in and kissed her inner thigh, then the other. Then higher. Then higher still.

She whimpered.

I smiled.

"Use your words," I said, brushing a fingertip along her slick entrance.

"Please," she breathed. Barely audible. But it counted.

"Please, what?"

She swallowed hard. "Please, touch me."

I traced lazy circles with one hand, watching her hips twitch. "Oh, councilor. I am touching you. Be more specific."

Her eyes fluttered. "Please... please make me come again."

There it was.

I rewarded her with my mouth, deep and deliberate. No teasing this time. Just hunger. I devoured her like she was mine because she was. Nothing else existed at that moment. Just her thighs trembling around my shoulders, the silk scarf pulling tight when she strained against it, and the low, desperate noises spilling out of her like a confession.

When her third orgasm hit, it was harder. She cried out, high and sharp, and I didn't stop. I let it crest and keep going, pushed her past the threshold and into something messier, wetter, less composed. She wasn't the elegant woman from the gala anymore. She was wrecked. Glorious.

I sat up, wiped my mouth, and studied her. Her skin was flushed, her lips parted, and her hair clung to her damp forehead. She looked dazed. She was beautiful but completely undone.

I didn't give her time to recover.

I slid two fingers inside her, slow at first, then deeper, until she arched against the silk bindings and gasped my name. Her body clenched around me, still trembling from before, so close to overstimulation it was nearly pain, but she didn't say stop. She whispered "please" again.

So I gave her exactly what she asked for. I curled my fingers against that perfect spot inside her and pressed down hard with my thumb. She twisted in the scarves, eyes rolling back, moaning something that might've been a thank you, might've been a curse. Either way, it turned me on even more.

I leaned in and bit her neck lightly, not enough to mark, just enough to remind her that she was mine right now. "You're going to come again," I said, and I meant it. "Because I said so."

And she did. One more time.

Her body obeyed before her mind could catch up, like she had given it to me entirely.

When I finally pulled my fingers out, she was boneless. Breathless. Quiet in the way that means a storm just passed through.

She blinked at me like she couldn't quite return to earth. I kissed her shoulder, her temple, and the corner of her mouth. Gentle now, reverent.

"You did so well," I whispered.

She smiled faintly. "You are dangerous."

I grinned. "Only to people who say yes."

Her wrists were still red from the scarf, but she didn't flinch when I took the scarves off. She let me soothe her. Let me kiss her hands like they were precious, like she hadn't just used them to claw at the sheets. Her breathing had finally slowed, but her eyes stayed locked on mine.

There was something there. Unspoken. Waiting.

I brushed her hair back from her face. "What is it?"

She hesitated, just for a second. Then her lips parted.

"Can I ask for something?"

I raised a brow. "Of course."

She bit her bottom lip. This wasn't a performative act; this wasn't a gala flirtation anymore. This was a woman weighing the risk of exposure—real exposure.

"I want you to fuck me," she said, voice barely above a whisper.

I tilted my head. Not shocked. Very interested.

"That is what you need, counselor? "

She didn't answer with words. Just nodded, breath shaky.

I straddled her hips again and leaned in so close our foreheads almost touched. My fingers drifted up, framing her jaw. Holding her steady.

I murmured. "If I do this, it won't be cute. It won't be for show. It will be real. And you will take it because you need to. Not because you want to impress me."

I could feel how close she was. Every twitch, every tightening pulse around me gave her away. She was falling apart, beautifully, coming undone by the minute.

And then she gasped. "I'm yours. God, I'm yours."

I leaned down, grabbed a fistful of her hair, and pressed my mouth to her ear.

"I think there is a more southern deity at work here," I whispered.

Her eyes flew open, wide and wild. Her whole body clenched.

I stood and went to get the bag with the straps, the promise, and the threat. I took my time coming back, letting her feel the absence like a hand around her throat.

"You want me to fuck you with this?" I asked, holding it up like a weapon. Like salvation came in inches and could be strapped on.

"I want... please..." Her voice cracked as she begged, as if she knew it wasn't enough.

I dropped the bag on the floor. Peeled off my clothes slowly, like a strip search. Slipped into the harness one strap at a time, watching her the whole time. Watching her watch me. Letting her feel just how unholy redemption could get.

"You want this?" I grabbed it with both hands, and still there was room to spare.

She nodded. Mouth open, barely breathing. She looked wrecked already. Beautiful.

I tightened the straps. Palmed the silicone. Lubed it up soft and viciously given it's acreage.

No god. No salvation. Just this. Just now. Just the two of us burning.

I folded her into position: face down, legs folded beneath, arms pinned to her legs, ass arched high, glistening and perfect, begging without a sound.

I spread her open and slid in. Deep. Savoring a final course not because you are still hungry, but because you can.

She moaned into the sheets, her whole body trembling from the inside out. She couldn't move. And I leaned in close, lips brushing the shell of her ear.

"Look at you," I murmured. "This is what you wanted."

She gasped as I thrust again, her fingers curling in tight against her thighs.

I gripped her hips and snapped into her hard enough to make her cry out.

"You needed this. To be used. To be bent and fucked and wrecked by someone who doesn't give a damn what name is stitched inside your skirts."

She sobbed. Yes, sobbed. Because it was true. Because hearing it aloud broke something wide open inside her.

"You could have said no," I murmured, my mouth pressed hot against the side of her throat. My breath hit her skin in short, ragged bursts. I wasn't panting. I was unraveling. Controlled only in the way a storm controls when to hit. "You could have kicked me out. Slammed the door. Pretended none of this lived inside you."

She didn't speak. Just shook her head, barely moving. Her cheek was pressed into the pillow.

"You wanted this," I said, slower now. Letting each word sink in like teeth. "...to be this. A body. A need. "

She made a noise. A soft whimper pulled from somewhere low and aching. And that was enough.

I moved inside her. Took my time. Let her feel the shift in the bed. Let her hear the slide of my palm along the base of the dildo, the slow press of it against her again. Then I drove into her. Hard. The thrust punched the air from her lungs. I didn't give her a second to catch it. I grabbed her hips and pulled her back onto me, forcing every inch deep inside until there was nowhere left for either of us to go.

She gasped, trying to arch and move, but I held her steady. I was too wound up to be gentle. Too far gone to fake softness. I used her body like it was mine because at that moment, it was. And she wanted it that way. She needed to be taken past language. Past thought. Past the pretty little manners she wore in daylight.

I fucked her, hard and relentlessly. Measured. Brutal in its precision. Every thrust was a decision. Every movement said I own this. I own you.

She was trembling now. Moaning into the pillow. Her hands clenched and opened and clenched again, searching for something to hold on to, but the only thing holding her was me.

And then I reached around.

Found her clit. Slapped it hard, like it had misbehaved. Like it could tell me all her secrets if I pressed just right.

She came. Violently.

Her whole body spasmed, her mouth open in a silent scream. Legs kicking uselessly against the restraints, her back arching in a desperate, beautiful curve. She looked divine. And I didn't stop.

I fucked her through it. Every contraction, every aftershock. I kept her on the edge of breaking, kept her body trembling with overstimulation until her thighs shook and her voice was gone.

I stayed inside her, moving with long, deep thrusts, as if drawing something into her that wouldn't wash away. My hands ran over her back, sides, and hips.

I came with a violence that comes from holding back for hours, looking at a beautiful woman moaning over and over because of what I did to her. After I was done, I pushed her ass down and fell on top of her, spent like loose change at a casino.

She was quiet now, her breath slowing. Her body was slack and limp, but still open and warm around me. I leaned over her and bit the back of her neck. I didn't say anything. There was nothing left to say.

She lay on her stomach, arms beneath the pillow, her cheek turned to the side, and her mouth parted. The sheets beneath her were a mess of sweat, slick, and something sacred. Her body was flushed and glowing, the kind of glow that comes after surrender, after being undone by hands that knew exactly how far to go and how much further to push.

I brushed her hair from her face and just looked.

About half an hour passed. I slipped out of the harness. I sat beside her, holding an oil bottle in my palms, warming it. Then I placed my hands on her back. There were no commands now.

Her muscles twitched under my touch, the last of the adrenaline burning itself out.

"I can't feel my legs," she murmured, voice muffled in the pillow.

"That's because you don't have legs anymore," I said calmly. "You're just mine now. A beautiful, trembling puddle of expensive perfume and good life decisions."

She laughed. It cracked slightly at the edges, like she didn't know whether to lean into it or cry.

I moved lower, massaging the base of her spine, then down to her hips. I worked silently for a while, hands slow and sure, and I leaned in again when I felt her fully relax.

"I think you should get my name tattooed."

She let out a tiny groan. "Please don't start."

"I'm serious."

"No, you're not."

"Oh, I am. Very small. Very classy. Just above your hip. Right where I can see it when I pull you apart."

"You are the most arrogant—"

"And attentive," I interrupted. "And talented. And thorough. Don't forget that part."

She turned her face toward me, barely managing to open her eyes.

"You want to put a brand on me now?"

"I want to make sure no one ever gets to see you like I did unless they ask politely and sign something in blood."

She smiled at that. And it wasn't just amusement. It was that kind of secret smile that only happens when a woman knows she's been cherished, not just fucked. Worshiped in the dark.

I leaned down and kissed her shoulder. Then the edge of her jaw. Then the corner of her mouth.

"Do you want water?" I asked.

"Yes."

"Bathroom's closer."

"I can't walk," she said.

I grinned. "Then crawl. Or I'll carry you. I haven't decided whether to be gentle or cruel yet."

She raised a lazy eyebrow. "I thought we were in aftercare."

"Oh, we are," I said, grabbing the glass off the nightstand. "But I didn't say you were free."

I helped her sit up. Her body folded slowly, as if it wasn't sure how to recall the motion. I sat behind her, legs around her, supporting her back as she drank.

She leaned into me without asking. Her hair fell over my chest, and I wrapped my arms around her waist.

She sighed.

"You really don't stop, do you?" she asked.

"No. I don't."

And I didn't have to say it, but she knew I meant more than sex.

I kissed her temple. Let her rest against me.

Minutes passed like that. The kind of quiet you only earn. I felt her weight soften. Her breathing evened out. Her pulse was calm.

"Will you stay the night?" she asked finally.

I considered it.

Then I smiled against her hair.

"You're lucky I like beautiful women."

I moved lower, my thumbs working the tight muscles above her hips. Her breathing was steady now, body softening under my touch, the silence between us thick and warm.

She lifted her head and shot me a look. Pillow-creased, makeup-smudged, still glowing. She looked like a goddess who had been caught in a thunderstorm.

I kissed the middle of her back, slow and warm.

She dropped her head to the pillow again. Still laughing. Still wrecked. Still letting me trace my name on her skin with oil instead of ink.

And that, for now, was enough.

Because this wasn't about a two-hundred-dollar bottle of champagne. I'll play the part when necessary. I can dress up, make nice, let you drag me through your Michelin-starred mating rituals. But none of that touches me.

Power does. Surrender does. That moment when someone stops pretending they're in control of anything, that's the reservation I care about.

And I always get the table.

It's just not that important to me.

You can dress me up, take me out, and get a table at Philomena or the Diplomat. I'll play along.

We weren't aligned because she wanted a show pony, someone polished and pliable, a partner who knew when to smile for the camera and when to shut up and look grateful. She wanted to slide me into her curated life like a designer accessory, a conversation piece she could flaunt at donor dinners and whisper about at brunch.

I am not going to be paraded around like a plaything.

She might have loved getting raw dogged into her mattress by me, spread open, shaking, pleading for more, while I reminded her she didn't own a goddamn thing about me, but that does not mean I was ever going to roll over and beg. I was not born to be a lap dog. I don't heel. I don't fetch. I don't smile on command.

And that, ultimately, is what broke us apart.

Not the sex. Not the silence after. Not even the secrets she tried to hold behind her perfect little smirk. It was power. What I hold. What I don't give away. She couldn't quite figure out how to claim it.

It was something.

It was incredible, actually. The kind of thing that leaves a mark in the blood and the bone. The type of thing that flickers in your memory when you least expect it. I won't lie and pretend it didn't mean something. It did.

It just wasn't enough.

Still, I will never forget what she looked like. Bent over and begging. Her voice broke as she whispered my name. Her hands gripping the windowpane while the full moon spilled across her back. The Potomac glittering behind her like the stage lights of a city that will never really care how hard you fall, as long as you fall beautifully.

12

House Rules

House Rules was a doctor. The kind who had been in medicine long enough to stop pretending to care what people thought. She had short white hair cropped tight against her head, and a body that looked engineered. She weight-trained constantly. No chest to speak of, and an ass that could've been the result of divine intervention or just a decade of deadlifts. Either way, it worked.

She drove a sleek, overpowered sports car and treated traffic laws like suggestions for other drivers. At one point, she had so many speeding tickets that the state threatened to take her license. Her insurance company panicked. She paid what she needed to and kept going.

Out in the world, she didn't listen to anyone. She made her own rules, and she didn't apologize for them.

In bed, she wanted rules. She wanted to be told what to do. She liked it when I took control and didn't offer choices. That was where she let go. She was never more striking than when she was kneeling in front of me, quiet, waiting, stripped of all that outside-world arrogance and looking up like she needed nothing but my attention.

She satisfied me in all the right ways and confused me in a few others. She didn't fit into one category. One day, she had the swagger of a middle-aged surgeon who thought he knew everything. Next, she was sweet, eager, and needy. And sometimes both showed up at once.

She was the Swiss Army knife of sexuality. She came with more settings than I knew what to do with, and I never knew which one she'd hand me next.

The first time it happened, I was fucking her with a huge cherry Imitation Ivan in the vag. Missionary style because even I run out of ideas sometimes. I was wearing a lacy push-up bra, holding my uncooperative Double Ds back from their planned meeting at a lower part of my body.

I had just settled into the rhythm. Deep thrusts, clean angle, full pressure. Her legs were loose around my hips, her breath hot on my collarbone. The room smelled like lube, sweat, and whatever overpriced musky cologne she had rolled onto the insides of her wrists.

She was moaning, low and steady, her skin flushed and slick. Her mouth hung open just enough to keep me watching it between thrusts.

And I'll admit it. For a second, I thought I was some kind of sex goddess. Like I was about to summon a string of orgasms with my magic cherry red wand and ride this girl straight through the gates of strap-on sainthood. I had coordinated the whole setup. I looked like control, and I fucked like I meant it. She was making all the right noises. Everything was going to plan.

Until it wasn't.

She bit the back of her hand so hard I saw her wrist tremble. Her breath hitched, fast and shallow, and then she started making these choked fu-fu-fu sounds. It was like her body was trying to smother whatever was about to come out of her.

Then it hit.

"Fuck me in the ass!" she bellowed like she was the main character in a slightly bawdy opera.

She screamed it. Loud. Raw. It was not framed like a request. It came out sharp and strange, like her mouth had betrayed her before her brain could catch up. Her voice cracked in the middle of the sentence. Her face flushed deep. Her eyes squeezed shut as if she couldn't see me, and I couldn't hear her.

She kept her hand clamped over her mouth like she thought she could shove the words back inside.

And then she started moaning again. Guttural, not pretty moaning, more like a wildebeest stuck in quicksand. Just the kind of noise people make when they realize they have already gone too far and there is no way to pull it back.

We hadn't been together long. A few months of steady play. Enough to build trust, not enough to know what kind of wreckage lived under the surface. Our scenes had range, but nothing brutal. She liked to be tied sometimes. She wanted my voice in her ear.

I don't generally like surprises, but what girl could say no to pegging a hot masc girl?

Usually, anal requires prep, and I wasn't prepared. I didn't have the size I would typically use for that. There's a whole world of talk that's supposed to happen first. And while I had enthusiasm, I also had questions. This hadn't come up before. It was dropped on me like someone suggesting Chinese takeout or drinks before a movie. You don't spring that on someone. You definitely don't do it while you're the one bottoming. But even if you're topping, it's not something you jump into. It's something you agree on. It's something you plan for. That said, I occasionally accept requests. And this one was hot.

So I rolled her over, pulled a pillow from the bed, folded it once, and tucked it under her stomach. It gave me the angle I needed. And there it was. Her definitely divine ass, lifted and offered, waiting for me. She didn't say another word. Just stayed still. Even I paused.

That first moment always matters. If I pushed in too fast, it could hurt. If I hesitated too long, she might close up. There are too many variables. Her ass was still up in the air. Her back was arched just enough to keep me focused on what I was about to do. I used a glove I had in my bag, lubed my finger, and worked her slowly. One finger. Then two. She clenched around me and shivered. If I was reading her right—and I hoped to God I was—she was terrified and excited all at once.

I pushed deeper. I used my other hand to press the Silicone Steve into her pussy, sliding it just enough to keep her open everywhere.

I worked both entrances at once. She started to shake. I waited until her breath calmed, until her hips tilted back to meet me.

I pulled out and I put a condom on the Decoy Doug and steadied myself for what was going to be a bumpy ride.

I drowned her ass in lube.

I tapped it at the entrance to her asshole. Let her feel it. Just the tip. In and out, shallow and slow, until I was sure she was open for it. I stood on my knees, bent forward, and moved like someone who knew exactly how to take what had been offered.

"You want it?"

She whimpered.

"That's not an answer." I wanted this totally fucking clear.

"Yes. Please. Put it in." She consented.

"Keep your ass up!" I ordered. This was not the kind of operation where close enough counts.

I lined up and pushed in, slow for the first inch.

She screamed.

"More?"

"Harder," she said.

"You sure?"

"All the way."

I slammed into her. One thrust.

She cried out.

"More?"

"Yes. Yes. Fuck me."

"Say it louder."

"Fuck me harder," she screamed at me. Damn, she is a Bossy Bottom.

"Say please."

"Please fuck me harder."

I grabbed her hips and started pounding her. Full strokes. Skin slapping. Her body bouncing off the bed like she was built for it.

"Fuck, yes. Just like that."

"You like getting your ass plowed?" I dirty-asked.

"Yes. God, yes."

"You like getting used like this?"

"Yes. Please."

She braced herself on the bed frame. Her knuckles went white.

"Say it."

"Fuck me, bitch."

I stopped.

"What did you just call me?"

She turned her head. Her voice was lower now. Steadier.

"I said fuck me, bitch." Where did my sassy, sweet bottom go, and who the hell am I fucking?

She wasn't begging anymore. She was snarling. Her whole body shifted. The sounds, the words, even the angle of her back. She was leaning into it. Claiming it.

I went to bed with a woman, and now I was fucking a frat boy.

She growled. Her muscles locked, then opened for me. I slammed into her again. And again. She shoved her ass back into me like she was starving for it.

"Harder."

I went harder.

"Fucking whore."

"Repeat it. And I will stop." I clarified.

"Fucking dumb bitch."

"Who am I fucking?" I said that more in a rhetorical sense.

She growled like an animal.

I grabbed her hair, pulled her head back, and pounded her like we were in a scene with a camera and a paycheck and a cumshot countdown.

Except it was real.

She reached down to her clit with her hand and with just a few strokes came so hard she slammed all the way back so the BackUp-Barry was all the way in her to the ring.

Of course, I wasn't finished. My clit was not used to all this, but I was still swollen. And still high from the way she had let me use her. I laid her back down, grabbed her wrists, and twisted them towards me.

"Don't move," I told her.

She grinned like she wanted to disobey.

"You're such a fucking whore," she spat. "A filthy, desperate little slut."

I am not the one begging for a pegging, but okay....

That did it. I went straight back in, deeper this time, rougher. Her back arched, and she moaned like she hated me for it.

"Stupid bitch," she hissed. "You like this, don't you? You fucking *cunt.*"

"We're going to need a shower after this, and I'm going to wash out your dirty little mouth." I barked at her.

I was past thinking. Past performance. It wasn't about how long it lasted or how loud we were. I was too turned on to pace it. Too locked in to stop. I pounded her hard and fast, sweat dripping, her insults getting more ragged by the second.

I came hard, ploughing her face into the mattress, mainly just to shut her trash talk, for one last hard thrust, sending me over the line and deep into her fucking ass.

When we finally stopped, the room was wrecked. Pillows on the floor. Sheets twisted. We looked at each other like strangers. Like people who had just confessed something they couldn't take back.

"Shower, now!" I barked

We would see who the dirty bitch in this relationship was.

If you are going to gender play as a man, my advice is, don't be an asshole. There are many kinds of men you can role-play: Mr. Darcy, Ed Sheeran, or Xaden. You don't have to be the kind of man that I would block on social media.

She was sitting at the foot of the bed, still wrapped in the towel she had barely bothered to dry off with. Coffee in hand. Eyes tracking me like I might say something she couldn't walk back from.

I leaned against the window frame and kept my voice calm.

"So umm"

She tensed.

"I fucked a woman. But about halfway through, she turned into a man auditioning to be an ex-husband."

Her face cracked. "Jesus."

"That wasn't an insult," I said. "That was a description."

She looked down at the mug like she wanted to climb inside it.

"You called me a stupid bitch," I added. "A cunt. You ordered me, a point we will return to in a minute, to fuck you harder like some drunk frat boy." For the record, frat boys do like to be pegged, but they don't want to talk about it.

"Where the hell do you get off giving me orders? Do you want to flip the script now and top me? Because if that is the plan, you are just a few aces short of that deck." I swiped at her.

She let out a sound that might have been a laugh. Might have been a sob.

"I need to ask you something," I said. "Not to make it weird. Just to be clear."

She nodded slowly.

"Are you trans?"

Her head snapped up. "No."

"Okay."

"That wasn't about wanting a male body," she said. "It was about trying to be someone else."

"You picked an angry man as your character. Of all the people that you could choose, you picked an angry man who demeans their partner indiscriminately?" I countered.

"I know," she sagged a little.

"You didn't warn me." I offered.

"I didn't know it was going to happen."

I nodded. "Were you afraid I would say no?"

"I wasn't trying to dominate you."

"You think you could?" I was only half-teasing; there was no way. On the infrequent occasion that I am topped, I prefer a dashing pleasure dom/domme. If you want to call me a princess and get me off 4 times in a night, I would probably do it. But I am nobody's bitch.

She exhaled. "I'm sorry for the language."

"I'm not fragile," I said. "But next time, if you're going to scream at me like your alimony's overdue, I want a heads-up."

That got a real laugh. Soft. Relieved.

"I am sorry," she said. "Could I dominate you?"

Dominating me? Oh no. But it's cute that she thinks she can. Perhaps she needs a downgrade to some fish she can fry.

"If you have to ask..." I just nodded.

I've witnessed many dynamics in my time, but this one was particularly new. Unique. Esoteric, even. She, in the dick-ish male-ish persona, wanted to bottom get pegged and shout insults at me. I have shouted insults at men before, but they are usually carefully chosen to excite or humiliate. Calling me a bitch is never a good idea if you want to fuck me again.

House Rules had this fantasy; she described it like a joke at first. To be with two women. Me in my dominance and the other, a stone-cold top with a big strap and no patience. She wanted to be on her knees for her. My role was to walk in and see her already performing acts that are definitely illegal in Texas. And that's precisely how I found her.

Face buried in the other Butch's crotch, sucking on a huge lifelike Deputy Dick. Spit was already running down her chin. Gagging, but not in rhythm. Trying too hard and still getting it wrong. I didn't say anything at first. I just stood behind her, arms crossed, watching her embarrass herself.

Finally, I spoke.

"You are going to need both hands for that! You would never make it in a frat house during pledge week." Yes, that happens, and no, I will not be elaborating further.

She froze.

I stepped in closer. Bent down. Spoke just behind her ear.

"You look pathetic. You begged me for this. Set the whole thing up. And now you're here slobbering all over someone's fauxcock like it's your first time on your knees."

She whimpered and kept going, messier now, desperate to correct herself.

I smacked her ass. Once. Then again. Harder. Pushing her down on the pseudo-member, making her gag.

"You're a worthless little cocksucker."

The other butch chuckled low in her throat and looked down at her, running fingers through House Rules' hair like she was petting a dog, then pulling her down farther onto her Stand-InSteve.

"She said she was ready?" The butch said.

"She's not," I replied, spanking her again. "But she's going to keep trying anyway."

I stood behind her, not penetrating yet. Just watching her perform for both of us. I let her squirm. Let her panic a little. Let her feel what it meant to beg for a scene and then fall short.

"Back straight," I ordered. "Spread your fucking knees, princess. Open your throat or I swear I'll fuck her and make you watch."

She obeyed.

"Good boy," I muttered, finally unzipping. "Now maybe I'll fuck you."

The other butch smiled—tight and slow—and looked up at me as I moved behind House Rules.

"Is she always this bad, or is she just nervous because I'm here?" The butch said.

"She is hardly worth your time," I said plainly. "But if you want to fuck her hard up the ass bent over, she is worth it, if you can shut the bitch up long enough." That was about two bitches more than I usually do, but turnabout is fair play.

She chuckled, still stroking House Rules' face, but now her eyes were on me. Focused. Intent.

"She listens to you," The Butch said, voice low. "That's hot."

The butch reached for my waist. That's when House Rules tensed.

Even with her mouth full, even as she gagged on the Synthetic Saul between her lips, she noticed. Her body locked for half a second. She knew exactly what was happening. She had asked for this scene, but she hadn't expected that Butch would want me. She hadn't expected me to *enjoy* it. I leaned in, not pulling away.

"This is what you wanted," I said softly, right above House Rules' ear. "Now spread your fucking ass cheeks wide because I am going to peg you until I come. And then you are going to watch me and her." I reached over and started kissing the Hot Butch.

Some fantasies don't work out like you planned. She really should not have called me a bitch unless she wanted to see the side of me that was one.

Outside the bedroom, House Rules was utterly different. We'd go to the best restaurants in town. She treated me like royalty — queen, princess, goddess, you name it. She doted on me. Observed every detail. It was almost jarring, the contrast between our polished public life and the deeply submissive persona she unleashed in private.

One night, we had dinner at a French restaurant in Georgetown. Very old-world, very white-tablecloth. The kind of place where the butter arrives in little porcelain plates and everyone pretends to have delicate appetites.

We sat right next to the fireplace, and the glow from the flames made her look enchanting.

House Rule was in rare form that evening. She wore a perfectly tailored navy suit with a crisp white shirt, which made her silver hair look as if a Renaissance sculptor had styled it. She looked, for lack of a better term, *distinguished.* If you didn't know better, you'd have mistaken her for an ambassador, or a partner at a boutique law firm with a yacht docked in Annapolis.

We sat across from each other, knees touching under the table, sipping wine and dissecting the menu with the kind of quiet intimacy that comes from knowing exactly how far you can push someone before the real games begin.

"You should let me touch you," she said softly, almost lazily, like she was commenting on the wine. "Right now."

I glanced around. Our waiter was two tables away, explaining the specials with unnecessary fanfare. Couples nearby murmured over duck confit and steak frites. It wasn't the kind of place where you let someone slip a hand up your skirt.

"I don't think so," I whispered back, smiling with only the corners of my mouth.

Her eyes flickered. Mischief. Challenge. A beat passed.

Then she took one of the ice-cold butter pats and dragged it slowly across her bread—except she wasn't watching the bread. She was watching *me* and watching my reaction.

Before I could stop her, she reached under the table and smeared a thick swipe of the butter between my legs, dodging around my panties with tremendous confidence and a gleam in her eye like she'd just dared a match to catch fire.

I nearly choked on my wine. It was cold and silky. She rubbed my clit in little circles as I tried not to moan. The waiter was only one table away and heading over.

The waiter approached, and House Rules did not stop; the waiter asked what I wanted. I faked a sneeze to cover up my orgasm and buried my face in a napkin.

House Rules asked the waiter if they could bring some more ice-cold butter.

The server shot a glance at the full bread bowl and the absence of butter, and shot me a knowing glance in the few moments that I could actually meet their gaze.

The waiter said they would give us a few minutes and scurried off.

"Don't worry," House Rules said. "I'll clean it up."

When we left the restaurant after just the right amount of wine, a car service was waiting for us. The second the door closed behind us, she dropped to her knees and buried her face between my thighs like a woman starved. She licked the butter away with reverent, slow, indulgent strokes.

No one could fault her in the cunnilingus department. She obviously had spent some time kneeling in the back of limos before. I came twice on the way.

I know she was trying to be dominant, and I appreciated the orgasms, but initiating is not dominance. Dominance is complicated; it ties into your idea of who you are and your relationship to the person on top. House Rules just didn't get it, and she probably never would.

We were headed out to a memorable evening. There was a play party—one of the more infamous ones—where the hosts had laid down a massive plastic sheet across the entire living room floor, transforming the space into a kind of hedonistic crash pad. Air mattresses were arranged and taped together into one large soft landing zone, like a perverse patchwork quilt. People moved between them like dancers in a deliberately unchoreographed ballet. It wasn't an orgy so much as an ecosystem.

Five women were lined up in a row, propped like centerpieces on a buffet table—legs parted, eyes flirty and welcoming. They were rewarded for how many women they could get to dive in. You could move down the line, as if browsing the specials. And I did. With reverence, with glee. Think diner counter, but the menu is moaning and wet. And yes—we used dental dams. We were decadent, not dumb.

House Rules didn't participate, not in that manner. She preferred to watch, throbbing, silently vibrating with the electricity of the scene. I sent a girl over to her—someone who liked kneeling—and watched from across the room as she was serviced. It grounded her. Gave her an anchor while I explored. I think it made her feel like she belonged.

Later, I arranged for something even more enticing. She was underneath me, face buried between my thighs, while another woman—someone strong, someone who knew how to take control and fine-tune the engine of a Chevy—entered her from behind. When I came loudly, as points were awarded for enthusiasm, I realized I didn't care if it was House Rules or someone else at that point.

The performance never came to an end. She wanted to be in the scene everywhere: in the kitchen, at the grocery store, mid-brunch. She'd try to kneel next to the stove while I was stirring risotto, ask for praise, and demand correction. She'd drop her voice and slip into character as if we were backstage instead of living real life.

It was exhausting.

One of the things about living in a role is that you forget to live outside of it, and I didn't want to be on stage 24/7. I didn't want to have to cue the lights every time I entered a room. I didn't want to be someone's fantasy *all the time.* No matter how hot it was at the moment, I needed a place to land.

She didn't.

Last I heard, she tried to settle down with someone else. Moved to another state. Planned a wedding. The girl left her, of course.

I've always needed clarity. Either we're building a real relationship—something with roots, routine, and maybe even children—or we're just playing for a while and then parting ways. And I don't regret either choice. But I do require honesty about what we're doing.

House Rules couldn't give me that. Not without rewriting who I was. And I wasn't willing to trade my identity for her kink.

13

Triple D

We met at Mr. Henry's on Capitol Hill, a beloved hotspot for the neighborhood and probably the best place in town to eat peel-and-eat shrimp on the patio with an ice-cold beer. I was sitting at the bar, minding my business, and she came up behind me. Ostensibly, she was trying to get the bartender's attention, but really? No. She came up behind me with her breasts—her *huge,* magnificent breasts, which were basically on my neck. I turned around, and I was suffocating in a wall of tits. And I remember thinking, if I die right now, it would be a good way to go.

I looked up, emerging like a diver coming up for air between her cleavage. I knew her immediately. It was the face you recognized. Like, *'Oh, hey, you're that woman from that thing,'* except that thing is the Sunday morning news shows. I'm not a person who gets starstruck; I am from Los Angeles and grew up around stars without caring a bit about them, but at this moment, I was utterly, embarrassingly starstruck.

She was the woman I wanted to be when I grew up—powerful, strong, bright, beautiful in that high-gloss, devastating, impossible way. She was among the most intelligent people I'd ever heard, and I hadn't even *met* her officially.

I did what any normal, slightly tipsy Hill person in a t-shirt and jeans would do when confronted by a literal goddess in silk: I offered to buy her a drink.

"Can I help you get the bartender's attention?" I asked. "Or, can I buy you a drink?"

I *fully* expected her to demur. A polite, *'Oh no, thank you,'* probably accompanied by a smile that could crush me gently. I'm sure she got offers like that twenty times a day, and I didn't exactly think I had a shot. But at that point, I was too far in to her décolletage to care.

From the moment I met her, I would've done anything to stay in her orbit. Carry her luggage? Sure. Buy her dinner? Absolutely. Book her a jet plane to the Bahamas? Why not? I was reacting to her like a barometer to an oncoming storm, my every impulse bending to the pressure of her presence. Never mind that I could barely afford dinner, let alone a jet plane. Logic didn't play a role in the equation. It was pure adrenaline, pure awe, and the sheer magnetic pull of wanting to do whatever it took to stay close to her. Breasts and adrenaline had replaced my brain.

And then it hit me. I was acting like a bottom. Oh no.

Now we were officially in uncharted territory. I hadn't bottomed for anyone since I moved to D.C., and suddenly I was wondering if I even remembered how to do it. Do I get on all fours? Do I fake an orgasm? Do I say "thank you" in a breathy voice and stare off into the middle distance?

I was spiraling. Fast. My nerves were shot, my brain was buzzing, and if I didn't get on a beta blocker or pour a cocktail down my throat immediately, I was going to screw this up with sweaty, over-eager enthusiasm.

Somehow, despite all that, I charmed her. It could be my overall geeky panic. Maybe it was the fact that I was still half-flustered from nearly suffocating in her cleavage. But I leaned forward, trying to reclaim a cool sliver, and said, "Hi." *[Redacted].* I gave her my name, and she gave me hers.

And, of course, I was like, "Oh. Right. Of course. Yeah, sure."

Like I didn't already know. Smooth. So smooth.

I wasn't in a suit. I wasn't trying to pick anyone up. I looked like someone who had gotten lost on the way to Whole Foods. But somehow—somewhere, she said yes.

I asked if she was there with someone. She nodded no. "Can we sit on the patio?" I asked. "I'll bring drinks."

And she said, "Sure."

I don't even remember reaching the bartender; I remember *demanding* two ice-cold beers and ordering a basket of peel-and-eat shrimp, as if I were on a mission from God. I didn't know if she even liked shrimp.

The panic was setting in. A complete internal monologue: Don't blow this, you dupe. Don't say something stupid. Don't curse. Don't overshare. Don't badmouth anyone in her orbit. Don't try too hard. Don't talk too much. Don't fumble. Don't *blow* this.

And then I had to pee. But I didn't want to leave her alone too long, let the beers get warm, the shrimp go cold, or, heavens forbid, give her the chance to *leave.*

So I skipped the bathroom and bolted to the patio.

And thank God—**thank God**—she was still there.

She hadn't left. She was sitting exactly where she said she'd be, and when I saw her, I felt something unclench inside my chest. Maybe. Maybe I hadn't blown it.

I put the drinks down and sat without asking. At that point, it was going to go one of two ways: she'd either call the police, or we were going to have a great conversation. There wasn't much in between.

And then I ran out of things to say. Immediately. My mind blanked. Wiped clean. Just me, beer, shrimp, a goddess on a patio, and nothing in my brain but static.

So I pulled myself together, barely, and looked at her and said the one thing I knew was true. "You look beautiful tonight."

And that's when I felt the shift.

I wanted to say something extraordinary, something that made me seem like I wasn't just some total freaking groupie.

I asked, "Were you just coming from work?"

She said she was.

And I jumped right into panic mode: *Don't talk shop. Don't talk shop. This is not a policy dinner, you idiot. This is shrimp and beer; stay in your lane.*

But she said, "Yeah. I work a lot."

The shrimp arrived at the table. I cracked open a shrimp with my fingers, feeling the shell snap as the briny scent mixed with the cool evening air. I watched her as she deftly peeled her own, her movements unhurried, almost elegant. How she brought the shrimp to her lips, then slipped her fingers into her mouth to savor the flavor, was effortless. She rubbed the remnants of seasoning on her lips with a slow, thoughtful ease. It was all so effortlessly sensual, a simple pleasure shared in the middle of the bustling patio.

I latched onto travel—the safest ground I knew. Everyone in D.C. travels, and politicians love talking about it. It's neutral, secure, and full of stories. There's always something: the best places, the worst meals, packing disasters, lost luggage sagas, airport purgatory at 3 a.m. It's easy ground if you're quick on your feet.

"Have you been traveling a lot lately?" I asked.

I mentioned that I'd just returned from Bermuda, and suddenly, thank God, she lit up. She loved Bermuda. We talked about the white roofs, the not-quite-pink sand, and the coral reefs. We wandered from one travel topic to another for nearly an hour, just... floating.

Somewhere in there, I realized I still had to pee, but it wasn't going anywhere. This isn't good. I got considerable bottom energy. Not until I booked a real date with her. I wanted to pick her up, okay, fine, *meet her*, take her out, maybe even go dancing. Wouldn't that be something?

But I didn't know if she was out. It wasn't a well-kept secret, but still. Outside D.C., who knew? I didn't know if she went to gay bars or lesbian bars, or if she even could. That's the thing about this city. There's a whole world of hidden lesbian circles. Private parties in Capitol Hill row houses or old-money Dupont mansions, where discretion isn't just expected; it's enforced. These were gatherings for women who couldn't afford to be seen—women with security clearances, women with husbands, women with power, real power, who couldn't risk the wrong kind of attention.

Some were in lavender marriages, quiet understandings written in tax returns. Others lived in carefully maintained Boston marriages, such as those between two wealthy older women.

I'd been to a few of those parties. The houses were filled with antiques, oil paintings, and heirlooms that whispered of generations past. The air smelled of old leather and polished wood, and the rooms were filled with the quiet hum of money, old money. I remembered one conversation overheard on a balcony between two younger women. They were trading notes about their partners, jobs, wealth, and family names, and laughing about how soft the beds were in those houses.

And at that moment, remembering the parties, I felt it. The fear. The quiet, crawling knowledge that I could be one of them. It was just another pretty thing, a distraction, something someone would grow tired of once I wasn't new anymore. I hadn't earned enough yet. I wasn't as accomplished as I wanted to be, and I knew it. I wanted to be seen as someone formidable, not just someone entertaining.

That's why I was so careful around her. Because even though she made me feel powerful, part of me still worried I would end up discarded, just another story someone else would tell. But all I wanted, at that moment, was to get her to say yes to a date despite my trepidation.

I started telling my best travel stories—Narita Airport at 2 a.m., the insane layover in Singapore, and the five hours I once spent stranded in the old TWA terminal at JFK, which I believe is now a hotel. I told her about losing my luggage on the New Jersey Turnpike at a service station and somehow ending up in a diner with a man who claimed to have worked in three White Houses.

I've spent a lot of my life traveling. And for once, it came in handy. If we'd drifted into politics, I'd have been completely outmatched—she knew *everything* and *everyone*. I only knew my tiny sliver of it.

But she laughed at my stories, smiled, and kept looking at me like I might be worth her time. I looked straight into her eyes and lost my balance entirely.

Her eyes were warm brown, flecked with gold, the kind of eyes that didn't just see you—they *took you in.* She wore her hair in braids that night, and her whole presence was... devastating. Immaculate. Elegant. She wasn't from the South, but she had that grace, that stillness, that power you sometimes find in women raised with rituals of presence.

Her suits always fit perfectly. Her nails were always done. Her makeup was minimal. She never wore much, but she didn't need to. She had *that thing*—the thing only a few women ever have—the composure that stops a room cold.

And I remember thinking, *Wherever you're going... I'll go.*

And I'm sure she always gets beautiful, powerful, unbothered. I mean, I'm not a child. I'm an educated woman. I can hold my own in most rooms. But with her? I was one hundred percent in groupie mode.

Still, I managed to summon some courage I didn't have. I looked up at her with something like determination—maybe a little lust—and said, "I would love to take you to dinner this week if you have time. And if not this week, then next. You tell me when, and I'll be available."

Which was about as clear as I could be.

Whenever she was free, I was free. It was golden retriever mode, full tilt. I should have returned to being the black cat; I usually am aloof, poised, and skeptical. But no. I was practically wagging my tail.

She looked at me for a long moment, then lowered her eyes, fingers tracing the gold jewelry on her wrist. "Give me your card," she said softly, "and I'll call you... Once I consult my diary."

Her diary. That shy glance, almost submissive tone, was a definite maybe, but it also put me right in my place. My life didn't have a diary. It barely had a calendar. A few Outlook meetings and a general sense of vibes. But she had a diary. That told me everything I needed to know. Would I be just another item on her calendar or a standing appointment with a small red heart and no name? I would work hard to convince her that I was the kind of person who stuck around.

I handed her my *work* card because I was too rattled to give her anything personal. "I'd love to text you later if I might?" I asked, trying to sound casual.

She just smiled. "Let me call you," she said. Oh no. Was that the brush-off? The polite freeze? The slow ghosting that starts with one missed call and ends with you crying into your beer?

But she took the card. And I thought: *If she calls, I might have a chance.*

She said she had to go.

I watched her walk away, her hips steady, her every step controlled, as if she knew I was still watching her.

The moment she turned the corner, I bolted for the bathroom. Not because I needed to pee, though I did — but because I needed a second to breathe, to recover, not to throw up the two beers I had barely finished. My hands were shaking. My mouth was dry. The adrenaline hit harder than the alcohol ever could. I barely made it.

Then came the waiting. Three days. I told myself I wasn't counting, but I was. I checked my phone every ten minutes. I reviewed what little we'd said. I second-guessed my tone, outfit, jokes, and even the shrimp basket. I imagined her tossing my card in the trash. I imagined her handing it to a staffer with a note to avoid my call at any cost.

I prepared myself for the silence. For the letdown. For the politeness, nothing would confirm I had been entirely out of my depth. And then she called. Not a text, not an email. She called.

She said she was free on Sunday and asked if I was interested. Interested? I was ready to get a tattoo of the reservation on my chest.

She said brunch, not dinner, and I wasn't about to quibble. Brunch was something I could do, and I excelled at it. I offered three places; she suggested a fourth. We went with hers.

Now, the real panic began: what to wear. What do you wear to brunch with a goddess?

Do you wear a suit? Pants? A dress? Sunday brunch typically means hungover leggings and dry shampoo for me, but this was *not* that kind of Sunday.

I stayed up half the night doing my hair, trying to figure out how not to embarrass her. I settled on black pants, a crisp white shirt, and a short black blazer. Professional. Polished. At least, I hoped so.

She walked in kakis, a campaign t-shirt, and sneakers. Her hair was flawless, her makeup was perfect. She looked like she was dressing down to seem casual.

I nearly slid off the vinyl seat.

How does a woman look like that on a Sunday morning?

What does she see when she looks in the mirror? And how is it not illegal to look that good before noon?

We had a sparkling brunch, despite my nerves, or maybe because of them. She was charming, composed, and a magnet for attention. People stopped by the table to say hello, chat, ask about upcoming events, fundraisers, or request photos. She handled all of it gracefully, introducing me simply and politely, letting me orbit beside her like some stunned little moon.

I was just happy to be there. To be anywhere near her.

When brunch ended, I hesitated. I didn't want it to end. So I asked casually if she golfed. Hains Point was just down the road — a charming city course right by the water.

What if we just went to the driving range and the putting green? That was fine with me. I got, I don't know, tokens for seventeen buckets of balls in case she felt like going all in. I was ready for anything. Nothing was going to stop me from spending time with this woman.

We went up to the upper deck because it's a double-decker driving range, and if you go far enough left or right, you get space to yourself. Nobody's up there. The ball gets a little flight, and you can stretch out without anyone bothering you.

I set her up with my clubs. She's a little taller than I, but we could share. I handed her my good driver, smiled, and said. "Show me what you've got, gorgeous."

She stepped up, planted her feet, and I swear to God, she d*estroyed* the ball. She just smacked the absolute hell out of it. Not two hundred yards, maybe, but damn close.

I was speechless.

"Wow," I said. "I'm impressed."

She glanced over her shoulder.

"You haven't seen anything yet."

I didn't even want to hit. I didn't care about golf anymore. I just wanted to stand there and watch her eyes locked on the ball, her swing fluid and powerful. I was in full groupie mode again.

She asked for a seven-iron, and I handed it to her. She didn't just take it; she used it. She hooked the end of the club around my waist and pulled me toward her. I stumbled half a step, laughing, and then she kissed me.

She kissed me. Right there, on the driving range, under the bright sun.

It wasn't a shy kiss. It wasn't tentative. It was confident, commanding, and full of promise. And I just about collapsed from happiness. This was my happy dance moment. Whatever she wanted, I wanted. Right here, right now.

I didn't say the thing; I was thinking that I wanted to fuck her right there on the deck. I tried to strip her down, lay her out on the turf mat, and bury my face in her until she screamed my name to the golf gods.

But I thought it.

Instead, I kissed her again and asked softly, "Do you want to stay here? Or... would you like to go somewhere else?"

And I meant it. Whatever she wanted.

I knew it couldn't be my place. Not because it wasn't clean, not because it was bad. Just... I didn't want her to see my secondhand desk.

My mismatched chairs. My thrift-store bookshelves. I didn't want her to think I wasn't good enough.

So I asked, "Do you want me to take you home?"

She nodded.

Her place. Of course.

We drove back, and I wasn't prepared for what I would experience.

Her home was stunning—a beautiful row house in a prime location—the kind of home that made you feel like you should take your shoes off at the door, which we did. The inside smelled like flowers and candles. It was not lit; it was just there, tucked into corners. There were antiques everywhere—plants, textures, and care. She lived in her space like someone who *owned* her self-worth. It was beautiful.

I turned to her and kissed her, deep, sure, reverent.

I didn't know what she was into, but I was ready to find out.

Sometimes, confident, even commanding women turn out to be pillow princesses. I had a sneaking suspicion she might be one. That was fine with me, as I was still grappling with the idea of having to bottom to anyone after all this time.

She offered me a glass of wine. "I have an interesting little chardonnay," she said.

"I would love some," I replied.

She handed me a tall, chilled goblet, and I looked at her, dead as I took it from her.

"Do you have anything I can eat?"

I hadn't meant it to sound provocative, not at first. But by the time it came out of my mouth, it was. I saw it land.

She raised one eyebrow. "I believe I do."

She didn't have to say anything else. We both knew.

"Shall we go upstairs?" She suggested.

She led me up. Her bedroom was just like the rest of the house: elegant, intentional, and layered. It featured a dark mahogany four-poster bed, an antique mirror, and richly textured fabrics. It wasn't cluttered, yet it was powerful in its stillness. Was I just another piece of expensive furniture?

I turned to her. "You brought me here. You kissed me. Shouldn't I be the one ordering off the menu?"

She smiled, slow and knowing, with a tease that lingered.

I could ruin everything if I played this wrong. So I went safe. A soft option. Worst case, she'd toss me on the curb like yesterday's *Washington Post.*

"I asked around about you." Her eyes ran over me like a full-body scan.

Oh fuck.

"I got the distinct impression that you like to be in control. Was I misinformed? Are you not who I thought you were?"

"What did you hear?"

"That you can make a woman scream—in bed, in the street, in the West Wing supply cabinet, in a Senator's office, even in the cloakroom at the Capitol. Quite frankly, you've got a reputation as a stud."

"If only I was flattered. Whoever you've been talking to doesn't know me as well as they think. It was a Congressman's office. Although—" I let my tongue flick across my lips, slow and deliberate. "They might not be wrong about everything."

"Well, that's good to know. Still, I have it on excellent authority from one of your exes, who was very sorry to see you go."

Oh, Jesus Christ. Who the hell was talking? There were too many possibilities.

"I'm pretty selective," I said carefully. "So I'm not sure who you mean. Maybe you should make up your own mind."

I leaned in, let the moment hang, then dropped it low and deliberate. "Forget everyone else. What do you want me to do? Because I'm already getting ideas. Like laying you back on that bed and making you scream until your bedroom becomes the epicenter of a 5.0 earthquake.

I dropped my voice as I stepped toward her, something lower and smoother than I usually let anyone hear. I pulled off my shirt and jacket, allowing each item to fall to the floor without ceremony.

As I walked, my pants were next, and now there was a trail of fabric behind me like a roadmap to where we were going. I reached her and kissed her, deep, deliberate, slow. Then I kissed her neck, her collarbone, and the top of her chest. I lifted off her shirt and slid it down her arms until it fell to the ground around her feet. I took my time. She didn't rush me.

I dropped my voice as I stepped toward her, letting it sink lower with every word.

"You are beautiful," I whispered.

I kissed her — slowly, thoroughly — and then kissed her neck, letting my lips linger as I moved lower. I kissed across her collarbone and down toward her breasts. I slid my hands to the buttons of her pants and undid them, one by one, before letting the fabric slip from her hips and fall to the floor.

I turned her gently and reached behind her to unclasp her bra. It fell forward, easy and graceful. I pulled it away from her like I was unwrapping something precious.

She melted under my mouth. Her breath hitched, her body softened, and everything about her changed: the way she clung to me, the way she opened, the way her hips lifted to meet each kiss like a prayer answered.

I was doing this right. I could feel it. You don't get that quiet, aching kind of surrender unless someone trusts you.

I lay her back and parted her thighs, resting them carefully on the edge of the bed. I moved slowly, kissing her, stroking her, building her up little by little until her whole body felt like it was humming beneath me.

She was wet, responsive, and completely engaged. Her sounds, her movements, everything told me exactly where she was, and I listened. I watched. I read her the way you read someone you've wanted for a long time. And when I found the rhythm she needed, I gave it to her. I didn't stop. I wouldn't stop. Not until she told me to.

Having her legs up by my ears and my face bobbing up and down on her clit as she tensed up, angling towards coming, I put three fingers inside her and was working her spot like it was a video game.

She arched hard. She came beautifully, a full, shuddering wave that rolled through her like it had been waiting to break all night. She clamped around me and bucked hard, and I held her through it, steady and grounded. She nearly broke my nose, and I would have thanked her for it.

She screamed, "Fuck yes!" and grabbed me with her legs to pull me closer to her.

I crawled up and rested on her breasts. But not for long. It would seem there were more courses to be served today.

Then she said it. "I want you to get dressed."

My whole body stilled. "You want me to leave?" I asked warily. I was getting put out like the cat.

She nodded, her voice rough, her eyes glazed but certain. "Not that. Look in the drawer," she said. "Harness. A few options."

I had no hesitation. I stripped off the rest of my clothes and opened the drawer, finding what she'd offered. The harness fits perfectly—snug, strong, and functional. The toy she'd picked was big and realistic. It was still soft but with weight. She lay back, pillow-princess perfect, ready for me.

It was becoming abundantly clear that she was topping from the bottom, and I was getting used to the idea. However, we need a much longer conversation about what is on the menu in the future. But for now, her intentions and my earnest desires were obvious.

I lifted her legs and brought her to the edge of the bed, adjusting until she was right where I wanted her. I moved slowly at first — easing in, teasing, testing her reactions. One hand on her hip, the other rubbing gentle circles on her clit. I watched every breath and every shift in her body, and I followed her cues until I found the rhythm that made her moan.

When I picked up the pace, her body answered me. Again and again. Her hands gripped the sheets. Her breath caught. I hoped she would tell me if I was doing something wrong, but she didn't say a word — just kept meeting me, kept rising to meet the pressure like she wanted to lose herself in it.

And I gave her everything I had. For what felt like fifteen minutes. Maybe more.

And I moved slowly, taking my time, watching every flicker of expression cross her face.

We found the rhythm together—not from instruction but from listening, watching, and knowing what it means to hold someone and not break them, to build them into something trembling, open, and safe.

Whatever else happened that night, I knew this part was real.

I gave her what she needed.

I wasn't watching the clock. I couldn't. I couldn't tear my eyes away from her. She was so beautiful, I kept forgetting what I was doing.

Now and then, I leaned forward and kissed her breast or pressed my body against hers to feel more. It was awkward sometimes. Clumsy. But I didn't care. I just wanted her to feel everything I had to give.

At some point, I shifted. I pulled her legs up and wrapped my arms around her thighs, lifting her slightly and holding more of her weight and moving with more rhythm, more control. Her ass was off the bed, braced by my body. And she moved with me.

She gave me that.

I didn't want to come. Not yet. Not before her.

I needed to wait. I needed her to get there first.

She gave me that. Her body moved in sync with mine, trusting, steady, and open. I could feel it — the way she offered herself without hesitation. It nearly undid me.

So I tried talking to her, my voice dropping low, testing the edge of it.

"Hey, beautiful... are you going to come for me?"

She laughed, breathless. "God, you're so fucking hot. All I want is to watch you come."

That almost did it. I held on anyway, somehow. "Are you close, honey?"

She wasn't. Not quite. I could tell — something in the tension of her breath, the way her hips stuttered instead of surrendering. So I adjusted, turned her gently, and repositioned us until she was in the correct position. I touched her clit softly. I watched her body shift from pleasure to focus to that delicious, teetering edge.

And then, finally, she let go.

So did I. Almost at the same time.

The relief was almost overwhelming, not just physical but emotional. It was like I had passed some unspoken test; she had allowed me to give her something, and she had accepted it.

I took everything off, finally. I tossed the strap to the side and climbed into bed with her. I didn't want to assume, so I waited a second, hovering on the edge like I needed an invitation. But she shifted, curled slightly, and that was all the permission I needed.

I wrapped my arm around her and traced her skin with my fingers. Up and down. Nothing rushed. Nothing more is expected.

Then she started to cry.

It wasn't a sob, exactly. It was just quiet tears, a release. She said softly, "Sorry. That was good."

I smiled into her hair. "You don't have to apologize for that."

Inside, I was screaming. *She liked it. She liked it. Oh my god, she might let me back into her bed someday.*

She turned toward me a little. "I loved how you were talking to me," she said. "That was hot. You're... you're so hot."

I was trying to play it cool. "Thank you for noticing."

Did it sound stupid? Maybe. I didn't care. She was complimenting me. I wasn't going to ruin it.

Then she looked at me and asked, "Did you come?"

"Yeah," I said. "Almost right after you."

"Really?"

"Of course."

And then, because I couldn't help myself, I added, "Would you like me to go down on you again? If you're still hungry, the kitchen's still open."

She laughed and curled closer.

"Again?" she asked.

"In a heartbeat," I said. "Right now, even."

She grinned. "Maybe not right now."

"Just give me a sign," I said. "Raise a finger, a toe, glance in the general direction — whatever you want."

She was quiet for a moment, thoughtful.

"So... what are you into?" she asked.

I looked at her and tried to read her tone. It wasn't small talk. It was real—opening a door.

"At the moment? Anything you want," I said.

She blinked slowly. "That's a lot."

"I mean it."

She sat up slightly, searching my face. "Would you tie me up?"

I held her gaze. "If that's what you want... yes. I would be happy to."

"Do you have any ropes?"

"Not on me," I said. "Do you have handcuffs? Scarves? Belts? Just tell me what you want."

And she paused long enough that I knew she was thinking about it.

And I waited long enough to clarify — I wasn't moving until she gave me the signal.

I kept my voice low, dropping it lower with every step I took toward her. I moved close enough to kiss her ear, to look into her eyes without flinching.

"What is it that you truly want?" I asked.

"Would you like to be out of control? Would you like to be tied up? Do you want me to fuck you again?" My voice was almost a whisper now, softer than my breath. "I can make that happen. I can make any fantasy you have come true. All you have to do is ask. All you have to do is tell me, princess. Tell me what you want... and I will do it."

She shivered in my hands, like nobody had ever talked to her like that before. It was almost too much to be offered everything at once. It was still Sunday morning, technically. We could have been eating bagels and flipping through the crossword puzzle. I would have done that, too. I would have done anything to be near her.

I was happy that I had enough skill, enough instinct, enough hunger to keep her wanting me around.

She was breathless, staring at me, still trying to decide if I was serious.

I was.

"Do you have any rope?" I asked her quietly.

"Do you want to be tied to your beautiful four-poster bed? Would you like to be whipped in the living room? Bent over the shower bench while the water runs down your back? Tied outside in the hammock where only the stars could see you?"

Her breath caught again, just slightly.

"You just have to tell me," I said.

It felt like I was offering her things she hadn't even let herself imagine yet.

And I meant it—every single word.

It was the first time I fully grasped the idea that what she needed was not just a lover or a Domme. She needed service, too—someone who would take away the burden of decision but still cater to every hidden want she had—someone strong enough to let her stop being strong for once.

It was intoxicating. It was dangerous. It was real.

If she had wanted to dress me up and parade me through her world, holding her purse at fundraisers, I would have done it. If she had tried to tie herself to my bed and let me tease her until she forgot her name, I would have done that, too. If she had wanted whips, cuffs, floggers, silk ties hanging from the ceiling beams — I could have made it all happen.

And if I didn't know how yet, I would have figured it out.

There was nothing she could have asked for that I would not have tried to give her.

We lasted longer than I thought we might.

A string of secret parties, gala nights, stolen hours tucked into corners of a city that never really sleeps. We were public in certain rooms, but never *public*. There was always a wall. Always a separation. Always a line I wasn't allowed to cross.

At first, I didn't mind.

In the beginning, it was enough to be near her. To belong to her in private. To be the one she sought when no one was looking. But over time, that wasn't enough for me. I started to want more. I wanted to be seen, not hidden. I wanted her to look at me across a crowded room and smile, yes, but not in secret — I wanted her to claim me.

And she couldn't.

Not because she didn't care, I believe she did, but there were parts of her life that couldn't be shared with me, at least not entirely.

In the end, we let it go gently, the way a candle extinguishes itself when the wick has burned too low to hold a flame. There was no anger, no betrayal. Just... an ending. Quiet. I was done. Finished. I knew it before I said it.

And still, some nights, I miss her.

Nights when I remember how we would come home from some event, half-drunk on champagne and adrenaline, tearing each other's clothes off before we even got up the stairs.

Flirting in public like we had a secret no one could touch.

Kissing in the car before walking into a ballroom like nothing had happened.

In D.C., you could fill every night with something if you wanted to. But some nights, I still hear her voice, no matter how loud the city buzzes.

She couldn't take me into the light; I was never meant to stay in the dark.

14

Continuing Resolution

The Assistant Secretary was young for his age. Or young for the job. Either way, someone at the White House decided that the son of a campaign donor needed some "real-world" experience and had him parachuted into my agency several levels above me.

He was adorable, of course. Sandy blond hair, bright eyes, the kind of boy who looked like he'd just stepped off a polo field or out of a Vineyard Vines catalog. He had that Ivy League polish, or rather, the polish money buys you when your actual GPA doesn't. There was a donation involved. There is always a donation involved.

And for reasons I still can't quite explain, he took a shine to me. And I... well. I didn't mind the attention.

When I first met him, I thought he must be brilliant. Some prodigy. A policy wunderkind who had rocketed through school and landed here to serve the public with intelligence and integrity.

I was wrong. The man was as dumb as a box of rocks.

Charming, yes. But dumb, and desperately uninterested in the actual work. He didn't read the briefing memos. He barely skimmed emails. He took calls from his "bros" during prep meetings, conversations filled with phrases like "dude" and "let's rage Cabo." He wore khakis when he should have been in a suit, called people "man" in front of ambassadors, and managed to remain blissfully indifferent to the fact that his entire team loathed him.

But he was hot. That was the one redeeming factor.

We were in negotiations one day when he tried flirting with me. I told him, flatly, "You have to read the damn documents, asshole."

He looked like I had slapped him. I don't think anyone had ever talked to him like that before.

It wasn't supposed to be romantic. There was no enemies-to-lovers arc happening. But still, there was a spark. Not because we were opposites or fated. Just because I challenged him, and no one else ever had.

Eventually, I cornered him on a trip in Singapore.

"You are an asshole," I told him. "You can't keep floating through this, grinning and making me do all the work. People are starting to notice."

He blinked. "I don't understand it."

That floored me. But okay. Honesty, even if it's simple, is better than fake competence.

"Then I'll explain it," I said. "But you have to be serious. This is actual work. I'll tutor you, but you've got to show up."

I offered to walk him through it, just as I had learned myself. Reading the documents aloud. Diagramming concepts. Building decision trees. If-this-then-that logic. Visual workflows. The stuff that got me through my first year. It wasn't elegant, but it worked.

He agreed.

So later, after everyone had left, I walked into his office to get started.

And he had no pants on.

Underwear. No pants. Just standing there like that was normal.

I didn't flinch. "Put your fucking pants on," I screamed in my dom voice.

He looked shocked. "They've got stains."

"And that's why you're standing here, pantless?" I asked, grabbing his trousers and throwing them at him. "You think that's going to play? You think this doesn't make the front page of the *Washington Post?* Because your staff hates you. This is exactly how they get their revenge."

He laughed, but he was nervous. And I was already imagining the headline.

"Do you want help or not?" I snapped. "Because I'm not going to help you if you're going to act like a creepy little jerk about it."

He raised his hands like I'd accused him of murder. "No, no, it wasn't like that."

"It's never like that," I muttered. "Fine. Whatever."

He tugged on a clean pair of pants — well, technically, some moisture-wicking golf-adjacent workout pants he probably kept in his gym bag. That was the best he could do under pressure. But as he pulled them up, I caught a glance—a real one.

And I'm not too proud to say it — my jaw may have dropped.

Because, frankly? Whatever this man lacked in brains, he was making up for in... proportions below the belt.

It felt cosmically unfair, as if he had made a secret deal with some D.C. back-alley genie. Ivy League legacy admission, political appointment, hot as hell, and *that* too?

Was there no balance in the universe?

But then again, he was as dumb as a post. So the scale tips back eventually.

We sat down. I took the armchair. He slouched on the couch, all long limbs and clueless energy.

"Here's what's going to happen," I said. "You're going to read this aloud to me. Slowly. When you hit something you don't understand, you stop. Then I explain it."

"Okay," he said. And then, quieter, "... about earlier."

"I should have knocked," I said. "And I will from now on."

He nodded. It felt like the closest we were going to get to an apology from either side.

He started reading. His voice was smooth, pleasant, and well-trained. He had no trouble with the words. It was everything *behind* the words that let him down.

These documents were dense. Contextual. Layered. You couldn't just read them, you had to live in them. They were legalistic, profoundly political, and cross-referenced with a five-year diplomatic backstory.

After one paragraph, he stopped.

"What's that part mean?" he asked. "Like, why do we import this stuff? Why can't we just make it here?"

I was smoldering. "Because God put the metal only in this country, and if we want it, so you can have your cell phones and video game consoles, we have to get it from them. And they don't want to give it to us for nothing. That is what we do here. We get people to buy America's stuff and we get the world to sell us their stuff."

"Wow, that is really cool," he said with the enthusiasm of a toddler who has just learned they can fake cry to get mommy's attention.

It took twenty minutes to explain. There were sixty pages left.

"I'm never going to get this," he said eventually, slouching further. "How am I supposed to do this job?"

I gave him a long, level stare. "Well, you're going to have to figure that out. Because the alternative is you go back to the White House and tell them you're not up to the task, and they reassign you to something soft like speechwriting. And I have seen the way you spell, it will not work out well for you."

"I can't do that," he muttered. "I can't ask for help. I need to prove I belong here."

"Then act like it," I said. "Because you are fucking up our entire negotiation posture."

He looked crushed and just wilted. And for a moment, I felt almost sorry for him.

Until I glanced down.

He was hard. Very hard. Visibly hard.

"What the fuck?" I said.

He looked down, then up, sheepish. "I... I like it when you talk to me like that."

Oh no.

Oh no no no.

"This is not happening," I said. "You're my boss's boss's boss. You do not get to make a pass at me."

"I'm not," he said quickly. "I swear. I— I don't know. I like it. The way you talk to me. I like the way it feels when you're in charge."

My brain did a complete restart.

"I'm not your secretary," I said. "I'm not going to sit in your lap, and I'm not going to call you sir. Whatever you think is about to happen, I promise you, it isn't."

He swallowed. "I just meant... I'd let you do anything. You could do anything. You could, I don't know, take it out on me when I screw up. Teach me. Make me better. I'd learn from you. I want to learn from you."

"Oh, so I get you off *and* I have to tutor you?" I said. "Charming. That's a hell of a deal for me."

"I mean," he said, trying a smile, "I'm good at going down on a woman. At least, that's what I've been told."

"Of course you've been told that," I said. "What the hell else are they going to say? Do you think anyone's ever been honest with you in bed?"

"I don't know," he said, still smiling. "But I bet you would be."

And that was the moment. That was when I realized what he liked.

This idiot liked female rage. It got him hard. It made him obedient.

Which meant... I could use that. If I wanted to.

I stood up slowly, took a breath, and looked down at him, shirt rumpled, pants barely disguising how turned on he was.

"You want to be useful?" I asked. "You want to learn something?"

He nodded, eager now. Hopeful. Like a puppy who'd just been told he might get to keep his toy.

"Then listen closely," I said. I walked over and leaned against the desk, arms folded. "This is not a game. I don't play games. I don't do secretaries or interns or any of that creepy Beltway shit. If anything happens here, it's because I decide it happens. And it will never interfere with work. Not once. Are we clear?"

"Yes," he said quickly. "Crystal."

"And you don't get praise for free," I continued. "You don't get hand-holding or soft-spoken encouragement or fake little gold stars. You get told what to do. You do it. And if you earn it — if you show me something worth seeing — then maybe I'll give you what you've been begging for with your fucking eyes since the day you walked into this office."

He blinked. "I've been that obvious?"

"Sweetheart," I said, dry as gin, "you've been obvious since your second meeting. The one where you called an ambassador 'dude' and stared at my legs under the table for forty-five minutes."

His ears flushed bright red. I let him sit in that embarrassment for a moment. Let it sink.

Then I pushed off the desk and walked toward him, slowly, letting my heels click against the tile like punctuation. I stopped in front of him and tilted his chin up with two fingers.

"If you want to serve," I said, in a low, quiet voice, "you'll have to prove you can be of service."

He swallowed.

"Take off your shirt."

He hesitated—just a second. But I raised an eyebrow, and that was enough.

He pulled it over his head clumsily and sat there, waiting, bare-chested and blinking.

"Not bad," I said, pretending to study him. "You've got the build. But that's not the part I'm interested in."

"What... what part are you interested in?"

"The part that listens," I said. "The part that follows the instruction. The part that doesn't need to be told twice."

He nodded.

"Good," I said. "Now get on your knees."

And he did.

Just like that.

"Here's what I want you to do," I said, circling behind him. "I want you to learn this. Read it out loud. Again. Louder."

He hesitated. I didn't.

I pushed him gently but firmly forward, bending him over as he should be. The only place he'd shown any aptitude was from this position — looking at the paperwork he should've read days ago, spine bowed, ready to be corrected.

I didn't have my flogger. Not that day, but I made do with what was available. A paddle from his fraternity, I assume. It worked well enough.

He read. I corrected.

And every time he hesitated, fumbled, or got the clause wrong, I struck—sharp, precise swats across the back of his thighs. Not to injure — just enough to make sure the lesson stuck.

"Reread it," I said. "And this time, get it right."

His voice trembled, but his spine straightened. Focus returned. He was sharper when he was being watched. It was better when there was pressure; it was almost impressive.

Almost.

"You do better with a little stress," I observed. "Good to know."

He didn't answer, but his body gave him away.

It was a strange phenomenon. Every time I raised my voice or tightened the leash of discipline, he came alive. His attention sharpened. His comprehension improved. He retained more in one punishment session than he had in a week of briefings.

Day by day, spanking by spanking, we made progress. He was finally learning. Whether it was fear, adrenaline, or some deeply buried craving to be told he was worthless and still found helpful, I didn't care. It worked.

Eventually, I brought in proper tools. A flogger. A paddle. Real instruments of reinforcement. He never complained. He improved. And he wanted more.

One day, after a particularly grueling session over the final section of the trade agreement, he looked up at me, glassy-eyed and flushed. "If I finish this document," he said, "will you let me go down on you?"

I paused. Looked at him.

"You finish this entire thing," I said, "and I might consider it. But after that, it ends. No more pretending this is a learning strategy. You're not going to string this out just to get spanked."

He looked devastated. Which is how I knew he had been dragging his feet for days.

Still, we got through it. Barely. And when the considerable negotiation came, he sat across from the delegation with a raging hard-on, scarcely able to speak. I carried the entire discussion, stepping in to clean up every half-baked sentence he started.

But he didn't completely humiliate us. That was something.

Afterward, over drinks, he leaned in and murmured, "I got a room at the hotel. I want to take you there."

I raised an eyebrow. "Why should I?"

He made a gesture that was... persuasive.

"Well," I said, "maybe."

It was like lighting a fuse. The second we stepped through that hotel room door, he was all over me. Clothes everywhere. His hands were reverent. His mouth? Focused. Determined. Eager to impress. He worshipped like a man who finally understood what excellence demanded.

I let him—more than once.

When he finally asked for permission to take it further, I laid out the rules. Protection. Control. My pace. My decision. He agreed to all of it, breathless.

He was... overwhelming, at first not just in size, but in intensity. Like this was what he'd been made for — not running offices or heading delegations or attending briefings he couldn't follow, but this. Pleasing someone. Following instructions and occupying space only when permitted.

When he asked me to talk to him — dirty, sharp, degrading — I obliged. I told him he was only good at this; he was a waste of a title, but a damn good ride. That was the only time he showed promise, when I was on top of him, using him like a toy.

He loved it.

I slid off of him, breathless, dazed, not entirely sure if I was going to laugh or scream. His chest was heaving. His eyes were closed. And then

"Oh my god," I said. "Did you just—did you seriously—?"

He blinked. Winced. Then blinked again.

"Oh my God. You came in your *eye*."

He looked at me, like a red-faced pirate, eyes watering. A single trail of something unfortunate was making its way down his cheek like a tragic little tear of regret. I lost it.

He tried to say something. I waved him off. "No. No, let me have this moment. You shot yourself in the face, with enthusiasm."

I wrapped myself in the hotel sheet like some victorious Roman senator and sat back on the bed, watching him try to blink his way to dignity. I wasn't sure I even wanted to see him again. Not because the sex wasn't good — it was alarmingly good — but because I wasn't sure how long I could keep doing mental gymnastics around the fact that he was *pathetic.*

But then, softly, he looked up and said, "Can I give you a massage?"

I raised an eyebrow.

He was already reaching for his bag. "I brought lotion," he said, like it was a peace offering. "Unscented."

I'll admit, I was curious. I'd already experienced the himbo apocalypse. There may have been a glimmer of usefulness left.

To my surprise — and it was a surprise — the massage was good. Not the fake kind men try to pass off as foreplay. He took his time. He focused. Shoulders, spine, hips, thighs. His hands were strong but careful. For once, he didn't talk. He didn't try to show off or make it weird. He just... worked.

When his hands found their way between my legs, it wasn't clumsy. He didn't ask. He didn't fumble. He just read me. He touched me like he was paying attention, like he was trying to learn something, and by the time his fingers were inside me and his thumb started circling just right, I forgot how unimpressive his résumé was.

I came again. Slowly. Fully. Without any of the usual performance or pretense. And just when I thought he might be done — that this might be the part where he rolled over and passed out like a frat boy with a trophy — he flipped me over and went down on me like a man with a mission.

I let him. Gladly.

In the end, that was the trade. He wasn't smart. He wasn't driven. He would never be a policy architect, a thought leader, or a man whose name would appear in any history book worth reading. But he had *one* talent. And I am not above admitting I made full use of it.

We carried on that way — torrid, intense, wildly inappropriate — for a few months. Three, maybe four. I stopped keeping track.

It was clandestine, high-pressure, and stupidly fun. He'd text me from boring meetings asking if I wanted to "review briefs" after hours. I'd make him show up with copies of real documents before I'd let him into my apartment. We had rules. We broke them. He called me ma'am once by accident at a staff happy hour and almost swallowed his tongue.

But of course it couldn't last. These things never do.

He made the mistake of insulting the wrong person in the office — someone who wasn't me, and someone who had actual power. The kind of power that gets people quietly reassigned.

One day, he was there, taking up oxygen and stapling his tie to reports. Next, he was being "transferred for a new opportunity in the private sector." Which is D.C. speak for *you pissed off someone honest, and now you're being shipped off to commercial purgatory to do compliance for a defense contractor in Ohio.*

I didn't even get a real goodbye. Just a voicemail that said, "Hey... I think they're moving me. I wanted to thank you. For, you know...everything."

He was never going to be a forever guy. I knew that. You can't build a life on sexual humiliation and glossary notes. And besides, some genes really shouldn't be passed on.

Still, sometimes I think about him. Not often. But once in a while. Usually, when I'm stuck in another endless policy meeting, someone gets flustered reading aloud.

I think, God, I hope nobody ever lets that man negotiate anything more complicated than a sandwich again.

15

Foreign Affairs

My pussy is so good it almost caused an international incident at the United Nations. I'll explain. As part of my former government job, I traveled frequently, so I apologize for being a little cagey about it. On this one occasion, I was sent to Geneva to help negotiate an international agreement. I was part of the U.S. delegation, and somehow, against all logic and caution, I found myself hopelessly entangled with the head of the French Delegation, a man who was fifteen years older than me. What happened between us was foolish and fabulous.

He was smitten with me, and I with him. I thought it would be some hopeless, meaningless flirtation, one of those fleeting things that burn bright and vanish just as fast, leaving you only with a bittersweet memory.

He picked me out even across a room of nearly seventy negotiators from all over the world at the United Nations headquarters in Geneva. Every time he spoke, he spoke directly to me, not addressing me by name but fixing his gaze so intently on mine that it was as if the rest of the world had gone silent.

I thought he was the most handsome man I'd ever seen. He spoke four or maybe five languages, his voice a dark velvet ribbon wrapping around every word. He was tall, six-three, maybe six-four, with honeyed skin and thick black hair that curled wildly, like he barely tried to tame it. His presence radiated determination, power, and a kind of

old-world grace I hadn't even realized I was starving to experience. I had spent too long dating Peter Pans and Pretty Princesses, and the sight of a grown-up man who knew what he wanted was like a drug.

He was the kind of man you read about in romance novels, the sort of man Erica Jong might have written about, the kind you imagine whisking you away into a wild, lost weekend, driving through the French countryside in a battered convertible, eating sun-warmed, slightly overripe peaches with juice running down your chin, the air thick with the kind of reckless freedom that makes you forget everything you're supposed to remember.

From the first coffee break on the first day of negotiations, he found me, and once he did, he wouldn't stop. He asked me endless questions, ostensibly about the talks, though there was nothing strategic about it; we were on the same side of the issue, French and American positions aligned, so there was nothing to be gained. It was attention for the sake of attention.

Even my lead negotiator, a political appointee way above my pay grade, noticed and tried to wedge himself into the conversation, maybe out of curiosity or concern. My boss, who was also on the trip, saw the heat between us. I would learn much later that both were trying to get me into bed and were jealous. Men can be work sex predators sometimes.

"Are you staying long in Geneva?" he asked me, and I, like a giddy idiot, felt like I had just won some cosmic lottery.

He smelled intoxicating. Some impossible mix of cologne, skin, and danger that made me want to drown in him, lose myself completely.

I wanted to climb him and pull him into me until there was nothing else. It was a level of want so primal and raw that it scared me.

Usually, when the Delegation traveled for international meetings, the American team stuck together, having lunch, dinner, and brunch, constantly moving as a pack. But I was already drifting away from the group, looking to devour a hot French dish for dinner.

We met for coffee, slipped away early from the negotiation tables, and snuck out for lunches that turned into long walks. We ran up the hill near the U.S. mission to the chateaus of old money that have now become restaurants. He knew every hidden room and neglected garden. We kissed under the heavy summer trees, drunk on adrenaline and desire.

Once, he vanished into the UN cafeteria when it was closed and returned, grinning, with a whole bottle of wine. He saw my surprise. "This is Geneva," he said. "Anything is possible here for a price."

Another afternoon, we took his car to the far side of Lake Geneva, where public swimming meant naked swimming, where men and women shed their clothes and caution without a second thought. The water was freezing, but the sun was warm, and we played like children, grabbing at each other, splashing and laughing until our sides ached.

I adored his Frenchness, his lack of apology for pleasure, his effortless sensuality.

My terrible French, battered by years of neglect, bloomed under his teasing corrections; my words tumbled out, clumsy but eager, and he would laugh, kiss my forehead, and beg me, in mock agony, to please stick to English.

We stayed out late, eating raclette-heavy melted cheese, pickles, and wine. We wandered into after-hours clubs hidden beneath the city, places where the night only ended with the dawn, where the imagination and the body could find anything it craved.

One night, just as we were slipping out of the conference hall, still flushed and reckless from stolen touches and whispered promises, we nearly ran straight into a group from the American Delegation. I saw them, a wall of suits and smiling faces, turning the corner, laughing too loudly, scanning the halls for stragglers. My heart stopped cold. For one dizzying second, I thought we were caught, that our secret would spill out under the fluorescent lights like something cheap and sordid. And if they had seen us and put the pieces together, I doubt I would have been fired on the spot, but I might be when we return. It would have been a scandal, a career-ender, the kind of thing that clings to your name forever. But he grabbed my hand, steady and sure, and without a word, pulled me down a side corridor and through a heavy glass door into the garden. The air was cool and sharp with night-blooming flowers; the sky was ink-black overhead. We ducked behind a hedge, breathless and laughing into each other's mouths, invisible again in the darkness.

That night, he took me to a private club where pleasure wasn't just implied; it was mandatory. Just inside, a vendor sold fetish attire of lace and leather; he chose a black crocheted dress for me, so short that everyone could tell if I femscaped. "No bra," he murmured. "No panties. Just this."

He was right. I felt powerful and desirable; judging by the number of looks I received, others did too.

It was a dark room with red pleather sofas, moody lighting, and black carpet, which I imagine was meant to hide the stains. It felt like a room designed to focus all your attention on the little vignettes created for specific pains and pleasures.

We wandered past scenes of raw, unfiltered desire, people bound in intricate shibari, lovers tangled in swings, acts of worship and surrender played out without shame. Women in latex towered over men who licked their boots, grateful to serve. Massages turned into happy endings; anxiety and shame blurred and bled into each other.

He held my hand through it all, steady and sure. He made me feel invincible, like the most beautiful woman in the room. And for one long, wild, perfect night in Geneva, I was.

We started with champagne, brought to us by a slender, submissive woman whose leather collar gleamed under the low lights. She wore nothing except a black apron tied tightly at her waist and a long, silken horsetail plug swaying gracefully behind her with every careful step. When she reached us, she sank to her knees, balancing the tray high above her head, her arms trembling slightly with the effort. Her knees spread wide in practiced submission, and her gaze dutifully locked onto the floor.

I reached out and took my glass. The Ambassador followed, plucking his flute from the tray with the same unhurried grace he applied to everything. Yet the submissive remained frozen in place, arms raised, legs braced, trembling harder now as she waited for something, anything.

Confused, I glanced at the Ambassador and muttered, "Is she going to stay like that?"

He smiled without looking up, the edge of it cutting slowly and deeply.

"She stays," he said quietly, "until you dismiss her."

I blinked, absorbing it.

Human furniture play. I'd seen it before, from a distance, the concept was simple enough, but it was a different matter to find myself part of it, to feel the weight of TrayTable's obedience hanging thick in the air between us.

Leaning forward slightly, I spoke to her in a low, measured voice.

"Would you be permitted to touch yourself?"

The transformation was instant. She gasped audibly, nearly tipping the tray in her eagerness, her voice rushing out in a breathless exhale.

"Yes, Mistress!"

I smiled, slow and deliberate, and whispered against her ear, letting my breath tease the sensitive skin.

"You're useless to me as a table," I said, soft but merciless. "Spread your legs. Show us your pussy. Pleasure yourself until I say otherwise."

Without hesitation, she obeyed, repositioning herself with a raw, beautiful kind of eagerness that should have been thrilling to watch but unsettled me just enough to make me wary.

Something was wrong with the way she moved, a note of brittle desperation clashing with the natural rhythm of surrender. Her eagerness wasn't blooming from joy; it was scraped from fear.

Whoever had trained her, whatever she belonged to, hadn't taught her trust or confidence; they had forced obedience into her. I observed her as she fumbled with herself, asking in a quivering voice, "How should I get off, Mistress? With a vibrator? My fingers?"

That was all the confirmation I needed. A submissive who trusted her dom wouldn't ask that. She would know instinctively how far she could go and how best to serve. Whoever had broken this one had stripped her of that inner knowing, leaving only the hollow need to please and the terror of failing.

It was only a guess, but an educated one. It was instinct, pure and sharp and unshakable, a way of reading the silence between words, the tremor in a held breath, the twitch of a muscle under too much tension.

I trusted my instincts. They rarely lied.

She slipped her hand between her thighs, trembling fingers disappearing under the black apron, and began to touch herself with small, desperate strokes. Her breathing quickened almost immediately, soft little gasps rising in the still, heavy air between us, her body shuddering with each slow, shame-soaked movement. She was beautiful like this, raw, trembling, exposed, and for a moment, I watched, savoring the way her body bowed and writhed, the way pleasure and fear warred across her face.

Heat curled low in my belly, blooming fast and furious as I leaned back in my seat, cradling my glass of champagne like a queen surveying her entertainment. I could feel the Ambassador's eyes on me, watching my reaction with a hunger he didn't bother to hide, and it only made the moment sharper, more electric. The submissive's whimpers grew louder, her hips grinding up into her hand in frantic, needy circles, and I smiled, slow and wicked, letting the pleasure of it all flood through me. God, it was intoxicating, the sight of her desperate devotion, the knowledge that all of it, every sound, every trembling arch of her spine, was happening at my feet, under my gaze.

Ambassador leaned in, his voice molten against my ear.

"Let me," he said, possessively, and I melted.

He knelt between my thighs, pushing my legs open with broad, steady hands, not caring who watched, and plenty was watching now, an eager, growing circle around us like moths drawn to a flame.

He buried his face against me, his tongue finding my clit with a slow, devastating certainty that made my head fall back, my mouth open in a silent, shuddering gasp.

"Oh God," I whispered, not caring anymore who heard, not caring about anything but the way he worshiped me, the way he tasted me like I was something holy.

I clutched the bench behind me, hips trembling, breath ragged, and somewhere in the distance, I knew: this was a performance now, an offering. But it didn't feel like a show. It felt real.

It was shocking, being the one on display, receiving, not giving, not orchestrating every move.

I was usually the one in control, the one directing the scene. But here... I was the center of gravity, the sun they orbited around.

I came hard, the pleasure crashing through me so violently that I slumped back against the bench, dazed and boneless, riding the aftershocks like a wave that wouldn't let me go.

Somewhere in the haze, I heard it, soft, trembling, almost lost under the thundering rush in my ears.

"Please, Mistress..." she whimpered. "Please let me come."

I turned my head lazily, heavy-lidded, studying her where she knelt. Her hands were fisted between her legs, her whole body locked in a desperate arch, every trembling line begging without daring to speak again.

"You want it that badly?" I murmured, my voice a lazy purr, silk dragging over steel.

"Yes, Mistress," she gasped, nearly sobbing. "Please, I need to, please, let me."

I let her squirm for a breath, two, savoring the sight, the way need had hollowed her out, the way obedience had strung her tight like a bow about to snap.

"You've earned it," I said at last, smiling slowly, letting her see the indulgence, the mercy she had bled herself for. I leaned in just enough to make her chase my voice.

"Yes," I whispered, barely more than a sigh. "You may."

The moment the words left my mouth, she shattered.

She broke apart at my feet with a helpless, broken sob, surrendering to the orgasm she had held back for what must have felt like an endless lifetime. Her body convulsed against the ground, gasping and shuddering in that raw, beautiful way only the truly devoted ever managed.

I watched her fall apart, letting it wash over me, feeling another, sweeter wave of satisfaction bloom deep inside my chest.

"Good girl," I murmured when she finally slumped, her forehead pressed against the floor, still panting.

It wasn't entirely clear to me at first, some of it tangled up in the language barrier and the swirling chaos of Geneva's multilingual underground, but slowly, the shape of it emerged.

I smiled, sharp now, blood-warm and fully returned to myself.

Fabulous, I thought, laughing inside. Now I get it.

I reached down, brushing a few strands of hair from her damp forehead, and let my voice dip into the velvet register she wouldn't dare disobey.

"Such a good little slut," I said, each word a caress and a slap at once. "Now go."

And she did, crawling away on trembling hands and knees, grateful tears still shining on her cheeks. I can only hope she brings a positive experience back to her dom, realizing that she could do so much better.

The Ambassador led me to a spanking bench tucked against one wall, a heavy sawhorse setup with metal manacles and thick padded leather, and he offered himself without hesitation, bracing his body against it, presenting himself to me. That fucking ass of his looked beautiful, spread open and ready.

I wasn't sure what you called this kind of bondage equipment in French, but I would bet it has a classy-sounding name that somehow dulls the reality of the brutality inherent in it.

Before I did anything else, I picked up the key and pressed it into his hand, a simple, sacred ritual.

Consent is made visible.

"You hold the key," I whispered, bending low so my breath tickled his ear. "You can free yourself any time."

He nodded, his eyes heavy-lidded with trust.

"You want a warm-up?" I teased, trailing my fingers down the curve of his ass. He smiled and nodded no. Oh, this was going to get intense.

I laughed, a low, delighted sound, and picked up a cane, soft and teasy at first, drawing a shiver from him.

"Then you'd better brace yourself, darling," I whispered, stepping into my power and feeling it wrap around me like smoke. "Because I'm just getting started."

"I want you to mark me," he whispered, bracing himself against the sawhorse, his voice thick with need. "I want to feel it for days."

I crouched low, pressing my lips close to his ear, letting my breath dance against his skin.

"I can't," I murmured. "You know I can't. You're not mine."

He shivered, a tremor rippling down his spine, and I smiled, savoring the ache I was leaving behind.

Instead of blood and bruises, I went for precision, the sting without the scars.

The cane whistled through the air, slicing the silence just before it kissed his feet, sharp and shocking.

The soles were perfect, sensitive, and brutal, but unlikely to leave damage. Pain without evidence. Just the way I needed it.

The crack echoed through the dungeon, pulling a gasp from his throat, and another, and another, as I painted him with careful, clinical strikes.

I crawled up beside him, my body draped over his back, my mouth grazing his ear.

"I know you want more," I whispered, dragging my fingers over the trembling muscles of his arms. "I know you want me to lose control. But I don't. I won't."

He groaned, low and desperate, and I smiled against his neck.

"Do you want more?" I asked.

"Yes, ma Belle," he breathed.

I pressed one more sharp kiss to his shoulder, then helped him off the horse, his cock hard and straining, his balls tight and drawn up, trembling with the effort of holding himself back. We needed something more...extreme.

I didn't chain him to the St. Andrew's cross; I didn't need to. I just pushed him against it, letting him brace himself with nothing but trust and obedience. I picked up the flogger that was there and ready. I scrutinized it to ensure that no studs or nails were in it. I gave it a tap on my leg to see how it felt. Perfect.

The flogger sang across his skin, left, right, figure-eights, building heat, building sensation, building the need between us until the room around us disappeared.

People watched. I knew they were watching. I could feel their eyes, their hunger, their fascination. An American woman, no less, handled a powerful man like he was her toy. And tonight he was mine.

The club was dark and thick with heat, the scent of sweat and sex hanging in the air, and when I finally led him away, deeper into the back rooms, the crowd parted for us like water.

The room we chose was padded, laid with soft mats covered by thin sheets, little pillows scattered around like offerings. It smelled of clean, fresh linen and the faint tang of anticipation.

I pushed him down onto the mat, straddling his hips with easy, unhurried confidence, planting my hands flat on his chest and feeling the wild thunder of his heart beneath my palms. At least two men followed us in, hovering at the threshold, eyes wide and hungry, hoping, praying, to be allowed a part of whatever was about to unfold. I smiled to myself, slow and wicked, savoring the sharp edge of being watched. An audience. Perfect.

Reaching into the shallow pile of toys beside the mat, I found a blindfold, soft, worn leather, still warm from some earlier scene, and without asking, without explaining, I slipped it over his eyes, tying it snugly at the back of his head. He didn't flinch. He didn't even hesitate. His body was already tuned to mine, waiting, trembling with the need to obey.

"Trust me?" I whispered, leaning down just enough that my breath stirred the hair at his temple.

"Yes," he rasped, voice hoarse with devotion, thick with need. I ripped a condom packet open and rolled it on his cock slowly, then mounted him with his hips already straining to buck like a wild horse.

I rode him slow at first, lazy and teasing, savoring every tense shift of muscle under my thighs, every shallow hitch of his breath. His head rolled back, arching his neck like a swan. He put his hands up to touch my hips and then paused. Holding for permission. I guided his hands to my hips silently.

Ten minutes passed, maybe more, a slow dance of friction and denial, and still he didn't come. He held back, grinding his teeth, bracing himself against the storm, and waiting and waiting for my permission. God, I loved him for that, for the iron control he wore like armor and would strip off only for me.

When I was ready, when my pleasure had built into a slow, greedy shudder that rolled through me like thunder, I leaned low, my mouth grazing the shell of his ear.

"Now," I whispered, and shifted my hips in one tiny, devastating roll, pulling his cock deep into me. I used my muscles to latch on and squeeze tight in two-second contractions.

He shuddered with a low, broken cry, his body jerking beneath me, the force of it almost lifting me off him. I had never seen anyone hold back like that, not in a club, a bedroom, or anywhere else. It was porn star control. It was pure, reckless devotion.

As he came down from it, trembling and wrecked, I raked my nails lightly over his chest, slow, deliberate strokes, back and forth, back and forth, leaving red trails on his skin that would sting but not bleed. Just enough to remind him. Just enough to brand him.

He wasn't soft. Not even close.

Without breaking the rhythm, I slid up his body, pulling the condom off with a quick, practiced tug, straddling his face in one fluid movement. He didn't hesitate for a second. He opened his mouth like a man starved, and licked me clean, drinking down every shudder, every last taste of me with a reverence that bordered on worship.

God, he loved it. And God, I loved him for loving it.

A man who adored pussy, who truly worshipped it, who craved it like water and air, was a rare and precious thing, and he devoured me like he could live on nothing else.

Across the room, the two men who had followed us still stood frozen, rock hard, openly stroking themselves, desperate for a glance, a gesture, a word of permission. I looked at them, smiling lazily, indulgently, but shook my head, slow and deliberate.

"No," I said, voice clear and soft and final. "Tonight... he's all mine."

And he was—every last trembling, worshiping, ruined inch of him.

I didn't know if I wanted it. He wasn't really into guys, but he would have done it if I asked, and I wasn't into forcing him. You have to want it. That's the whole point of BDSM. You ask for what you want. You give your consent. You build something tangible from that.

Now, I would have been all in if there had been a woman there. No hesitation. But two men? That wasn't for me. It's not like I hadn't had the option before. More than once. It just never called to me.

We didn't have much in the way of clothes, just the dress I was wearing, so we wandered, bare and wild, through the beds, watching others, taking in the raw, electric thrum of sex and pleasure vibrating through the club.

I ended up getting a massage from one of the submissives kneeling beneath their Mistress. Asking was a ritual in itself—awkward, formal, breathless. I approached the Mistress and asked, in clumsy French, "Madame, puis-je emprunter l'un de vos soumis pour un massage?" She smiled regally and amusedly, nodding her permission.

The submissive led me to a padded table, and I, naked now, gleaming under the low lights. He poured oil over my skin, warm, rich, slick, and his hands moved slowly, reverently, smoothing it across my back, over my ass, down the trembling line of my thighs. It was clinical and sensual all at once, making my whole body hum with awareness.

The Mistress was breathtaking, a woman I might have gladly knelt for, given half the chance, but I stayed with the Ambassador, feeling his heat close to me, anchoring me.

While the submissive massaged me, the scene deepened. They presented me with a large dildo and asked if they could slip it inside me, slow and careful, while I lay sprawled on the table, half-wild already.

The Ambassador pressed a vibrator against my clit, the trembling buzz almost too much, nearly vicious in its precision.

I whimpered softly, trembling on the edge, and he whispered, his voice dark and ragged, "Please, Belle, let me make you come. Please... I want to watch you arch your back for me."

And I did, fast and hard, shuddering around the dildo, bucking against the vibrator.

One of the ever-attentive submissives appeared, offering a towel at precisely the right moment. Subs do come in handy sometimes.

The Ambassador and I kissed afterward, messy and sweet, trading soft, lingering touches, basking in the haze of pleasure. We drank another glass of champagne, naked and still humming from the electricity of it all, before finally pulling our clothes back on, what little we had, and stepping out into the Geneva night.

He dropped me off at my hotel, and I did the Walk of Shame through the lobby, thank God no one from the Delegation saw me, still flushed, still tasting him on my lips, still slick between my thighs.

I crashed into bed, boneless and buzzing, only to be jarred awake four hours later by the hotel alarm screaming at me, in German, no less, and for a few heart-pounding seconds, I thought the world was ending.

I dragged myself into the shower, barely got into my blue power suit, and stumbled into the next day's negotiations, feeling every delicious ache from the night before.

The French Ambassador, my French Ambassador, could not take his eyes off me. Every time I moved, I felt the weight of his gaze settle on my skin, warm and constant, a silent caress that pulled at the center of me, tethering me to him no matter how large the room or how many bodies moved between us.

People were starting to notice; whispers drifted, glances sharpened. They would know soon enough, but for those four or five days in Geneva, it didn't matter. In that small, stolen corner of the world, we were untouchable, wrapped in a fever dream that neither politics nor propriety could penetrate.

We never saw each other again after that week. I never went back. But those days left their mark, carved deep under my skin, some of the most passionate, disarming moments of my life, still vivid, still trembling with heat in my memory.

It was the kind of thing you write novels about, the kind of thing that still makes you wet just remembering it years later, the kind of thing that, no matter how the world spins or who else touches your life, no one can ever take from you.

Romantic tones, always, because it was a fling, but it was the great fling, the once-in-a-lifetime, sexually charged, breathtaking kind. You know the kind I mean: where you know it can't go anywhere, where it won't go anywhere, and somehow, that makes it burn even hotter.

You want what you want, right there in the moment, no future, no promises, just skin and heat and breathless, selfish need. It's as close, I think, as women ever get to having sex like men do, without any expectation that anything will come from it beyond the immediacy of touch and sweat and surrender.

Maybe women really can have sex like men, if we stop thinking about tomorrow, stop thinking about marriage and babies, and all the invisible contracts society writes for us in the back of our minds. Perhaps if we focus solely on what we want, right then and there, that's when we become powerful.

16

After Hours Session

Some nights in Washington, D.C., are so crazy and wild that they defy understanding, comprehension, and, well, a bit of good sense. It was not meant to be that kind of night. I planned to have a simple, lovely, happy hour at Sequoia on the waterfront in Georgetown.

Bathed in the shimmering night view of the Kennedy Center, with its white stone glowing above the Potomac, I stood at the edge of the city's polished charm. A glimpse of the Pentagon sat just beyond the water, squat and silent, and behind it, the corporate towers of Rosslyn pierced the sky, lit up like a second skyline pretending not to be Virginia.

The plan was simple. I was supposed to meet a friend for a drink, exchange a few stories, flirt with the idea of something more, and then call it a night. No drama. No intrigue. Just a clean, easy evening.

I had told myself that before, of course. That it would be just one drink, just one conversation, just one hour away from the mess of real life. I meant it when I said it. But standing there, heels already sinking slightly into the soft earth near the water, I could feel the edges of that plan unraveling. Something about the air was off. Not wrong exactly. Just charged. As if the city had other ideas for me.

The night veered off course almost immediately. Before I could even find my friend or order a drink, I ran into three old acquaintances—men I had known for years, the kind of friends you don't see

often but never quite shake loose from your orbit. All of them were bachelors at least for the night. One wore the role like a uniform, proud and permanent. Another had just slipped the ring off for the evening, looking to lose himself in something far from the routines of home. The third straddled the line, living in that vague gray area between commitment and escape.

They were already half a drink in and fully leaning into the kind of night the darker corners of D.C. tend to offer up to those who know where to look. They weren't wandering aimlessly. They had intention in their eyes, that mix of restlessness and hunger that usually ends in trouble—or at least a story you can't tell in the morning.

I knew them well enough to read the signs. The sharp grins, the casual brushes of the shoulder, the way they moved as a pack, scanning the room like predators dressed in charm. And I also knew what they were hoping for.

So before anything could get twisted, I made one thing perfectly clear. We were not ending up at that gloryhole bar again. I said it directly, with enough force to cut through their smirks. Whatever else they had in mind, that particular chapter was closed for me. I had no interest in repeating that kind of chaos, not tonight.

I've come to understand that among a specific class of Republican men in Washington, there exists a quiet, habitual ambivalence around sexuality. Under the right conditions—usually late at night, after just enough scotch or just enough power has been exercised—they will cross over. Sometimes eagerly. Sometimes often. What begins as a calculated pursuit of a socially acceptable female companion can shift without much resistance into a different kind of encounter entirely, one that takes place in the shadowed corners of a bar, where a man's needs are met with skill and silence. It isn't treated as scandalous, not within the circle that understands how these things work. If anything, it's barely acknowledged. We carry on as if it never happened. Just as you wouldn't mention it if your married friend spent a little too long chatting with a stripper, you don't bring up what happened at the bar because you know it didn't mean anything. Not to them. They weren't exploring identity. They were seeking release, and they went to the person best equipped to provide it. I'm not even convinced it has anything to do with orientation. For many of them, it's simply about access to the most competent mouth behind the hole in the wall.

I had just broken up with my partner and wasn't ready for wise decisions. When they invited me to join them for the evening, a normal person, someone with sense, would have gone home. But, of course, that wasn't me. For someone who understood men this well, you'd think I'd have developed the good sense to run, but no. There I was, a certified expert in male stupidity, voluntarily signing up for extra credit.

One was married; we will call him The Chief of Staff; one was single, the Hill Hound, and one was dating somebody, the Defcon, short for Defense Contractor. No other women around. There are no plans to eat dinner—just oysters, drinks, more drinks, and enough bad decisions to pave the road straight to hell. Technically, we did eat later: sushi and lox artfully arranged on the bodies of naked submissives at a flesh buffet. But that little culinary detour wouldn't happen until much later—after a few more drinks, a few more disasters, and a headlong tumble into the kind of night you only survive by accident.

Old Ebbitt Grill is practically in the shadow of power, just across the street from the Treasury and within spitting distance of the White House. Its walls have absorbed 170 years of secrets and deals, and its tables serve as neutral ground for people who would never admit, even under oath, that they know each other well. We went for oysters, because that's the ritual. You don't just grab drinks at Ebbitt. You order oysters on the half shell, laid out across enormous platters chilled with crushed ice and garnished like trophies. It is part theater, part appetite, and fully a display.

That night, the oysters became something else. The men I was with began turning the act of eating them into a kind of sexual demonstration. No one announced the competition, but it was apparent.

One by one, they picked up oysters—slippery, briny, absurd little things—and did their best to simulate how they'd go down on a woman. What followed was nothing short of a disaster parade. It was a tragic showcase of clumsy, overconfident moves: too much tongue like they were licking a postage stamp in a wind tunnel, too little tongue like they were afraid of being electrocuted, awkward flicks that looked more like seizures than seduction, and suction techniques better suited to eating pudding than pleasure.

Watching them fumble was almost painful. It does matter how you go down on a woman. It's not just "the thought that counts." It's about paying attention—matching her rhythm, building slowly, adjusting when she moans, tenses, or grabs your hair. It's about not being in a damn rush. About making her feel worshiped, not attacked. And what were these guys doing? It was like they were trying to eat Jell-O with chopsticks.

I nearly choked on my drink, watching them. "Jesus. No wonder women fake it," I said.

"Watch closely," holding it steady in my hand like it was the floor of the Senate and I had the mic. I demonstrated the proper technique. Just focus, patience, and rhythm. Gentle pressure. Tongue with intention, not panic. "See that?" I said after I set the shell down. "That's how you do it. Not like you're licking peanut butter off a spoon in the dark. Like you give a damn whether she walks away smiling or wondering what she even married you for."

They were silent for a second, maybe the first time all night. Probably calculating which women in their lives had been faking it out of mercy.

I wiped my fingers clean and reached for my drink. They laughed, assuming I was joking. That was their first mistake. I wasn't.

These were men who played at power all day, who negotiated influence in language coded and polite. But here, with raw oysters and too much martini, they could be crude and direct, at least in gesture.

We talked about sex, about life, about their girlfriends and wives, and their stupid, predictable questions.

"Hey, do you think she means it when she says..." the Hill Hound asked, eyebrows waggling like he thought he was clever.

"Does size matter?" the Defcon asked, glancing around like he didn't want anyone quoting him later. For the record, yes. It does. I don't know why anybody still wonders.

Somehow, I'm always in the rooms where men ask these questions. Maybe I had the bad sense not to leave. Perhaps they sensed I would tell them the truth.

And here's the truth: "Women want a man who's charming, disarming, decent on the dance floor, who opens the car door, who can plan a fucking date, who listens when they talk—and who fucks them." I said, flat as a C-SPAN broadcast, like I was listing the basic criteria for public office.

I set my glass down and let the truth roll out, because someone had to say it. "Women want their oyster eaten. Regularly. Enthusiastically. This is not advanced calculus. You go down on your woman once a day—or at the very least, *offer* to. Whether or not she takes you up on it. Whether or not she returns the favor. It's about wanting to please her. About being generous. About not making her feel like intimacy has to be negotiated like a mortgage rate."

"And while you're at it," I continued, "don't turn the house into a goddamn disaster she has to clean up like your unpaid maid. Don't burn through the bank account like you're trying to speedrun bankruptcy. Don't sleep around like your dick has diplomatic immunity. Offer a back rub. Ask how her day was. Then listen to the answer. That's it. That's the whole formula."

"You do that, and guess what? You don't need a prenup. You don't need a divorce lawyer. You get to see your kids *every single day,* not just alternate weekends while she moves in a massage therapist named Fen into the house you are paying for, who has great arms, owns a French press, plays guitar in a band, and actually listens when she talks about her job."

They blinked at me, wide-eyed and slightly slack-jawed, like a group of interns who just realized the bill they co-sponsored was going to bankrupt their home district. Then came the laughter. Too loud, too forced, the kind of nervous laughter men use when they've been publicly outmaneuvered and don't know how to regain control of the room.

These were men who closed deals on Capitol Hill, who handled billion-dollar contracts, who swaggered into hearings without notes. But put a raw oyster in front of them and ask them to demonstrate basic sexual competence. Suddenly, they turned into overgrown frat boys with performance anxiety and no functional roadmap.

If there had been a grading rubric, none of them would've passed. Frankly, most would have had their licenses revoked.

And the night was still young.

We were chatting away when someone—probably me—had the brilliant idea of going to a strip club.

Not like I needed to pay to see it, usually. But honestly, I've never really understood men's obsession with strip clubs—paying to stare at something you can't touch, like dogs at a butcher shop window. Perhaps it's about the fantasy of being catered to; perhaps it's about outdoing other men, or maybe it's just baked into the DNA of making bad decisions. Whatever it is, men end up in strip clubs at an alarming rate. And so there we were.

Men hanging out together are fucking hysterical. Especially when they're a little drunk. Especially when they think they're kings of the night.

We stumbled into one of the strip clubs that used to scatter D.C.-like landmines—low ceilings, sticky floors, and the faint smell of regret baked into the wallpaper. Many are gone now, paved over by condos and craftmade cocktail bars. Pity. There was some wild shit that used to happen here.

This one was tucked into K Street—not far from the White House, but far enough that plausible deniability stayed intact.

Inside? Packed. Wall-to-wall men, glassy-eyed and craning their necks.

The women? Professionals. Smiling like animatronics, leaning close, walking that fine line between flirtation and absolute disdain.

The guys tried to play it cool.

The Chief bought the first round of overpriced drinks, pretending it was just another networking event.

The Hill Hound was already angling for a private dance like a Labrador with a steak.

The Defcon kept muttering about how "this place used to be better," like a man mourning his lost innocence.

And me? I perched on a barstool by the stage, drinking in hand, watching the farce unfold.

Because here's the thing: Strip clubs aren't noble. They aren't sexy. They're contempt dressed up as chivalry.

The men call them "ladies"—like that makes it better. The women flirt back—like they don't hate every second. Everyone lies to everyone else, and nobody wins.

I wasn't there for solidarity. I was there for the sheer absurdity of it all—and a little bit for the tits and ass.

At one point, The Hill Hound shoved a fat stack of cash into my hand—five hundred dollars in twenties, sweaty from his pocket and his bad ideas. "Time for some girl-on-girl action," he said, grinning like an idiot. "Go tip the dancers. All of them."

So there I was—slipping twenties into my cleavage, laughing as the dancers pulled them out with their wondering hands. It was a power move disguised as a party trick—and the dancers, God bless them, played along like we were all in on the same delicious scam.

For a few shining minutes, it was me they leaned against, me they flirted with, me they wanted to impress. And my boys? They grinned like proud idiots, convinced their money was making it happen, when it was never about the cash.

It was about being the center of gravity in a room full of men who thought they were the sun. The boyfriends who stole from them. The bail money. The dreams that died under the glare of cheap stage lights. There was some strange balance to it all—women who had been scammed by scummy men, now charming money out of upstanding guys willing to pay fifteen bucks for a bottle of cheap beer to stare at naked butts and boobs. A closed loop of bad choices and broken dreams, spinning round and round.

The real city, not the one you see on TV, is filled with noble people doing their best for the poor and the downtrodden. It's also dirty men in dark corners doing savage things out in the open, living in this strange, grinding dichotomy between better angels and lesser demons.

The moment that got the most attention from the men wasn't the dancing. It was when the women cleaned the mirrors and the pole between sets. Watching a half-naked woman scrub a chrome pole? The room went still. Hypnotized. I think it's further proof that men, at their very core, want to see a woman subservient to them—sexually, physically, symbolically. Some deep, grimy part of them lights up at the sight of it, even when they're too drunk or too proud to admit it.

Maybe it was the Madonna-whore complex all rolled into one: The virgin in high heels, cleaning up after herself. Either way, it was fucking weird. And it was only going to get weirder.

One of them—probably the Hill Hound, though it could have been the Defcon, they were both operating at frat house IQ levels—suggested we "find somewhere a little more...adventurous."

We ended up outside a bondage warehouse club. No sign, no lights. Just a thick pulse of bass bleeding through concrete walls. The kind of place you find if you know someone, or if you're dumb enough to think you belong everywhere.

The bouncer gave us a once-over. We were still in business clothes—collars wilted, shoes scuffed—but I dommed my way in with a withering gaze, my husky voice, and a "these aren't the droids you're looking for" Jedi mind trick. I shot the bouncer a "good boy" and walked on through. He must have thought that I had brought three subs along with me to play or display. And maybe I had.

Inside, the air hit like a hammer: sweat, latex, cigarette smoke, cheap vodka. Techno music grinding so hard it rattled your teeth.

Everywhere you looked: leather, chains, latex, ropes. People bound, flogged, gagged. Some suspended from the ceiling like dark, broken angels.

The Chief froze, deer-in-headlights. The Hill Hound looked like he was trying to figure out how to expense this. The Defcon just muttered, "Oh, fuck me," under his breath—and not in the good way.

"Welcome to the church of pain and punishment," I said, deadpan.

We pushed deeper into the crowd. Bodies everywhere. A woman with silver nipple clamps attached to a leash. A man in a dog mask barking for attention. A line of submissives waiting at a whipping station like sinners queuing for communion.

A woman was bound to a Sybian machine, her body jolting and seizing as she was forced into orgasm after orgasm, each one ripped from her at the whim of her Master, while the men standing around her—casual, smug, drunk on their importance—started betting among themselves, wagering whether she was faking it, whether the trembling in her thighs, the shuddering of her breath, the raw, broken moans spilling from her lips were *real enough* to satisfy their pathetic little standards.

I stood there, rooted to the spot, the disgust rising in me almost too fast to catch, because *there's no way she's faking it*—not strapped to that machine, not locked into that brutal setup that was built to obliterate you, not wearing that frontless bra and tight corset with no underwear, her body offered up on display like a dare, knees pressed against the floor, stockings tight against her thighs, high heels still digging into the ground as she writhed, bound and helpless and utterly exposed.

And still, even here, even in a place that was supposed to understand, that was supposed to *know better*, they stood around her like hecklers at a sideshow, jeering, laughing, judging, reducing a woman's pleasure to a performance to be audited, inspected, graded like a fucking term paper, still pretending like her body, her reactions, her raw, involuntary need were somehow theirs to *verify*.

It was exhausting—soul-crushing, bone-deep exhausting—and without saying a word, we moved deeper into the club, into the dark where the lights thinned out and the music thickened like smoke and the scenes around us grew even heavier, more brutal, more broken.

In the back, the space opened up into a grim, electric landscape, with racks lined up like butcher's tables—except instead of carcasses, it was people strapped down, tied, spread, their bodies straining helplessly against cuffs and ropes, skin flushed pink or blooming purple under the relentless strobe lights, every exposed inch of them offered up without apology or shame.

Nobody here was shy; nobody here was pretending; there was no coyness, no hidden blushes, only the raw, ugly, beautiful honesty of people who had long since stopped giving a damn about what anyone thought.

Off to the side, a whipping post had drawn a crowd, a grim little procession of submissives waiting their turn like kids in line for a carnival ride, each volunteer murmuring consent like it was a prayer, sacred and private, even as the crack of leather splitting the air rose louder than the pounding bass and made even the bravest among them flinch.

Behind me, my three bachelors—half-drunk, half-horrified, thoroughly out of their depth—stood frozen like mannequins dropped in the middle of a war zone. One of them, voice barely above a whisper, muttered, "Jesus," while another, clutching his drink like a lifeline, leaned in and asked, "Are we even allowed to be here?"

I smiled, but there was no warmth in it, no mercy, just the hard truth.

"You're allowed," I said. "You're just not interesting."

As if to underline my point, a Domme in six-inch stilettos and a latex corset swept past us, dragging a male submissive on a leash behind her, not even sparing them a glance, and I watched with grim amusement as my guys nearly broke their necks trying not to gawk too obviously.

"Don't stare," I said, almost sweetly. "You'll get slapped."

One of them, still desperate to break the tension, managed a weak joke. "Would it be...bad?"

I shrugged, tossing it off like it didn't matter at all.

"Only if you like being slapped," I said, and by the way they squirmed and shifted on their feet, it was suddenly a very real fucking question.

We wandered through the maze, drifting from scene to scene, and everywhere you looked, someone was flying, someone was sobbing, someone was coming apart at the seams in the best, most brutal, most necessary way possible.

In one corner, a suspension rig spun gently, a woman dangling mid-air like a spider caught in the middle of an impossible, elegant dance, her body wrapped in intricate ropes that glowed electric blue under the UV lights, every line a map of trust and surrender.

In another corner, a medical table gleamed coldly under the strobes, laid out with needles and scalpels and gloves—an altar for those who knew what they were doing, who had negotiated every second of what would happen on that steel surface, because nothing here was for amateurs and nothing, not one goddamn thing, happened by accident.

Everything here ran on trust, on boundaries you couldn't always see. Still, you could feel thrumming in the air like static against your skin, on a thousand silent negotiations you never witnessed but were woven into every breath, every glance, every careful, deliberate touch.

This wasn't chaos, no matter how wild it might have looked to untrained eyes; this was sacred, serious, and deeply, viscerally real—the kind of real you could only find when you stripped away every lie you wore outside these walls.

I caught the guys before they could stumble into a scene mid-play, reaching out without thinking and blocking their path with my arm.

"Rule number one," I said quietly, my voice cutting through the low throb of the music, "you don't interrupt. Ever."

They nodded, their faces pale and wide-eyed, their cheap bravado draining away with every step we took deeper into the real heart of the club.

I stood still for a moment, letting it all wash over me—the weight of it, the truth of it—and I thought about how out there, out on the sidewalks and in the boardrooms and the endless bars lined with glassy-eyed sharks, women performed because they had to, because survival demanded it, because being desired was sometimes the only armor they were allowed to wear.

But in here—in this strange, unholy place—they performed because they chose to, because they trusted, because they had built consent not as an afterthought but as a fortress, brick by brick, every minute, every look, every breath and brush of skin asking and answering without a word.

There was a difference, one you could feel deep in your bones if you were paying attention, if you hadn't already drowned out the part of yourself that still recognized the sound of truth when you heard it, raw and undeniable.

I wasn't sure if my guys felt it—maybe they were too overwhelmed, too busy trying to look casual while everything inside them was screaming—but I thought it, running under my skin like a live wire, cutting through me with a sharpness that left no room for pretending.

Near the back, a massage table was set up—but not for massages. A woman lay splayed open, ankles and wrists bound to the corners, as two masked doms demonstrated the fine art of cunt worship in front of a crowd.

It was the most honest thing I'd seen all night. Raw. Worshipful. No pretense. Just mouths and hands and the kind of attention I had begged those idiots to understand over martinis and oysters.

I elbowed Defcon. "That," I said, pointing, "is what I was talking about."

He stared, slack-jawed.

"Every day," I said.

He nodded slowly, like the universe had just cracked open and handed him the answers to the SATs.

I smiled to myself, sipped my drink, and was about to push deeper into the dark when Hill Hound—God bless his delusional little heart—started inching toward the massage table. You could see him working up the courage, fueled by a lethal cocktail of bravado and bad ideas.

He shuffled up to the nearest dom, a massive man in a leather vest and boots who looked like he could bench press a pickup truck, and mumbled something about "giving it a shot."

The dom raised an eyebrow, looked him up and down like he was appraising a rescue dog, and—after a long, heavy pause—gave a single nod.

Permission granted.

The Hill Hound practically bounced in place.

He knelt awkwardly at the table, hands trembling, before leaning in like a man about to dive headfirst into holy water. And then—God help me—he did his best. It was earnest. It wasn't perfect. It was like watching someone try to read Braille with boxing gloves on.

The dom watched him for about thirty seconds before stepping in, tapping him on the shoulder like a teacher redirecting a clueless kindergartner.

"Slower," the dom said, voice low and amused.

I called over, unable to help myself: "She's not a damn oyster, Hill Hound. Take your time like you want her to come."

The dom shot me a grin, then turned back to Hill Hound with theatrical patience. I walked over, leaned in, and mock-whispered to the dom, "I'm so sorry—my sub is undertrained."

The dom chuckled darkly, grabbed a fistful of Hill Hound's hair, and shoved his face back down between the woman's thighs. "Stick out your fucking tongue," he growled, moving Hill Hound's head in slow, deliberate circles, showing him exactly how it was supposed to be done.

The poor bastard tried to keep up, tongue out, desperate and clumsy, while the crowd howled with laughter and cheers.

I stood back, arms crossed, smiling sweetly. "Extra credit if he survives," I said.

I nearly fell over laughing. Even the submissive on the table—bless her patient, generous soul—smiled around her restraints.

The dom wasn't done. He kept a firm grip on Hill Hound's hair, dragging his face in slow, careful motions. "Flatten your tongue! Broader strokes! Listen to her body, not your damn ego!"

Hill Hound, the cunnilingually challenged, looked like he was about to have a religious experience or a stroke.

The submissive shifted again—this time with a small, genuine moan—and the crowd lost it.

"What kind of man does not know how to eat pussy?" someone bellowed from across the room, nearly choking with laughter.

I elbowed the Defcon. "Two minutes before he passes out or cums in his pants," I said.

The Chief stood frozen like a man watching the Hindenburg crash in slow motion.

The dom turned back to the table, wiping Hill Hound off him like an annoying mosquito.

"Maybe he likes cock better." the dom grabs Hill Houndby the scruff and puts his face to his own crotch. The Hound's face was inches from the leather.

"Is that what you want? To suck my cock?" The Hound just nodded slightly too enthusiastically.

It does look like it might turn into one of those nights afterall.

The dom got into The Hill Hounds' face and said, "Go back to your mistress on your knees."

The floor was grimy, filed with beer and lords knows how much DNA, but the old dog did it. I will be he was very disappointed.

"Next?" he barked at the crowd.

Nobody moved—nobody but me.

I cocked an eyebrow at The Hill Hound — smug, still sweating in his business shoes — and gave him a look that said, "Take notes, asshole." he said, his voice low and certain, a quiet command wrapped in deference.

The Chief shook his head hard, like he could physically reject what was happening. Still, the dom saw it too—the crack in his armor, the surrender blooming just beneath the surface—and before he could pull The Chief forward himself, I stepped toward the massage table, not waiting, not hesitating, already knowing the space was mine to take.

I climbed onto the table smoothly, parting the crowd with a look, and settled between the bound submissive's thighs like I belonged there. I met her eyes—silent permission—and then leaned in.

I started slow. Gentle. Mouth open, tongue flat, moving in a steady rhythm like I was painting her pleasure in deliberate strokes. The crowd that had been laughing and jeering a second ago went silent.

She gasped, arching against her restraints, her body answering before her mind could catch up.

I heard a stunned noise from Hill Hound. Saw the Defcon's jaw drop.

I wasn't performing for them. I was worshipping her, and she responded, writhing, keening, her thighs trembling around my head.

When I finally pulled back, she was wrecked, and the whole room erupted in cheers. I wiped my mouth delicately and smirked at the boys.

"That," I said, "is how it's fucking done."

"You," the Dom growled, pointing directly at The Chief. "Step up."

There's a moment in every man's life when he realizes he is no longer in control of the room.

This was his moment. The Chief hesitated, but only for a breath. Then he stumbled forward like a man walking toward his own execution. The Dom didn't bother asking him what he wanted. He shoved a thick leather collar into the man's trembling hands.

"Put it on," he said.

A low murmur rippled through the crowd, the kind of anticipatory sound that signaled blood in the water. Laughter followed, sharp and growing, as the Dom snatched the collar back, fastened it himself, and yanked the strap tight around The Chief's neck. Then, with a theatrical flourish, he handed the leash directly to me.

"You have to keep your bitch on a leash," he said, smiling widely.

I didn't waste a second. I gave the leash a savage pull, hard enough to send The Chief stumbling forward, collapsing onto his hands and knees. The crowd erupted as my heels struck the concrete in crisp, echoing clicks. Cheers and whistles bounced off the warehouse walls while I led him slowly around the massage table like he was the saddest, most pitiful show dog ever trained.

The submissives clapped louder, boots stomping in rhythm, voices shouting encouragement with cruel delight. Every few steps, I gave the leash another sharp tug, just enough to make his throat catch with a sound that was part gag, part moan. He didn't fight it. He couldn't.

Now he was on the floor, tethered to my grip, transformed into the living contradiction of a man who had built his whole career on control. To him, power had always meant a tailored suit and a firm handshake. But not tonight. Tonight, his power belonged to me.

I dragged him in a deliberate, slow circle, leash held high like a prize ribbon, showing him off to the room. Around the table we went, again and again, as the crowd began to clap in time with the pulse of the music. Their rhythm fueled me, and I leaned into the spectacle, savoring every second.

By the time we completed the second loop, I had him right where I wanted him—on display, humiliated, and obedient. I walked with the proud posture of a champion handler, leash in one hand, high heels carving sharp punctuation into the floor, like I was presenting my finest animal at the Westminster Kennel Club.

And he, poor thing, played his part to perfection.

He crawled behind me, the knees of his tailored suit already torn, his face flushed with humiliation. Each slow shuffle across the cold warehouse floor seemed to scrape away another layer of pride. The submissives lining the walls clapped louder with every movement, stomping their boots in a steady, mocking rhythm until the entire space vibrated like a living heartbeat. The humiliation was the show, and he was giving them exactly what they came for.

I tightened the leash with a swift jerk, forcing him to heel properly at my side. The room quieted just enough to hear the squeak of leather as he dropped into place. I didn't need to raise my voice. "Sit," I said, low and precise. He obeyed instantly, folding to his knees, settling on his heels with his head bowed so wholly and quickly it almost made me laugh.

Good boy.

I paced slowly around him, letting my heels echo deliberately against the concrete. Every step was a reminder of the reversal at play. The power dynamic wasn't subtle, and I had no intention of softening it. I was going to make sure the entire room felt it, savored it, envied it. With a flick of my wrist, I gave the leash a playful tug and turned to face the crowd.

"Now," I said, drawing out the word, letting it drip with the kind of wicked delight that only comes from absolute control, "anyone here got a congressman who needs his cock polished tonight?"

That brought the house down. Laughter cracked like a thunder-clap. Boots pounded the floor again in a wave of appreciation. The warehouse lit up with noise, the kind that vibrated in your bones and made your skin prickle. My Chief flinched, a visible jolt running through him like I had just fired a pistol next to his ear, but he stayed kneeling. His hands curled into fists on his thighs, knuckles white. He was shaking, red-faced, humiliated beyond measure—and still, he didn't move an inch. He knew better. In this city, control is the one actual currency, and tonight, every ounce of it was mine.

I lifted my glass and tipped it in his direction, just enough to let the crowd share the toast. Then I leaned down close enough that only he could hear me, my voice velvet-wrapped steel.

"Now this," I murmured, "is bipartisanship at work."

The Human Buffet

Across the room, the so-called "human buffet" immediately drew the eye. Two women lay stretched out on a low platform, their bodies arranged in a crisscrossed X, each one carefully adorned with sushi and narrow breadsticks that had been balanced with unsettling precision. Some of the breadsticks were placed into their canals, resting there like props in a decadent, slow-moving performance. Sheets of nori covered most of their skin, but not enough to conceal the details from anyone who actually bothered to look. The instructions were clear: guests were encouraged to take food, but only in a precise manner, only with their mouths.

I felt the temptation to reach out, maybe to tease a smile from the nearest woman while lifting a piece of tuna with her tongue from a delicious thigh. But she looked like she was having a good time, and so did the buffet table, which had a big smile on its face. It must have tickled a little bit.

It took me a good ten minutes to get the roe out of her Bermuda triangle and the wasabi out of her cleavage, but I love sushi and don't mind having to wait to eat. I really wanted to go back for seconds, but the men were hogging the buffet as always. I would have loved a chance to dive into her California roll.

The Whipping Station

Toward the far wall, a whipping station had been set up, complete with a padded St. Andrew's Cross and a display of floggers, crops, and whips hung in neat rows. I didn't even have to ask. One of the submissive men offered himself up with almost comical eagerness, and within minutes I had him in place—shirtless, braced, and bound.

He had strong arms and pale skin, which always looked better once marked.

Someone handed me a single-tail and asked if I wanted a demonstration. I smiled and shook my head. "Old fucking hat," I said as I began flicking the handle in tight, practiced figure-eight loops, warming up. I took a few steps back, enough to let the whip break through the air with a clean, piercing crack. It wasn't about pain. Not yet. It was about sound and control. The sudden pop echoed through the space and made several people twitch involuntarily. That was the point.

The man I was whipping was someone recognizable, at least to me, even with the eye mask on. A Republican Congressman. I knew his name, his voting history, the kinds of bills he'd helped sneak through committee. If anyone captured a photo of him like this, stripped and bound under my hand, his reputation would collapse by Monday morning. But here, in this moment, with his arms stretched wide and his eyes fluttering closed in anticipation, none of that mattered. It was, in its own way, beautiful.

There was something undeniably erotic about it. Not because I wanted him. That was never the point. But watching someone powerful yield, even just a little, had its own kind of intoxication. The sight of a man like that brought to heel, restrained and responsive, stirred something darker, sharper. Honestly, the world might be a better place if more Republican men spent their evenings being whipped. It certainly couldn't hurt. We might even get more money for mammograms.

The Kneeling Bench

In another corner of the warehouse, a kneeling bench sat beneath a dim spotlight, its surface covered in black leather that gleamed faintly with polish. A Madame presided over it, her nails long and lacquered like claws, her Mary Widow corset so tight it looked like it could split with one deep breath. Her breasts, clearly enhanced and displayed to theatrical effect, were practically a shelf. She offered sensory play to the crowd in a voice that was both amused and predatory, asking which of the men wanted to kneel.

They all rushed to volunteer.

She started with ostrich feathers, gliding them softly across exposed backs and shoulders, tracing lazy, circular paths over their necks and down their arms. Then she switched to her nails. No warning, no smile. Just slow, deliberate drags down their spines, measured and precise enough to draw gasps. The contrast between soft and sharp made them shiver.

She flirted without shame, asking if any of them wanted to go home with her after. One of mine—the one who still had a girlfriend—turned crimson on the spot. The others laughed it off, hesitating just long enough to remember what waited for them outside this room. A different life. A different set of rules. Another night? Maybe.

The Bootlicker's Station

Just past that setup was what some people called the bootlicker's station. A man sat patiently on the floor, legs folded neatly, offering to lick the boots or shoes of anyone who chose to sit before him. I didn't take him up on it, but I respected the offering. It takes all kinds to make a night like this work. Everyone has their role, their ritual, their need.

Mummification

A few feet away, another scene was unfolding. This one involved mummification. Bodies were being wrapped tightly in layers of Ace bandages, neoprene, or cling film. Some of the subjects squirmed as they were compressed, nerves lighting up under every inch of pressure. Others went still, their muscles relaxing as they gave themselves over to it completely. Whatever the response, one thing remained constant. Each person trusted the hands that wrapped them. Total restraint requires absolute faith.

Bullwhip Guy

Near the DJ booth, a man wielded a massive bullwhip, performing with the kind of showmanship that could stop time. He timed each crack with precision, letting it snap through the air above the crowd in rhythm with the music. Even over the pounding bass, you could hear it clear as day—a sound like a gunshot, sharp enough to slice through every conversation in the room. After each strike, the entire warehouse went quiet for a breath, as if the whip had cast a spell. It was thrilling.

Glory Holes

Near the far end of the room, there stood the glory holes. Of course, there were going to be glory holes. How could we get away from the fact that there were going to be glory holes? Of course, the men wanted to run up to it and put their cocks into that hole and just hope for the best. But what I did notice was that a certain Congressman had just ducked behind the wall right as my three guys ponied up and dropped trowel. It was one of those pleasant little D.C. secrets. You know, there was a strategist from Health and Human Services back there, a twink submissive who must have been on his off night from being the favorite receptacle of the current Speaker of the House. He was a slight guy with a talent for things you would not expect, and no, it definitely was not the one you are thinking of. No, definitely not.

While the boys were busy, I took a turn on the sybian machine while the two lovely ladies from the buffet table licked my nipples. It was a great evening. I obtained both their phone numbers and a date later that week for Whips and Chips.

It hit me then, in the middle of everything. This—this was the real D.C. Not the polished think tanks or the carefully worded press releases. Not the lobbyists crowding happy hours or the interns sprinting down K Street with latte orders and unpaid ambition. The truth lived here, in the dark, where permission and power tangled so tightly you could no longer tell which one came first. Here, people stopped pretending. They found out what they were made of.

I was nearly to the exit when the married Republican, the same one I'd dragged through half the night on a leash, called out to me with one final pitch. He grinned like a man offering a favor.

"Hook up with my wife," he said. "She likes women. We've got an arrangement. Sometimes I sleep with the guys she brings home, too."

He called it civilized.

I gave a short laugh. "Well," I said, "If I were married to you, I would be looking at an off-ramp too." But I didn't take the offer. I wasn't looking to become a tourist attraction in someone else's circus. I wasn't there to be the garnish. I have big main course energy.

It was a shame, really. Because it could have been a spectacular night. In some ways, it still was one of the wildest, most unfiltered nights of my life. But it could have been something else, something more, if I hadn't just been part of the décor. A living prop in someone else's performance.

Later, sitting alone, turning it all over in my head, the pattern started to take shape. What so many of the men really wanted wasn't connection. It wasn't even a woman. What they wanted was to learn how to impress women—while quietly craving each other. They played straight when it was convenient. They chased our attention with polished charm, but never gave us their whole truth. And women like me? We followed the breadcrumbs. We got swept into stories we didn't realize we were only there to decorate. Bystanders in someone else's confession.

It happens all the time in D.C.

Men here—especially the ones tangled in politics and power—live double lives so naturally they don't even flinch. They're buttoned-up husbands during the day, perfectly presentable for campaign photo ops and donor brunches. Then, after dark, they become leather-clad submissives, crawling across the floors of private clubs, begging for discipline they won't admit they need. They pass through strip clubs, sex clubs, gay bars, and hotel hallways like it's part of their commute, while their wives and girlfriends stand somewhere in the background—either oblivious or choosing not to see.

It's not because they're cruel. It's because they're trapped. Somewhere along the line, they bought into the lie that power demands secrecy. Desire can exist here, but only in the shadows. Their vulnerability must always be hidden under layers of control.

Washington feeds on that lie. Here, even the liberals are conservative underneath. Everyone's protecting something—security clearances, campaign futures, family names. You're allowed to be wild, but only in secret. You can want men, or pain, or worship, or humiliation—but only if nobody ever sees you bleed.

It's not a secret—not really. Everyone here knows the signs, even if they pretend not to. Grindr crashes every time the Republican National Convention comes to town. The sex clubs, the real ones, used to run unlisted events and discreet backroom parties, the kind you could only attend if someone vouched for you first. There were always names to protect, reputations to manage. And in this city, the closets weren't just metaphors. They were deep enough to hang coats and hide classified files.

That's how Washington works. You can be anything here—any fantasy, any kink, any version of yourself you're brave enough to touch. But only if you lie well enough to keep it buried.

That night, I didn't just learn something about the men I played with. I knew something about the city itself. About the price of performance. About how easy it is to vanish into the dark when the light feels too dangerous to bear.

Sure, there are gay bars. There are pride flags. There's whatever version of acceptance people think counts as progress.

This town still runs on silence.

There used to be gloryhole bars across the city. Not just one or two tucked away in forgotten alleys, but an entire underground network that thrived in the dark margins of D.C. It was a city alive with sex clubs, themed nights, and places where people could indulge their desires without pretense. You could pay for it, pick it up, or find yourself in the middle of it by accident at three in the morning.

The scene was rough and often unsafe, but it existed with a kind of raw honesty that is hard to find now. That part of the city, once pulsing with possibility, has faded into memory. It is strange, even a little tragic, that a city founded on the ideals of life, liberty, and the pursuit of happiness never truly made space for that kind of freedom. Instead, pleasure had to be hidden. It was denied, suppressed, and driven underground.

Only certain people were ever allowed to express themselves fully. Everyone else had to navigate in the shadows, building a kind of private joy that the world refused to acknowledge. There was no public celebration of desire for them, only secret gatherings and whispered invitations.

To me, that has always felt like a fundamental injustice. People should not have to hide their desires. They should not need coded language or back entrances. Everyone should have the right to be fully themselves, in public, in daylight, without shame. That freedom should not be conditional. It should be perfectly ok if a Republican Congressman wants to suck cock in a dark bar wearing nothing but a pair of leather chaps, a chain mail g-string, and high heels. I support all their rights and their wrongs. Now I just have to get them to support mine.

17

Recess Appointments

There's something about New Year's Eve. We have such ridiculous expectations about how it should go, and it makes us jump into situations and stuff that—well, we probably shouldn't. I've had many of my most chaotic, unhinged, unforgettable nights on New Year's, year after year.

One year, I was dating someone who ended up dating a friend of mine. Then they both just showed up at the same New Year's party. Surprise! One year, a friend of mine got arrested at a party. Another year, I was reeling from a breakup, newly single for the first time in a long time, and it was my first New Year's alone. That one led me to take a risk. A big one. A bad one. Probably one I shouldn't have.

It all started on Craigslist, as all bad ideas often do. There used to be a personals section. It was New Year's, and I didn't want to go to the bar with this other couple because, well, being the third wheel at a lesbian bar on New Year's is *bleak*. My ex and I had broken up just days before, and I felt wrecked. Like emotionally blindsided, dumped-before-the-holidays wrecked. I didn't want to sit at home and feel like a rom-com cliché with a broken heart and a TV dinner.

I did the unthinkable: I answered an ad. A butch woman had posted that she was new in town and looking for something to do on New Year's Eve. She seemed nice enough—Rachel Maddow vibes, but with something else—something more deliberately masculine. I wasn't sure if I liked it or not, but it was New Year's and I just wanted

someone to clink glasses with, maybe dance a little, and go home. Alone. Ideally, buzzed and lightly glittered.

I invited her to join my two friends and me for dinner. We'd eat, we'd head to the lesbian bar, and whatever happened after that...well, we'd see what else the evening might bring. At dinner, things seemed promising enough. We met at the bar at Cafe Berlin and had a cozy table, good conversation, lots of laughs. She was polite, a little stiff, but who isn't awkward on Craigslist Blind Date New Year's?

My friends were charming, the drinks were flowing, and it all had the potential to be perfectly forgettable in the best way.

Then we drove to the bar in my car. She was very skittish like she thought the world might harm her at any minute. Maybe it had before. She laughed awkwardly. Like it took effort.

We found parking, walked into the bar, and it was packed. Glitter everywhere. People hugging, kissing. The DJ was terrible, but that's par for the course.

"Wanna dance?" I asked.

She looked at me like I'd asked her to solve a differential equation.

"I don't dance," she said.

"It's New Year's Eve! C'mon, just one song."

She shook her head. "Not my thing."

Strike one.

We stood at the edge of the dance floor for a bit, sipping drinks. She started doing this weird thing where she tried to correct how I spoke, the way I stood, like I was some unruly schoolgirl who needed guidance.

"You know," she said, looking me up and down, "you really should let someone take the lead sometimes."

I stared at her. "What are you talking about?"

She leaned in close, too close. "I could show you. If you let me."

"Let you what? Stand there and neg me all night, so I will be desperate and worn down enough to let you fuck me. Hell no."

She smiled, smug. "You want this night to go a different way. I can tell."

I am going to go out on a limb here and just ask.

“Do you think that just because I wear the heels that you should be calling all the shots?”

“Well, no. I am just used to being in control,” she retorted.

Finally, she led me out to the dance floor, probably just to shut me up. She tried to take the lead, and I humored her. "Oh, you want to lead?" I said, raising an eyebrow. "Go on then, but so that you know—I'll back-lead you if you fumble."

It didn't go as well as she thought. After a few awkward spins and a mistimed dip, she got flustered and frustrated. And she was already strapped for battle. She was wearing a dildo and holster.

She looked wounded. Like I'd insulted her core identity.

"I thought we had a connection," she muttered.

"You thought wrong," I said. "The only thing you are topping tonight is the dildo you can go fuck yourself with."

She scoffed and turned away.

"Happy New Year, Sprinkels," I added. "That bitch couldn't top ice cream."

"Well," I muttered, watching her retreat into the crowd, then out the door, "this might officially be the worst New Year's Eve ever."

And that, dear reader, was the end of my Craigslist adventure. Honestly? It was a relief. There I was, surrounded by two hundred lesbians, most of whom were single. I could either sulk or salvage the night.

That's when another woman approached me. Gorgeous. Seriously, goddess-level. She wore a pintucked tuxedo shirt, unbuttoned just enough to make me dizzy from peering into her grand canyon. No bra. You could see her perfect little nipples through the pleats. Around her neck was silver jewelry that shimmered under the bar lights. Black jeans, a leather belt, black motorcycle boots. Her hair—fine, tousled, very James Dean—completed the whole androgynous dreamboat vibe. She was tall, lean, and confident.

"You look like you need rescuing," she said, her voice low and playful.

I raised an eyebrow. "I'm not a princess who needs saving," I replied. "But, if you wanted to dance, I wouldn't say no."

She smiled. "My lady."

She extended her hand, and I let her lead me onto the floor. This time, I didn't backlead. She was a solid lead—fluid, strong, attentive. I let myself be swirled around, dipped, and spun. She knew every step. Swing, salsa—like she'd been dancing professionally on the side.

"Where have you been hiding?" I asked between songs.

She laughed. "Just moved here. New in town. I don't know anyone yet."

"You came to this party alone?"

She nodded. "No expectations. I just wanted to dance."

I clinked my glass to hers. "You're already miles ahead of my last date."

We danced, talked, and laughed. She charmed my friends and struck up conversations with acquaintances. Everyone was taken with her, but her attention always circled back to me. She draped her arm casually but protectively over my shoulders when we sat. When I turned to face her, I caught a hint of her scent—something warm, musky, and devastatingly sexy.

"What are you wearing?" I asked, leaning in.

"At the moment? Way too much clothing," she teased.

She chuckled and leaned a bit closer. Her tuxedo shirt gaped at just the right angle, offering me a peek at her bare chest. I swear, she opened an extra button just for me.

At midnight, when the countdown hit zero and the crowd roared, she took my hand, pulled me close, and dipped me. Right there, on the dance floor, in front of everyone. And then she kissed me passionately, thoroughly, like she already knew my favorite flavor of desire.

It was electric.

After feeling dead inside from the breakup—and then getting negged by a Maddow knock-off-date—I suddenly felt alive again. Radiant. Desired.

This woman, this tall androgynous dream, had swooped in like some queer New Year's fairy godparent and turned my shitty night into an absolute fairy tale.

"Happy New Year," she whispered against my lips.

"It is now," I whispered back.

Somehow, I knew everything would be okay after that. I mean, I can't say that it was, but after that kiss on the dance floor, I was like, *more please.* Where can I get more of this?

About an hour after midnight, she walked me out to my car.

"I'd like to call you," she said.

And I wanted to say, *you're not coming home with me tonight?* But I wasn't that bold. I wanted to jump on her. I wanted to jump on her and clasp my thighs around her ears and get on top of her. That was the kind of reaction I had to her.

"I'd like to take you out," she said.

"I'd like you to take me," I blurted. "That sounds lovely. I know a great restaurant—if I can recommend it, if you're interested."

She smiled. "Absolutely."

"Great. Let's make a plan."

We meant to go to dinner later that week. And after we made those arrangements, she gave me this incredibly passionate, ten-minute kiss. She pressed me hard against my car, then opened the door for me—driver's side, like a damn chivalrous noble person—and kissed me again before letting me get in.

I wanted to scream, *No, don't go! Come back here! Let's go home together! Let's make this a night to remember!*

Instead, she asked, "Are you going to watch the Rose Bowl tomorrow?"

"No, but I'll watch the parade. It's on in a few hours. Call me and we'll watch it together."

She laughed. "I'd like that."

And I'm sitting there thinking, *Oh my God. She wants to watch the Rose Parade with me on the phone. Like we're teenagers.*

Red flag? Maybe. Maybe something was going on that I didn't know about. Perhaps she had somebody at home. Maybe she wanted to take it slow. But after that kiss? My God. I was floating.

I woke up for the last half of the Rose Parade, grabbed my phone, and sent her a quick text. She responded almost immediately.

Up and caffeinated, she wrote.

I texted, *Call me?* I padded into the kitchen in my bathrobe and poured a cup of coffee. My phone rang before I even made it back to bed.

"Hey," I said.

"Hey there," she replied, warm and relaxed.

We chatted about the parade. I told her I was originally from Los Angeles, and I had fond memories of attending the parade in person.

"Wait—you went to the Rose Parade?" she asked.

"Once. Total madness," I laughed. "There's a whole story. I'll tell you over dinner."

We didn't get too personal, but I told her I was single and asked if she was. She said yes. Told me she was new in town—moved to D.C. for a job at the National Institutes of Health. She was a scientist. Later that week, we made plans to meet for dinner. I was counting down the hours. She kept texting me cute things throughout the day. Not over-the-top. Nothing overtly sexual. Little stuff.

Did you see the Washington football team pull off a miracle today?

I replied, *That's wonderful. I have no idea what that means.*

She sent, *There's a new Smithsonian exhibit coming up. Maybe we could go?*

I wrote back. *That sounds delightful.*

We hadn't even had our first dinner, and she was already planning date number two. I was smitten.

We met at an adorable Chinese restaurant in Chinatown—somewhere halfway between our places. We ordered dumplings, noodles, and spicy string beans. Our taste in food? Identical. Except I liked mine a bit more spicy. Naturally.

After dinner, we walked back toward the cars, and she turned to me.

"Do you want to come back to my hotel?"

A hotel? I blinked. She was staying at a hotel?

"Absolutely," I said. Because she was hot. And during dinner, she'd been stroking my thigh under the table—not overtly, but enough to make me want to take a bite of her *dumpling*.

As we walked, I hesitated.

"Maybe we should talk before we get too involved. I mean... what are you into?"

"What's your thing?" I asked, watching her expression closely.

She grinned. "I like being told what to do. Then I do it. Then I make you happy."

She said it with such obscene levels of confidence that I was floored—and completely wet at the same time. It was so straightforward.

"Yeah," I breathed. "That sounds great."

She tilted her head thoughtfully. "I can also take control if you'd prefer."

Now that was an interesting proposition.

"What would I prefer this evening?" I mused, theatrically stroking my chin. "I feel like I'm ordering off a menu. Hmm. I'll take fisting for $800, Alex, and a side of shibari straps with a mild flogging."

She laughed. "You're ridiculous."

"So, when you look at me," I asked, still half-joking, "do you feel like bottoming? Or topping?"

"I think you could go either way," she said. "I think both could be interesting."

"Then maybe we do both," I suggested. "We switch. Flip situation. You top one night, I top the next."

"That would be lovely." And just like that, the terms were set. She was staying at the Hinckley Hilton—infamously known for the shooting of President Reagan. It's not called that, of course, but that's what locals call it, because D.C. humor is gruesome

We drove back to her hotel, electricity buzzing between us. The room itself was unremarkable—nice, but plain. Still, we barely noticed. We fell into the room kissing, grabbing at each other like crazed lovebirds.

"This doesn't happen to me that often," I admitted as she pushed me back on the bed.

"Let me lead tonight," she said.

"Abs-a-fucking-lutely," I agreed. "Very Sex and the City, and I am here for it."

She slowly undressed in front of me, holding eye contact the entire time. My pulse thumped in my ears.

She was naked when she crawled up between my legs and grabbed my underwear with her teeth.

"Oh my god," I said, laughing. "That's either going to be adorable or awkward."

She pulled them down delicately, expertly, and it was more charming than I'd expected.

She kissed my thighs, ran her hands up and down my legs, exciting every nerve ending in her wake. She unbuttoned my skirt, and slid it off. Her movements were confident, measured.

"Spread your legs," she murmured, guiding me so that my thighs hung off the edge of the bed.

She went down on me then—slowly, intentionally. Then she stripped off my T-shirt, draping it over my eyes.

"Hold on," I said, slightly alarmed. "Blindfolds this early? Might be a bit much."

She pulled the shirt away immediately. "Okay," she said gently.

Then she took her shirt and tied my wrists with it, looping it loosely through my hands.

"You can get out of this easily," she said. "I want you to feel safe."

"Would you like a gag?" she asked.

"No," I said. "I want to talk. I want to be able to talk dirty. And I want you to talk dirty to me, too."

She smiled. "Yes, Princess." I shivered.

She lay herself over me, pressing her weight into me. Her kisses were soft, languid, trailing from my neck down to my clavicle. She licked my ear so delicately that I shivered.

"You're killing me," I whispered.

"That's the plan," she replied.

She made her way down, slowly, deliberately, until she reached my breasts. She lavished them with her mouth, sucking and licking until I was squirming.

Then she traveled down my stomach, teasing every inch, before diving full-face into me.

She was outstanding.

She slid a finger inside me and tapped my G-spot with precision, all while flicking her tongue across my clit in tiny, rhythmic strokes.

"Fuck," I gasped, my whole body arching. "Do another finger." I can't stop giving orders.

She obliged, then added another. Her mouth and hands worked in tandem like a symphony of pleasure.

"You're gonna make me scream," I warned.

"I hope so," she said, voice muffled against me.

She kept going, building me up, riding each wave with grace and pure hunger.

I know she was duck-billing her hand and at the same time tapping her tongue on my clit, and I came so hard I thought—honestly—I thought I broke her fucking nose. Like, for real. This is it, I thought. I've broken her nose with an orgasm. Emergency room, here we come. Honestly? Not the worst meet-cute ever. I'd already done worse.

I was curious what she'd do next, or what *I* could do next, because I was feeling that itch to retake control. Maybe I'm not a great bottom. I didn't want to starve at the flesh buffet—especially not when I'd already worked up such an appetite.

"I want to go down on you," I told her.

She looked a little surprised. "I don't know..."

"Honey," I said, leaning in close with a wicked smile, "you don't know me. And I don't know you. So let me show you what I can do. Maybe we'll both learn something."

I was riding a wave of cocky confidence. Some women—especially more masculine-presenting ones—aren't into being eaten out, but if you do it with the right tone, the proper reverence, it can be electric. And with her, it was.

She didn't want fingers. I asked, she said no, and I respected that. So I focused. I gave her that slow, rhythmic suction, almost like the way you'd nurse on a blowjob, but with more finesse. Smaller scale, sure, but the same principles apply.

Her whole body shuddered and bucked like she'd been holding that orgasm back for a decade. There's a kind of woman like that—buttoned-up until something cracks open and then, *whoosh,* the dam breaks.

Tuxedo Shirt, as I was now calling her in my mind, collapsed like she'd been hit by divine lightning and shattered in the best possible way. And while she lay there in the wreckage of her climax, I curled up beside her, wrapped us in the blanket, and ran my fingers through her thick black hair.

"That was nice," I whispered. "But we're not done."

She groaned a little. Not in protest—more like in *possibility.* I let her rest a bit longer, but I already knew I was going to ride her until the stars fell out of the sky.

Eventually, she stirred, smiling with that flushed, euphoric look. "So," I said, stretching luxuriously, "I'm happy to bottom. But I'm gonna be in control, alright?"

She raised a brow. "Isn't that topping?"

"Shhh," I said, pressing a finger to her lips. "Let me have my delusions."

She grinned, then pulled out a harness—sleek black leather—and a dildo that looked like a sparkly purple galaxy.

"Oh wow," I said, holding it up. "Is this a unicorn's cock? It's adorable. And weirdly intimidating."

She laughed. "You want to try it?"

"Hell yes. But only if I get to *boss* you while doing it."

"I wouldn't have it any other way," she purred.

I got her settled, strapped in, and worked that starry beast with my mouth. Just the tip, soft and slow. Up and down. Gentle suction. Over and over until the base pounded her clit with every movement. She moaned, trembled, and I knew she was getting close.

"Alright," I said, wiping my mouth. "Your turn. But remember the rules. I'm riding you, and you don't move until I say. Got it?"

"Yes, Belle," she whispered.

I smirked. "God, I love it when you get obedient."

I climbed on top of her, lining myself up. The dildo was thick, but I was wetter than sin and determined to make her squirm. I slid down slowly, inch by inch, until I was seated all the way, hips pressed to hers, legs wrapped tight.

She gasped. "Holy fuck."

"You're not allowed to move," I growled, rotating my hips in tight circles. "Feel that? That's control. That's *me.*"

"Yes, Belle"

I gave her a few slow thrusts, just enough to make her beg. Then I leaned in and whispered against her ear: "Now you can move. But not too fast. We've got all night."

“Feel what it's like for me to ride you. For me to tell you what to do—to make you mine, just for tonight. To have you follow every single command like it's gospel."

She moaned, nodding eagerly. "Yes, Belle. I want to be bad. I want to do bad things to you."

I leaned in, eyes glinting. "Good. Because I like it when you're bad."

I unwrapped my legs and pushed her back into the mattress. Her hands flew to my waist, gripping me like she might never get the chance again. I leaned into it—knees planted wide, thighs flexing, riding her hard. My fingers slid into her mouth. "Suck," I ordered. She did, tongue wrapping eagerly, eyes wide and locked on mine.

Still riding her, I reached between my legs, flicking my clit, working it as the dildo pounded deep. I gasped, body shivering, and came hard, legs trembling, back arched, hips grinding deep against her.

"Do you want more?" I whispered, licking my lips.

She didn't hesitate. "God, yes. Please. Again." "Then get on all fours. You're going to take it. Hard."

I dropped onto the mattress and let her flip me, my ass up in the air, knees apart. I grinned over my shoulder. "Is this what you want? This view? You want to fuck me like this?"

"Yes, Belle," she breathed.

"Good girl. Now show me what you've got."

She slid the harness back on, guided the strap in, and slammed into me with a force that made my entire body jolt forward. I cried out in sheer, breathless pleasure. She grabbed my hips and pounded into me, over and over, each thrust more precise than the last.

"Say my name," I demanded.

"Belle, Oh god, Belle."

"Louder."

"Yes, Belle!"

I was lost in it. Her rhythm, her strength, the way she was nearly growling with every movement. I reached around and rubbed my clit while she fucked me, and it took barely thirty seconds before I exploded around her. My arms gave out. I collapsed onto the mattress, gasping, soaking, stunned.

She eased out slowly and collapsed next to me, wrapping her arms around my waist. "You okay?"

I laughed weakly. "I think you broke me. In the best way."

She smiled and traced a finger down my spine. "You're incredible."

We lay like that for a while—quiet, entangled. Then she got up, stripped down, and gave me a slow back massage, tracing patterns across my skin. She kissed my shoulder, then my neck, and rested her chin on my back.

"You think this is something?" she asked softly.

"I do," I admitted. "I don't know what it is, but it's something."

And for a while, it was. We had a wild, excellent relationship—full of sex, chemistry, and little surprises. She liked to switch sometimes, and we'd trade places, playing at dominance in clubs, teasing each other with little leather whips and ropes. It was never overly serious, but it was fun. Sweet. Sometimes she'd pretend to top me at one of the local kink bars, and I'd snicker into my drink while she gave orders like she was practicing for a play.

But there were cracks. She was still getting settled in a new city. I wasn't really ready for something serious yet. We weren't quite ready, either of us. Our timing was off, even if our chemistry was perfect.

"We should be together," she'd say, brushing hair from my face.

"I know," I'd whisper back. "But now's not the time."

Nine months of blissful chaos. Then she got a job offer out of state—something too good to turn down. And just like that, she was gone.

She packed up her books, her harness, her little whip, and kissed me goodbye at Union Station. There were tears. Mine, not hers. She held it together. She always did.

"I'll miss you," she said.

"Then stay."

She shook her head. "You'll always be the one who showed me how to let go. I'll never forget that."

The train pulled away.

I stood there long after it was gone. D.C. sometimes is just a place for people passing through.

18

Spin Doctor

The Spin Doctor was a political operative of the highest order. The kind of guy who swoops in to save campaigns. His body was fueled by adrenaline, black coffee, beer, and scotch.

"Are you from Boston?" someone once asked him.

"Yeah," he said proudly. "Southie. What of it? Ya bastard." And suddenly, everything about him made sense.

He drank. He swore. He had a dirty joke ready for every moment. He knew everyone. Like, *everyone.* He had an actual Rolodex. He could get anyone on the phone, any time, anywhere. He was the consummate DC guy.

He had a lovely little row house bought with what he proudly called his "ill-gotten political gains." And before I even met him, the warnings started.

"He's a player."

"He'll love you and leave you."

"Don't be fooled by the tuxedo or the charm."

"He'll fuck you once and vanish." And honestly? I wasn't even looking for a boyfriend at that point, so I just shrugged. "Thanks for the PSA, I guess."

One Friday night, after getting sloshed with friends at the beach house, I stumbled back alone around 11:30 p.m., high on Dewey Devils and ready for some bad decisions. I had the full drunken bravado going, wobbling in my heels, beach dress stained with neon-red cocktail

disaster down the front, and I went looking for the Doctor to take for a Spin.

I swung open the door to find him... asleep. Alone.

"Wait a minute," I slurred. "You're alone?"

He sat up, bleary-eyed. "Am I supposed to apologize?"

"No, it's just..." I hiccupped. "Everybody said you're a player. Shouldn't you be... You know, balls deep in some intern or something?"

He laughed. "Wow. Harsh."

I crossed my arms, or tried to. I wobbled instead. "I was *warned* about you."

"And yet," he said, grinning, "here you are."

"I mean, I guess," I muttered.

"Maybe," he said, stretching out like a cat, "I was waiting for you."

"Oh, please," I snorted. "Don't lay it on so thick. I'm drunk, not stupid."

He laughed again and tried to pull me into bed.

"Nope," I said, wobbling backwards. "I'm not looking for some charming disaster. I want a *real...*" hiccup.

"A real disaster?" he said, smugly.

"Don't get cute with me," I shot back. "You don't get a crack at me if you're out here running through every bimbo with a voter registration card."

"Who says I only date voters?" Spin quipped.

"Jeeezuuusus Please tell me the girls you chase are at least old enough to vote," I mumbled with bravado.

I tried to spin with the dramatic flair of an evil soap opera villain, my drink-stained sundress clinging awkwardly, but instead fell into bed with Spin. I crashed into his bed and stayed there until morning.

I woke up and he was gone. I was still in my dress, but my heels were off...somewhere.

I stumbled downstairs, nursing a hangover from hell.

There was coffee. Of course, there was coffee. But no cream. No sugar. Just sludge out of a giant industrial tin someone had bought for five bucks.

"Welcome to political life," someone muttered at me. "If you want good coffee, bring your damn beans."

I poured myself a cup of bitter punishment and shuffled outside.

There was a Spin Doctor. Sitting on the deck and reading *four* newspapers, *The New York Times, The Wall Street Journal, The Financial Times,* and *The Washington Post.*

"Morning, sunshine," he called.

I winced. "Ugh. What time is it?"

"Seven," he chirped. "Plenty of time."

"Plenty of time for *what?*" I groaned, shielding my eyes from the nuclear blast of sunrise.

"To read the papers. Stay informed. You want to be good at your job, don't you?"

"I'm an analyst," I muttered. "Not a political hack like you."

"Still matters," he said, flipping a page. "Besides, crosswords build character."

"Hand me the crossword," I grumbled.

Even hungover, with a migraine trying to tunnel out of my skull, I could still crush a crossword. Spelling, not so much. But riddles and clues? I could do it blindfolded. And that's how I spent my morning: sipping terrible black coffee, squinting into the sun, eviscerating a crossword puzzle, and wondering how the hell I had ended up hungover at the feet of Spin Doctor, King of Political Fuckery.

We did the crossword together, and he was incredibly good at it. I had him write in the answers so I could hide my terrible spelling.

"Hey, what's this one?" he called out.

"Ulysses," I mumbled, and he spelled it perfectly, no hesitation.

We sat there, sipping bad coffee and reading the papers aloud to each other.

"Did you see what so-and-so just did?" he'd ask.

"Since you worked on his campaign," I'd tease, "how's he still breathing?"

He'd volley back, "What do you think this story means?"

"Not much," I'd shrug. "The news coming out is garbage."

We bantered back and forth. Somewhere in that haze of crossword puzzles and political gossip, I could see it happen: he stopped seeing me as just another pretty face. He started seeing me as someone who might matter.

He spent the rest of the day just a few feet away, orbiting me.

"Want to walk down to the water?"

"Want to get in the ocean?"

"Want to walk the beach with me?"

He was every inch the quintessential Boston boyfriend, persistent, loyal for precisely five minutes at a time, endearingly pushy.

By four o'clock, someone yelled, "Is it time for margaritas?" and honestly, yes. Yes, it was.

We usually went straight for Dewey Devils, but even I couldn't stomach another pack of sugar and regret. Margaritas it was. We sat on the balcony, talking, laughing, drinking, watching housemates drift by like clouds.

By midnight, he looked at me and said, "Let's go for a walk on the beach."

"Oh, I've seen this movie before," I said, rolling my eyes.

Still, I went. Of course, I went.

He brought a blanket, like a proper gentleman of sleaze. We walked to the so-called "private beach" in Dewey, where the giant mansions loom and the cops can't bother you. We sat, cuddled up under the stars, listening to the waves.

It was beautiful, I won't lie. Quiet. Moonlight shimmering off the water. Almost no light pollution. It was the kind of setup you dream about.

And the kiss he gave me? Honestly, it was good. Soft. Gentle. The kind of kiss you want to sink into.

But then...

He skipped *everything*.

No slow build, no tracing kisses along my neck, no tender exploration of my body. Nope. He dove *straight* into my underwear like he was a drunk man falling into a well.

"There are a few stops before you get to that destination," I muttered. Did he listen? Of course not.

He proceeded to *miss* my clit entirely, despite it being exactly where it has always been, and started vigorously rubbing the *left side* of my labia like he was trying to start a fire.

If my left lip could have reported him for arson, it would have.

Meanwhile, he tried to maneuver my head southward for a beach blowjob.

"No," I said firmly. "Not happening."

I sat up. "You haven't even made an effort. I'm not giving a sandy-ass blowjob while you rub the wrong place and call it foreplay."

He looked confused. Like genuinely bewildered. He may have gotten this far with other girls who were too polite to correct him. I just was not that impressed.

"I'm going back to the beach house," I said, brushing sand off my dress. "You can stay here and rub your own damn left labia."

"I don't have that." He grabbed his left nut. "But I have this, and you are welcome to rub the left or the right any time you want."

That did it.

"Listen. You're cute. You're adorable. I'm sure women throw their panties at you all the time. I get it. You're used to being worshipped for just existing. But I'm not some desperate little intern hoping for a pat on the head and a disappointing round of sandy sex. I don't need anything from you. I *wanted* something more. Something real. Not clumsy fumbling and misplaced confidence. You talk a big game, but honestly, I don't understand how you *still* can't find the clit. It's not some secret treasure map. It's exactly where your dick is. And I'm damn sure you manage to find *that* just fine. I hope you find it again tonight. Really. Because I'm out of here."

And I walked unceremoniously away, trying to keep my underwear from falling. Spin Doctors sat there looking at the ocean as if they had just been peed on.

The rest of the weekend, he followed me around like a sad puppy.

"Hey, want to go to a game?" he'd ask. "Wizards? Nationals? Orioles?"

He kept pitching sporting events at me like he was trying to win me with baseball caps and cheap beer. And honestly? After that sad beach performance, he should have been pitching *apologies.*

Still, because I am nothing if not occasionally merciful, I agreed to meet him for a drink.

We met at one of the million Capitol Hill bars, low ceilings, sticky floors, older men in khakis yelling about the Fed.

He was charming. Of course, he was.

His stories were incredible, tales of campaigns won and lost, moments of glory on the trail, dirty jokes whispered at the right moment.

I sat there thinking, *'God, you are everything I should want.'* And also: *You couldn't find a clit if it came with a goddamn treasure map.* Both things were true. Welcome to dating in DC.

I mean, Spin Doctor was gorgeous. Rugged. Tall, 6'2". Fit, but not muscle-bound. He had a stomach, just enough to make him look real, not gym-obsessed.

He told me he was approaching campaign season.

"I'll be going away for a while," he said. "But I want to keep in touch. See you whenever I'm back in town."

"That's fine," I said, shrugging. "Open to that. But I'm going to make sure this is something we both *want.*"

He grinned. "I heard you're into domination."

I raised an eyebrow. "Oh? Who did you hear *that* from?"

He gave a little shrug, playing it cool. "Congressman Ma...."

I shushed him. "No names, some fucking discretion."

If you're into that... I'd be into it too."

"Uh-huh," I said, internally rolling my eyes. "Something to look forward to, I guess."

But I was cautious. I wanted control over the situation, over access to me. I needed to know what was going on in that messy, brilliant little brain of his, which wasn't easy, because he was so good at gliding across the surface of every conversation. Slippery as hell. Charm oozes everywhere out of him like an oil spill.

"I'm not gonna be just another item on your checklist," I told him.

He laughed, leaned back, confident as ever. "I'm a bit of a dominant, too," he said. "I'd be interested in trying to dominate you."

I gave him a long, slow once-over.

"You think you can dominate *me?*" I said. "You think that's where this is headed?"

He just grinned, cocky.

I laughed. "Okay, sure, buddy. Good luck with that."

Look, I know within ten seconds whether a man can pull it off. Whether he has that weight, that *gravitas,* that *thing* that makes submission even *possible.* And he didn't have it. Not even close.

I could picture him *up against* a St. Andrew's Cross, flogged senseless, but dominating me? Not in this lifetime.

Many men get it twisted. Every time, these types ended up begging to be tied up and pegged anyway.

"Tied up and pegged" was practically the unofficial motto of half the 'doms' I'd met in DC.

The idea of *domming* a so-called dom like Spin Doctor? That was starting to sound way more interesting than anything he'd offered so far.

Friendship? Sure. Sex? Maybe. Heavy maybe.

He left town for campaign work, somewhere like Philadelphia, and disappeared for about four weeks.

When he was gone, he called.

"Hey," he said. "When I'm back, would you go to a black-tie gala with me?"

In DC, black-tie events are like Starbucks: one on every corner. Fundraisers, charity balls, embassy parties, you name it. Ten or twelve formal dresses in your closet? Normal.

Men have it easy: one tuxedo, a few bow ties, maybe a spare vest. But as a poor government worker, I had to hustle. Vintage stores. Consignment shops. Rental places in Georgetown where you could rent designer dresses like they were library books.

I altered the dresses myself, restitched them, added scarves, gloves, tiaras, jewelry, whatever it took to make them look new.

"Of course I'll go," I told him, thrilled.

It was a fundraiser for the Heart Association, or another alphabet soup non-profit. Didn't matter. It was a big night, and I was excited.

I selected a full-length, red satin dress. Gloves. A massive glass heart pendant I found at a local jeweler. I was ready.

That dress? Definitely couldn't afford it. Bought it anyway. Pulled my hair into some Jackie Kennedy situation, because Boston, right? Thought he might find it attractive.

I wore my best dancing shoes and waited. He picked me up, got us a cab, and we headed to the dance at the Waldorf. The Wilson? Honestly, I can't remember now, some beautiful old hotel.

The venue was lovely. A live band. A small dance floor. Very romantic.

I'm not even sure now how attractive he was... but on the dance floor? He was *incredibly* handsome. He knew how to show off his partner, making her feel delicate and dazzling. Like a prize.

And I did. I felt like that.

When he looked at me, all serious and earnest, and said, "You look beautiful tonight," and kissed me lightly, reverently, on the lips right there on the dance floor?

Yeah. I melted a little.

"You look so incredibly sexy," he whispered, brushing my ear. "I want to take you home tonight."

Oh. Well. Carts *definitely* before horses, but... okay, Spin Doctor. I see you.

We danced all night. I met his friends. We swapped stories. Everyone in DC always has a backlog of crazy stories: the campaign trail, crazy bosses, politicians misbehaving, and trips that went wrong.

My stories weren't bad, traveling a lot back then, but theirs? Legendary.

Someone told a story about chili crabs in Singapore, another about an assistant secretary who landed in the hospital after eating something way too spicy.

I told the infamous "Thailand Brothel Incident," an undersecretary caught in a full-service massage parlor on official government travel. Official government embarrassment. Thankfully, it was an *adult* establishment, small mercies, and not something even worse. Still, they buried him in paperwork and put him on "indefinite leave."

Nothing stays buried in DC forever. Nothing.

After the dance, we hit a nearby bar for a nightcap, very DC: whiskey and cigars.

He flirted shamelessly. Drew little circles on my thigh with his finger. Smiled at me like I was the only woman alive.

Maybe it was the martinis. Maybe the whiskey. Perhaps the way he cleaned up in a tuxedo.

But yeah, I was willing to see where this went.

My apartment was nearby, imagine that. Probably planned it weeks in advance. That's how guys like Spin Doctor work: 42 steps ahead, always thinking about how to get you exactly where they want you. And tonight? He wanted me. I was curious. Curious enough to let him.

And then... reality.

Besides his inability to find the clit, which, frankly, should have disqualified him from ever holding a passport, he was... not as big as I'd imagined. He was packing light.

Curse of the Irish. Below average. Not tragic, just... disappointing.

"Six foot two," I thought bitterly, watching him undress, "and this is what you're packing?"

You can never tell. Sometimes you think you can, but nope. Nature has jokes.

(And for the record? If you want a preview? Look at the nose. That's all I'm saying.)

He stood there, naked, eager, expectant.

I stepped out of my red dress, revealing nothing but a black merry widow and stockings.

He gasped, *audibly,* like I'd just walked out of his wildest fever dream.

I looked at him, calm and deliberate.

"Kneel," I said.

And he did.

Without hesitation. Hands between his knees. Head bowed.

Just like that.

I smiled to myself.

This? This was why he could never dominate me.

This was why it was going to be my way, or he could get the fuck out.

"I know you *wanted* to take control," I said, circling him. "I know that seemed important to you."

He stayed silent.

"But clearly," I continued, "that's not what's happening tonight. Or ever."

I crouched down beside him, making him look up at me.

"You can stay," I said sweetly. "Or you can go. Your choice. But if you stay,"

I grabbed his chin, lightly but firmly.

"You're mine."

He swallowed hard.

"Tonight," I said, "I'm going to flog you. Then you're going to go down on me. And *if* you do a good job, *maybe* I'll let you come."

He nodded.

"Yes," he whispered.

I raised an eyebrow.

"Yes, what?"

He straightened just slightly. Shoulders pulled back. Chin lifted.

"Yes, my beautiful Belle."

I let the pause stretch between us, savoring it.

"Good boy," I said softly, letting it linger just long enough to settle into his chest. "Now. We understand each other."

I rose without hurry and crossed the room to the bed. My heels were silent on the floor, but I knew he could hear the shift in my breath. I knelt, reached beneath the frame, and drew out a large plastic storage bin. The kind most people use for holiday decorations or forgotten sweaters.

But not me.

This one was mine. My private archive. My curated collection of consequences.

I popped the lid and peeled it back slowly, letting the contents speak for themselves. Coiled ropes. Neatly bundled, worn soft with use. Leather cuffs. Cold steel nipple clips. A selection of floggers and paddles arranged by intensity. And the toys, lined up like instruments in a surgical tray, each with its own purpose, each ready to test exactly how much he thought he could handle.

I didn't look at him. Not yet. I wanted the silence to thicken, to settle around him like smoke.

Tonight was going to be instructional. Not just for him. For me too. I wanted to see what he'd do when stripped of the last illusions of control. When obedience stopped being performance and became a reflex. When he stopped trying to impress and started trying to endure.

If Spin Doctor was very, very lucky? He'd make it through the night with his pride just slightly bruised. If he wasn't? He'd learn what it truly meant to beg.

Women are told to be mysterious. But what they really mean is invisible. Quiet. Controlled. Decorated, but not devoured. Pleasing, but not pleasured. We're taught to tuck it all in. Cross our legs. Lower our gaze. Make everything smaller. Neater. Easier to manage.

I'm not interested in being manageable.

I want to be the kind of woman they never recover from. The kind they think about during meetings. The kind they search for years later, drunk and alone, wondering what it was they touched and lost.

Our power isn't in hiding. It's in the reveal. In the precision of showing exactly what *we* choose, when we choose it. It's in making a man ache with hunger and then denying him the bite. Or letting him kneel and taste it straight from the source.

Men should be obsessed with our pleasure. Terrified of it. Grateful for every second they're allowed near it. And if they understood that? If they truly *understood* what a woman sounds like when she comes without apology, what she looks like when she's not shrinking for anyone?

This entire planet would rearrange itself in awe.

The more time a man spends going down on a woman, the better his world gets. The better *her* world gets. That's just the math. Give, and you *get*; a fundamental universal law.

Women, we're not always programmed for it, but let's be real, we tend to lean into giving more naturally than most men do.

Anyway. I took out my big box of toys and dropped it in front of him.

"Choose," I said.

He chose the flogger. Of course he did. They always did.

He picked a dildo, small, three or four inches, skinny. Designed for pegging beginners.

If he thought he was gonna *fuck me* with that?

No, honey.

I was going to fuck *him.* And he was going to *thank* me for it.

I tucked the rest of the box away and covered it. Distraction was the enemy.

I had him stand, bent over, spread-eagled, balls dangling between his thighs, hands gripping the bed frame.

"Here's the deal," I said. "I'm going to start flogging you. If you want me to stop, raise your right hand. I'll stop immediately. No questions asked."

He nodded, wide-eyed. "Okay."

"Okay *what?" I prompted, flicking the flogger against the bedpost for effect.

"Okay, Belle," he corrected.

Accuracy in flogging is everything. And it only comes with a lot of practice.

I started.

Shoulder blades. Butt. Thighs. You can't go too hard on thighs, but you can go hard on someone's ass. Especially when their balls are dangling there, adding a whole extra layer of anxiety, which, honestly, makes it hotter.

"Count for me," I said.

"One... two... three... four," he panted.

Whack, right across his ass. Shoulder blades. Thighs. Repeat.

This went on for almost twenty minutes.

Light touches. Harder ones. Enough to build him up without breaking him down.

At no point did he raise his hand.

Judging by the raging, angry 3 inch hard-on between his legs? Yeah. It was working.

When I decided we were done, I put the flogger down.

"I'm going to stop now," I said.

"Yes, Belle," he breathed.

"Good. Crawl up onto the bed. Lie down."

He scrambled onto the bed, still flushed, still buzzing.

"Now get up on all fours."

I ran my hands all over his body, his back, his thighs, tracing every mark, every welt, every patch of hypersensitive skin I'd awakened. I wanted him to *feel* it. To stay inside it.

"Spread your ass cheeks," I ordered.

He obeyed, lying face down with his arms stretched out above his head.

The position was challenging, bent over the bed, ass up, cock pressed down against the mattress where I *wouldn't* touch it.

Not tonight.

He wasn't going to come because *I* touched him.

If he wanted to come, he would have to *work* for it.

I grabbed the lube. Slathered it generously over the dildo. Over his ass.

"I'm going to start slow," I said, my voice low and calm. "I want you to talk to me. Tell me what you feel."

"Okay," he whispered.

I pressed just the tip of the dildo against him. Waited.

"Tell me," I said.

"It feels good," he said, breathless. "It feels great. But... I'm scared."

"Good," I murmured, pushing in just a little further. "Fear keeps you honest."

I smiled to myself.

He was scared.

And *he should be.*

"It's okay to be scared," I said. "You've never done this before."

"No," he admitted.

"That was a statement, not a question. Listen, you're going to have to say 'stop' really loud and clear if it hurts or if it's too much. Understand?"

"Okay," he nodded.

I got just a little bit in and felt him tense up.

"Do you want me to stop?" I asked.

"No," he said quickly.

"Good."

I moved behind him, reached around, and played with his balls a little. He sighed, *actually sighed,* with passion.

"Open your ass," I said, firm. "Not like you're trying to take a shit. More like you're trying to fart, relax it."

And just like that, it happened.

Slowly, carefully, I slid in. A little deeper. Then a little more. Moving gently, working him open until the whole thing was in. I let it sit there for a minute. Complete skin contact, my breasts pressed against his back, my hair brushing his skin, my stomach pressed to his ass. Making him feel it and making it real.

"I'm going to start moving it now," I whispered. "Is that what you want? You want to get fucked?"

"Yes, Belle, please," he begged.

I started very slowly, halfway in, halfway out. Then a little deeper. Then a little more. Until it was a full stroke. No pulling out. Just rhythmic, controlled thrusts.

He started moving his hips with me.

Every stroke. Matching me.

He came *violently.* So hard he collapsed onto the bed, the dildo pushing out of him as he shuddered and gasped.

I rubbed his back, dragged my nails lightly across his skin, soothing him.

"How do you feel?" I asked.

"Wonderful, Belle," he breathed. "That was... wonderful. Let's do it again soon."

I smiled coldly.

"Oh, sweet boy," I said. "We are *not* fucking done."

I called him by his real name, sharply.

"You're not getting out of this bed until you get *me* off. Twice. You worthless piece of shit. How *dare* you even *think* about getting off without finishing the fucking job"?

He scrambled up onto the bed, flipped over, ready.

No more erection. His dick was practically inverted. Sad. Pathetic.

"You're going to get me off now," I said, climbing up onto the bed, stacking pillows behind me.

"This is your only mission now. If you don't? You're a half-baked loaf of bread. Fucking useless."

He needed a full tutorial.

"Where's the clit?" he asked.

Blank stare.

"You're fucking kidding me," I snapped. "You're going to *learn* today."

I grabbed his head and shoved his face between my thighs.

"Put your fucking tongue *right here*," I ordered, pointing. "And don't you DARE do the goddamn alphabet. That shit doesn't work. That's for amateurs."

He nodded, desperate to please.

"You know why people can't find the clit?" I said. "Because they don't fucking *care*. That's why."

He mumbled something. I ignored it.

"Use your tongue right here, consistent pressure. Gentle circles. You fuck up? I pull your hair. Got it?"

"Yes, Belle," he whispered.

I sat back and let him work.

"Now," I said, grabbing his hand. "Put your finger up inside."

He did, clumsily.

"Do you feel that little rough patch?" I said.

"Yeah," he said, eyes wide.

"That's the G-spot, genius. You treat it like a goddamn treasure map. G marks the fucking spot."

"Okay," he said, nodding frantically.

"You want pussy to be nice to you?" I said. "Then you be nice to the pussy. Jesus Christ."

I lay back, sighing dramatically.

"You're supposed to be this big-time operative. Mr. Campaign Sex God. And you don't even know where the basic buttons are."

I shook my head.

"Honestly? After all the women, and, who knows, maybe men, you've been with? You're *still* this bad?"

He just whimpered.

"I wouldn't let your cock NEAR me until you can manage basic *fucking courtesy.*"

I grinned wickedly.

"And *if* you ever figure it out? The entire female population of DC will throw you a fucking parade."

I pushed his head back down between my thighs.

You have to be able to do four things in this world if you want to call yourself a successful man.

One: throw a punch. Take one, but throw the other.

Two: hold a fucking job.

Three: dance.

And four? Eat pussy.

If you can't eat pussy, I'm sorry, but you're not a het man. You might have the equipment. You might have the paperwork. But spiritually, you're not in the club.

And that's where Spin Doctor failed. Miserably.

He could dance, sure. Throw a punch? Probably. Hold a job? Obviously. But when it came to the most basic of basic skills?

He was lost. Helpless.

"It's not that hard," I snapped. "There's ONE spot. Put your mouth on it. Move your fucking tongue."

But no. He treated it like he was licking a damn ice cream cone.

"You're not a fucking cat," I said, grabbing a handful of his hair. "This isn't a bowl of cream. Although, frankly, it is one of the best things you'll ever taste, so maybe act like it."

He just blinked up at me, clueless.

"You have to get in there," I barked. "Mouth ON, tongue MOVING, sucking a little. This isn't complicated. This is basic bullshit material."

I sat back, furious.

"You don't learn how to do this," I said, "you are NEVER touching any part of my body again."

Was I clear enough? I think I was.

It took a while. It took coaching. It took demonstrations. It took patience, I didn't even know I had.

"Just move your fucking tongue," I hissed. "It's not a goddamn SAT exam. It's a clit. FIND IT."

Eventually, he started to get good at it. Sort of.

"We're gonna need another session," I muttered. "If you even manage to get me off tonight, you're still on probation."

He had the nerve to say, "Well, I could just use a vibrator..."

I sat up straight.

"No," I said coldly. "You're not using a vibrator. "

I looked at him as if he were a freshman intern who had just mixed up 'appropriations' and 'authorization' in a committee hearing.

"You managed to get through four years at Harvard," I said. "Two years in a top political program. You chased after every disappointed undergrad in Massachusetts and every campaign worker you could grab, put a Kennedy to shame, and you STILL can't find a clit?"

He just whimpered.

"You're going to remedial boot camp," I said, yanking his head back down. "You either get me off or you get the fuck out."

"I'm sorry," he mumbled. "I'm trying,"

"Not hard enough."

At this point, I felt like I needed a whiteboard. Diagrams. Maybe a fucking gynecological chart.

Sometimes guys are too good-looking for their own good. They think they don't have to work. Think their pretty faces will carry them forever.

Not with me.

"Every woman deserves to get her pussy eaten," I said. "Every. Single. One."

If he failed? Kick him to the curb. Period.

I tried, though. I *tried.* I had an okay orgasm. It wasn't magic. It wasn't even memorable. It was "fine."

Whatever.

I sat up.

"Next time," I said coolly, "if there *is* a next time, you need to be better. If you can't pass the oral exam, you're not getting anywhere near the rest of me."

He nodded sheepishly, put his clothes back on, and left.

I rolled over, grabbed my vibrator, and finished the job correctly.

"I didn't even want that dick," I muttered, half-laughing at myself.

I stared at the ceiling.

"Geez Louise," I sighed. "Seriously considering flushing this turd down the dating toilet."

That could be it. Maybe all the women before me had figured it out, too.

Maybe that's why he got passed around like bad hors d'oeuvres at an inauguration party. Looked good on the tray, but Nobody wanted it once they got a taste.

Two weeks later, he was back.

Campaign trail. Poughkeepsie. Ohio. Wherever the fuck.

And me? I wasn't exactly chasing him. After that dismal performance? Let's say my enthusiasm had cooled.

But part of me thought: *Maybe he could be trained.*

Like a big, dumb golden retriever.

Maybe.

He called. We made plans. We went to a glorious dinner with his friends, this big, loud, hilarious group swapping political war stories at one of the few wood-paneled steak houses for politicos.

And for a little while?

It felt easy. It felt fun.

It felt almost like it could be something.

Almost.

We even smoked cigars together sometimes, like real DC types. I know, I know, it's tacky, it's smelly, it's gross, but every so often he liked a cigar. And once, I even brought him some back from Paris.

No, not *those* cigars. I had the yellow bands taken off, discretion, you know.

We'd go outside, light up, drink whiskey, so very Old DC. So very "power player in a bad suit." And yeah, I humored him.

One afternoon, I asked, "You coming over tonight?"

"Yeah," he said. "I'd like to."

"Good," I said. "Have you been practicing? Have you been reading up?"

"Yes," he said quickly. "Yes, Belle."

"Good," I said. "Because it's time to prove it."

When he got to my place, I sat down on the sofa, threw my legs open, no underwear, and said, "Okay. Show me what you can do."

He moved the coffee table out of the way and crawled over.

And... honestly? It wasn't that much improved.

He managed to *find* the clit this time, which, sure, was a small victory. He didn't hurt me as much when he tried to finger me. Progress.

Did he find the G-spot? No.

"Look," I said, exasperated. "This isn't going to work if you can't get this right, after *multiple* demonstrations."

I gave him the full tour again, as if it were a field trip.

"Lick *here.* Nowhere else."

"Keep pressure. Gentle but steady."

"Give me *suction.*"

"Finger *inside,* curl it slightly."

"Circles, tap-tap-tap right on the G-spot. When you're licking my clit."

"You do those two things together? You'll get a woman off *every single fucking time.*"

I sat back.

"If you don't, it's *your fault,*" I said. "Not hers. Yours."

He looked overwhelmed. Good. He should be.

Eventually, he managed to eke out a small orgasm for me that barely raised its hand at attendance.

He pulled away at the worst moment, just when he should have doubled down.

And I knew.

This? It wasn't going to work.

"All right," I said, sighing. "Let's just get on the bed."

I climbed on top of him, thinking, *Maybe there's some redeeming quality here. Maybe.*

He was hard. That was something.

As I mentioned before, there wasn't *much* there. It was fine. Utility-grade dick. It'll do the job, like that. Like renting a U-Haul when you needed a moving company.

I've seen two guys with actual micro-penises. That's another story for another time.

But Spin Doctor? Just... smaller than average. Which was *surprising.*

I rode him. Rocked back and forth. Made circles with my hips.

And... nothing.

It wasn't happening.

I whispered in his ear, "Do you like this? Do you like the feel of my cunt on you?"

"Absolutely," he said immediately.

"You're not responding," I said, grinding down. "I want you to *respond.*"

He tried. Half-heartedly.

And it hit me like a cold wave.

Women are told our whole lives not to fake it. But men? Nobody tells *them* not to fake it. Nobody tells *them* to try harder.

"Fake it," I hissed. "Tell me you like it. Get into it."

He did his best.

I fingered my clit and got myself off while riding him because, well, someone had to.

I climbed off, rolled away, and sighed heavily.

"I just don't see a future for us," I said to the ceiling.

I took a shower. Didn't care if he was still there when I got out.

When I got out, he was still sitting there, sheepish.

"I disappointed you," he said.

"Yeah," I said bluntly.

"I'll try harder next time," he said hopefully.

"Next time?" I said, tilting my head.

For the next year and a half, he tried everything he could to get back into my bed.

Texts. Calls. Invitations. Dinner plans.

As if he were going to improve magically.

Or bigger.

Or, God help me, both.

You know, look, if a guy's got a small dick, that's not a problem.

If a guy's got a small dick *and* a bad attitude? That's a whole different story.

Like, if you've got a small dick, you better have some fucking skills. You'd better be *excellent* at something else. You better be great at eating pussy, because if you're good at it? She won't even care.

I was fine with the dick. It wasn't the size.

It was everything else.

He wasn't good at it. He wasn't good at fingering. He wasn't good at communicating. He wasn't good at *me.*

At some point, you just sit there and think: "Why am I doing this? Why am I putting up with this when there's fresh dick in the city?"

So that's what I did. I went and got myself some fresh dick.

He tried to get me back into bed. A lot. Thirty times. Maybe forty.

He even tried real dates, movies, dinners, the whole nine yards.

"I've gotten better," he said.

Spoiler alert: he hadn't.

I gave it one more try. Nope. Still bad. Still sad.

I started thinking maybe he was gay. Perhaps he wanted something more extreme. Maybe he was just confused.

But honestly? If you can't communicate what you want, you don't get what you want. Simple.

But he never really said it out loud. Never asked for it. Never made it a thing.

We even went to that lesbian Mexican restaurant down at Rehoboth Beach. Had a grand old time, margaritas, patio laughs, total vibe.

When I stumbled back from the bathroom, half-drunk, and walked into a wall of lesbians at the bar?

I thought, "Oh. This looks like a hell of a lot more fun than what I'm doing right now."

Maybe we were always just friends. If he'd played his cards right, we could have had some real fun.

But he didn't have any cards to play.

I couldn't let him near anyone else I cared about.

We drifted apart. But those first heady days, the dinners, the drives to the beach, the funny jokes, the shared newspapers, that was the kind of relationship I wanted. It's a shame the sex part never worked out.

19

Third Party Candidate

That awkward moment when you realize you're dating a couple accidentally. He asked me out. I said yes. Seemed simple enough. Then she found out. Then he suggested we all sleep together, because apparently, group sex fixes everything. But unless I miss my guess, she was the one who actually wanted to sleep with me. He was just handling recruitment. At that point, do you have a husband or do you have a pimp?

I started wondering if this was just a case of a girl who did not want to come out of the closet. There are a lot of advantages to staying in. You get to keep your opposite-sex marriage, avoid disappointing your family, and still do whatever you want on the side. If your husband is in on it, even better. It is a very 1950s setup. She wants to look respectable. She stays closeted. They both receive Social Security benefits and matching luggage. So which is it? Is he a philanderer, or is he a full-time recruiter for his wife's secret sex life?

They were what we'd now call poly or open. It was a surprise to me in every possible way.

I met this charming guy, and he asked me out to dinner. We went to a café in Adams Morgan, had a lovely meal, then went back to my place to watch movies, cuddle, and snuggle. He laughed at all my jokes. It was sweet. He left in the wee hours, no sex, just chemistry. He promised to follow up later that week. I was thrilled.

"Cool," I said, grinning.

He was part of my beach house share. So I went out that weekend expecting to see him, but he wasn't there.

Instead, there was this girl.

"You know that's his girlfriend, right?" one of my housemates whispered.

"His what?!"

"Long-term girlfriend. They've been together forever."

Cue instant mortification.

"Nobody told me he had a girlfriend," I hissed. "He didn't mention it. At all."

Nobody had sat me down to explain that they were in an open relationship. This was something they did. Often.

And yes, I was smitten with him. But I was **very** smitten with her.

Over the years, I had kept seeing them, but only as friends, until one night at the beach house when she was asleep on the floor, and I was in bed. He crawled into bed next to me and tried to initiate something.

"Dude," I whispered, "she's right there on the floor. How could you disrespect her like that?"

He blinked. "She wouldn't mind."

"I mind," I shot back. "Not happening."

Another time, I bumped into her in the hallway in the middle of the night.

"Hey," she whispered, surprised.

"Hey," I replied.

Then she kissed me.

"Oh," I said, breathless. "Wait... yes. More of this. Please."

I pressed her against the hallway wall and we made out, barely containing ourselves while twenty people snored nearby.

"Privacy," I muttered.

"Shower," she whispered.

We snuck out to the beach shower, one of those outdoor rinse-off stalls, and turned on the water. She was tall, with chestnut-colored skin, curls that fell like poetry, and the kind of athletic build sculpted from joy and boxing classes.

We soaped each other down, giggling, breathless. I went down on her first. Then she dropped to her knees and returned the favor.

"I want more," I gasped.

We didn't have toys or lube, but I tried to finger her anyway. Ambitious, sure, but partial credit for effort, right?

She was soaked, a result of the combination of water and her body heat. I slipped two fingers into her canal, moving slowly, deliberately. She straddled me as I sat, and her breasts pressed into my face while my hand remained inside her. She rocked back and forth, moaning softly.

"God, you're beautiful," I whispered.

She moved like water. I could have stayed there forever, surrounded by heat and steam and scent. It was dizzying. Electric. We both came, again, before tiptoeing back inside and crashing together on the couch.

She was gone in the morning, back in his bed.

I didn't know what would happen next. Would we talk about it? Pretend it didn't happen? I was exhausted, stunned, and buzzing with energy.

But I knew one thing for sure: I wanted more.

Saturday night, we all went out dancing. Too much drinking, too many bad decisions. I was burnt out and headed back early.

Later, they came home, both of them.

He sat in the corner, in what I mentally dubbed "the cuck chair."

She walked over to me, undressed slowly, and lay beside me.

"Okay," I said, sitting up. "Ground rules. I don't do performances. If I'm here, I'm not the one being managed."

She grinned, leaned in, and kissed me. Deeply.

We made out as he sat silently across the room, rock hard and mesmerized.

"I can do this," I murmured, tugging her closer. "But I get *her*. Not him." And that night, I did.

He got a show, sure, but I still didn't know where this was going.

I had her flat on her back, legs in the air, within minutes, because that's just how this girl rolls. She was incredibly sensual, passionate, and animated, always eager to try something new, and would often stand and bend over. She wanted it all.

This time, I managed to finger her fully. And she screamed when she came, loud and raw. It was explosive.

After that, she wanted to go down on me.

"Sure," I said, breathless. "Go ahead. Take your time."

She was incredibly skilled, slow, sensual, and filthy in the best way. She talked dirty with this whispery, delicious confidence, and then she did something with her tongue, this wet, rhythmic sound that made me squirm.

"Oh my god," I gasped. "What even *was* that?"

She just smirked and kept going until I came hard, nearly crushing her head between my thighs.

Afterward, I lay there panting. "Okay. So in this little game you two play... what usually happens next?"

He sat across the room, still watching. Quiet. Expectant.

"I mean, I'm curious," I said, "but also... I'm not sure how much more I want to do. I want to hear what's on the menu, sure, but I'm not guaranteeing I'm ordering off of it."

I propped myself up on my elbow and looked at both of them.

"Up until now," I continued, "you two have been in control. And that's not my thing. I like being in control. I like knowing what's going to happen. I enjoy making people happy and helping them feel better. If we're going to continue, the script needs to change. Someone gets tied up tonight, or we all go to sleep."

They exchanged a glance. I had a feeling I knew how it would go. However, I had limits, and it was time we discussed them.

"I'm not the passive one here," I added. "And I'm not the one sitting in the cuck chair. So... let's talk." And we did.

They were down to play. Always looking for that elusive bisexual unicorn, I guess, in swinger-speak. They'd done this before, clearly.

"Look," I said, "main character energy only. If we're doing this, it's going to be on my terms."

She laughed. "God, I love that."

He smiled. "Yes, ma'am."

They were both spectacular. Gorgeous. Magnetic. And while I was open to a shared experience, I also wanted some control of my own.

"The idea of tying you two together," I said slowly, "and fucking you both? That's kind of hot."

They didn't object.

Later that night, I let him go down on me.

"Damn," I muttered. "You're good at that."

He looked up, eager. "Can I?"

"No," I cut him off. "You don't just get to fuck me. That's not how it works."

I stared him down. "This may be a regular game for you two, but you haven't met someone like me before. So maybe, just maybe, it's time you lay back and enjoy *my* show."

I gave him a choice. He could jerk off quietly in the corner chair. She could get him off with her mouth. Or she could fuck him, *but* if she did, she'd have to go down on me at the same time.

They chose the latter. As he fucked her hard, God, he went at it like a jackhammer, she buried her face between my thighs. I was turned on. The whole dynamic was incredibly intense.

He came first, obviously. I mean, how long could you last watching your wife go down on another woman while you're inside her?

When he tried to finish me off, I stopped him.

"No," I said. "She can do it." And she did.

When we were done, I sat up and looked at them both.

"We'll have a longer conversation sometime soon," I said. "But that's it for tonight. Thank you."

We drove back to the city together. It was... awkward.

I thought we'd feel closer after the experience, but instead, I felt like an interloper.

This isn't a relationship, I thought. *This is an adventure. A rom-com detour, not a destination.*

And it wasn't great. I knew that.

We didn't talk for nearly a week. Then she called.

"Want to meet for drinks?" she asked.

I hesitated.

"Fine," I said. "Let's talk."

"Yep. Just you and me?"

She smiled. "Yeah. Just us."

I liked the sound of that.

We met at this super fancy bar on Pennsylvania Avenue, The Prime Rib. It had dark wood paneling, brass fixtures, and that old-school elegance all the Hill types still adore. She showed up in a soft lavender dress, low neckline, high hem, and no stockings. That alone was wild for D.C. But on her? It worked. Beautiful jewelry, heels, hair down, glowing. She looked incredible.

She greeted me at the bar and handed me a dirty martini.

"Classic," I said, raising it. "Thanks."

She smiled. "One of my favorites."

We sat there for a while, chatting. Travel. Work. Mutual friends. Nothing overtly sexual. It felt like a first date, or even less intense. But under all that calm? She radiated heat. She was *smoking*. Steam practically poured off her.

After we shared an appetizer, I leaned in a little. "So... what's on the menu? With you and your boyfriend, I mean. What's the deal?"

She didn't flinch. "Well, we both like girls. We like each other. We like threesomes. Sometimes we have more casual setups, other times more ongoing ones."

"Why didn't you say something sooner?" I asked.

She shrugged. "Discretion. He has a clearance. I do too. Can't risk blackmail. It's D.C. You get it."

I nodded. I did. But I also wanted to know where *this* night was going.

A few drinks in, I couldn't help myself. "So... you want to come back to my place?"

She didn't hesitate. "Absolutely."

We grabbed a cab. She was on me immediately, hands on my thigh, whispering in my ear.

"I'm not wearing any underwear," she breathed.

"Is that right?" I teased, sliding my hand slowly up her leg. "Mind if I check?"

She gasped softly. "Please do."

And yes, she was dripping wet. I kept teasing her all the way home. We ran into my building, laughing, kissing, giddy. In the elevator, I pressed her against the back wall and slid my hand under her dress, right to her clit. She moaned.

"God, you're soaked," I whispered.

"I've been thinking about this all night."

We made it to my top-floor apartment, praying that no one had gotten on the elevator. I didn't want witnesses. I wanted *her* to come in the elevator, but I didn't want *anyone* else to show up.

Inside, it was go time. I had everything: restraints, rope, wax, whips, toys, whatever she was into, I had it. My four-poster bed was made for this.

"Do you trust me?" I asked.

She nodded, unzipping the dress herself. "Show me what you've got."

"I want to tie you up."

"Yes."

"I want to drip wax on you."

She hesitated. "Never done that before."

"Well, tonight's your night. Cross it off the bucket list."

"And what's your goal for me tonight?" she teased.

"Five orgasms."

"Five?!"

"Yep. Only one with the vibrator. The rest? Freestyle."

She grinned. "Hot."

"Very."

I tied her to the bedposts with my favorite silk rope. She looked unreal, red ropes against that beautiful skin, open, trusting, glowing. Her eyes locked on mine.

"Ready?" I asked.

"Please," she whispered. "Do your worst."

She had no idea what was coming. And that? It was precisely the way I liked it.

All I wanted was to heighten her sensuality. I started with a feather, slow strokes across her skin, not to make her laugh, but to light up every nerve ending she had. I kissed her neck, played with her breasts, and asked gently, "Would you let me use my nipple clamps?"

She blinked. "I've never done that before."

I grinned. "Tonight's the night for firsts."

They were beautiful, soft leather with a delicate grip, and she loved them. Her breath caught every time I touched them. It was like flipping a switch inside. Her body came alive under my hands.

As the room got darker, I lit a candle. I let a single drop of wax fall on her stomach. Then one over her breast. Another down her thigh.

Each one made her inhale sharply. "Oh, God."

"You're stunning," I whispered. "And so different with me than with him."

The thought crossed my mind. I wanted her. Just her. Not to break up a couple, but women like her didn't come around often.

I kissed her nipple clamps, tugged on them just enough to make her moan, then kissed my way down her belly, down to her clit. I started slow, just a tease, then pressed hard, adding a finger inside her, searching until I found her G-spot. Her entire body tensed as she came hard.

"One down," I murmured, "four to go."

I reached for the big dildo I kept for special occasions, long, girthy, soft silicone, and built for women with serious strength. I slid into my harness and said, "I want to fuck you."

She nodded breathlessly.

I unbound her hands from the posts and cuffed them to her thighs instead. She climbed on top of me, balancing carefully, and then started to move.

It wasn't the typical up-and-down rhythm. She ground into me, slow, deep, intense. Her hips rocked side to side, front to back. She wasn't just riding me, she was *working* me. Using her pussy like a weapon.

"Jesus," I whispered. "You're going to kill me."

She smirked. "That's the idea."

I came so hard watching her, her body glowing, breasts bouncing with the clamps, red ropes hugging her skin. She was everything.

But she didn't stop. She kept moving.

I reached forward, pressed my thumb to her clit, and whispered, "Come for me."

She did, violently. Her whole body shook.

"Two down," I said, grinning.

I gently removed the clamps, licking her nipples to soothe the sting, and wrapped my arms around her. We lay there for a few moments, skin against skin, warmth and breath and softness.

She teared up a little. I didn't say anything. Some people cry after an intense experience. This felt like something more profound.

"Relief?" I asked quietly. "Something you've been looking for?"

She nodded. "Maybe."

I went to get a warm washcloth, gently cleaned her, and massaged lotion across her body, light, soothing touches.

"You doing okay?" I asked.

She nodded again, voice barely audible. "I'm better than okay."

"Want to go for another?" I teased. "I have a rabbit vibrator, rotating shaft, G-spot stim, and the little ears for your clit."

She hesitated. "I don't know if I have another one in me."

I leaned in close, whispered in her ear, "Yeah, you do. Of course you do."

"You're just used to men falling over after one orgasm," she teased.

"Let's go again," I said, catching my breath. "Unless... you want to use it on me?"

She smirked. "Maybe."

"Well, I only have one, so we'll have to make a choice."

We decided I'd use it on her. At first, she wasn't totally into it.

"Just give it a second," I said.

It took four minutes.

And then she started to come. Hard. Her hips bucked, her ass lifted, her G-spot fully engaged as the vibrator did its work. I started slow, building the intensity gradually.

She screamed loudly and kept coming. Her body shook.

"Okay," I said. "That's number three. Two more to go."

She collapsed onto the bed, panting.

"I can't believe I just came again," she whispered.

"You've still got two more in you," I grinned. "Maybe even six."

She laughed weakly. "Let's aim for five. But God... I don't know if I can."

"The trick," I said, "is being so turned on by the other person that you *want* to keep going. And when I look at you... I'm so incredibly turned on. Whatever you want, I'll do it. Tonight, consider me your personal service top. Anything to get you off?"

"Then why don't you lie back," she said, rolling over, "and let me return the favor?"

She slipped between my legs, placed her mouth on my clit, and began sucking gently. Not a lick, not a kiss, something more intense. Deep suction, like a mouth-made vibrator.

I moaned instantly.

Then she slid her tongue inside me.

It was sensual, slow, utterly devoted. She grabbed my breasts, her body in a posture of near prayer, her ass lifted behind her like a work of art. She kept sucking, alternating with soft, rhythmic strokes of her tongue.

I came fast. Embarrassingly fast. If I were a man, it would've been a one-and-done. But I wasn't done.

"All right," I said, still breathless, "two more for you. What do I have in my bag of tricks?"

I pulled out my most dangerous bedroom weapon, a curved double-sided dildo.

"Let's do this," I whispered, holding her upright on her knees from behind, one hand on her breasts, the other between her legs. I moved her in small circles, teasing until she came. Quick. Intense.

Now she was dripping. Perfect timing for me to fuck her.

I reached for the dildo, part inside me, part outside through a harness. Hands-free.

I crawled under her.

"Climb on," I told her.

She did, grinding down onto me. I started thrusting into her, slow at first, then harder. Sparks. Literal sparks, it felt like. The room faded away.

Then I flipped her, reverse cowgirl. I held her hips, pounding her rhythmically.

"Faster," she moaned.

"Almost there," I said.

I reached around and rubbed her clit, feeling the heat, the slickness, the sheer intensity of her arousal.

She came hard. And that was number five.

She rolled off, utterly spent. I lay beside her, equally exhausted, happy, and satisfied. All I wanted was to curl up in her arms and stay there all night. But I knew I might not get that as the other woman.

I didn't want to make it difficult for her, or *them*. I didn't want to force a choice she wasn't going to make. I didn't even know how long I had with her.

All I knew was I wanted to make sure she had a *good* time, so that she'd think of me when she was back home.

God, I was starting to sound like a mistress. And I didn't want to be the mistress. I didn't want to be the side chick, his or hers. But in my defense... she was breathtaking. Kind. Wild. Intoxicating. I was just lucky to be there.

It didn't feel like cheating. I assumed he knew. Or I didn't want to ask. Some questions are too complicated. And honestly? I wanted it to be easy.

I wanted her. I wanted to be with her. And somehow, I was always trying to negotiate around him.

At some point that night, she got up and said she had to go home. I wanted to ask her to stay. But I knew she didn't belong to me. I only got her for these short, wild, blindingly sexual bursts of time. The kind that rewired my whole nervous system. But the future? That still had him in it. He was always going to be there. And I was just... the guest star.

That wasn't all that appealing.

Still, it went on like that for, I don't know, maybe four months? She'd leave my bed, thoroughly wrecked, completely spent, glowing from orgasm after orgasm... and then go right back to his. It was more than I could bear.

After one of those nights, we all went to a dungeon dance, one of the big BDSM parties in D.C. Think rave meets fetish showcase: flogging, bootlicking, rope play, latex, bodies writhing in time to music so loud it vibrated in your ribs, and of course, dancing.

She was mine that night, but he was there too. Still, she was the only one I had eyes on. Well... mostly.

"Want to flog him?" she asked me, teasing.

"Oh, absolutely," I said without missing a beat. And so I did.

I got him onto a St. Andrew's cross and gave one of my patented whipping demos, methodical, artful, just painful enough to keep him breathing hard. And oh, he was turned on. His body told the whole story, no secrets. That bulge in his pants was practically waving a white flag.

"You liked that, didn't you?" I whispered into his ear.

He nodded, eyes wide. "Yes, Belle"

Honestly, I was enjoying myself. For a moment, I thought, *This could work. I get to fuck his girlfriend and flog him?* Win-win.

But here's the thing: I don't hold space for people who don't have space for me. I had space for her. That night. In my bed.

He wanted to come too. And so, for one last evening, we were all together.

He never got to fuck me. Oh, he wanted to. Desperately.

"Not gonna happen," I told him. "You're not my priority here."

"I just thought," he said sheepishly.

"You thought wrong."

Look, I do fuck men, but I didn't want to fuck *him.* I wanted to fuck *her.* I wanted to start a life with her and buy a house. But she didn't choose a life with me, and she would never leave him. I don't take love that comes in meager doses.

If you can't shuck the pearl you want from the oyster, you don't really have the pearl.

20

Beltway Bandit

There's an awful lot of money in D.C. Many people get rich being Beltway bandits, feeding America's endless desire to purchase weapons, software, guns, butter, and computers. There's always something to sell to the government, and one of the most lucrative things you can sell is your time and expertise. Being a consultant is a very popular option here. You sell your time or other people's time, to run a machine, create a report, or do a review, and you can charge just about anything you want.

Entire companies, accounting firms, and strangely-branded tech companies will sell you just about anything. "Oh, you want a document review of 500,000 documents? We can do that for you. Here is the bill." Invariably, some people become incredibly rich from this. This is the story of just one of them.

He was not even 29 when I met him. He had a massive house in Potomac, with an indoor swimming pool that he might have installed illegally in a walkout cabana. The house sat on many acres up a long driveway, down a very dark road without streetlights, leading to a massive home with multiple cars in the garage and a constant inclination to buy more. He was always buying and trading in vehicles. Sometimes, he'd barely have a car before finding someone else to sell or trade it to.

He had friends who lived with him. Technically, you'd call them roommates, but I honestly don't think he collected rent. He probably

paid them for various jobs, like ensuring the shopping was done. In another era, it resembled an upstairs-downstairs arrangement. They had their wing of the house. Somebody had to be there to meet the plumber. He had these friend-servants managing these arrangements, and it worked out well for everyone. He traveled frequently, and the house stayed immaculate in his absence. They'd have their girlfriends stay over, cook meals, and stock the fridge with food for days.

A lot of pizza was delivered, Chinese food, too. And probably, though not my department, a good amount of hookers, cocaine, viagra, and pot.

So, there I was in this huge house, his latest interest. I didn't expect it to be a long-term romance because he was pretty young, and marriage didn't seem to be on the table. Although plenty of people might think 29 is a fine age for a guy to marry, or even younger, this guy had a lot of growing up left to do. He had all this money from government software contracts, probably classified. Nobody who deals in classified software ever talks about it, which is the first clue. If you don't discuss your work in D.C., people assume you're a spy or selling to spies. So when someone doesn't volunteer information, you don't ask. I never bothered to care; it's so common in D.C. that locals no longer even think about it.

We met at a bar through friends of friends during happy hour. He was on the short side, not shorter than me, but short for a guy, maybe 5'7", and incredibly built. He had a certain "let's buy drinks for the whole bar" energy, always ready with funny stories. Money never seemed to enter his mind as something to worry about, so I made a point never to bring it up.

He'd casually say, "You want to go to New York for the weekend? Let's go."

If I said, "Hey, let's go horseback riding," he'd immediately respond, "I know someone with stables. Let's do it."

Or I'd suggest, "Wouldn't it be great to take a pasta-making class?"

"Absolutely," he'd say. "Let's do it." Followed by a call to his travel guy to book tickets to Naples.

"Let's go to the museum," I'd suggest. "We can have lunch there and take funny pictures like tourists."

"I'm down for that," he'd agree. Then he would call his buddy on the board and have a wing closed down for us to go roam in together.

Being with him was like hanging out with a toddler. It was more of a playdate than a date. There was never a need for a "where is this going" conversation, and he appreciated that. A lot of people were trying to marry him, but I wasn't one of them. If he had asked, I might have considered it strongly, but he needed a little more time to ripen. His lifestyle was impulsive, living in what felt like a multi-million-dollar frat house, and that's not exactly what one would consider marriage material.

Still, we got along well. He was handsome, fun-loving, and incredibly charming. When he was in town, we spent all our time together, dining out wherever we wanted. Reservations never seemed to be a problem for him, though I'm not sure if he had connections or was paying people off.

One night, we visited an adorable French restaurant in Georgetown, renowned for its central fireplace and classic dishes. We split a bottle of wine, and he had arranged a driver for the evening so we could relax. On the way home, flushed from wine and food, we found ourselves having a fling in the back of the limousine. It was tacky, but these drivers are paid for discretion.

He was a virtuoso in the oral culinary arts. He adored it, often murmuring passionately, "I could eat your 'snack' all day." He sheepishly suggested, "Maybe you could be more assertive with me."

I smiled. "Assertive? Now you're speaking my language."

He seemed relieved. "I'd love to show you something when we get back home."

"I'm down for that. As long as you keep going down on me all the way home," I replied enthusiastically.

As we continued home, he continued dining as well, building anticipation for whatever surprise he had waiting, clearly eager and ready for more adventures together. He was about average girth but had a massive set of balls, which was the secret to his success in many aspects.

When we arrived back at the house, I noticed that none of the guys were there. The whole house was dark, but the proximity lights snapped on as we walked past the meticulously manicured gardens, featuring hydrangeas, hostas, and other plants that deer probably munched on. He had a koi pond filled with enormous fish, and as we approached, lights inside flickered to life.

He took me to a room I'd never seen, though, given the house's size, that wasn't surprising. Inside was a full-on red-room dungeon, exactly like something out of *Fifty Shades of Grey*. My breath caught, and I tried to play it cool, but I was already dripping wet with excitement. The room was stocked like an adult store from Los Angeles or New York, filled with vibrators in every imaginable color, nipple clamps, anal beads, and even what looked like a fancy cattle prod (probably not real). There were spreader bars, whips, chains, and a large St. Andrew's cross. A bed stood in the corner, not quite as elaborate as the movie version, but impressive nonetheless.

Stepping into the persona he hadn't yet fully experienced, I slowly walked around the room, touching items, inspecting everything. He began to speak.

"No talking," I ordered.

His words halted immediately. I approached him, grabbing him firmly by his bearded chin, tilting his head up. "Well, well," I purred, "I guess the secret's out. Kneel."

He instantly dropped to his knees, spreading his legs, his hands raised and palms out, his eyes cast down obediently. "Oh my God," I thought, "this is going to be easy. He's completely self-trained, like a puppy who's already housebroken. Perfect."

"Do you have anything for me to change into?" I asked.

"Yes, Belle," he replied eagerly.

I raised an eyebrow sharply. "I haven't given you permission to call me that yet."

"Yes," he corrected himself quickly, gaze still lowered.

He showed me a selection of outfits, each more fabulous than the last. None had labels, suggesting they were custom-made, perhaps from Trashy Lingerie or some discreet tailor. Realizing he must have been secretly checking my sizes from clothing labels and mentally measuring my height against his, I realized he'd planned this carefully.

"Face the door," I commanded, and he turned obediently. I chose a stunning black velvet Merry Widow, complete with deep blood-red piping, stockings, and a garter belt. The shoes were absurdly high, so I opted for just the stockings and lingerie. The fit was perfect.

"Turn around," I said confidently.

He nearly stammered in excitement, "Yes, Belle."

"I told you," I said sharply, eyes narrowed with a playful threat, "you haven't earned the right to call me that yet. You think you're worthy? You're trying to impress me, but you haven't earned this privilege. If you ever want to touch me again, you have to earn it. Do you understand?"

"Yes," he murmured, flushed and eager.

"Answer me clearly," I demanded, stepping closer. "How are you going to earn it? How are you going to prove your worth to me?"

He looked up with intensity, ready and waiting.

"How are you going to earn it?" I demanded.

He hesitated briefly, then answered softly, "By tolerating pain. By absorbing pain."

Now, I had his number. I grabbed his face firmly, looking into his eyes. "You're not fucking worthy of that yet," I whispered sharply, and he visibly quivered in excitement. I'm not sure if he doubted my ability to step into this role, but it came naturally to me. Frankly, I think more women should embrace it. So many men secretly crave humiliation, to lick patent leather heels, crawl up stockings, and feel hands grinding them into submission.

"Find me a ridding crop," I ordered, pointing across the room. He eagerly crawled across the floor, obediently returning with his chosen implement.

"Stand at the cross," I instructed him, stepping forward. "Look at me and listen carefully. You need to tell me your safeword."

He nervously replied, "Whatever you want it to be."

I shook my head firmly. "Here's how this works: no green light, no yellow light. If you say the word 'stop,' we stop immediately. Your responsibility is to communicate your limits. My job is to read you, and trust me, I'm good at it. Do you understand?"

"Yes," he said clearly.

"And what should I call you?" I asked, eyeing him expectantly.

"Servant," he quickly answered. "I want to be your servant."

"Good. Now disrobe," I commanded softly.

He stripped slowly, maintaining eye contact with the floor. Once naked, I evaluated his body, deliberately echoing how men have appraised women's bodies for centuries.

"It looks like you've been around," I said disdainfully. "Not fresh, used. Too many have touched you. Why should I bother touching something so shopped around?"

He trembled slightly, a mix of embarrassment and anticipation.

"Apologize," I demanded.

"I'm sorry," he whispered earnestly. "I know I have little value to you now, but maybe I can earn your forgiveness."

"Maybe," I responded coolly. "If you endure enough pain, perhaps you'll please me. But there are no guarantees."

I circled him, tapping the riding crop across his back, shoulders, and buttocks, critiquing him relentlessly. "Tighten up here," I ordered. "Hit the gym more. Do some squats, your ass needs to be better. If you're going to serve me, you must be in top condition. I only accept the best."

I slapped the crop lightly on his chest and stomach, maintaining a rhythm of humiliation. "Give me more," I insisted. "If you want my attention, my approval, you must give me more to work with."

Coming up behind him, I rested my hands gently around his neck, feeling him tense with excitement. Choking kink confirmed. Good to know. Without squeezing, I whispered into his ear, "Remember, you're nothing to me right now. But you can become much more. Absorb my pain and provide me pleasure, and I will stay. Disappoint me, act bratty, or displease, and I will walk away, and never fucking touch you again."

"You worthless piece of shit," I hissed sharply. "Get down on your fucking knees."

He immediately dropped, clearly eager and aroused, his jr member fully erect. I took the riding crop and gave his junk a sharp tap, making it bounce even harder, standing at absolute attention.

"I'm going to sit down on the couch," I commanded firmly, "and you're going to crawl over to me. You're going to lick my feet through these stockings, give them a proper massage, and be useful to me. Maybe I'll let you eat my pussy. That depends entirely on how good a job you do."

He obediently crawled across the floor to me, and as he touched my feet, I deliberately pointed out his mistakes.

"No," I snapped. "You're doing it wrong."

"Yes, Mistress," he stammered, correcting himself quickly.

I raised an eyebrow, smiling coldly. "You can call me Mistress, for now. But you'll need to earn the right to call me something better, something that suits the pain you're about to endure."

Every time he faltered, I bent him over, smacking his ass just firmly enough to reinforce my dominance. "Bring me a flogger," I ordered. "Something red."

He quickly returned, dropping to one knee and presenting it ceremoniously, as if offering a sword.

I smirked, "In the name of St. Michael, the Marquis de Sade, Casanova, and the Fifty Shades of Grey, I dub thee my fucking servant."

I stood over him, guiding his tongue between my legs, pressing his face into my kitkat just long enough to tease, then pulled away abruptly, denying him further satisfaction.

"Stand," I ordered, leading him toward a padded spanking bench. "Hold onto the front."

"I'm going to flog you," I explained calmly, "but I'll start softly. We'll build up slowly."

I began gently, tracing a figure-eight pattern across his upper shoulder blades, carefully avoiding the spine and kidneys. Gradually, his shoulders turned a glowing shade of red. Then I moved lower, focusing on his ass and the back of his thighs, painting them crimson with precise, controlled strokes.

"Can you take more?" I asked softly but firmly.

"Yes, Mistress," he gasped eagerly, pushing back slightly in anticipation.

"Good," I whispered, increasing the intensity slightly, still careful and controlled.

Though we kept the session sensual, intense enough to ignite his skin but not cause real harm, I was careful to maintain clear boundaries. For first encounters, caution was paramount, safety first, always with enthusiastic consent. Typically, my rule was to avoid penetration in dungeon scenes, reserving that intimacy for the bedroom. It helped clearly define our dynamics and maintain boundaries.

However, there was one exception: pegging. One of my favorite activities, it always took place in the red room, fittingly named and humorously reminiscent when I finally watched the movie.

It was amateur hour, of course, but I had him open his ass wide. I leaned in and whispered, "I'm going to put a dildo in and I'm going to fuck you hard on this bench. Would you like that?"

He enthusiastically responded, "Yes."

I slowly inserted the dildo using plenty of lube, observing that he didn't seem unfamiliar with the process. He'd done this before. At least he wasn't a virgin, not that I cared about virginity, which is vastly overrated. I tapped his back, thighs, and ass gently with the riding crop, carefully maintaining control. Consent has always been my priority; I prefer enthusiastic consent.

Gripping his throat lightly, I fucked him with the dildo, not aggressively enough to cause pain but assertively enough to make it clear who was in charge. His body responded willingly and eagerly.

Afterward, I guided him to crawl over to a nearby chaise. "Come here," I instructed softly, "lick me until I come."

He obeyed immediately, pleasing me expertly until I climaxed. Feeling satisfied, I gently commanded, "Let's move to the bed."

"Of course," he replied, taking my hand as we ascended the stairs together. Once in the bedroom, we talked briefly about what we had done, establishing more precise boundaries.

But by this point, I wanted to enjoy regular, passionate sex, just lights-on, straightforward intimacy. Our dynamics and his limits would be explored more deeply in future discussions.

Afterward, we ran naked through the expansive house, laughing and jumping into the indoor pool. The water was shockingly cool, contrasting sharply with our heated bodies. To warm up, we quickly moved into the hot tub. His back and thighs were vividly red from our session.

"How do you feel about tonight?" I asked softly.

He sighed happily, "I loved it. I want to do more of it with you. I want us to be a real couple who explores this together."

"This requires real commitment," I said seriously. "There are rules. You can't have sex with anyone else, no dating, no flirting, no sexual contact whatsoever. If you're with me, you belong to me entirely. Respect and trust are non-negotiable. Do you understand?"

"Yes," he agreed earnestly.

"Are you sure?" I continued firmly. "I'll collar you, and you'll wear it discreetly under your shirt. You belong exclusively to me. I can fuck you whenever I want, tease you whenever I please, and you'll obey me. Do we have an agreement?"

"Absolutely," he nodded eagerly. "But can I still go down on you at least once every time we're together?"

I smiled warmly. "That's a deal, though only if I want it. And believe me, you'll know exactly when I do."

We never delved deeply into the personal history or trauma that might have influenced his submissive desires. I wasn't interested in hearing about past mistresses or relationships. I occasionally took specific requests, but only outside of our dynamic, not when we were actively engaged in play. I didn't live in the BDSM world 24/7. I enjoyed the balance of going out, having fun, and returning home to assert control, to whip him gently, manacle or blindfold him, and explore deeper sensations together. Mutual enthusiasm was key.

We maintained a fantastic dynamic for about a year, at which point I sensed we'd reached a natural conclusion.

He wasn't any closer to getting married, and I wasn't any closer to believing he was ready. It wasn't as much fun as it used to be. Once you've dominated a millionaire, or billionaire, as he had become, with a big house in Potomac, you start wondering, what's next? So many other men, so many other women, and so little time.

21

Food Insecurity

There are more spies in Washington, D.C. than most people realize. You would never recognize them on sight. That is the point. They are recruited precisely because they can disappear in a crowd. They know how to listen without drawing attention, how to hold eye contact without revealing anything, and how to blend into the professional background noise of the capital. Many of them are chosen not just for their intelligence, but for a particular psychological profile: strong under pressure, emotionally detached, able to manipulate and observe without becoming entangled.

There is one particular category of spy in D.C. who rarely, if ever, sees the field. These are not the agents who cross borders or wear disguises. These are the ones who sit behind screens, piecing together fragments of communication, an overheard conversation, a deleted email, a glance caught on surveillance footage, and assembling a coherent map of someone's inner world. Their work is about patterns, motivations, and vulnerabilities.

Intelligence agencies recruit heavily from psychology and sociology departments for this kind of work. They want analysts who can not only understand human behavior but also anticipate it. The goal is to identify pressure points. What would push someone toward betrayal? What hidden craving or insecurity could be used to lure them into a honey trap? What financial weakness or addiction might be

quietly exploited? There are only so many core reasons why people turn. The right analyst can isolate the trigger.

These are the people who are trained to think like predators without ever stepping into the open. They live quiet, fabricated professional lives. They rarely say what they really do. If you meet them at a party, they will tell you they work in consulting or policy research, maybe something vaguely adjacent to data analysis or behavioral science. They are employment-based ghosts, blending seamlessly into the D.C. ecosystem, watching and waiting for a crack to appear in someone else's armor. And when it did, she was ready.

She was a lover like you'd only find in an erotic thriller with a twist ending. Advanced degrees in criminology, sociology, and probably three other '-ologies' she never mentioned. We met casually at a networking event, and I asked her out right away. She was curvy, with big breasts and a nice ass, wearing a pristine white designer suit with a blush-pink top that screamed Easter Egg Roll at the White House meets Elle Woods Goes Fed.

She said she worked at the FBI as an "Analyst," of course. A behind-the-desk spy was probably recruited out of a top program. But her vibe? It was more forensic accounting meets I could kill you with a fork if I needed to. I stopped asking too many questions. People like that tend to avoid discussing their jobs. They're trained not to. The vaguer the job description, the more dangerous they are.

She was nearly 40 when we met. Light brown hair with expertly placed blonde highlights, cut in a soft curls that said "don't fuck with me" but whispered "I might let you if you ask nicely." Her energy? Smooth. Controlled. As if she had undergone some specialized training, spy school for attractive women.

She had this uncanny ability to get you talking. Within five minutes, I had already shared with her my childhood, my relationship with my mother, and how I had once tried to become a Pilates instructor during a breakup. Meanwhile, I didn't even know if she had siblings. Classic operative behavior.

We had our first official lunch outside the J.(read: Gay) Edgar Hoover Building in honor of the closeted allegedly gay icon himself. I picked a patio café with good espresso, excellent people-watching, and just enough distance from the Bureau that it wouldn't feel like an HR training module. We sat in the sunshine, early summer warmth flickering across the metal table. I talked. She watched. I gestured. She sipped. At one point, I think she nodded. It was subtle enough I might have imagined it.

She was bubbly that day. Bright eyes, quick smiles, and a kind of deliberate, polished charm that felt both natural and carefully managed. Her college stories were hysterical. Something about stealing a mascot costume and using it to bluff her way into a rival university's frat party. Her travel stories were just as funny, jet lag in Zurich, a broken bidet in Rome, a disastrous attempt to flirt in Portuguese that turned into a diplomatic misunderstanding. She told them with flair and rhythm, like someone who knew how to hold a room. And then came the story about her office.

It started with the copier. A mix-up about a shared login. She needed a password. But no one would give her the password. So she called tech support. They gave her a different password. That password didn't work. So she went back to her supervisor, who was out sick, and then tried to reset the password herself using the internal ticketing system, which, wouldn't you know, had just migrated platforms, and now, I stopped listening.

I nodded, smiled politely, stirred my espresso like it might contain an escape plan. Meanwhile, she kept going. Now she was explaining the PowerPoint she eventually made once the copier was working again. Something about logistics. Supply chain documentation? She lost me at "document version control." And the kicker? She actually laughed. Not a nervous laugh. A sincere, warm, this-was-such-a-weird-day kind of laugh. Like it was a story you'd tell a roommate over a glass of wine.

I sat there thinking, this is the most boring story I've ever heard. How could a woman who just five minutes ago had me in stitches over a malfunctioning bidet now be monologuing about an office copier? Why would anyone tell this story, out loud, on purpose?

That's when it clicked.

Oh. She's a spy. Because here's the thing: this was a rehearsed story intended to deter nosy civilians from asking questions. A woman who is sharp, funny, and socially nimble does not suddenly lose all sense of storytelling unless she is making damn sure you stop being curious.

Did she work at the FBI? It could be a cover, or she could be on loan from another agency. Whatever her job was, I knew at that moment it was one she couldn't talk about. Which usually, invariably, means spy.

Then, she asked if she could come to my place that weekend for dinner.

"I'd love to cook for you," I offered.

She smiled. "Only if I can bring dessert."

Spoiler alert: She brought a dessert bar.

She showed up that Saturday with a whole reusable grocery bag of mysterious items. A bottle of wine? Sure, classy. A pint of gourmet ice cream? Love that. A whole-ass pie? Unexpected, but okay. Then came the whipped cream.

"For the pie?" I asked.

She just smiled.

Next out: fruit cocktail, Nutella, a tub of frosting. FROSTING? No cake?.

Then she pulled out honey. And a second tub of whipped cream.

"...Okay. You're not making dessert, are you?" It was beginning to dawn on me.

She looked up at me, deadpan, like we were planning an op. "I want to put this all over your body." She said it like she was offering love, not kink. Like this was the most intimate thing she could imagine doing for someone.

Ah. There it was. She's a *Spy Splosher.*

So now she was "out". Not just out as a spy, if she was one, but out as a full-blown splosher. A whipped-cream-wielding, frosting-loving, fruit-cocktail-obsessed splosher. And I sat there thinking, splosher spy? That's a combination I hadn't seen coming, like James Bond if Q packed his gadgets in a lunch box.

How could she have a kink like that and still hold a security clearance? I mean, forget the whipped cream for a second. We're talking full grocery store kink. That had to be something you declared, right?

But believe it or not, it's usually not a problem. The clearance system isn't as much about what you're into as it is about what you're hiding. You can be gay, kinky, poly, into latex clown cosplay, whatever, as long as you're out about it. The risk isn't the behavior. It's the secret. Being gay wasn't automatically disqualifying anymore, at least not in civilian agencies. You just had to be out. And more importantly, your family had to know. Your mother, specifically. I am not kidding. That was the benchmark. Because the most significant risk wasn't blackmail from a foreign agent. It was a call to Mom.

So sure, you could be queer and serve. You could be non-monogamous. Hell, you could probably be into cryogenic latex sleep pods if your references backed you up. That's where things got sticky. No pun intended.

Of course, I never asked. We never got as far as the big reveal about her actual job, let alone her clearance process. And even if I had asked, she probably would have lied. That's what they do. You don't get a complete resume with spies. You get a cover story and good sex, intense orgasms.

But I kept wondering. Had she told her clearance officer about the food thing? Had she sat down with a straight face and said, "Listen, just so you're aware, I get off on frosting women. And yes, my mother knows about the women, not the frosting." Because if so, honestly? That's impressive.

"Is this your thing?" I asked, hands on hips, trying to play it cool.

"One of them," she said, pouring wine like a Bond villain with a plan for my destruction.

"And you... Usually, do you bring all this stuff?"

She shrugged. "Not always this much. But I like being prepared."

Was she going to pull a can of Easy Cheese out next? Shove a baguette up my backside? Torture me with fondue forks?

"Look," I said. "I've never done... food play." She gave me a smile that was way too confident for someone holding a tub of Cool Whip.

"You'll enjoy it," she said. "I promise."

While skeptical, I wanted to believe her. My boundaries are negotiable when the girl in question looks like a cross between a French pastry and a dominatrix accountant. I told myself I'd roll with it. I'd cooked dinner already, might as well lean into dessert.

She wanted to go out into the middle of my backyard garden, a huge yard with lots of trees, and have a kind of food-body-paint picnic. A plastic tarp, candles, and a privacy clothesline strung up between branches. Romantic-ish.

There we were, buck naked. Me, out of my depth, and her with grocery bags full of kink. But I was game. I mean, I ask people to cross lines with me all the time. Who am I to shy away from a bit of frosting?

So I set it up, a tarp near the trees, privacy rigged up, candles ready for dusk. We started clothed, drinking wine. Perfectly normal. Until she spilled wine on me and decided to lick it up. Thoroughly.

"Oops," she said, locking eyes with me, her tongue already flicking against my skin.

"That's one way to handle it," I said, smirking.

She laughed, pushed my breasts together, and filled the cleavage with more wine. "Just... stay still," she whispered, and began to drink me in.

Next came the whipped cream. She put little dollops on each nipple and spent an eternity licking them off, only to reapply. Sometimes she painted it back on with her tongue.

"You're going to make a mess," I warned.

"That's the point," she whispered, giggling.

There was something almost tender in it, beneath the giggle. Like every swipe of wine across my skin wasn't just playful, it was generous. Like she was decorating me. She was offering something of herself. Her authentic self, the one who didn't get seen at work.

She grabbed the Nutella next and painted little spirals on my stomach. Circles. Polka dots. Licked them all up like the world's kinkiest finger painter.

Then came the frosting. She squeezed it onto my inner thighs, drew hearts with her fingertip. Switched colors. Painted my labia in pink, my clit in green. Rubbed it in, rubbed it off, with hands, with tongue. Her concentration was that of a pastry chef and a lover all rolled into one.

"You realize this isn't how I normally play," I said, breathless.

"I know. But you're doing great," she whispered, looking up at me, her lips sticky with frosting.

It was sweet. It was sensual. But we were covered in goop and hadn't even gotten down to it yet. I was turned on. I wanted more. Needed more. It was time to break out the strap-on.

I lay her down on the sticky blanket, covered in dessert, and mounted her. My fingers. My tongue. I found every curve, every moan until she was gasping my name, clutching at the dildo I was wearing with frosting-sticky hands. Jacking it off as if she were churning butter.

"You're mine now," I whispered.

"Yes, Belle," she panted. "Yours."

I got the goop all over me as I repositioned her, pressing her body down into the mess on the blanket. I grabbed a huge handful of whipped cream and smeared it over her face, dragging it through her hair, down her neck, all the way to her toes. I took a glob of Nutella and spread it over her belly button, then slid whipped cream between her thighs, right on her clit.

"Oh my god," she gasped. "Let me blow you."

"Open," I told her. "Eat this."

She tried. She really did. But the strap-on was thick, and she'd slathered it in frosting first—thick, white, supermarket frosting with artificial vanilla and a gritty sugar bite. It clung to the silicone in swirls, and her lips smeared it with every bob of her head. It stuck to her lashes, her cheeks, the corner of her nose. She looked up at me with her mouth full and her face covered like dessert left too long in the sun.

She gagged again, and I pulled back, not to let her off the hook but to give myself a better view. The fake cock glistened with spit and frosting and a little smear of Nutella from where I'd dragged it across her chest. I wrapped one hand around the base and started stroking it right in front of her face.

I pushed the head against her lips and started sliding her hand faster, twisting at the tip, working the frosting into a mess of froth and spit. She kept her mouth open while I used her like a surface to stroke against. Her tongue darted out, lapping at the underside every time my hand reached the top.

"Suck it like a candy cane," I barked, completely making this up as I went along. If this goes on any longer, I am going to start making Christmas references.

She moaned, louder now, her whole body trembling. I reached down with my free hand and scooped up a fistful of whipped cream, dragging it down her chest, over her nipples, between her legs. She gasped when it hit her clit, already overstimulated and soaked from everything I had poured on her and into her.

This is going nowhere, and I am getting bored. It is like being stuck at a bad play, and I am begging for an intermission to sneak out.

She nodded, whimpering, obedient. I pumped the strap-on harder, faster, spit and sugar flying with each stroke as I dragged the slick mess across her lips. She didn't flinch.

"You're going to take it. All of it. Frosting, cream, and whatever else I decide to smear on that pretty mouth."

"Yes. Yes, Belle. Please."

Her whole body slid beneath me, skin skating over the tarp and cream like we were in some deranged adult version of a backyard slip-and-slide. She screamed for more. So I gave her more. She started yelling for pie like it was a safe word. Fuck I forgot about the pie thing. I picked it up. So do I throw it on me or her? What part of the body? I guessed and chucked it to her abdomen and pushed it between us. She came screaming something about cherries.

And then all I wanted was a shower and eight hours of sleep.

I dismounted with the grace of a moose and landed face-first in the damn thing. Afterward, I pulled away and sat up. "You know, usually my idea of a sexy night includes dinner beforehand. Maybe dessert later."

She giggled. "This was both."

We were sticky and exhausted. "I don't even know how you're going to walk through the house like that," I said. "I should've set up an outdoor rinse station or something. "

We took turns showering, then sat down to talk.

"I have to say," I began carefully, "I'm not bad at improv, but we really should've talked about this ahead of time."

"I know," she said, nodding. "But this is something I love. Like... I fantasize about it a lot."

She sighed, honestly. "I've spent the week fantasizing about what I wanted to do to you. And this was it."

"I get it. But... can we have regular sex sometimes?"

She just lay there when I tried to have a more regular sexual experience, even making out wasn't her thing. She just froze. The same woman who had been wild and uninhibited, writhing with whipped cream and Nutella all over her body like a damn sundae, couldn't seem to connect without that fantasy element.

She needed the food, the gooey, sticky, decadent performance of it all. And don't get me wrong, I'm open-minded. But I asked her, gently, "Is there anything we can do that's... maybe less sticky? Like whipped cream only?"

She shook her head. "It doesn't work unless it's the full thing," she said, severe as a diabetic coma.

I nodded slowly, trying to wrap my head around it. "You mean like... full grocery aisle, buffet-on-a-bed, frosting and fruit cocktail situation?"

"Yes," she said. "The fruit cocktail, especially. I like the way it feels when it drips down."

"I mean... help me understand," I said, leaning back. "Is it just the mess? The taste? The texture?"

She looked at me carefully, like she was deciding how much to share. "It's all of it. The sensory overload, the feeling of something cool and wet, or sticky and warm. It heightens everything. It turns me on."

"So... sensory," I echoed, nodding.

"Right," she said. "And... It's taboo. It's messy and ridiculous. I was raised to be perfect and polite. This is the opposite of that. It's freeing."

"Okay," I said, trying to keep an open mind. "And it's not just about you being covered in food?"

"No," she said. "Sometimes, it feels comforting. Like... weirdly nurturing. I know that sounds bizarre."

"Honestly? Not that bizarre. I've seen stranger."

She smiled faintly. "It's also control. Performance. I set the scene. I bring the props. I know exactly how it's going to go."

"How far does it go back?" I asked. "Like, do you remember when this started for you?"

She told me that the food thing started when she was a kid, not in a sexual way, not at first. It was emotional. Tactile. Ritualistic. Her parents were cold, the kind who schedule affection between extracurriculars. But dessert? That was allowed. That was safe. Her mother didn't hug her, but she plated pudding with precision. Her father didn't praise her, but he'd scoop ice cream like it was an act of penance. Sugar was the only reliable tenderness in the house.

So she learned young that sweetness meant attention. That food was the language no one punished her for needing.

Later, when she discovered sex, the wires got crossed. Or maybe they were never separate to begin with. She learned to associate arousal with mess, desire with indulgence, and love with a particular kind of chaos. Sploshing wasn't just about sensation; it was about reclaiming the parts of herself that had been ignored. It was about being touched, seen, worshipped, and still being good. Still being lovable. Even sticky. Even out of control.

Psychologically, she understood it. She could analyze it six ways from Sunday. She was familiar with imprinting, sensory reinforcement, and early developmental attachment patterns. She could write a whole dissertation on how the brain encodes touch, shame, and reward. But knowing the theory didn't make the need go away. If anything, it made it harder. Because she knew how rare it was to find someone who would indulge her ritual without mocking it. Someone who wouldn't flinch at the grocery bag of kink.

That was the thing about her. She wasn't chasing shock. She was chasing comfort. Control. Consistency. In a world where she watched people lie and betray each other professionally for a living, she wanted something stupid and honest and strange. Something so absurd that it couldn't be faked.

The mess was the point. "And now it's non-negotiable."

There was never going to be a second date. Some cravings are meant to be satisfied once, then sealed away like an overindulgent memory. And honestly? One night was enough.

Perhaps someone else would view the entire sundae setup as foreplay. But for her, it was the relationship. The food wasn't decoration. It was love, in the only language she'd ever been safe speaking.

And that was when I knew. Spy chick, FBI girl, wasn't going to be my match. I just wasn't the one to help her reenact whatever fruit-cocktail-espionage-romance she had going on in her head. Someone else could be, someone with a tarp and a sense of humor.

It's a shame, though. She was brilliant. Funny. Hot. I even liked her mystery. But we didn't talk after that. Not even a text. And honestly, maybe that was for the best. Because I'm not sure I see the love of my life as a splosher or a spy.

22

Op-Ed

We met at a social group, one of many here in D.C., which is desperately trying to connect workaholic, Type A individuals into a community. She was shorter than me, with thick black hair and a curvy, petite figure. A writer, working for nonprofits and the occasional commercial publication. She was the original golden retriever girl: eager, enthusiastic, loyal to a fault. Anything I did or said, she loved. She hung on every word. And I? I wasn't in a great place to appreciate her particular lapdog tendencies. I wanted someone more challenging, someone who'd push back. She never disagreed, never questioned—always smiling, constantly nodding.

It made me feel like I didn't know her at all.

She came from an interesting family. Political, certainly. Rich? Absolutely. She didn't talk about them much, which only made the silence more telling. In D.C., there's a class of people who can afford to work for peanuts because of family money, who graduate from Ivy League schools with no debt and stroll into jobs that pay in "experience." They're the ones who can take the prestigious but underpaid gigs, and she was absolutely one of them.

She was a social butterfly. Incredibly good at hiding her feelings. While I found her charming and interesting, she was also a bit of a mystery. She presented a perfectly polished exterior to the world, and it took real work to peel that mask away and get to the person underneath.

But when she let go? Oh, when she dropped the mask...

That only happened during sex, specifically, during our hot-as-hell bondage sessions. That's when I got to meet the real her.

We officially connected at a massive lesbian nonprofit gala. It was a Whitman-Walker or Mautner Project event—something huge, like Lesbian Prom. One year, I decided to go full glam rogue: a giant red strapless satin ball gown paired with a 1920s vintage men's tuxedo jacket. No shirt. Just the dress, the tux jacket, and a black-and-white bow tie. So yes—plunging neckline, a whole lot of skin, and enough cleavage to be considered a structural hazard.

The dress was tight—no bra, no underwear. Just my boots underneath. I think they were lace-up, or maybe I wore my black motorcycle boots. Either way, the vibe was chaos couture: curled hair, great makeup. I walked in, and the moment our eyes met across the room, that was it.

She did not leave me alone all evening.

She changed placecards to sit next to me. She followed me around like a shadow. There was a moment on the dance floor—of course, I led. I was taller when she tried to kiss me, but I dodged it. I am not that easy.

Meanwhile, I was attracting attention like a disco ball dipped in pheromones. People stopped me to compliment the dress and, let's be honest, stare at my tits. Men, women, gay men—it didn't matter. My cleavage was magnetic. I've never understood gay men's fascination with boobs, but there it was: jaws dropping, eyes wide, absolutely no subtlety.

At one point, we took a stroll around the silent auction tables. That's when I realized just how attentive she could be. My little golden retriever never left my side. She fetched me drinks, ensured I was comfortable, and made sure I was having fun. If I'd asked her to crawl under my skirt and get me off right there, she'd have done it. Hell, I think she would've *preferred* it. Attention to me meant less pressure on her.

Honestly? Sometimes that's helpful. I don't always love being the center of attention—it can be exhausting. But when it happens, I know how to ride the wave.

Anyway, I mentioned I needed food. Not even tipsy yet—just hungry. Before I could blink, she'd spoken to the catering staff. And I swear to God, I don't know how she did it—bribery? charm? Jedi mind tricks?—but she managed to get a whole tray of hors d'oeuvres brought over. From another event, no less.

She handed me a plate and said, "You shouldn't have to wait in line."

That was the moment I thought: Oh. Oh, I could ruin you in the best possible way.

I shudder to think how much cash she put in their hands, but that's the kind of person she was. "Oh, you need something? I can fix this. I can go do it." It was charming, honestly, because that kind of attentiveness? It's intoxicating. That level of focus, of care, of presence—it makes you feel like the only person in the room.

She shepherded me around that gala like I was her date to the Oscars.

"Come talk to these people," she'd say, tugging at my hand.

"Do I have to?"

"Yes. They're delightful. Just trust me. I'll do the talking, you smile."

And she knew everyone. I wasn't even sure I'd committed to this situation, but I certainly wasn't complaining. It was, well, lovely.

"Would you like this?" she'd ask, standing in front of the silent auction table.

Before I could answer, she was already signing my name to some silent auction form.

"I'm not sure I want to spend money on that," I said, watching her flourish her pen.

"Oh, I'll pay for it," she replied with a wave of her hand. "It's for charity, after all. What's the difference?"

And for her? There wasn't a difference. She gave without thinking. Like, money wasn't even real to her.

Eventually, we were called to our table. There was a long, somewhat boring program before dinner finally showed up. Midway through, I must've sighed or something.

"What's wrong?" she asked.

"They don't have martinis. Only wine."

"Say no more," she said, standing up like a woman on a mission.

"Wait, where are you going?"

"You'll see."

Next thing I know, she's vanished. Ten minutes later, she reappeared with an ice-cold martini in hand.

"Where'd you go?" I asked.

"You wanted it, didn't you?" She handed me the glass, beaming.

She must've sprinted to a bar in another wing of the hotel—or bribed someone. Who knows? But it was perfect. Bone-chillingly cold and precisely what I needed.

Over dessert, I started teasing her.

"Do you want a taste?" I asked, scooping up a spoonful of whipped cream.

She nodded.

I brought the spoon to my lips, slowly licking off the cream with a swirl of my tongue.

"You like that?" I whispered.

She didn't answer. Just stared, wide-eyed, lips slightly parted.

I leaned in. "You're not saying anything."

She swallowed. "I love it. I love watching you."

I don't know if anyone else at the table noticed, but I wouldn't have cared if they had.

It wasn't lust, exactly. There was a romantic vibe between us—cocooned, soft, like some fairy tale version of a relationship. I didn't know how she saw me, but around her, I felt taller. More vivid.

When the music started, I stood up and extended my hand. "May I have this dance?"

"I thought you'd never ask."

I led her to the dance floor for a waltz. God, I love waltzing. Any schlub can get the girl if they know how to dance. If you can make her feel like a princess, like she's safe, adored, and the only one that matters, you win. That's it. That's the whole game. You could look like a mother fucking troll that crawled out from under a damn bridge and you could still get the girl. I am not promising forever, but you will have her attention; the rest is still up to you.

"You're leading like a dream," she murmured, following my every move.

"You're easy to lead."

"Only with you", she said. Her voice was breathy, reverent.

Three songs in, and she was all mine.

We shared a cab back to my place.

"You're staying," I said as we pulled up.

She blinked. "Am I?"

"It's too late. Too dangerous to get a ride on your own. Come on."

She didn't argue.

In my kitchen, I didn't bother with more wine. She hadn't drunk much anyway. I just slowly undressed her, piece by piece, peeling away the layers until she was perched on my countertop.

"We should talk," I said, stepping between her knees.

She nodded. "Yes."

"About what you want. What do you want me to do to you tonight?"

Her breath caught.

"I'll do anything," she said, voice trembling just a little.

I tilted her chin up. "Anything? That's a dangerous word."

She met my gaze. "Then it's dangerous."

That was the moment I knew—this wasn't just about sex.

I'm like, "Okay, but that's not how it works. You can't just say I can do anything—you have to tell me what you want."

I looked at her, trying to gauge if she understood. "If this is the stopping point, we will stop. If you want to go further, we'll go further. But you have to tell me."

She shook her head, nearly whispering. "I can't. I don't... I don't have the words."

There it was. The entrance into her psyche. She'd spent so long people-pleasing and cutting off her own emotions that she had nothing, in that moment, to offer of herself. Nothing clear, nothing honest.

So again, we couldn't do much. No bondage. Not with that kind of dynamic. Expectations become unrealistic and unbalanced.

I poured her a glass of water and handed it to her.

"Hydrate," I said. "You're going to need it."

She drank, eyes locked on mine.

"Okay," I said, softening slightly. "Tell me what you want to do."

She looked down. "I can't."

"Alright. You tell me yes or no. We're doing this menu-style. I'm the waitress, you're the customer. Order what you want."

Her shoulders relaxed a little. "Okay."

"Do you want to kiss me?"

We'd already kissed, but I needed to hear it.

"Yes."

"Do you want to kiss my neck?"

"Yes."

"Do you want me to touch your breasts?"

"Yes."

"Do you want me to suck on your breasts?"

"Yes."

"Do you want to touch my breasts?"

A breath. Then, "Yes."

"Do you want to suck on my breasts?"

Another "Yes."

"Do you want me to bite your breasts?"

"Yes," she whispered.

"Enthusiastic compliance?"

She smiled, nodding. "Yes."

We were getting somewhere. This was the only path forward, a strange erotic game of red light, green light.

She got visibly uncomfortable when I asked if she wanted me to go down on her. So we didn't. That was her boundary, and I wasn't going to push it. Vaginal sex, yes, anal yes but I vetoed it anyway. That's for another night.

"We're going to save that," I told her. "That's for when we've got more trust."

She nodded, relief washing over her. I lead her into the bedroom. I undressed her slowly, kissed her softly.

"Do you want me to do this?" I asked.

"Yes."

"Say it out loud."

"Yes. I want you to."

"Good. Bonus points for enthusiasm."

I kissed her cheeks, her mouth, the corners of her lips. Her ears. Her neck.

She let out a gasp. Her hands clutched the sheets.

"You like that?"

"Yes. Oh my God, yes."

"Good," I whispered, staying at her neck, letting my hands roam slowly.

We were finally getting somewhere real.

I circled down to her clavicle, then traced my hand slowly down her chest, over her breasts. They were full, round, and already eager—nipples hard, her breathing shallow. She had big, beautiful, natural breasts that were utterly enthralling to me.

"You like that?" I murmured, watching her eyes flutter.

"Yes," she gasped. "God, yes."

I spent an extraordinary amount of time on her nipples, using my tongue, alternating with the gentlest graze of my teeth. She shivered. I flicked one nipple gently with my finger, teasing.

"You like that too?" I asked.

"Yes," she said again, her voice higher, breathless.

"Noted," I smiled. "We'll circle back to that."

Then I began to move lower. As I traced my fingers toward her thighs, she tensed, noticeably uncomfortable as I neared her center. I paused immediately.

"Okay," I said softly, backing off. "We're not doing that. Not tonight."

She nodded, visibly relieved.

"We've got all the time in the world," I added, redirecting. I focused on her legs instead, trailing kisses down to her feet.

There was lotion on the bedside table—a simple hand cream. I took some in my palms and began to rub her feet, hoping it might help her relax.

She yelped, giggling. "I'm so ticklish!"

"Ohhh, really now?" I said, grinning. "Is that so? Well, lucky for me, I can work with that."

I leaned into it, tickling her gently, playfully. Her laughter filled the room, warm and disarming.

"Okay! Okay! Mercy!" she said between laughs.

I had her roll over onto her stomach, and I slowly dragged my nails down her back, not scratching, just light pressure, a whisper of sensation. I did that little teasing serpent pattern that always drove people wild. She giggled again, shoulders shaking.

The view was beyond thrilling: her back arched, breasts pressed against the sheets, and that incredible ass just begging to be touched. My hand hovered over it, resisting the urge to grab or spank.

"Tempting," I whispered. "But not tonight. Not without a conversation first."

Still, there were signs. She'd be into it. Eventually.

"Alright," I said, flipping her gently. "Now it's my turn. You're going to serve me."

"Okay!" she said brightly, like I'd just handed her an extra credit assignment.

I handed her the lotion. "Start with my arms. Slow. Then legs. Take your time. Focus on the task."

She nodded with full attention, like she was preparing for a test.

"You're doing this for me," I said, watching her. "Just for me. Can you do that?"

"Yes, Belle."

God, she said it so naturally I nearly melted.

She began to work the lotion into my arms, deliberate and reverent. I wanted her to stop overthinking, to let go of the anxiety. Sometimes, service allowed a person to drop into focus, to calm the nervous chatter, and exist in the moment.

And yes, I wanted her. Badly. But I also didn't want to spook her. Some people have a hair trigger when it comes to body stuff, to sex. It's better to move slowly and err on the side of caution.

I watched her as she rubbed the lotion into my calves, then my thighs. Her touch grew more confident. She was now focused, deep in the service headspace.

I wanted to fuck her with violent passion, with biblical energy, and with a lover's touch. But more than anything, I wanted her to feel safe enough to let me.

So I waited. And I watched. And I planned the rest of the night.

And oh, what a night it was going to be.

I leaned in and kissed her, slow and deep. "Stay with this," I whispered, letting the kiss linger. My hands found hers and guided them toward my clit.

"Just touch me here," I murmured. "Get used to the feel of me."

Her eyes sparkled. "Yes. Absolutely."

And she was great—really, really great. Her hands were attentive, reverent, and when her mouth followed, it was with practiced, focused joy. She used her fingers with just the correct pressure, hitting my G-spot perfectly while her tongue rolled and danced over my clit with such dedication, I almost came from the sight of her alone.

"You like that?" she asked, glancing up between my thighs with those big, dark eyes and her thick black hair spilling all over.

"God, yes. Don't stop. You're so good at this."

She smiled, and her head dipped again. The side of her face between my thighs, her dark hair like silk, the look of absolute hunger—it was intoxicating.

When I finally arrived, it was sharp, clean, and satisfying. I stroked her hair, catching my breath. "That was perfect," I told her. "Now it's your turn."

I reached for the harness and chose one of my favorite dildos—long, curved, a little ambitious for a first time. She eyed it warily.

"We don't have to—"

"No," she cut in, breathless. "I want to. Just... slow."

"Slow is good," I agreed, and lay back on the bed. "Climb on top of me. We'll take our time."

She straddled me, nervous but determined, and with each slow inch, she sank on it, her tits bouncing in my face, warm and soft and perfect. I kissed them, sucked on them, played with them, while my hips bucked ever so slightly beneath her.

"You're so beautiful," I said between licks. "Take your time. Just feel."

It took a while—ten minutes, maybe more—of her easing into it, learning the shape of it, how it moved inside her, and her hips started to roll on their own. Little circles. Slow thrusts forward, then back. I reached up, grabbed her hair, and kissed her breasts.

"Grab the headboard," I instructed. "Hold onto the slats. "

With her leaning forward, I could reach her hips, guiding her rhythm, tilting her just enough to hopefully stimulate her G-spot. She moaned, her hands gripping the headboard tighter.

I reached for her clit, trying to stroke her into climax, but she twitched away. "Too much," she gasped.

"Okay," I said gently. "How about this?"

I grabbed a small vibrator from the nightstand, flicked it on, and placed it gently on her clit.

"Oh, fuck," she gasped. "Yes—yes, Belle—"

She came in seconds. Violently. Her whole body shuddered, and then she collapsed onto my chest, panting, melted.

I pulled the covers up around us. We curled into each other like lovers who've known each other for years, not hours.

In the morning, I made coffee and brought it to her. I thought we'd talk.

"What are you thinking?" I asked, sipping mine.

She just smiled and shrugged. "It was good."

"That's it? You're a writer. Give me more than good.'"

She laughed. "I'm just... not used to talking about it."

"If you can't talk about it, we are going to get into trouble soon if we continue."

She blinked, not offended—just startled.

"I want to understand you," I said gently. "What do you like. What do you want?"

"It's hard to say," she admitted. "I've never done anything like that before."

"You seemed like you had," I smirked.

"I just... trusted you."

The next time we were together.

She wanted to be good for me. That was the first problem.

She lay across my bed in the soft gold light, wrists already bound above her head, rope wound snug but gentle, as if tied by someone who could read nerves like braille. I had taken my time, wrapped her in silken coils, but never touched anything else. Not her breasts, not her thighs, not the ache gathering between them. Not yet.

"I'm here," she whispered, breath already shaky. "I'm yours."

I stepped in closer. I touched her cheek with the soft edge of a black feather, let it drift down the column of her neck, stopping just above her collarbone. Her body flinched, but she didn't make a sound.

"That's not what I asked," I said.

She blinked up at me, trying to stay brave, trying to be good. That reflex would ruin her if I let it.

"You keep offering yourself like an apology," I murmured. "Like sex is something that happens to you. Something you endure. Something I invented."

I lowered the feather again, tracing a curve under her breast, not touching skin, just skimming the surface of want. Her nipples pebbled hard. Still, she stayed silent.

"You think being passive is being pleasing," I said. "But you're not here to please me. Not yet. You're here to tell me what you want. Until then, you get nothing."

She writhed slightly, the rope pulling taut against her wrists. She looked so sweet in the soft glow, lips parted, lashes trembling, thighs pressing together as if they could conjure pressure from friction alone. But I wouldn't reward silence.

"You get to ask for it," I said, running the feather between her thighs, hovering just over the thin silk of her underwear. "You get to be selfish. Or you get to stay untouched."

The whimper she let out then wasn't from pleasure. It was from panic. The panic of being seen.

"I don't—" she started. Her voice cracked.

"Yes," I said gently, "you do. You've thought about it. Tell me."

She twisted her hips toward the feather. I pulled it away.

Her mouth opened again, then closed. Her breathing was shallow. Her knuckles were pale from the rope's tension. I waited. No punishment. No reward. Just silence and her own pulse.

"I want you to touch me," she said finally, barely more than a whisper.

I tilted my head. "That's a start. Where?"

Her chest heaved. She closed her eyes.

"Say it."

"My—" She swallowed. "My breasts. I want your hands on me. I want to feel like they belong to you."

The feather dropped to the floor.

I leaned in, finally laying my palm against her breast, skin to skin, thumb brushing over the nipple so slowly it made her sob.

"There," I said. "That's what I wanted. Now we begin."

Her arms were already bound above her, wrists crossed and fixed to the headboard in a figure-eight knot that gave her just enough play to squirm but not escape. Now I slipped down her body, watching every shift in her breathing, every flicker of resistance. Her thighs were still parted for me—she wanted to surrender. She just didn't know how yet.

I picked up a second length of rope.

Her eyes widened as I slid it under her right thigh and looped it around the bedframe, pulling the leg wide and securing it in place. Then the left. Now she was open completely, legs spread, wrists fastened, spine arching faintly off the bed. She looked fragile, almost deer-like in that position—flushed, breathless, caught in her own instincts.

"Better?" I asked.

She blinked at me, confused.

"I saw your jaw unclench," I said. "You're safest when you're most restrained, aren't you?"

She gave the slightest nod.

"Good."

I took another piece of rope and looped it around her chest, just under her breasts, wrapping her ribcage until it compressed slightly with each breath. I could feel her letting go with every turn of the cord, her focus narrowing. Then a second line above her breasts, framing them, holding her in place like an offering.

Then one last knot, a simple line between her ankles and her wrists. Not so tight that it hurt, but enough to remind her of the architecture of her own helplessness. She was held. Tethered. Open.

And her eyes—finally—went soft.

Her body stopped trying to correct itself. Her hips no longer tried to tip away. Her hands, clenched for so long above her head, relaxed into the rope. Her chest moved in a slow, even rhythm.

I knelt between her legs.

Her vulva was pink, glistening, still untouched. I hadn't put my mouth on her yet. I hadn't even teased. I had kissed her thighs, worshipped the inside of her knees, held my breath just inches away from her, but I had denied her anything direct. That denial had done its work. Now she was ready.

"I'm going to go down on you now," I said, voice low, lips almost brushing her inner thigh. "You don't have to perform. You don't have to do anything. You don't even have to come. You just have to feel me."

She swallowed. Her hips stayed still.

"Say it," I said. "Say you want my mouth."

"I want your mouth," she whispered.

"Where?"

"On me. Please. On my pussy."

I smiled.

"There you are."

I lowered myself until my mouth was just above her. I didn't tease. Not now. Not when she was finally quiet inside. I licked her, slow and deep, a flat sweep of my tongue from her entrance to her clit. She gasped. Her thighs jerked slightly against the bindings, but the rope held her open. She couldn't close herself off anymore.

Good.

I licked her again, this time circling her clit, letting the motion build. She was warm, wet, and responsive now. She moaned, a soft, broken sound that didn't try to sound pretty. It just escaped. That was what I wanted.

I sucked her clit gently between my lips, flicking it with the tip of my tongue in small, rhythmic pulses. Her breathing quickened. Her hands pulled against the rope above her head, but not in protest—only in instinct. She had nowhere to go. Nothing to do. Her job was to receive.

I slid two fingers inside her. She clenched around me.

"You're doing so well," I murmured against her. "So open. So fucking soft for me."

She cried out, head rolling against the pillow.

I stayed steady. My tongue worked in rhythm with my fingers, slow and deliberate, reading every twitch, every moan, every tremble as feedback. I didn't need words. Her body was speaking fluently now.

And still—she hadn't come.

Not yet.

But she was close. I could feel the tension coiling low in her belly. I could feel her cunt fluttering around my fingers. I could feel her thighs begin to shake against the ropes.

Not long now.

But not yet.

Her moans were building, but uneven. Her hips moved, but not in rhythm. Her body wanted to fly forward, but her mind was still in the room. Watching. Assessing. Holding a leash I had not yet cut.

So I pulled back.

Her whimper at the loss of contact was real and raw. Not because I had teased her. I hadn't. I had worshipped her. But she hadn't dropped yet. She hadn't truly let go.

Her eyes met mine.

"I need more," she whispered.

I nodded.

"Then you'll have it."

I left her legs tied wide to the corners of the bed. I didn't loosen a thing. I added rope across her thighs, a diamond pattern over her hips that crisscrossed her lower belly, and cinched down just tight enough to limit movement. Her whole pelvis became an altar—bound, framed, exposed.

She was breathing hard now. But not from panic. From relief. She was sinking into the ropes like they were silk sheets, like they were hands of the divine.

I took out the blindfold.

She watched me as I knelt beside her and slid it over her eyes. It was soft, thick, perfectly opaque. She twitched slightly when it settled across her face, and then—finally—she exhaled.

Deep. Long. The kind of breath people take in church.

Without sight, her body stilled. Without visuals to perform for, she stopped performing.

I brushed my lips across her inner thigh. She gasped. Her legs pulled against the ropes, but they didn't move. Her body had no choice now but to stay exactly where I placed it. I could feel her start to float.

I kissed lower. She whimpered.

"I'm going to gag you now," I said softly. "Not to silence you. But to free you."

She nodded.

Her voice had dried up anyway.

I slid a ball gag between her lips, smooth and firm, held in place by a leather strap that buckled behind her head. Her breath came through her nose now, fast and shallow. Her hands clenched and then stilled above her, still tied to the headboard.

Now she was bound completely.

Arms spread and fixed. Legs wide and tied down. Hips cinched with rope. Blindfolded. Gagged. Her world had narrowed to sensation. No choices. No role to play. Nothing to offer. Only the body she could not hide, and the mouth she could not use.

Now I went down on her again.

This time, she didn't flinch. She didn't try to move. She didn't do anything except exist.

My tongue pressed into her clit with focused pressure. Direct. Right there. Over and over. I slid two fingers inside her and curled them upward. She arched against the rope.

Her moan came through the gag, low and rough. Beautiful.

I didn't change rhythm. I didn't need to.

She was mine now. Not figuratively. Fully. Completely. I could feel her body giving way, melting under me. Her hips strained against the binds, but only in surrender. Her moans deepened. Her breath quickened.

Her orgasm came like a flood.

It started with a single sharp cry muffled behind the gag, a wrenching sound from deep in her belly. Her whole body trembled, not jerking or flailing, but vibrating. A locked door opening at last. Her cunt clenched around my fingers in tight, pulsing waves. Her thighs shook. Her breath came in gasps. Tears slipped beneath the blindfold.

I stayed with her.

I kept my mouth on her, steady and grounding, even as the tremors rolled through her. I didn't let go until the last aftershock passed, and her body sagged back into the rope.

Only then did I stop.

She was utterly still.

Silent. Gagged. Blindfolded. Bound. And finally—at peace.

I wiped my mouth and kissed the inside of her thigh again, reverent now. Just to mark the moment.

She had never looked freer.

I untied her slowly.

Not just because the knots were precise, but because she needed it done with care. She had let go so entirely under the rope that bringing her back had to be just as intentional. I loosened her ankles first, rubbing the red lines gently with my thumbs, then her thighs. I kissed the places where the rope had pressed. I spoke softly while I worked, nothing commanding, just the cadence of someone watching over her.

The gag came off next. I held her face in both hands and kissed her forehead. She didn't speak. She just looked at me like she was still underwater.

Last came her wrists. I eased them down one at a time, guiding her arms to her sides, and then I pulled her into me, wrapping both arms around her, cradling her head against my chest. She curled into me like a child. I didn't ask questions. I didn't say anything at first. I just held her.

Her breath slowed gradually, the way it does when someone's nervous system is recalibrating after a hard drop. Her body relaxed, inch by inch. It took time. I stayed with her the entire way.

When I finally spoke, my voice was low and even.

"I think I understand what you're asking for," I said.

She didn't pull away. She nodded faintly against my collarbone.

"You want me to make decisions for you. Not just in the moment, but in advance. You want me to know what you want without you having to say it."

Another small nod.

"I get it. I do. That's part of what I do, part of what I love. But if we're heading in that direction, what you're talking about is consensual non-consent. And that's serious. That's not something we fall into. That's something we negotiate."

I looked down at her. Her eyes were open now, listening, not panicked.

"It means there are boundaries. Firm ones. Pre-cleared actions. Scenarios. Language. Hard stops. It means we talk about it all when we're not in the heat of the moment. And then, once it's all understood, yes—within that box, you can let go. You can be taken. You can be ravished. You can pretend you don't want it while knowing you're safe. But only because we both know the rules before it starts."

She swallowed.

"I don't want to break that trust," I said. "And I won't ever play rough without consent, that's already clear and confirmed."

I felt her tense slightly. I tightened my arms around her, not restraining, just holding her still.

"But here's one way we could do it," I continued. "If speaking the words is too hard for you—if saying 'I want this, I need that' makes you shut down—you could leave me a list. Somewhere I'll find it. Something private. You write it beforehand. Check off the things you're craving. Tell me what you want to give up that night. What do you want to surrender? What you want to keep."

She looked up at me now.

"You wouldn't have to vocalize it in the moment. You wouldn't have to fight your instincts to please or to hide. But I'd still know it was real. Still know it was yours. And once I read it, then yes—I'd make the decisions. I'd take control."

She blinked, her eyes glossy but alert.

"But this only works if we both agree that your needs matter. This can't just be about you pleasing me. That's a broken dynamic. It would always tilt too far toward performance, toward guessing, toward you disappearing. I want both of us to be satisfied. I want you to ache for what I give you because you know it's exactly what you asked for, even if you never said a word."

She was silent for a long time.

Then finally—quietly—she said, "I think that's the only way I could ever really ask for it."

I brushed a strand of hair back from her face.

"Then that's the way we'll do it."

I'd love to be able to tell you that everything blossomed after that night. That we found our rhythm, that she opened up, that it all clicked. But that's not how it went.

It was a slog.

Three steps forward, two steps back. Every time I thought we'd made progress, the next night she'd fall silent again. She kept waiting for me to decide everything. To drive every touch, every word, every inch of it. I know some dommes want that—complete subservience, no resistance, no hesitation. But not me.

I like a little fight.

Not brattiness, not games. Just presence. A partner who's there because she wants to be, not because she's afraid to say no. Not because she thinks obedience is the price of admission.

You'd think she'd be the perfect partner on paper. Beautiful. Talented. Willing to do anything I ask. And she did. But it was like sleeping with an emotional ghost.

I could tie her up a hundred ways, fuck her ten different ways, draw every sound I wanted from her throat. But it was hollow. She wasn't *in it.* Not with me. Not fully.

And I don't want that. Not from a partner. Not even from a lover. Sure, it can be hot in short bursts. You can build a weekend scene around it. But it doesn't sustain you. You can't come home to that. You can't make a life on silence and guessing.

Eventually, we broke up. She found someone else—a man, I think, who was deeply dominant but also passive in his own way. Warm. Gentle. Friendly. I imagine it worked better. Maybe he didn't push her to speak. Perhaps he was content being the gravity she orbited around.

And I hope it worked. I really do. She deserved someone who made her feel safe enough to let go. And he probably didn't mind never being let in.

But we weren't a match. She wasn't someone I'd start a family with. And I'm not talking about the kink. I'm talking about everything else. Because sex alone never sustains anything, no matter how twisted or sacred or hot it is. You need someone who meets you where you are. Who stands beside you? Who's there to give, not just to serve.

It has to be a partnership. Even when one of you's wearing the handcuffs.

Otherwise, it's not a power exchange. It's just an imbalance. And if that goes on long enough, it starts to feel abusive. Not in a sexy way. Not in a consensual way. In a soul-eroding way. The kind where you stop recognizing yourself because you're the only one doing the work. And I wasn't going to live there. Not even for her.

23

Filibuster

We met at a bar in D.C.—a friend-of-a-friend situation. It was that Georgetown spot made famous by *St. Elmo's Fire*. He asked for my number, and—shock of all shocks—he called the next day.

After many hot and spicy phone calls and flirtatious emails, I did my due diligence. A little light research told me he was in finance at one of the big firms. Recently divorced. She got the house in Connecticut, and he'd just moved into a new place in New York City, which I was assuming was a freshly claimed bachelor pad. I was hoping he hadn't brought women there before the split—but when I checked the deed, I saw he bought it solo. Clean title, clean conscience. Nice.

He met me at the train station.

I took the Acela up from D.C. and appreciated him paying for the ticket. I like a man who's just a little old-fashioned. He met me at the platform's top like a gentleman out of a movie, all buttoned-up confidence and that half-cocked Wall Street smile. A black car was waiting—naturally—and he opened the door for me like he'd been practicing for the role his whole life. We barely spoke on the drive, but the energy between us was crackling like a third rail.

Still, I made it clear: if this was going to happen, it had to start like a *date*. Not a transaction. Not a hook-up. A proper beginning. I

didn't want to feel like a fetish consultant. I wanted lunch. Conversation. Connection. Then—and only then—could the game begin.

So we went to lunch. He was a charmer. He got us a bottle of champagne, and I sat there in my sundress and floppy hat, already half in love with the fantasy. He was beautiful. I don't understand how anyone wouldn't want this man.

We were perhaps a little tipsy from the wine when we made our way upstairs to Chelsea Piers—the double- or triple-decker driving range, I can't remember which. We found a quiet corner on the upper deck, away from the crowd. I'm guessing not many people knew how to go up there.

He was very good at golf. And I wasn't bad myself—I'd taken lessons for a while at D.C.'s Hains Point. We joked about the clubs, about how strong they were. Then he came up behind me, *Tin Cup* style, wrapped his arms around mine, and started whispering the filthiest things I've ever heard into my ear. And it was delightful.

I was utterly enthralled by his touch, his scent, the heat of him behind me. I wanted to tear into him. He was like a drug.

He enthralled me. I would've done anything he asked if he'd just said it clearly, and on all fours. He joked about the golf clubs and what we could do with them physically later, and I found that intriguing, but I also had his number after that.

He was looking for...Let's say: leadership. He wanted someone to take control. I believe what he'd been doing was purchasing my goodwill—with the charming lunch, the dirty talk, the champagne, the golf.

During our flirtatious golf swings, he had grown incredibly hard. And he was huge. He was packing a baseball bat down there, and I was all for it. I swear—I've never... it was just—it was sick. It was huge. It was gigantic. And it was all mine—all weekend.

By this time, I was fucking dripping wet, and I wanted nothing more than to have his head buried deep in my crotch, worshipping at the divine temple.

Of course, who wouldn't want that from this macho man who'd been tossed on the discard pile? I mean, if he could go down on me like a married man *should* know how to, this was going to be an incredible weekend indeed. I was looking forward to seeing his ass up in the air when I fucked it hard with a dildo. That's what he'd asked me for—he wanted pegging —and I thought that was just about the hottest thing I could imagine.

I know some men are squeamish about these sorts of things, but really, wanting to get fucked up the ass can be very pleasurable for him.

Well, I was soaked, and he was hard as a rock, so we jumped in a car and went back to his place. It was a strange Manhattan apartment in Murray Hill—floor-to-ceiling windows, 15-foot old-school frames, and a loft bedroom you had to climb a ladder to reach. Small kitchen. Smaller bathroom. Big space. Mostly empty. I'm guessing the wife took everything—or maybe this was his escape hatch.

I didn't want to ask too many questions about the divorce, but I was curious. Still, it was early. I wanted to know what was going on inside his head.

This was the moment we had to talk about sex. About what he wanted. About what he was willing to take, what he wasn't, and what he'd brought with him. I hadn't brought anything—I wanted him to handle all that. It was a little teasing. I made sure he hadn't had an orgasm in at least four days. Which, let's be real, probably killed him. But he was ready. So ready.

He had everything laid out. The toys are still in their packaging. He picked out a very ambitious dildo to be fucked with. I respected the hell out of that. There were smaller ones, too, but I could tell he was aiming high. He told me he hadn't tried it before, and I believed him.

He wanted to be pegged hard by me, wearing nothing but a harness, high heels, and a bra. Me, not him. I could get behind that. He didn't want me in all black, and he didn't want me overly girly either. The red lingerie he chose went perfectly with my features—long, thick black hair, skin soft as hell, and lips made to ruin him. He'd even gotten the bra size right. You have to love a man who shops with focus.

Just for fun, he brought a riding crop. He wanted to be whipped lightly to get in the mood. But I didn't think that was going to be a problem—he'd been hard since Chelsea Piers and stayed hard straight through.

The negotiations were easy. He agreed to everything. I got dressed in the items he'd brought me, slipped the giant strap into the harness, and had him give it a blowjob. I think he found it humiliating—in a good way.

I like a man who enjoys being humiliated sometimes. He liked it too. It was passionate.

He was so grateful. He wanted to clean my shoes with his tongue. Then he worked his way slowly up my thigh. The bedroom window gave us a perfect view of the neighbors—I wondered if anyone was watching.

I told him that if he wanted this, he had to receive it like a woman would. Open. Brave. Hungry. And god, he responded. He got even harder.

Honestly, if I were the one being penetrated, I don't think I could've taken the whole thing either. I might've needed backup.

He started kissing up my leg, then took the massive dildo in his hands and treated it like it was real. Mouth, hands, and eyes closed. He did an excellent job. And he knew I was reacting—because I was enjoying it immensely.

I'm one of the few who can be strapped and still climax, just like a man. And I was close. I told him to make me come. And he did.

I took his cotton undershirt and gently put it over his head. I turned him over, dragged my nails lightly down his back to his ass, and told him how hot he was. He didn't respond much to praise, so maybe he needed a bit more degradation. We all have our kinks. No judgment.

I heightened his senses—light fingernails down to his ass. Then a smack. Open-handed, not hard. No marks. Just sound. He tensed up, and when that happens, you *pause*. You check in.

I grabbed the riding crop and began tracing. Slight taps—shoulders, back, thighs. Testing. Watching.

I found it—his spot. Just under the curve of his ass, at the top of his thighs. What a perfect ass. I spanked and teased, had him lift his butt and spread himself so everything hung through his legs. I kept him there, in that moment. Letting it build and letting him *feel* it.

Then, I reached through—where his cock and balls hung. He came. All over the bed. So much of it. He was *so* excited.

That was a turn I didn't see coming. But a delightful one. First one out of the way. Now he'd be more patient. More receptive. But honestly, it didn't go down. He stayed ready.

He was spent, lying face down, pillowcase still on. I unstrapped and lay next to him. No rush. We had all weekend.

He eventually came out of his stupor. I was eager to see where he was emotionally. He was embarrassed that he'd go so fast. I wasn't. It was a *great* sign. But some men get self-conscious.

Honestly? It doesn't fucking matter. As long as she's happy—and you can make her happy again—no woman is ever going to complain, especially when you haven't even gotten to the main event yet. These were just the preliminaries.

And wasn't that *delightful*!

We sat by the fire for a little while, sipping champagne and talking. I wanted to know what he was thinking—what he was feeling. He admitted he felt like he was disappointing me.

I assured him he wasn't.

Okay, maybe some of it could have gone better, but we got the small one in, and for the first time? That was a real accomplishment. He told me how incredibly hard he felt when I was holding him, moving on him—how it felt like he was fucking himself. I was thrilled to hear that. Watching a man give in to that kind of energy is hypnotic. And on a man that beautiful? It was a sight I wouldn't forget.

I had him clean up, then give me a massage—worshipping every part of my body with his hands, his lips, little kisses on my shoulders, my back, all the way down to my legs. I made him use a lot of oil so that my body gleamed in the firelight. He said he liked it. I believed him. A lot of "Yes, Belle" and "You're so beautiful, Belle." He asked if he could touch my breasts. I let him. He kissed them, licked my nipples, and teased me expertly. It was arousing, indulgent, and intimate.

I love this kind of time, when we worship each other's bodies without the weight of expectations. No relationship drama. No outside noise. Just skin, breath, heat. This is what we're made for—to delight in one another in whatever form that takes.

He navigated down toward my clit—still in training, bless him. Good God, the man needed training wheels. But I figured practice makes perfect, and this was as good a classroom as any.

I gave him specific instructions: what to do with his tongue on my clit, how to work the labia, how to make small circles, how to flick, how to use his hands *and* tongue together. How to make the little claw. How to look for the G-spot. It took nearly an hour of "earnest searching." Truthfully, he found it immediately, but I made him search longer. It was more fun that way.

I taught him how to make soft, slow circles with his fingers, how to warm up the area, then how to put his mouth back on my clit and suck, then flick—flick, flick, flick—until I was so turned on I could hardly sit still.

And it worked. Oh, it *worked.*

I wanted to go further, but I also wanted to save something for the evening. I had plans. So I asked him, "Would you be open to me tying you up and riding you—*hard?*"

There wasn't much discussion after that. He was incredibly into it. A little sheepish, a little shy, but intensely eager. He got into a submissive posture immediately.

It's incredible how quickly a man will bend when the right woman permits him. He was dying for it. I could see it in every muscle.

I couldn't help but think—if only his wife had been more forgiving, more imaginative. She could've had *all* this.

We got dressed for dinner, though the ritual of dressing was almost as intimate as anything we'd done so far. He put on a beautiful suit—something that probably cost more than my first car. I slipped into a little black dress, but not before teasing him first. I walked into the room in just a bra, panties, a garter belt, thigh-highs, and heels. I left the dress outside the room so I'd have to go back for it, giving him a full view of my body.

My body looked terrific. Chest forward, attitude engaged. I don't *need* a push-up bra—but damn if it didn't look good.

Even in that expensive suit, he knelt at my feet. I made him ask me if he was going to take me out to dinner, made him tell me what we were going to do that evening, and then I told him whether or not that would please me. He was good. Very good. I told him I'd tie him up and ride him like a stallion—and then I was going to fuck him hard, just how he'd asked. I think he came close to losing it just hearing that.

I had him get my dress and put it on me like a proper servant. He zipped it slowly, grazing my backside. I stopped him.

"Don't you dare touch me unless I tell you it's okay? Mind your place, or I swear to God I'll leave."

He stammered, "I'm sorry, Belle."

"No excuses," I said. "What I say goes. Understand?"

"Yes, Belle."

I had him retrieve my jewelry and place my grandmother's pearl necklace around my neck—she'd be so proud, truly. She had married three men and outlived them all. She was a very Merry Widow.

I told him I'd brought something for *him*. A small velvet submission collar. Symbolic, of course. We weren't ready for public display—yet. But the meaning was clear.

He knelt, back turned to me, and I placed the collar around his neck beneath his tie. It had a little silver ring dangling from the front. He understood. We exchanged adornments—he gave me pearls; I gave him powerlessness.

As my grandmother always said, training a man benefits all women. Though I am not sure she meant it in this context.

Before we left, I gave him the rules. "When we're outside, you're the perfect gentleman. You open doors, order for me, and lead on the dance floor. But when we return—when that door closes—you're mine. Knees on the floor, no questions asked."

He looked me dead in the eye. "Yes, Belle. I'll do anything you want."

The car was already waiting.

At dinner, he was utterly devoted. The restaurant was Manhattan-fancy: so many forks, I wasn't even sure what half of them were for. But I let him lead. I don't care about ambiance as much as taste, but the way he treated the moment—like it was part of our larger performance—made it delicious.

Every so often, I reminded him I was wearing thigh-high stockings. He was visibly distracted. It was delightful. He shifted between being this solicitous, respectful gentleman to something far more desperate and worshipful—only I could see it.

After dinner, we wandered and ended up at a cigar bar. He ordered a brandy and a cigar. I watched. Not my thing, but it gave me ideas.

In that moment—sitting in a wingback chair, legs splayed, laughing and commanding attention—he looked like a king. Not like the D.C. types. He was his own man—a man who'd lived a life and was still open—still seeking. Still hungry.

And when he sucked on that cigar? I was thinking about earlier. And later.

I touched my pearls. He leaned in across the table. "Yes, Belle?"

"I'm jealous of the cigar. Let's go."

He got the check so fast I didn't even see him signal for it. Just dropped two hundred in cash, and we were gone.

In the black car on the way back, I reached over, traced his cock through his slacks—massive, hard, impossibly eager. I stopped before he exploded, but I let him touch me. His hand slid up my thigh, past the stocking, brushing my clit. I could've come right there.

I unfastened the top of his collar and ran my finger around it—a reminder.

When we got back to the apartment, I flashed him as he stepped out of the car. Provocative. His eyes widened.

He walked me to the door, stared at my ass as I moved ahead. I didn't stop him.

Once inside, I told him to stop. "On your hands and knees," I ordered. He obeyed immediately. Crawled right to my shoes, head bowed, ass in the air.

I closed the door behind us.

"Now I'm in control."

And I had *plans.*

I told him to take down the mattress and blankets from the loft and place them in the center of the cavernous living room, right in front of the fireplace. I had him start a fire—not because it was cold, but because I wanted to see his body in firelight. I tried to watch it flicker across his skin like a dance.

My god, he was beautiful.

I had him kneel in front of me. I took a tie and wrapped it around his arms behind his back. It was a struggle—those arms were massive. I looped the tie several times and had him hold the ends in his hands so he could get out if he genuinely wanted to. A man of his size? Nothing would truly restrain him unless he allowed it.

He knelt—legs open, arms behind his back—and I started touching him, tracing his contours, reading his responses. I brought the riding crop back out and dragged it lightly over his skin, across his chest, grazing his nipples, down to his thighs. I watched for any twitch, flinch, breath hitch—any signal of where to strike.

It didn't take long to find his favorite spot again: just beneath the curve of his ass. Perfectly spankable.

I had him bend over, ass up in the air, and used the crop gently, teasing the backs of his thighs, tapping the crease of his hips. He was practically vibrating. Still hard. Desperate.

I figured it was time. I started with the smallest dildo from the set—something manageable, slicked it with lube, and began the slow, purposeful process of easing him into it. At first, his body resisted. So I stopped. Waited. Then whispered, "Push back onto it. You have to want it."

He got it. And it made all the difference.

He became greedy. Hungry. His ass moved back onto me, inch by inch, accepting more, adjusting, inviting.

I let him sit with it, kneeling before the fire. I poured champagne, let him sip it off my skin, kiss me, touch me, run his fingers over every curve. I told him to go down on me again. Practice.

He still wasn't great, but he was trying. Earnest. Learning. I gave guidance, direction, pointed him toward Eden, and let him taste the apple.

Eventually, I finished myself off while he watched. He seemed to like that. A consolation prize—but one he appreciated.

And we still had all night.

I told him to build the fire higher while I lounged on the mattress, watching every movement of his bare, beautiful body. He moved like a man owned because he was.

I instructed him to bring champagne—yes, of course, he had more—and he brought up two fresh glasses. He poured while I lay back, lounging, legs slightly open, garter belt taut. His cock was still hard. Still ready. It was like he was built for this.

I spilled a little champagne on the head of his cock and traced it with my tongue. He nearly lost it again. I told him, not yet. I wanted him to feel everything: the fire, the heat, the champagne, the anticipation.

I let him worship me—run his fingers all over me. Nothing rushed—just sensation. The sounds of the city echoed through the windows. It felt like we were alone in the world.

Eventually, I let him go down on me again. And this time? He was getting better. He found the clit. He used his hands and his mouth. He took direction. I came. Hard.

Then it was time.

I had him lie flat on his back. I climbed on top of him. Told him not to move. Not a muscle. If he moved, I'd stop. This was for *me.* I was going to use him. Ride him. Come as many times as I want. And he was going to lie there and take it.

He agreed. Of course he did.

I slid down onto him slowly. Inch by inch. He was massive—long and thick and perfectly cut. I rode him gently at first, just taking my time and feeling every bit of him and letting him feel every bit of me. I started to move faster, bouncing on my knees like I was riding a horse.

He watched as I touched myself, as I brought myself to climax on top of him. It was an overload. And I held him afterward. Still joined. Still inside.

I contracted my muscles—slowly, deliberately—around his cock. He jolted. I don't think he'd ever felt anything like it. I waited, then did it again. And again. And then I started moving.

Up. Down. Up. Down. My breasts full, my body glistening, my moans loud and shameless. I came again. He was still holding on. Still not coming.

Then I got off him, had him turn around, and get on all fours. It was time for his reward.

I strapped on the most enormous dildo—the one he chose himself—I removed the smaller plug he had been wearing.

Pegging someone well requires skill and patience. Pegging a man—especially a straight man—requires trust. Most have never experienced anal sex in a way that makes them feel open and safe. It has to be slow. Gentle. Controlled. Stay in. Don't thrust. Let him think it. Let him enjoy it. This wasn't about pounding—it was about pleasure.

I had him spread his legs wide. His balls dangled. Ass cheeks wide, hands holding them open. I guided him down onto the dildo. Slowly, the tip went in. He was silent. Overwhelmed. Not in that much pain— in ecstasy. He was finally getting what he wanted.

I got on one knee to angle properly, then both knees. I pulled his hips toward me gently. I pressed my chest to his back, grabbed his cock—still hard—and whispered to him.

"Are you ready for more?"

He moaned Yes.

"What was that?"

"Yes, Belle."

I pulled him back more, then pushed him away. Each time, a little more went in. I told him to reach between his legs, touch his cock, and jerk it while I continued.

And he came in 20 seconds. Beautifully.

Then he collapsed in a heap. I slowly pulled out, lay beside him, and we both breathed. We talked about what we felt, what it meant, and how it felt for him. He admitted he'd gone into sensory overload.

We wished it could be a regular thing. But D.C. and New York were far apart. I couldn't leave my job. He couldn't leave his. Still, it was a perfect weekend. And on Sunday morning, I took the train home. And I don't think I've ever quite stopped thinking about him—or what might have been.

24

Phoenix Campaign

The Phoenix was this blistering hot redhead I met at a bar—curvy, china-smooth skin, full, thick lips, and that mane of red hair. Not just wavy—no, naturally curled. The kind you can't fake. She wore it half up, half down, like she'd stepped out of some vintage movie. It was piled on top of her head in this soft, messy twist while the rest cascaded down her back in curls.

And her body? Beautiful breasts, beautiful ass, everything. She was stunning.

There was this tattoo, right in the middle of her back. A phoenix. Always a sign. A marker of someone who's risen from something—or tried to. Nobody gets that tattoo unless they've got a reason. Trauma? Probably. Abuse? Almost certainly. I didn't ask. I wanted to. God, I wanted to. But she never offered it, and I don't ask unless it's safe.

You can smell it on someone sometimes, you know? Like a current that runs underneath. Some submissives role-play out trauma in a healthier way through power dynamics—reclaiming control by giving it away. Maybe they were spanked, and now they like it, but in this context, it's consensual, negotiated. It's about choosing the story.

That was Phoenix. I could see it all in one look. That's my particular gift.

When we met, she was non-committal. I got her social media account instead of a phone number, which is okay, considering the modern era. That way, if she didn't like the vibe later, she could block

me. Fair. It's a weird world. A lot of creeps out there. I don't want to be one of them.

Her profile pic? It was her, bending into the camera in a slightly provocative top, those big eyes looking up. She was practically telegraphing it. People try to hide their tells. They think they're slick. But if you're with someone like me, someone who can crawl into your head and read what you're not even ready to say out loud, you shouldn't even bother. I could tell what made her submit. What made her happy? What made her *surrender joyfully?*

Some people say they're doms. They like the outfits, the aesthetic, the lingo. But being a Dom? It means you get inside someone's head and make it safe enough for them to share their truth with you. If they can't find the words, you help. That's the deal. And the clothes are pretty cool.

Phoenix lived in a cute little apartment, way across town—pretty much the opposite side of the Beltway. Geographically undesirable, but when you're in that honeymoon flush, who cares? I drove. Happily.

One of our first nights out, we went to a Chinese place—or maybe Thai? Doesn't matter. The point is, *they knew her there.* The waitstaff, the host, and even the guy bussing tables. She was greeted like royalty.

"The usual, Miss?"

I blinked. I was used to being the one who turned heads. My presence tends to fill a room—servers talk to me, people look me in the eye. Not that night. They zeroed in on her, as if she were the sun and they were orbiting.

"That was... new," I said once we sat down.

"What?"

"You're known here. Like, *known*-known. Do you have a loyalty card or something?"

She giggled. "I may have a dumpling problem."

"I respect that."

I didn't mind it, exactly. But it was rare enough to be jarring. Usually, even if I'm not *trying,* people pay attention to me. But she eclipsed me in that moment, and not because she was loud, but because she had *presence.*

"You okay?" she asked, sipping her Thai iced tea like nothing had happened.

"Yeah," I said. "Just not used to being second fiddle."

She smiled. "Maybe it's nice to let someone else take center stage."

I smirked. "We'll see about that."

And we did.

Under the table, I kept teasing her—rubbing her leg with my foot, hooking my ankle gently around hers, and tugging, playful, suggestive.

"You know," I leaned in with a smirk, my voice low and coaxing, "I've been wondering what it'd be like to tie your ankles together."

She raised her eyebrow, but didn't pull away. "Has anyone ever actually done that to you?" I asked, brushing my foot up the inside of her calf.

She bit her lip and smiled. "There was this one time..." she began, her voice dipping into a hush. "I was tied up, ass up, and she fucked me from behind for so long I lost track of time. I couldn't take it anymore—so she pushed me down on a vibrator, and I just exploded."

"Now that's a story worth revisiting," I grinned. "Let's start there."

We left the restaurant soon after, and she walked ahead but kept glancing back to make sure I was following. I was. Oh, I was following.

At the car, she stopped by the passenger door and waited.

"You want me to open this for you?" I teased, already reaching for the handle.

"It's just... nice," she said softly.

"Of course it is," I replied. I opened the door and leaned in, reaching for the seatbelt. As I pulled it across her chest, my fingers brushed her, and she let out the faintest shiver.

"You okay there?" I murmured near her ear.

She gave me a look, her lips parted slightly, breath hitched. "You're not playing fair."

"I never said I would."

I kissed her jawline, then the soft spot just beneath her ear, and down to her collarbone, where the scent of her perfume hit me—something classic, not trendy. Warm, like ambergris or something floral and vintage.

"You smell like secrets," I whispered.

"You smell like trouble," she shot back, laughing.

I cupped her chin, tilted her face to mine. "You look beautiful tonight."

She pulled me in by the lapels and kissed me hard, full-bodied, like she'd been waiting all night.

We made out like teenagers parked under a streetlamp—hands everywhere, breathless laughter, lips bruised with want—when we could've easily driven the few blocks to her place. But there was something delicious in the delay, something vintage and seductive.

"We could go now," she finally gasped, pulling back slightly.

I drove to her high-rise with one hand on the wheel and another inching up to her Delta Dawn.

"Lead the way, Phoenix. I'm right behind you."

At her building, we held hands as we walked in. In the elevator, we were a tangled mess of lips and limbs.

"You're lucky no one else got in," I murmured as I grabbed a handful of her ass.

"Are you kidding? I'd have made them uncomfortable on purpose," she said with a mischievous grin.

Once in her apartment, she tugged me out onto the balcony. The view of Arlington shimmered below.

"Champagne?" she offered.

"Only if you're joining me."

She brought out two flutes and a chilled bottle of champagne. We settled onto her lounge chairs, the city sprawling at our feet. She poured. I watched.

"To improbable nights," she toasted.

"And to the women who make them possible," I replied, clinking glasses.

I took one careful sip. "Just one glass. Doms and alcohol don't mix."

"I'll behave," she said with a wink, sipping hers.

She wouldn't. Not tonight.

The air was crisp, the sky velvet, and the moment stretched between us like silk being pulled tight.

I turned toward her, eyes locked on hers. "You know what happens next, don't you?"

She smiled. "I was hoping you'd tell me."

I set my glass down. "I am going to fuck you."

She didn't hesitate.

I slowly eased her out of her clothes until she was perfectly naked, her skin glowing in the moonlight. I started kissing down her body, lingering at her breasts. Her nipples were the most sensitive I had ever encountered.

As I trailed kisses lower, down to the golden triangle, I began licking her clit with slow, deliberate strokes, and slipped two fingers inside her. I found her G-spot within seconds, confirmed by the sound she made.

"Hnnnnnnnngg," she gasped, her body bucking slightly.

"Got it," I whispered, smiling into her skin.

She was like a bronco under me, bucking and twisting as I worked my fingers deep and complex. I wanted to get her off quickly, under the stars, before anyone started calling in noise complaints. Because my God, she was loud.

"Ohhh—oh my God, yes—don't stop, don't you dare stop," she moaned, so loudly I glanced around instinctively.

"You're going to get us arrested," I laughed softly, not letting up. And within minutes, she came hard, shuddering beneath me.

We went inside after that. As I led her into the bedroom, I asked, "What do you want to do tonight? What's your fantasy?"

"I want you to fuck me from behind," she said, eyes gleaming with heat.

"Permission granted," I said, practically growling.

I bent her over the edge of the bed, ass up, feet on the floor, face buried in the mattress. I slipped on my harness and slid into her slowly at first, savoring the tight, greedy grip of her body.

"You were made for this," I murmured.

"Harder," she begged. "Please, Belle. Harder."

I picked up the pace. We went at it for at least twenty-five minutes before I realized she needed more.

"Vibe?" I asked, panting slightly.

"Yes. Please," she said, breathless.

I flipped her over and tossed her legs to her ears. I dove deep into her.

She grabbed her vibrator and turned it on, holding it to her clit while I kept thrusting. Then, with perfect, almost telepathic instinct, she pressed the vibe against me, too, through the harness. It was awkward but electric.

We came together, bodies shaking in sync, gasping each other's names.

"Holy shit," I said, collapsing next to her. "That was impressive."

She grinned. "That was just the beginning."

And she meant it. We had sex four or five more times that night. She was insatiable, her body pulling me back in every time I thought I was done.

Every time I fucked her from behind, I saw the Phoenix on her back and thought, There's something more here. A story she hasn't told me. A tale she may never tell.

The next morning, I slipped out before she woke, leaving a note tucked under her pillow: Can't stop thinking about last night. I want more. Same time next weekend?

She agreed.

When Saturday came, I brought wine, takeout from her favorite place, and of course, my trusty red suede flogger.

"This weekend, "I told her over dinner, "I'm going to fuck you on the balcony. Bra on, ass bare. You'll be tied to the railing, and you'll take every inch of it."

She shivered and nodded, biting her lip. "Yes. Please. I want that."

That night, I tied her to the balcony rail. She wore a bikini-style bra that offered coverage from above, but from the street, no one could see her bare ass. Still, the idea that she might be caught was a risk that made her breath hitch.

I dragged the flogger across her skin first, teasing.

"Don't make a sound, "I whispered. "You don't want the neighbors to see you like this, do you?"

She shook her head frantically.

Good. But if you cry out—"I smacked her ass with the flogger. "They'll know exactly what's happening up here."

She whimpered, and I watched her try to stifle the sounds.

It was thrilling.

She collapsed against the railing, breathless, hair tangled, skin flushed. And I whispered in her ear, That's my good girl. My firebird."

Her skin was incredibly sensitive—some of the most responsive I'd ever encountered—and when I made my way down to the golden triangle with my fingers, I teased her clit with my fingertip while sliding my fingers inside.

"Oh my god," she gasped, hips twitching. "Right there, don't stop."

"Like a horse, huh?" I teased, grinning. "You're bucking like a bronco."

She nodded, biting her lip, too far gone to respond verbally.

I kept going, plunging deeper with my hand, and watching her twist beneath me. She was loud—so loud that I was starting to worry someone might come outside to see what the fuss was about.

"We don't even have music on." I whispered in her ear, chuckling. "You're gonna get us kicked out of the neighborhood."

But five minutes later, she came hard, trembling and gasping.

"That's it," I murmured, brushing her hair from her face. "I've got you now."

We moved to the bedroom, and I asked her what she wanted.

"Tell me your fantasy," I said, cupping her chin.

"I want you to fuck me from behind," she said without hesitation.

"Bend over for me, baby," smacked her ass hard.

I bent her over the bed, her feet hanging off the edge, ass high in the air. I strapped on the harness and slid into her with ease. She was so greedy, clenching around the dildo like it owed her money.

For twenty minutes, I kept her there, steady and unrelenting, until she reached for the vibrator pressed against the sheets. She screamed for me to drive her down into the mattress, and I was more than willing to comply. My thrusts grew sharper, harder, pounding until her first climax tore through her.

Then her head snapped back and she screamed at me, tears streaking her face.

Her voice broke, and she spat at me, wild and furious. The spit caught my cheek, hot against the sting of her words.

"Fuck me!"

I tightened my hold, shock turning to something sharper, darker. If she wanted cruelty, if she wanted to scream at me through tears and spit, then I would give her no relief. I slammed harder, refusing to let her breathe, pinning her open as the first orgasm faded and the second began to build under my hand.

"You're mine, "I said against her back. "You're not a person right now. You're my possession. Something I own. Something I control."

She gasped, moaning louder, hips jerking involuntarily.

"You love that, don't you?" I pressed the toy harder, just for a second, and she shuddered. "You love being used. Not asked. Not coaxed. Owned. You want to be something I can bend and hold and take however I want."

"Yes," she cried out. "Please... I want to be yours. Please keep me like this. Use me like I belong to you."

"You do belong to me." I pushed deeper, grinding until she whimpered like it hurt, like she wanted to break apart to take more. "You're not my good girl. You're my bitch. My whore. My filthy little possession. You'll come when I tell you, and you'll thank me for ruining you."

Her eyes were wet and furious, her voice tearing out raw. "I'll do anything. Just don't stop."

"You'll come again, and again, until there's nothing left in you but the sound of me owning you. Until your mind is blank and your body's used up. Until every time you open your mouth, it's only to scream my name."

She was panting hard, crying and spitting, trying to hold herself upright even as her muscles gave way. I slammed her hips back into me, one hand gripping cruelly, the other working her clit without mercy. She was soaked and trembling, thighs jerking, body caught between pain and hunger.

"You're going to come again," I said, calm and steady, even as I punished her body. "You're going to scream for me. You're going to beg me to keep using you. And you're going to do it because you don't have a choice. Because you're mine."

"Please!" she screamed, spit flying from her lips. "Please, make me come. Just keep going, don't stop, don't you fucking stop!"

"Good bitch, "I growled. "When will you give it to me?"

And she did.

She came with a scream that broke in her throat, collapsing forward as tears streaked down her face, sobs tangled with the sound of her orgasm. I caught her chest in one arm and held her tight as she shook, sobbing my name through the tremors.

"That's two," I whispered, sliding the toy between her legs again before she could even catch her breath. "You're not finished. Not even close. I'll take everything you've got, and then I'll take more."

We had sex four or five more times that night. She was insatiable. And every time I fucked her from behind, the Phoenix tattoo stared back at me—proof of pain, resilience, and rebirth.

I slept over and left early in the morning, slipping out while she slept. But I left a note: "Saturday night. My place or yours?"

We met up again that weekend. I brought over takeout and a bottle of wine. We ended up on the balcony again.

"You know what I want to do to you?" I asked, setting the takeout down without looking at it. My voice was quiet, but she heard the shift.

She glanced up at me, eyes already wide. "What?"

"I want to take you out onto the balcony, tie you to the railing, and paddle that perfect ass until you're trembling. Then I want to fuck you while you try not to make a single sound. Because if you do, the neighbors will hear. And they'll know exactly what you are."

Her thighs pressed together under the table. She nodded slowly. "Okay. But I'm not wearing anything except a bra."

I didn't smile. I didn't need to. "Perfect."

She followed me out into the warm night air, wearing nothing but that skimpy bra. Barely there. Not enough to cover anything useful. Just enough to give the illusion of modesty. I tied her wrists to the metal railing with nude color stockings, tugging her arms forward until her back arched and her ass rose like an offering.

She was exposed. Illuminated. Vulnerable.

"If you make a sound," I murmured, letting the paddle drag across her bare skin, "someone will hear. The guy is smoking on the next balcony. The woman across the courtyard who always waters her plants at night. You want them to see what kinky shit you are into?"

She shook her head fast, her voice catching. "Oh, Belle."

"When to keep your mouth shut. You know I won't stop just because I'm watching."

The first crack of the paddle echoed off the brick, loud and sharp. She jerked hard, but no sound came out. Just that raw gasp, she tried to swallow. I watched the bloom of red spread across her skin with satisfaction. I hit her again, harder, and her legs trembled. Another. Then another. Her breath came in short bursts through her nose, mouth buried in her arms, fists clenched tight. She was trying so hard.

And she was soaking.

I slid my fingers between her thighs and smiled. "You're dripping, sweetheart. Haven't even fucked you yet."

Her hips bucked back into my hand. Her body was feral—desperate—clawing for more. Her nails scraped at the railing.

"Easy," I said, gripping her hip with one hand and pushing two fingers deep into that wet, hungry heat with the other. "You're not going anywhere. You stay right here. You stay mine."

She was panting. Wild. Clawing at me like an animal, but still bound and silent. Her obedience was trembling at the edge of her need, and that made it even sweeter.

"You like this, don't you? Being used. Being fucked like a possession. No voice. No control. Just me inside you, telling your body what to do."

She moaned into her forearm. Just a sound of desperation, swallowed whole.

"That's right, "I whispered, curling my fingers, feeling her squeeze down around me. "You're mine. And when I decide you get to come, you'll do it without a sound. You'll come for me silently. Because you know what happens if you don't"

Her body convulsed. She was already so close. I didn't slow down. I rubbed her with precision, listening to the wet sounds of her vagina, watching the way she shook and writhed, and trying not to scream. Her legs trembled. Her jaw locked. And then she came—violently, completely, silently. Her body shook so hard I had to hold her up.

But she didn't cry out.

Not once.

I pressed a kiss to the back of her neck, tasting sweat and submission.

"Good girl, "I whispered, still inside her. "That's one."

And I started again.

After I made her come on the balcony, shuddering against the railing, we went inside to the bedroom upstairs. I tied her to the bed—simple but effective. "I need to get off, "I told her. "Oh, I'm just going to fuck you until I do."

She was on her back, her hands tied, her legs bent and bound together. I got on top of her and fucked her missionary-style, pushing deep, her moans muffled by the pillows. She was completely into it.

I went down on her a little to see how close she was to coming. Not quite there. So I stopped, untied her hands, and had her climb on top of me. She held herself still as I fucked into her, rubbing her clit at the same time.

She struggled to come into that position, though. "And the vibrator?" I asked.

"Yes, please," she gasped.

So I grabbed the toy, turned it on, and in about 30 seconds, she came hard. She needed the pressure—the vibration. Some women do. I've seen it before. It could've been the position. It could've been the ropes. Could've been a habit. Whatever. We'd figure it out.

The next time we got together, I prepped her.

"Here's how it's going to go, "I said. "You're going to come into my house. That's the last decision you're going to make."

She raised an eyebrow, curious but quiet.

"If you feel uncomfortable at any point," I said, "Just say 'stop', 'hold,' or even just 'hey.' I'll stop immediately. No questions asked. But unless you say one of those words, I'm making all the decisions tonight. Do you understand?"

She nodded. "Yes."

"Yes, what?"

"Yes, Belle."

"Good girl."

She arrived in a sweet little sundress, accompanied by floral panties and heels. Cute, not my usual thing, but she knew it would please me. And I liked that. They were sheer, delicate flowers embroidered across the fabric. Pretty. Sexy.

I stripped her naked at the door. No ceremony. Just peeled everything off. Then I wrapped rope around her torso—several times, up and down—so her breasts were framed, exposed. Not full shibari. This was quick, makeshift, and not about aesthetics. It was about control, pressure, and containment. Something she could get out of if she wanted to. Trust-building.

"You can say stop," I reminded her.

Nothing. She didn't want to.

So I went for it—legs up. I flogged her thighs with my red suede flogger—slow, rhythmic, building that crazy figure-eight pattern. Not too hard. Just enough. Then I finger-fucked her for twenty minutes straight, playing with her G-spot until she was begging me to let her come.

"Please," she whimpered. "Please let me come. Please, Belle."

I sucked her tits, letting the tension build even more.

When I finally gave in—let her come—it was wild. Her whole body arched. That gorgeous ass bounced under my hips when I fucked her from behind. Her tits smacked together with each thrust. She was beautiful.

Sometimes with her, I felt almost masculine. Not Butch—but something else. Power. A male-female polarity that I rarely indulge in, but damn it felt good.

She brought that out in me. Not many people do.

I don't even—I don't look butch. I don't act butch. There've been times in my life when I've presented more butch, sure, but at that point? I was full femme. Long hair, big tits, big hips, maybe even still wearing makeup. The kind of femme that gets stopped in the grocery store for directions and gets called Mis with a bit of extra sugar in the tone.

And all I wanted to do was fuck her. Hard. Make her come. Watch her go limp and dreamy-eyed and fall asleep tangled in the sheets like a satisfied kitten. She was everything you could ever want.

Outside the bedroom, our dynamic worked just as well. She was charming, disarming, and talkative in that "have ten tabs open in my brain" way. Fun. So fun. Not exactly someone I'd be just friends with—too much electricity—but that chemistry? It was undeniable.

I'd watch her scrunch up her face when she came, her lips parting, cheeks flushed, and those little gasping breaths? Yeah. She could go hard. Over and over. It was a lot. And I loved it.

But like most beautiful, scorching, made-for-TV kind of things, it had its cracks. She had a hair trigger when it came to certain things. Stuff we'd now call red flags. I suggested the party casually over dinner. "There's this event... a little off the beaten path, but I think you'd enjoy it."

Her fork paused halfway to her mouth. "What kind of event?"

I hesitated. "dungeon party. It's a safe space, all vetted. I thought it might be fun."

Her eyes darkened. "Oh."

"It could be an adventure," I coaxed. "chance to explore—"

"No," she snapped, surprising me. "You have to respect that."

"What's going on?" I asked, trying to keep my tone even. "You're usually open to new experiences."

Her gaze dropped. "Not this. There's someone there, someone I don't want to see."

"Who?" I pressed, but she shook her head.

"Does it matter? I won't go."

Frustration simmered. "You're safe with me. We can handle anything together."

She looked up, eyes glistening. "Not this. Please don't push."

I sighed, feeling the distance growing. "Alright. I won't"

But it was too late. The unspoken words hung heavy between us. Later, I learned the truth—someone had hurt her deeply. I wished then, as I do now, that I had listened better, understood more. But sometimes, even a phoenix fears the fire."

She looked away. That was the last real conversation we had. She never spoke to me again after that night.

No text. No explanation. No text. No call. No explanation.

Just gone.

And look, I've had endings before—messy ones. Civil ones. The kind where you both cry in a diner booth over pancakes and promise to stay friends. But this? A digital vanishing act? It felt like someone ripped the final pages out of my book and set them on fire. Like I was halfway through the best sex of my life, and she just slipped out the door, still breathless, never to be seen again.

I don't think I ever got the whole picture with her. Maybe I wasn't supposed to. Perhaps she was the kind of woman who only exists in one act—blazing bright, then smoke.

But I still think about her sometimes. About the Phoenix on her back and what she must have walked through to get it. About how she came, begging like she needed saving. About that tiny smile she gave me when I brought her tea the morning after—the kind of smile you'd miss if you blinked.

It wasn't love. But God, it could've been something.

25

Chesapeake Caucus

As a rule, I'm not the kind of girl who gets fixed up. I don't make a habit of it. I've never been a fan of online dating either. I prefer meeting people in person, the way you're supposed to—where it takes some skill, some courage, and a bit of conviction to walk up and start talking. It's a habit. Practice it enough and you get good. And I am. I talk to strangers all the time: at the gym, at the grocery store, waiting in line for coffee. I don't walk through the world with headphones in or my eyes glued to my phone. I pay attention. I stay in the room. And because of that, I meet people.

Still, I occasionally agree to a setup, usually against my better judgment. And it rarely works out. That first spark is hard to judge from a photo or a few curated compliments from a friend of a friend. You need chemistry, which can't be manufactured.

So, I had low expectations when I agreed to this one. A friend of a friend from work, kind of thing. I was already halfway out before I was even in. But, I said yes, and we met for a drink on Capitol Hill at this cute little bar. Very lowkey. We both ordered martinis—hers dry, mine dirty as hell—and we chatted.

Chesapeake was...nice. Not immediately electric, not setting me on fire, but there was something. I couldn't tell what I was picking up—maybe a kind of vulnerability, or perhaps she was just hyper aware of the setting. But something in me said: go out again. Maybe she'd warm up. Perhaps she was just slow to unfold.

And then she said something that caught me off guard. Something oddly specific.

"I wonder what you'd look like on the beach at New Year's."

I blinked. "Excuse me?"

Chesapeake smiled, like she'd said something perfectly ordinary. "I'm going to my Bay house—just me and a few friends. We're having a quiet New Year's this year. You should come."

It was still early December. She was inviting me to spend a holiday weekend together, as essentially strangers.

"That's...bold," I said, sipping my drink.

She shrugged. "I think you'd like it."

She didn't say much else, but I could read between the lines. The house was probably inherited—classic family property. I pictured ivy-covered brick or gray shingles, along with wraparound porches. While the whole backstory wouldn't be clear until later, I would come to learn she was, in fact, something of a political heiress—a legacy name. One, I recognized instantly when I finally heard it, though I would never repeat it here. Or anywhere.

She was discreet. She didn't date women publicly, which is why she was so nervous. She wasn't married—I checked. But she was guarded, cautious, like she'd lived her whole life with a press secretary hiding in her closet with her.

At that moment, I didn't care about the press. A fire pit by the bay. The wind and the water, and a kiss at midnight that might mean something. Maybe I was in the mood for a little romantic mischief.

I glanced across the table at her. She was undeniably beautiful, but oddly dressed—a blue pantsuit—nothing terrible, but nothing fabulous. Sensible shoes. Diamond studs—real, no doubt. A simple Cartier watch. A bracelet that whispered old money. Nothing ostentatious, but every item quietly said, *I have never needed to check a price tag in my life.*

Still, I couldn't quite get a read on her. And that's rare for me. Usually, I can sum someone up in ten seconds flat, but with her, it was like trying to decode a locked diary in a language I didn't know.

I've learned that when someone has that kind of emotional armor, it's usually for a reason. They've built a persona, often since childhood, something socially acceptable, perhaps even noble or impressive. But their authentic self is buried. Repressed. The only way to see it is to catch them off guard—tipsy or furious, laughing too hard, or caught in bed with someone they trust.

With her, I felt the shell. Polished. Pristine. Impenetrable. And yet I knew—I *knew*—there was something messy and hungry underneath. I just had to find the crack. God help me, I wanted to crawl through it.

I told her, "I'm happy to go to the Bay house. But I'm taking my car. I'll drive you if you like, but I'm having an exit plan."

She didn't flinch. Just gave a little nod, like she respected the practicality.

"Send me a list," I said. "Do I need an evening gown, a cocktail dress, or footie pajamas? What's the vibe?"

She laughed, surprised. "Everything you'll need will already be there."

Of course it would.

She mentioned casually that the house would be fully stocked with food and drinks—no need to go out, which I took as rich people code. Wealthy people like that don't go to restaurants on holiday weekends. It's too much effort, and it's too visible. Either the chef handles it, or everything's catered and waiting.

The list arrived later that night, via text. Simple and to the point: *If there was something special that you would like to bring to use, please do so.*

That was it. No emoji. No follow-up. No winking implication or even a polite qualifier. Just the sentence, floating alone like a dare.

I stared at it for longer than I care to admit. "Something special" is not neutral language. It is laced with invitation, with presumption, with a kind of baited silence that leaves you either feeling desired or exposed. I could not quite tell which she meant. Did she want me to bring wine? Something rare and aged, the kind of bottle with an origin story? Or was this more...specialized? Did she mean toys? Lingerie? Some accessory or token she had hinted at before but never quite requested? Was she testing whether I could guess what she wanted?

She is not the kind of woman who leaves things to chance. So if she left it open, it meant she wanted to see how I filled in the blank.

Of course, the possibilities multiplied like rabbits. I imagined her in those perfectly tailored cigarette pants, sitting with that calm confidence she uses to disarm senators. Maybe she had something elaborate in mind. Some game. A scenario. She's the one who joked that the only way to get Congress to pass universal healthcare was to tie them down and edge them until they agreed to feed the poor.

Maybe she would want to roleplay something like that. Perhaps not the whole fantasy, but some version of it. It was hard to tell with her. I could not ask for clarification. That would have broken the spell. I packed light but deliberately. A black dress, I guessed, she would like. Clean lines. No frills. A silk scarf that could double as an accessory or a gag. The flogger, just in case she wanted to test limits, and a bottle of French wine so obscure it might as well have been a bribe.

My heart was loud in my ears the whole drive. That humming ache of anticipation. The kind that makes you forget to breathe.

I still didn't know what she wanted. But I was ready to find out.

We drove over the many bridges of Maryland. Her hand crept up my thigh somewhere near the incline of one, her mouth close to my ear, whispering something I can't even remember now.

I slapped her hand back. Not hard. Just enough to make a point. My voice dropped into that deeper register, the one I save for when I mean business.

"No," I said. "Not on this bridge. You don't touch me unless I tell you to."

I didn't even really mean to. It just sort of slipped out—that voice. The one people listen to without thinking. The one that settles low and leaves no room for argument. She responded to it instantly, like it was an executive order from the White House. Breath caught, eyes fixed, posture perfect. She didn't question it. She didn't need to. Her body had already decided to obey.

She froze, and then she melted. Her pupils widened. Her lips parted. She went quiet in a way that wasn't silence. She looked at me like she wanted to climb into my lap and beg for forgiveness with her mouth.

She whispered, "God, I love that voice," more to herself than to me.

I let the moment hang, then leaned in just enough. "God isn't here right now. I am. He can have you back on Sunday. You're mine now."

That voice has stopped rooms, meetings, auditions, and lovers alike. It's my power switch, and she had just found it—without even knowing what she'd done. Later, if she's lucky, I'll let her find out where the other one is.

We crossed the bridge in that silence, her hand politely folded in her lap, my fingers gripping the steering wheel like a lifeline.

The house was exactly what I'd pictured, only better. A gravel driveway lined with tiny lantern lights curved up to a sprawling estate with panoramic views of the Chesapeake. An old stone fountain near the entrance. Everything smelled of salt, pine needles, and aged wood.

Old money, through and through.

I popped the trunk, reaching for my bag, but she ran ahead and grabbed it.

"I'll carry it," she said, already lifting it out.

"I thought we could just let the servants get it." I clicked my tongue—obviously joking.

But she turned to me with that unreadable look she does so well and said, almost too casually, "Oh, there are no servants this weekend. It's just us. All alone out here, where we can get up to whatever it is we want to do."

Then she looked at me. Not flirtatiously. Not playfully. She looked right through me and asked,

"And what is it that *you* want to get up to?"

I held her gaze with as much stillness as I could manage. Let the tension settle between us, heavy and full of possibility. Then I let my voice drop—just slightly deeper, just enough to shift the entire dynamic in the space.

"Then you can be my servant this weekend," I said. "Would you like that?" I whispered it, close and sure.

She looked at me like I had just spoken some ancient spell, the kind of phrase that bypasses logic and goes straight to the hips. Her lips parted. She didn't answer.

So I gave her the words. "Just say yes, Belle."

She lowered her eyes. Then she leaned in, slow and deliberate, until her mouth brushed the edge of my ear. "Yes, Belle," she whispered.

Her voice held a kind of gravity, the kind that settles deep and doesn't move. She knew exactly what she was saying and exactly who she was saying it to.

The room she gave me was lovely—cottagey, soft, the kind of place with plush bedding and more throw pillows than anyone would ever need. But notably, I was alone. That made sense. We hadn't crossed that threshold. Yet.

But, I wanted to test the air.

Her room was next door—of course—and massive. It had views of the bay, antique furniture, and nautical touches that screamed of generational wealth, along with a king-sized four-poster bed with a canopy that belonged in a movie about old money and mistresses.

She was there when I walked in. Sitting quietly on the edge of the bed like she'd been waiting for me, hands folded, eyes low.

No words.

So I made a decision.

I stepped toward her, slowly, deliberately. She didn't move. Her eyes lifted just as I stood in front of her, her gaze level with my navel. I ran my fingers through her hair and gently but firmly gripped a handful.

Her breath hitched.

"Are you waiting for me to decide what happens next?" I asked, voice low, just above a whisper.

"Yes," she said.

"Well, then," I murmured. "Let's make it worth the wait."

I gathered her hair low at the base of her neck and angled her head back slowly. I kissed her there, just beneath the ear, with pressure and presence.

She let go of whatever she had been holding. Her breath shifted. Her posture changed. She leaned in like she had finally been granted the thing she wasn't sure she was allowed to want. Her knees adjusted. Her spine released. The tension dropped from her shoulders like it had been waiting for permission to leave.

She was ready. Primed. Looking for her little adventure, and apparently, I was her toy for the weekend. And honestly? That was fine. Who says no to a beautiful woman, a political dynasty, and a delicious little secret?

I wasn't about to break out the flogger and bend her over the nearest piece of furniture, some antique showpiece that probably has a name I'll never know and a provenance longer than most marriages.

I nodded and looked around. Quiet house. Expensive furniture. Clean. Designed to look effortless. She sat in front of me like she didn't know what to do next, which meant she knew exactly what she wanted and was waiting for permission.

"I can make you very comfortable," she said. The kind of line that could mean guest towels and spa water. Or a paid-for apartment in Dupont Circle, a Mercedes-Benz, and a bank account that receives a deposit from a trust account with a name entirely unconnected from her dynastic name.

"Shh. I am in control now." I walked past her, into the sitting area, and sat down like I owned the place. "Take off your clothes."

She inhaled just slightly. Then she reached for the top button of her blouse and began to undress. Slow, deliberate, waiting for a reaction that I hadn't given her yet.

When she stood naked in front of me, she didn't posture. She just stood, eyes alert, hands loose at her sides. Her body was athletic, sculpted, but there was a softness to her hips, a weight to the way she carried herself that suggested control had always been the game. And she was tired of holding it.

"I can do anything you want," she said. Her voice wasn't sultry.

"I know you can." I rose and walked toward her. I didn't touch her at first. Just circled her, slowly. Let her feel the attention. Let her know she had been seen, and that being seen wasn't always comfortable.

I reached out and ran my fingers along her collarbone. I traced one hand down her shoulder, across her arm, and let the other press gently to her belly. I didn't grope. I touched the way a curator might inspect a rare object, noting every line, every detail.

I circled one hand around her breast, then touched her hip and slid my thumb over the inside of her thigh. Nothing to interpret. Just the contact of someone taking a complete inventory.

"You are exquisitely made," I said, calm and confident. "You were born to be adored."

Her throat moved like she was swallowing something heavy. Her hands twitched slightly, as if they weren't sure whether to reach for me or clasp each other.

"You don't have to prove anything here," I said. "You're already enough."

Her eyes flooded. She tried to blink it back. I let her have the silence.

I touched her cheek, then tilted her chin toward me. "You're beautiful when you cry. You know that?"

She nodded once, but her breath broke halfway through.

"Good girl," I said. "Now, stand still. I'm not done looking at you yet."

She tried to recover. Straightened her spine just slightly, then softened again as if remembering where she was. Where she wasn't in charge.

"We can talk about this later, can't we?" Her voice dropped into something warmer. "Isn't there something you want to do to me now?"

I turned and gave her the kind of look that makes people forget how to speak. Let the stillness do most of the work. Then I answered, quietly but with no room for negotiation.

"Stop asking questions."

Another rich bitch with a schedule to keep and a fantasy to fulfill. No staff for the weekend, just me, brought in like a specialist. She cleared her calendar for it. Friends arriving later, obligations postponed, but right now? She wants to come before the wine has time to breathe. That's the part they never say out loud. The richer they are, the faster the panties fall. They want rules. They want orders. They want to be told when they can speak and what they're allowed to feel.

And she'll love it. They all do.

"Touch yourself."

Her hand moved without hesitation, but her posture collapsed almost immediately—knees softening, shoulders rounding, breath escaping like she had already forgotten who she was standing in front of.

"No."

I stepped in behind her and straightened her spine with the flat of my palm.

"Head up. Shoulders back. Chin level."

She adjusted.

"Keep your legs straight. Ankles firm. I don't want to see your knees buckle."

She nodded.

"I didn't ask for a response. Stillness means stillness, that includes your head."

Her fingers resumed their motion, tentative at first, then faster, trying to find rhythm. Her hips began to tilt forward.

"Stop leaning. Square your hips. Center your weight."

She tried, but I saw it again—her right foot starting to shift.

"Plant your feet. Both. Flat. I don't care if it hurts."

Her jaw was tight now. Her whole body was tensed under the effort. She looked like someone trying not to fall, not to beg, not to break.

"You're curling again. Straighten your spine. Now."

She obeyed, but it came at a cost. Her hand hesitated for a moment before finding its way back to movement.

"Don't pause. Don't slow down. If you can't handle the position, I'll take the privilege away entirely."

She whimpered. I circled in front of her.

"Chin up. Keep your eyes forward. If you drop your gaze again, I'll bind your hands and make you watch me make someone else come."

She gasped. Not at the threat—at how badly she didn't want it to happen.

"You don't get to fall apart. Not yet. You stand up straight and you keep going."

She swayed slightly.

"Stop shifting. Lock your knees. I said still."

She was red now. Chest rising fast. Legs trembling. Tears brimming. Her hand moved faster out of panic than pleasure, desperation spiraling through her body while I gave her no room to hide in it.

"You're too loud. Keep your mouth shut. You don't moan unless I say."

Her lips sealed instantly.

"Good."

I moved close again and spoke just beside her cheek.

"Now breathe quieter. You're not a fucking animal. You want to come, then behave like someone worth watching."

Her entire body jerked once—her only mistake—and then steadied, even as the muscles in her thighs twitched and her fingers faltered from fatigue.

"Sloppy. That was lazy. Start again. Keep the pressure consistent."

She was shaking hard now. She adjusted. She obeyed. She kept going.

But she wasn't going to last.

I had no intention of letting her finish.

"Stop."

I said it loud enough to cut her wide open.

She froze, breath sharp, eyes wide and already glassy. Her hand hovered in place. Her body trembled like it had been caught mid-crash. She looked at me like she was about to cry—begging already without words.

I wasn't going to let her get away with silence.

"No. Say it. Use your words. Beg me."

She opened her mouth, choked once, then tried again. "Please—Belle, please, I need—"

"Louder. You think I can't hear you? You think I care what you need?"

"Please let me come—please—I'll do anything—"

I stepped in, close enough to see the sweat on her hairline.

"You'll do anything? Anything? That's cute. You think your desperation is special? You think you're the first rich bitch to fall apart in front of me like this? You get *nothing*."

She whimpered, shaking hard.

I kept going.

"You want to be used. You want to be ruined. You want to be my toy. Then say it. Scream it. *Beg me.*"

She sobbed.

I grabbed her chin, made her meet my eyes.

"You don't get to come. Not for me. Not even for yourself. I will leave you standing here with your thighs soaked and your dignity gone. I will leave you in this house, alone, aching, dripping, and silent. Do you understand me?"

She nodded, too afraid to speak now.

I didn't let her off the hook. "Say it. Tell me you understand." And then the house fell silent. One beat. Two.

Ding-dong. The doorbell rang.

She flinched again, harder this time.

I turned toward the sound, calm as glass. "Looks like the guests are here," I said. "Could be company. Could be an audience. Depends on how cooperative you are." I didn't wait for her to answer. I was already walking toward the door. Because now, finally, I was revved to go.

The other couple, D.C. power dykes. Names you might recognize if you read *The Hill* and *Politico.* Nothing personal, but the glances lingered longer than you'd expect from strangers. This meant they knew me, or were at least familiar with me. Still, it looked like a promising weekend.

The house had been pre-stocked by the house manager. Champagne in silver buckets, cheese boards that looked like magazine spreads, pastries lined up for morning, bagels, smoked salmon. This was wealth with foresight. That kind of planning only happens when you're used to having everything exactly how you want it.

Friday night

New Year's Eve was Saturday. We had a whole evening and a full day ahead, and I barely knew this woman. Didn't know these guests, and I was unprepared for what would unfold.

Wine came first, of course.

We gathered around the kitchen island—crackers, cheese, and someone pulled a baked Brie from the oven. Grapes, strawberries, olives. I plucked one of the big green olives with a pimento still inside, held it between my teeth.

"You watching?" I asked her.

My date nodded, slowly.

I used my tongue to dig out the pimento—slow, deliberate—and watched her reaction. Her jaw tightened. Her breath caught. She was hooked.

"Enthralled?" I teased.

"Jealous," she whispered.

We fed each other fruit. Strawberries and grapes passed from one set of lips to another. It was sweet, indulgent, just this side of dangerous. But there was still a question hanging in the air: Would this turn into a real party? Public performances? Partner-swapping? Or was everyone just here to flirt and drink?

No one had ended up spread-eagled on the buffet yet, but the night was young.

The Champagne—chilled and sharp—went down *way* too easily.

"I need a dip," I announced.

She cocked her head. "You're kidding. It's freezing."

"But the pool's heated, right?" I shrugged. "Run fast, jump in."

"I'll get my suit," she said.

But before I could even respond, the two other women—one a news anchor, the other, I think, a Phd—dropped their clothes right there in the kitchen.

Like, just—boom. Tits out. No warning.

I blinked.

"Oh," I said. "It's *that* kind of party. Got it."

She was already laughing. "Problem?"

"Not at all," I said, unzipping my boots. "Just clocking the room."

T-shirt. Jeans. Sweater. Off. No hesitation. My body, flawed or not, wasn't going to be hidden. I was all in now.

She stripped quickly behind me, and we bolted for the pool.

The water was *heaven.* I pulled her close and kissed her hard, right there in front of everyone.

The women brought out more wine. We drank it in the pool, hips brushing, fingers grazing. Someone fired up the jacuzzi, and we all shifted over. More wine. More fruit.

She fed me a grape. I licked her thumb.

"God, you're trouble," she whispered.

"And you love it," I said, wrapping her thigh around my waist.

She laughed and melted into me, her hands sliding over my breasts beneath the water.

If this was how Friday night started, I couldn't wait to see what New Year's Eve would bring.

The other couple. That's a story too. But let's say things didn't cool down anytime soon.

The couple in the jacuzzi with us was naked, but no one seemed inclined to swap or get performative. Which, frankly, was a relief. Because at that point, I still wasn't sure what the hell this weekend was supposed to be.

Someone *should've* explained the rules to me beforehand. But keeping me in the dark was part of her game. This may be something she does regularly. When you're that rich, that insulated, reality can blur. You start believing you can do anything, to anyone, whenever you want.

I'd disabuse her of that notion later, of course.

But for the moment? I was too drunk to leave. Too turned on to want to. The bubbles. The wine. The hot girl. The grapes. The *grin* she gave me. I could manage this.

The other couple brought us towels and robes—plush, obviously, like everything else in this house—and we wrapped up, heading back inside. I thought about showering off, but she took my hand and led me into her bedroom instead.

The primary suite.

Her plan, it turned out, was to shower me. Wash me down herself.

At first, I let her. The steam shower was enormous, featuring multiple jets, a bench, a rainfall head, and a handheld wand. She turned it on—the whole space filled with warm fog, cozy and close.

She started soaping me up—gently, reverently. Until she got just a little too bold, sliding her hand between my thighs like she was entitled.

I slapped her hand away.

"Uh-uh," I said, stepping in close, voice firm now. "No. I don't know what *you* had planned for this weekend, but your plan is over. I'm running this now."

She blinked. Stunned.

I tilted her chin up, eyes on mine. "You're used to being in control, aren't you?"

She nodded.

"Not here," I said. "Not with me. Nobody tells me what to do. Do you understand?"

A pause. Then: "Yes."

I leaned in. "Do you *agree* with what I'm saying? Is this what you want? Because if not, I'm more than happy to walk."

I was bluffing, sure—I was tipsy and wildly intrigued—but she didn't need to know that.

"I want to be of service," she said quietly. "That's what I want. I want to please you."

"Oh," I smiled. A service sub. "Now *that* I understand."

And it clicked. Not a masochist. Not a switch. A woman who needed purpose. Someone who wanted to be useful, helpful, and worshipful. My favorite kind.

"Soap me up," I said, reaching for the sponge she'd been holding.

She dipped the oversized natural sponge in the warm water and began washing me slowly and deliberately, as if I were something rare and irreplaceable.

She started with my shoulders, working her way down. Every inch. She took her time with my legs, her hands moving in soothing circles. She even cleaned between my toes, kneeling in the steam, hair damp and wild.

Then she poured shampoo into her palm—something expensive, lemon-rosemary—and started washing my hair. Twice. Massaging down to the roots with focused attention, as if she were cleansing more than just dirt and sweat. As if she were wiping away the world.

She rinsed with the handheld sprayer, carefully keeping the water from running into my eyes. Then she applied conditioner with that same devotion, working it through in long, patient strokes. I stood under the rain, letting it all cascade down my body as she wiped me with a washcloth, her touch feather-light.

It must've been an hour, just this. Just care. Just the kind of devotion you read about in fairy tales, if the fairy tale involved steam showers and very adult dynamics.

She toweled me off, wrapped me in one of those fluffy white robes, and only *then* ducked into the shower herself. Three minutes, tops. Efficient. Focused.

She emerged, wrapped in her robe, and walked me back into the bedroom.

"Would you like a massage?" she asked, her voice lower now. Softer.

I smiled. "I could get used to this."

The bedroom was warm, dimly lit by two low lamps and she lit the prepared fire, now it was crackling in the old stone hearth. The king-sized bed looked like something out of a gothic romance novel—four-poster, carved wood, swathed in soft linens and a velvet coverlet that practically begged you to ruin it.

She gestured for me to lie down. I dropped the robe slowly, letting it slip off my shoulders like silk, and stretched across the center of the bed. She took a bottle of oil from the nightstand—of course, she had oil, this was a woman who planned everything—and warmed it in her hands.

"Tell me if it's too much," she murmured.

"I'll tell you if it's not enough," I shot back, smirking.

That earned a flicker of a grin. She climbed onto the bed, straddling my thighs, and began with my shoulders, pressing her palms into my skin in slow, wide circles. Her touch was firm, practiced. I could tell she was trying to impress me.

"Where did you learn this?" I asked, half curious, half teasing.

"Ex-girlfriend," she said.

"Oh? And how did that end?"

"I still have the massage oil. She doesn't have me."

I chuckled.

She worked her way down my back, gliding over my spine, pausing now and again to knead a knot or press into a pressure point. I let my head drop into the pillow, eyes closed, breath slowing with each pass of her hands.

She leaned in and whispered in my ear, "You like that?"

"I like you, quiet and obedient," I said, not opening my eyes. "Keep going."

And she did. Down my lower back, over my hips, her fingers sliding under my waist, dragging the oil over my thighs. She moved slowly, reverently, as if touching me was her most incredible privilege.

"You smell amazing," she said, her voice a little hoarse now.

"I taste even better."

A beat passed.

She leaned forward, her lips just grazing my shoulder. "Do I have permission?"

"I'll let you know when you've earned it."

That got a little whimper out of her. She resumed her massage, adding a little more pressure, a little more speed. She was wound up, I could feel it in her hands, and the idea that I was keeping her from what she wanted made me smile.

When she reached my calves, I flexed under her, arching my back just slightly.

"Now." I murmured.

She paused.

"I want to worship you," she whispered.

"Then start."

I flipped over in one smooth motion, watching the hunger rise behind her eyes. My legs parted just a little, invitation and command rolled into one.

She lowered herself between them, almost reverently. Her lips brushed the inside of my thigh, then again, closer now, following the slick trail of her massage oil, kissing, tasting, slowing the rhythm to a crawl to torment herself.

I grabbed a fistful of her hair. "Don't make me beg for what you're already dying to do."

She moaned softly. "Yes, Belle."

And then she finally put her mouth on me.

She didn't need training. She was already excellent.

My hips rolled forward as her tongue circled, teased, then pressed. She kept one hand on my thigh, the other on my hip, anchoring herself in service, as if the act of giving me pleasure was a sacrament. I bucked against her, pulled her deeper, held her in place with firm fingers in her curls.

"Don't stop," I said. "Don't you dare stop."

And she didn't.

Not until my whole body tensed, arched, and then shattered beneath her.

When I finally opened my eyes, she was still on her knees at the edge of the bed, looking up at me, her lips slick, her cheeks flushed, and something like awe in her eyes.

"You're going to stay down there for a while," I said, voice low.

"Yes, Belle," she whispered, breath catching.

"And next," I added, "you're going to thank me with your whole body."

Her smile was radiant.

"I was hoping you'd say that."

When I let myself come again, it hit like a break in a dam. My body arched. My hands clenched the sheets. I cried out once, loud enough to echo off the walls, and then again when the second wave tore through me even harder. She had watched the whole thing unfold from her knees, her lips on my lips, her face flushed with wonder. She did not move. She did not dare.

I let the orgasms stretch through me, savoring it, letting it empty me and refill me with something sharper.

When my breathing slowed, I looked down and met her eyes.

"Now crawl," I said, voice still low but rougher now. "up here. Slowly. Show me how grateful you are."

She moved like she'd been starved for permission. Every inch forward was deliberate, her hips swaying, her breasts brushing against the sheets as she climbed. When she reached me, I held her there with just a look. Her breathing was shallow and ragged.

"Straddle my face."

She hesitated just long enough for me to slap her thigh.

"Now."

Her legs trembled as she obeyed, knees planting on either side of my head, her body hovering above me. I didn't move. Not yet. I let the waiting make her squirm. Let her feel the weight of being seen like that.

"Sit."

She sank with a moan. I slid my tongue along her folds, slow and steady, until she gasped, and her hands flew to the headboard to steady herself. I teased her like I had all the time in the world.

She was already soaked, the taste of her slick on my tongue. I circled her clit, soft at first, then firmer, then rough. She ground down harder, riding my mouth like she had something to prove.

I reached up and grabbed her ass with both hands, spreading her wider, digging my nails in deep until she cried out. I didn't stop. I held her like that, pulled her tighter, sucked her clit with the pressure she craved, and let her fall apart right there.

She screamed when she came. It was not a polite sound. It was wild, raw, almost feral. Her thighs shook. Her whole body arched. She came so hard I could feel it in the way she convulsed against my mouth, in the flood of slickness, in the way she kept trying to pull away even as I held her down and kept going.

She begged me to stop. I didn't. Not until she was gasping, pleading, clawing at the wall behind the bed.

Then and only then did I let her up.

Friday Evening

We came down the stairs to the smell of pizza—hot crust, roasted garlic, a hint of something sweet like balsamic glaze or caramelized onions. The kitchen was already humming. Music played low from a speaker on the windowsill. Wine glasses clinked. The light had that soft, gold quality that made everything look intentional, even the mess.

The island was covered in butcher paper, hand-labeled in thick black marker. "Margherita." "Hot honey and soppressata." "White pie with thyme." "Caramelized onion and goat cheese." Crumbs and oil stains had already taken over the corners. Stray basil leaves clung to the edges of the counter.

The couple was near the oven, glancing up as we walked in. The reporter was the first to speak. She was tall and clean-lined, wearing a silk blouse like she'd come straight from set but rolled her sleeves with purpose. She slid a bubbling pie out of the oven and spun it onto a wooden board like she'd practiced it for the camera. Her voice had that polish—the cadence, the projection—but her posture had gone loose with wine and comfort.

"Perfect timing," she said. "This one just came out. Four cheese with truffle. Still too hot to touch, but no one here's been waiting."

Next to her, the PhD leaned back against the counter with a glass of red in hand. She was dressed like someone who didn't care what anyone thought about how she dressed. Slouchy sweater, no shoes, curls pulled back into something functional. Her expression was amused, like she was keeping score in a private game.

"She's been performing since bottle one," the PhD said, not unkindly.

The reporter laughed. "I like an audience. Someone has to make sure the pies get photographed before they disappear."

"No pictures. We agreed," my blind date insisted.

A massive salad sat in a deep wooden bowl on the table—romaine, fennel, orange segments, mozzarella, toasted pine nuts. The dressing clung in glossy ribbons, glinting under the lights.

At the end of the table, dessert had already been started. A bowl of melted dark chocolate sat in a shallow dish warmed by a tea candle, with halved strawberries, sliced apples, and a few marshmallows arranged around it. One strawberry had been dipped, bitten, and left, the stem resting on a napkin like someone had been distracted mid-decision.

There were no formal seats. Just open chairs, full plates, scattered linen napkins, and butcher paper curling up at the edges. The wine bottles were already half-empty, the corks collected in a dish by the sink.

The reporter handed us glasses without asking what we liked.

"Get in there before the good ones are gone," she said, nodding toward the pizzas. "Though it's been a running argument about what counts as good."

The PhD met my eyes for a long moment and didn't smile.

"I've yet to be convinced," she said. "But I'm open to persuasion."

"Yes, you are," the news anchor, kissing her partner on the lips in a kissing sneak attack.

There was something in the way she said it. Not quite an invitation, not yet. But not closed off either.

I took notes.

The reporter was halfway through a story about an off-the-record embassy party in Kalorama, and the PhD was laughing into her glass, already a little pink from the wine.

Chesapeake wasn't laughing.

She shifted beside me, posture rigid, lips pursed into a silent protest that didn't stay silent long.

"I'm ready to go upstairs now," she said, with the artificial sweetness of someone who thought that volume and charm could substitute for authority.

I didn't respond. I placed my glass back on the counter and wiped a smear of oil from my thumb with the edge of a napkin.

"Belle." Her voice sharpened. "Take me upstairs."

I turned my head slowly. My voice stayed soft, almost gentle. "You're welcome to go upstairs if you'd like. I'll join you when I'm ready."

Her mouth opened, then closed again, as if searching for the retort that would land. But there wasn't one that would work here. Not with me. Not tonight.

She stood abruptly, chair scraping hard against the tile. It caught the edge of the butcher paper, sending a half-eaten pizza slice skidding onto the floor. Her cloth napkin fluttered down after it, as though it, too, had had enough of her.

"Upstairs," she snapped, planting a hand on her hip, "NOW!"

The room froze. No one breathed. The others turned toward their plates, pretending to be fascinated by olives or crust or the edge of their glasses. But the tension crackled through the air like a live wire.

I turned to her. I looked her dead in the eye and let every inch of control, every ounce of authority I owned settle into my voice.

"Veruca, you go upstairs now," I said, low and final. "And I will join you, if I want to." Referencing the demanding child from *Charlie and the Chocolate Factory.*

No room for negotiation. No warmth. She could storm and stomp and huff all she wanted, but this was not her scene to direct.

For a second, she just stood there, blinking—caught between the shock of being denied and the slow realization that she was outmatched. Her shoulders tight, spine rigid, each step louder than the last. She stormed toward the stairs because she wanted a reaction from me. The others kept their faces polite. They had the good sense not to intervene.

I didn't flinch. I reached for the wine bottle, refilled my glass with care, and said only, "She'll be fine."

I didn't say it to anyone in particular, just softly, like a passing observation. The strawberry on her plate had started to bleed into the butcher paper.

I returned to the conversation without explaining, without apologizing, without offering a single excuse for her behavior or mine.

I knew she was upstairs waiting—anticipating—and that anticipation was part of the experience. I let twenty, maybe thirty minutes pass before I followed her.

When I finally came up, I opened the door slowly, and there she was: kneeling on the floor, arms raised, head bowed. Naked. Waiting. Just waiting.

We hadn't even discussed boundaries, limits, or safe words—nothing about what was okay, or what wasn't. So there wasn't much I could do except start from zero—command-based play only, no pain, no surprises. I had to guide her through every move, getting verbal and enthusiastic consent for each step. That's how it works when you're doing it right. Not everyone does, but I do.

I crouched down, took her face gently in my hand, and looked her in the eyes.

"So that tantrum downstairs...that was your idea of seduction?"

Chesapeake didn't speak. The intention was obvious now. The stunt with the pizza. The shouting. The dramatic exit. All of it staged to provoke, to stir something dark and urgent in me. I let the silence stretch.

"You thought you could get into my head with that?" I asked, voice calm, almost curious. "Maybe you'd stir something in me by throwing a fit in front of your friends and pouting on a bed like a punishment-hungry debutante?"

I stepped forward, slow and deliberate, with the weight of absolute clarity. "I don't think you know how far off you are. You thought you could manipulate me into wanting you. You thought this little spectacle would flip some switch."

Chesapeake shook her head once.

"You self-absorbed little Veruca. All that noise, all that effort...and you couldn't have picked a worse strategy." Another beat.

"You don't live in my head. You don't even have a key to the front gate."

I let her eyes sweep over me.

"If you ever want to get close to me, you'll have to start with something real. Because this?" she gestured toward her body, toward the silence, toward the whole performance, "this isn't anything I want to touch."

I stood still for a moment, then took a slow breath and let the silence settle over the room like a blade.

"How did you think this was going to go?" she asked, her voice low and level. "Did you imagine I'd come up here furious? Violent? That I'd grab you, pin you down, and fuck you until you cried out?"

I stepped to the edge of the bed, looking down at Chesapeake without a flicker of softness.

"Was that the deal? Was that what you were trying to trigger? Because if it was... I'll tell you now. I'm not even sure I want to touch you at all."

Chesapeake didn't answer. I didn't wait for one.

"Right now, you're not a partner. You're not a submissive. You're just a problem. One I have absolutely no interest in solving."

She crouched slightly, lowering my voice so there was no mistake.

"I don't know much about you, Chesapeake. I don't know who trained you. I don't know what you're into. But I am a woman of very precise appetites. I know what I want. I know what I don't. And right now? You're not useful to me."

She stood again, slow and deliberate, stepping back.

"Whatever you were before—whoever made you think this kind of behavior would earn you anything from someone like me—you need to let that go. All of it."

I moved toward the dresser and picked up her keys.

"If you want me to touch you tonight, you're going to have to make yourself into my fucking dream."

"You're going to do what I say. Exactly how I say it. Or I take my keys and walk out, and you can sit here with your perfect little pout and think about how badly you misjudged me."

I waited, one final breath, eyes on Chesapeake. "Your move."

"Yes," she said.

"Yes, *what?*"

"Yes, Belle"

Before I left, I turned to her. "I'm sleeping alone tonight. You'll have to earn your place in my bed."

She nodded. "Yes, Mistress."

And that was that.

She didn't come knocking. Part of me wished she had.

But still—it was a good night—a strong first showing. I curled into bed alone and fell asleep smiling.

There wasn't much more I could do at that point, so I slipped into sleep. The house was already quiet, hushed like a secret, and before I knew it, morning had arrived.

New Year's Eve Day

I got dressed, pulled on my bathrobe, and headed downstairs in search of coffee. A tiny part of me had expected her to leave a cup at my door, but it was still early. And, to be honest, the situation is unclear.

Downstairs, the house was still. No one else was awake yet. I made coffee, found a blanket, and wrapped myself in it as I sat out on the porch. It was cold, but the coffee kept me warm. The bay was blanketed in a soft morning fog that felt like possibility. I always loved this time of day—the quiet, the softness of a world not quite ready to start.

It was New Year's Eve. The last morning of the year. And after the way things started, I wasn't sure if I was even going to stay. I grabbed the paper and scanned it, ignoring the crossword for once. Not because I didn't want to do it, but because I didn't want anyone accusing me of getting a head start. I read the op-eds and let my mind drift. *The Washington Post* had plenty to say, as usual.

I heard movement inside and padded into the kitchen to refill my mug. She was there already, draped in a silky pajama set with a matching robe and slippers. She looked like something out of a 1950s pin-up calendar. She walked over to me and kissed me, dragging her hand over my chest with a lazy grin.

"That body isn't yours, you know," I teased, catching her wrist mid-grope. "It's mine. You only get to borrow it."

She smirked and replied, "Then I'll take very, very good care of it."

Still, there was a part of me that considered the gamble. If I stayed, some other personality would appear. One less self-conscious, more intentional. Someone worth the effort. But that kind of thinking is how people waste weekends, and wardrobes, and perfectly good rope. And I don't do charity work before I've had my coffee.

We waited on the porch for the others, sipping coffee, wrapped in quiet intimacy. That's when we finally started discussing what she wanted, what she liked, and what she'd experienced.

"There was someone before," she said, almost too casually. "A woman. She was my...dominant, I guess. A powerful thing. She liked control, but she didn't... she never got me off. Wouldn't go down on me. I didn't care. If I wanted to come, I had to do it myself."

I blinked. "She didn't care if you came?"

She shook her head. "Didn't want to. Said it wasn't her job."

I laughed. "Sounds like an underqualified manager with a God complex. Let me guess—she's got a LinkedIn profile full of job titles and not a single clue how to make a woman happy."

She looked at me, eyes sharp. "You're not wrong."

"Well," I said, stepping closer and placing a hand gently on her cheek, "if you want to be with me, you follow my rules. That means no texting, no random interruptions. No disappearing into your phone when I'm speaking. Got it?"

"Yes, Belle," she said softly.

"Good," I said. "Because if you don't follow my rules, I will leave. No second chances."

"I'll be good," she whispered. "I promise."

And just like that, the other couple trickled in. Chesapeake disappeared to the kitchen, bringing out premade platters. The kitchen filled with chatter and the clatter of bagels being toasted. Lox appeared. Platters were laid out. We drank more coffee, laughed, joked, and bickered over the crossword. I got a few good ones. She was impressed. I could hold my own, even among these high-powered dykes.

After breakfast, we broke off. Back in the bedroom, she followed me into the shower. I let her rewash me, with a slow, reverent touch. As the steam rose around us, I looked down and said, "You've been a good girl. I'm proud of you. Ready for your reward?"

She nodded eagerly. "Yes, Belle. Please."

"Then get to work. Make it count."

She knelt before me without hesitation, mouth and hands already in sync. Her tongue curled around my clit, her fingers deep and sure. She asked first. Always. Three fingers, rotating perfectly on my G-spot. Her lips—God, her lips—alternating between the tip of her tongue and the flat of it, building a rhythm that unraveled me.

She knew what she was doing. And she knew exactly who she was doing it for.

And I let her. I let her please me until I came, gripping the edge of the shower wall, her name tangled in a sigh of approval that echoed in the steam.

And I told her, like she needed to hear it: "Good girl."

Because she was, and she knew it.

I could stay in this dynamic forever. We finished the shower, and I crawled into her bed—well, onto her bed—and I told her to rub lotion into my body. Not like a massage, but just a lotioning session for me. I told her, "You're going to rub it in like you are a Russian aesthetician." She smiled, eager, and got to work.

"Want me to brush your hair too?" she asked.

"Obviously," I said. "You think I'm doing my hair before dinner? Try again."

She giggled and nodded. "Yes, Mistress."

That kind of attention, that level of care, of control—it was intoxicating. Just the feeling of the lotion on my skin, the weight of her hands, and the intimacy of it all. We continued to explore each other's bodies in small, tender ways. It wasn't about sex right then. It was about presence. About being seen, served, and savored.

New Year's Eve

I must have fallen asleep because I woke up just before dinner. I laughed to myself out loud, even then got up, went to my room, twisted my hair up, and put on a beautiful dress for New Year's Eve. I don't often wear girly things, but I can fill out a dress, and this little blue taffeta number—cocktail length, with no underwear and no bra—was built to slay.

"Let them stare," I said to my reflection, fluffing my curls. "Let them wonder."

I descended the stairs like a princess in a romantic novel. No—like the motherfucking queen.

At the bottom of the staircase, I was greeted by... a buffet. A very unusual buffet. There was my delightful little date, spread out like a delicacy, wrapped in Saran Wrap on the kitchen island. Her legs were wide open, her body on display.

"Happy New Year to me," I muttered, sipping the Champagne that had suddenly appeared in my hand, offered by one of the other women, completely naked except for a frilly apron and heels. "Oh, it's that kind of party."

Two tops. Two bottoms. I could feel the dynamics vibrating in the air like electricity.

"Dominants can smell each other," I said under my breath.

No one here could top me. That much was clear. And no one seemed to want to.

"Is this for everyone?" I asked, nodding toward the human buffet.

The PhD smiled. "Only if you say so."

I took another sip of Champagne. "For this weekend, she is."

I walked over to Chesapeake—my date, my beautiful display—and leaned down. I filled my mouth with Champagne, then kissed her, letting the liquid slip between us.

"You like this?" I whispered.

"Yes, Belle," she whispered back, breathless.

"My delightful little snack."

I dragged my hands down her arms, across her breasts—cool and flushed—and then lower, between her thighs. She was soaked.

"Maybe you like being on display," I teased.

She moaned in response. That was enough.

"Has everyone had a taste yet?" I asked the room.

Heads shook. "Not yet," someone said.

"Well, I guess it's time to share. But you only touch her with my permission. Understood?"

The other top nodded.

"Come on, blondie," I said to the Phd curvy bombshell across the room. "Let's see how you handle instructions."

She smirked and sauntered over, her body made my heart race.

"You're going to kiss her here," I said, pointing. "Gently. Show me you know how to behave."

The blonde obeyed.

And just like that, the real party began.

I walked her over to my date on the buffet and said, "Would you like to touch her? I think she would like that." Then I turned to my date. "Would you like that? Would you like her to touch you?"

She nodded.

"I need to see more enthusiasm. You know we're out in public. This is different."

"Yes, please," she said breathlessly.

"Good. I'd like you to kiss her first. Then I'd like you to go down on her—just a little. Would you be into that?"

She nodded again, but I caught the sparkle in her eyes this time. Her voice was low and sweet: "Yes, Belle."

"The buffet," I said with a wink to the blonde, "is open."

Watching her get kissed and touched by another woman was unexpectedly thrilling. There was something both generous and possessive in the act, like I was letting someone borrow a rare book with strict instructions: no creasing the pages.

I turned to the other bottom in the room, the newscaster—a brunette, athletic, built like an action hero. No bra, probably no panties, just fishnets and black boots that screamed Rocky Horror chic. She was intoxicating.

I leaned in, close behind her ear, and whispered, "Would you like a taste of my date, too?"

She inhaled sharply, then said, "I'd love that."

"Good," I said, taking her hand and leading her over. "Be sure you do a good job, but I don't want her to come. Look, here like you mean it—but the cherry is mine."

She smiled, a wicked thing. "Understood."

She kissed my girl, sucked her nipples, and slid down between her thighs. Chesapeake moaned, her legs trembling, wrapped tight in Saran Wrap but barely able to hold still.

The way my date responded to being on display—shivering under every touch, melting under every glance—maybe she liked being watched more than either of us had guessed.

The Newsie brunette finished, and I stepped in. I poured a little champagne into my mouth and leaned over, dripping it slowly onto her clit.

"You like that?"

She nodded, lips parted. "Yes, Belle."

I put my tongue on her. I teased her slowly at first, using the flat of my tongue and then just the tip, circling her clit while I slid two fingers inside her. I angled until I hit her G-spot, and she moaned loudly—louder than I expected. Within four minutes, she was coming, her body jerking under the wrap, head thrown back, calling my name in front of the room.

There was a moment of silence, like a beat held in a piece of music, and then conversation resumed as if nothing had happened. But the tension had shifted. Dominance, after all, is a kind of gravity—it pulls attention. I could feel eyes on me, and I didn't mind. Maybe they were impressed. Perhaps they were aroused. Maybe both.

I kissed her, then whispered, "You were a very good girl."

She smiled. It was both shy and radiant at the same time.

I poured myself another glass of champagne, grabbed a few crackers and cheese, and let her rest on the table, still bound, still radiant.

Dinner was about to start. I carefully cut her out of the wrap, helped her into her heels, and left her otherwise nude, which seemed to be the required uniform for subs at dinner. The apron, once charming, had disappeared somewhere.

I suggested to the blonde Phd, "Why don't we sit down to dinner while the bottoms do the serving? Let them sit at our feet—or stand behind us in case we need anything. And if they're good, we'll feed them. But only if they do exactly what they're told."

There was a murmur of agreement. My date lit up at the idea, her body practically humming with anticipation.

It was going to be a very, very good evening.

Somebody had brought the candles and lit them on the dinner table. Bombshell waited at the table with Chesapeake and Newsie, naked except for their shoes, and got all the food to us. Once the table was set, I instructed Chesapeake and Newsie to remove the chairs, leaving only two for us. The subs remained standing beside their respective tops while we dined.

"This Bordeaux is excellent," sipping slowly.

"It pairs well with scandal," I said with a smirk.

Newsie and Chesapeake stood like obedient statues, each holding a slender tapered candle in both hands. They were to remain standing for the duration, arms up and candles steady, their only function to provide light. Their palms had started to redden from the heat. The wax had already begun dripping down their fingers, pooling at the webbing between them, running in rivulets down their wrists. Neither flinched. Not unless we allowed them to.

Chesapeake's arms were trembling just enough to draw my attention. I set down my fork, wiped my mouth with a linen napkin, and stood slowly. I did not speak to her. I simply reached out and took one of the candles from her shaking grip. She made a soft noise—not quite a gasp, not quite a moan—and stilled herself again. I tilted the candle just enough that the wax began to run freely.

She knew better than to drop her gaze.

I trailed the hot wax slowly across her collarbone first, watching her muscles jump. Then lower, across the tops of her breasts. Her nipples were already hard, anticipating what was coming, or maybe just aching from restraint. I brought the candle close—so close the flame kissed the air right above her skin—and tipped it again. A thick drop landed on her left nipple. She jolted. Not enough to move her feet, but enough for her knees to buckle slightly.

I said nothing. I simply let the wax drip again. And again. Until the entire tip of her breast was coated, pale and glossy, hardened into a swirl of heat and restraint. Then I shifted to the other side.

Across the table, Bombshell was watching with half-lidded eyes and a fork suspended in midair. Her steak was untouched. Her mouth twitched once, then she turned her attention to Newsie, who had already begun to squirm. Bombshell crooked one finger and beckoned her forward. Wordlessly, Newsie stepped away from her post and lay herself flat on the long, narrow dinner table, tucking her knees just enough to make room between the silver and porcelain.

"Don't spill the wine," Bombshell murmured, mostly to herself, and lifted one of the candles from the table.

The first pour was a punishment. She didn't test the heat or prepare herself. She simply let the wax fall in a thick stream down the center of Newsie's stomach. The girl cried out, arched up, legs kicking once before Bombshell pressed her hand flat over her navel and held her still.

"Oh no," she said gently. "You don't get to move. You wanted this."

Newsie whimpered. Her thighs flexed. She bit down hard on the corner of her lip, leaving a faint red imprint behind.

"You hold your position, or I'll find something more restrictive than dinner service to tie you to," Bombshell said, and her voice was all sugar.

I resumed my seat, let Chesapeake remain standing beside me with one candle, her nipples cooling beneath their shell of wax.

Bombshell poured another streak across Newsie's chest, this time over one breast, then the other, watching the way the wax spread and hardened as it touched her. Newsie gasped and moaned, but stayed flat. She kept her arms tucked obediently at her sides. Her eyes were wide open now, fixed on the ceiling, glassy and stunned. She wasn't blinking.

"You wanted to be on display," Bombshell said lightly, almost as though she were explaining something to a curious guest. "You get to be the centerpiece now."

She traced a fingertip through the wax on Newsie's sternum, letting it crack and crumble just slightly, revealing the flushed skin beneath. Then she leaned down and licked a clean line through it.

Chesapeake shifted beside me, legs clenching together.

"Feet flat," I said to her calmly. "Unless you want your turn on the table."

She swallowed and straightened her stance.

Wax continued to drip. Onto skin, into wine glasses, across the tablecloth. It had become part of the meal. A seasoning. A ritual. And we were nowhere near dessert.

The next course was almost as intriguing.

There was a lot of conversation, as there always is in D.C.—political intrigue, gossip, whispered truths. "Did you know so-and-so is two steps ahead of the FBI?" "That one's screwing her intern." The usual. The subs had to stand there, silent, observing, occasionally shifting their weight in anticipation.

I took a cherry tomato from my salad, rubbed it lightly along my date's clit—testing the waters—and found her very much aroused. With a teasing grin, I slipped the tomato inside her. Then another. Not too far, just at the entrance, right where it would keep her attention. If I was right, it was resting against her G-spot.

"Hold these for me," I murmured to her.

For dessert, I planned to retrieve them.

As the champagne was poured, I had Chesapeake clear the plates. Bombshell dragged her fingers down her sub's back as she passed.

I pulled my girl over my knee and gave her a sharp spank. The tomatoes popped out at just the right moment. Everyone noticed.

"You didn't hold them, pet," I whispered. "That was your only task."

I had her bend over like a misbehaving child, her hands on her ankles, ass and pussy displayed. She flushed beautifully and stayed perfectly still.

"You adore this, don't you?" I asked, trailing some softened butter between her legs.

She whimpered.

"That wasn't a no."

I licked it away without letting her come. The anticipation was delicious for both of us.

Bombshell followed suit with her sub, perhaps in solidarity, or maybe because I'd taken the lead and they liked the structure.

After dinner, we moved into the den. The space featured a large L-shaped couch and coffee tables—a kind of playpen for adults. Dessert was raspberry truffles, and I had an idea.

I laid my date down on the coffee table and arranged the truffles along her body—on her thighs, her breasts, even one resting just above her clit.

"No hands," I said. "That's the rule."

Bombshelle joined, licking dessert Chesapeake, tongues chasing chocolate as it melted. Newsie took a turn as she cleaned her belly button with a delicate flick of the tongue.

"This is the most fun I've had with sugar," Bombshell said.

When the music came on, Erasure's "I Love to Hate You" started playing. I couldn't resist.

"Come on," I told my date, hauling her to her feet.

She was still sticky from dessert but smiling wildly.

"Do you tango?" I asked.

"Not really," she said, laughing.

"That's fine. You have to follow."

I guided her into position, holding her tightly, one hand on her waist, the other at the small of her back.

"Step, step, turn," I whispered.

She followed, clumsy at first, but then—something clicked. We kept it simple: a few dips, a slow spin. Nothing fancy, just a connection. The feel of her body against mine, the way she relaxed into the rhythm—it was bliss.

The others watched. Some seemed curious or jealous. I didn't mind either way.

"You're showing off," Chesapeake teased.

"I am showing you off." I said, twirling her again.

Dancing with someone who would do anything for you, who was grateful for every second—it's kind of aphrodisiac.

New Year's Eve was just getting started.

My date looked incredibly hot, and I felt powerful and deeply appreciative. I dipped her low on the dance floor, dragging my hand down her thigh. She quivered. I spun her and dragged my leg up along hers. When the song ended, I stopped. She gave me that look—the one when your eyes meet on the dance floor and the only word unspoken between you is *yes.*

There was still plenty of evening left. I wasn't in a rush to race upstairs or dive into some spontaneous group scene—those things come with complications, and I prefer to negotiate those kinds of escapades in advance. Still, the night had already taken a wild turn, and I was only a glass and a half in.

Back in the kitchen, someone had laid out an assortment of toys—dildos, vibrators, even a sex swing. Floggers, too. This party was evolving into something else—a new level. I didn't know these people well—barely knew my date, honestly—and I was already violating her in six ways. But something about the atmosphere gave me this regal, devil-may-care air. Like I could get away with anything I wanted. I grabbed one of the floggers and gave it a few experimental swoops against a pillow, partly to test it, partly to announce myself.

"Showtime?" someone asked, raising a brow.

I smiled. "Maybe. Depends on whether anyone wants to play."

I wasn't there to dominate strangers coldly. I wanted to see who was open, who was curious. And more importantly, who understood the rules? I don't touch anyone unless I know what they're into. Who their partners are. Whether they want to be touched at all.

Still, I felt comfortable with the flogger in hand. It was soft leather—ideal for beginners or a showy warm-up. I can make a flogger dance smoothly and slowly off the skin, or make it bite—depending on the distance, speed, and rhythm. This wasn't the implement you'd use for severe pain. And I wouldn't touch anything heavier without multiple consent conversations and plenty of trust. This was just for show.

The sound of the leather slapping the pillow got everyone's attention.

"Well then," said the blonde top, "I guess the party's started."

"Does anyone want a turn?" I asked, half-playful, half-dead serious.

To my surprise, all three lined up. There were some structural pillars we could use, and a few sets of soft cuffs nearby. But I started with Chesapeake. I walked up behind her, laid my hand gently on her neck, and leaned close.

"Is this what you want?" I whispered. "Do you want me to flog you? Do you want pain? Or pleasure? Or both?"

She nodded. "Both, Belle."

"I need a sign from you if you want to stop. Raise your hand. If that fails, say stop. Loud and clear. Got it?"

"Yes."

"Because this turns me on. You're doing this for me—it pleases me. Are you willing?"

She exhaled, trembling. "Yes."

"This is going to be a perfect New Year's Eve."

I started by dragging my hands down from her neck to her breasts, then down her back. I pulled her hips backward gently so her ass arched out, her heels helping the posture. Bent forward slightly, she was a vision.

And then, I began the rhythm.

Flog. Pause. Flog. Whisper. Flog. Praise.

A symphony for the skin.

Very, very light at first—the sound and anticipation mattered most. The flogger whispered across her back, butt, and thighs, just enough to flush the skin. Not enough to leave marks, just enough to tease. After a few minutes, I wanted to escalate the issue, but I also wanted to check in.

I stopped and walked over to her, gripping her throat gently—but with a touch of pressure. "Do you want more? Do you want it harder?"

She gasped, her words barely forming. "Fuck!"

"No," I said firmly. "You have to say it clearly. Say, 'I want more.' I won't do it unless you tell me to. I need your consent."

"Yes, please! I want more, Belle!"

"You are fucking hot." I backed up and slapped her ass with my open hand, then again, a bit harder, pushing the intensity to maybe thirty percent. Just enough to leave her aching for more, but not overwhelmed. When I'd had my fill of her—for now—I stepped back, unclipped the restraints, and said, "Who's next?"

Surprisingly—or maybe not—both the blonde and the brunette raised their hands. I pointed to the blonde first.

As she walked over, I took her chin in my hand. "Are you ready for this? Do you want my style? Do you want me to flog you? Tell me where you want to feel it."

She nodded. "Yes, Belle. On my back. On my thighs. Wherever you want."

I smirked. "Good answer."

I ran my hand from her waist up to her neck and back down again, enjoying the way her body responded. I pulled at her hips, turning her just the right way, making her stand properly, then smacked her ass.

It was a gorgeous ass—round, high, and begging for attention. She was curvy in all the right places. I couldn't help but wonder what kind of domme she was to Newsie. Maybe they were into switching? D.C.'s full of surprises.

I could feel Chesapeake's eyes on me, and sure enough, she was pouting from across the room. Jealousy looked good on her, but this wasn't the time. I gave her a hard look, just a tilt of my head, and she dropped to her knees in a heartbeat.

That's right.

"Don't brat out on me now," I said sharply. "This is not how the evening's going to go. You brought me here. This is *my* playtime. If you want to sulk, go do it upstairs by yourself."

I dismissed the blonde reluctantly—she was fun—and called over the brunette.

She was lean and toned, all long lines and muscles. I guessed she did Pilates or yoga religiously. As I started to flog her, I noticed the way her ass tensed and released with each strike. She was built like a dancer. My mouth practically watered.

My mind wandered for a split second—could I get the blonde *and* the brunette in bed tonight? What would I do with my bratty little date? Maybe make her watch? That could be punishment enough. But I wasn't feeling that petty or cruel. Not yet.

She laughed nervously, but didn't move. Maybe she was too proud. Whatever the reason, I didn't push it.

Eventually, we retired to the den, sprawling on a giant couch that doubled as a bed. The TV was on, playing the New Year's Rockin' Eve countdown. All the toys had been brought and arranged neatly on the coffee table.

Just in case someone wanted to end the year with a bang. And I certainly did.

I brought back my date, who was being a little bratty at that point, and had her sit next to me. I wrapped my arm around her and gave her a soft kiss behind the ear before leaning in and whispering, "You're not done yet, are you?" She shook her head no, almost breathless.

"Good," I said, sliding my hand down her thigh. "Then get under my skirt. Show them how obedient you can be."

Without hesitation, she crawled under the hem of my dress and began to go down on me right there on the velveteen sofa. The other women barely blinked. Some smiled, and one poured another glass of wine. It was exhilarating to be so seen—on display like that, to be desired openly.

But I wasn't finished. I called out across the room, "Anyone else care to join?"

The curvy blonde domme from earlier smirked and set her drink down. "I thought you'd never ask."

Within minutes, the scene unfolded into a slow-burning orgy. My date was still beneath me, her tongue working expertly, and I could barely catch my breath when the blonde domme knelt behind me, her fingers tracing lazy lines along my back.

"Mind if I touch you too?" she asked, already pressing her mouth against my shoulder.

"Only if you behave," I teased, biting my lip.

She slid in beside me, and suddenly I was being worshipped on all sides. Newsie joined in, forming a sinuous, writhing heap of tangled limbs and gasps. One slid her hand into mine, guiding it to her breast. Another kissed the inside of my wrist.

My date, ever the good girl, kept her position while I was stroked and kissed from every direction. The couch turned into a theater of pleasure, the fireplace casting flickering shadows across our flushed, glistening skin.

"Harder," I commanded, gripping the edge of the cushion as my hips bucked forward. The blonde domme pulled my date up into her lap, kissing her while her hands explored every inch of her.

I was going to fuck in the New Year. No resolutions, no quiet reflection, just bodies, lube, and noise. Chesapeake went first. She straddled me and lowered herself onto a Silicone Steve—a realistic, uncut beast I picked for the evening. Because why not start the year with something a little over the top? The way she bounced on it, hungry and confident, it was almost ceremonial.

As the countdown started, I leaned in close and whispered in her ear. She was going to come at midnight. Not before. Not after. Exactly when the clock struck. I rubbed her clit hard and rotated her hips with my hands, guiding her in tight, agonizing circles. She was whimpering for seven seconds. At three, she was shaking. When the final cheer went up and the room exploded with noise, she let out a scream of her own and came hard, shuddering, collapsing onto the rug in a breathless heap. She'd done her job.

But I was just getting started.

Blondie was next. She was the type you just knew had a weekly CrossFit instructor who whispered in French and made house calls. Her body moved like it had been trained for this. Fluid. Responsive. Fuckable in every possible configuration. When I motioned her over, she didn't hesitate. She lay back on the coffee table with a little flourish, stretching out like she was modeling for a centerfold, one that somehow involved a lot of hardwood furniture and no shame at all.

I hooked her ankles and folded her legs back until her ankles pressed against her ears. She laughed, not nervous—excited—and held my gaze with something just a little bit cocky.

"You're flexible," I said, dryly.

She winked. "You're welcome."

I pulled a pillow off the couch and slipped it under the small of her back, elevating her hips until everything I wanted was on display. I poured lube into my palm, warmed it slightly with my fingers, then coated her slowly, generously, deliberately. She was already slick, but I wanted her slippery. Shiny. Ready.

For her, I chose a toy with a thicker base and a slow curve—designed to press and drag along every spot that could make her squirm. I pressed the head to her entrance and pushed in, watching her mouth drop open in a silent gasp. She arched into it, hips twitching upward, greedy for more. I paused just long enough to watch her settle around it, then eased deeper.

Her breath caught in her throat.

I started slow. Deep thrusts that made her body rise to meet me each time. I let her grind against the rhythm, let her find her own tempo before I retook control. She was vocal. Not just moaning, but allowing the words to spill—broken, needy, completely unfiltered.

"Oh god... fuck... please don't stop..."

Newsie moved in beside her, crouched low, holding Blondie's legs back by the ankles. Her mouth hovered just above one nipple, then the other, tongue flicking, lips tugging. Blondie's nipples turned hard as glass under the attention, and her whole body writhed between the two of us.

I picked up the pace, thrusting harder now, using the angle to grind right where I knew she was feeling it. Then I reached for the vibrator. I held it right on her clit and watched the change in her face. Her eyes snapped shut. Her back arched clean off the table.

She tried to say something, but it came out as a ragged scream instead.

She came hard, clenching around the toy so tightly I had to slow my movement just to stay buried in her. Her orgasm hit in waves—shuddering, panting, legs trembling under Newsie's grip. I didn't stop. I just eased off the vibe a little, dragging it in teasing circles, coaxing the aftershocks until she was gasping and writhing and finally swatting weakly at my hand.

Only then did I pull back. Blondie let her legs drop open, limp and shaking, her chest rising and falling like she'd just run a marathon.

"Holy shit," she said, somewhere between laughter and collapse.

And we weren't even halfway done. Then it was Newsie's turn.

She knelt between Chesapeake's thighs, already licking, already wet from watching. I bent her over from behind, lined up a longer, slimmer toy—my instinct said she was the type who liked precision over stretch—and eased in. She inhaled sharply and rolled her hips back, greedy for more. I was right. Blondie slid in beside us, humming and ready to play. I gave her the nod, and she started vibing Newsie's clit while I fucked her slowly, then hard.

There was a rhythm to it, each of us tuned to the others. A scene like something from a perfectly cast Swedish porno from the 1970s—collaborative, unhurried, slightly absurd in its athleticism but profoundly, beautifully effective.

Everyone was doing something. Touching, sucking, fucking, moaning. The room smelled like sweat, lube, and heat. I watched for a moment, still moving inside Newsie, letting myself feel it.

How often does something like this happen to a girl?

We completely ruined the sofa, which was unfortunate because it had been a lovely one. Chesapeake came first when I told her to. Then Blondie started riding Newsie's thigh like it owed her something, and I followed soon after. Everyone got their cookies except Blondie, but Newsie made up for it by going down on her while using one of those internal G-spot vibrators that should come with a warning label. It looked like a perfect time. I might get one for Valentine's Day—assuming I'm not bored with Chesapeake by then.

Then Chesapeake started getting bratty, saying she was going to go up the stairs. I was like, "Oh, so I fuck two other women and now you're going to act out?" Well, we'll see how that goes. She stormed upstairs, and after I came and helped the others finish off, I gathered up some toys and followed her.

I found her sulking and said, "Okay, it seems like you need my attention. Kneel. Now."

She dropped down, still pouting.

"Don't behave like that again," I said firmly. "You want to act like a brat, I'll treat you like one."

I bent her over the bed, slid my fingers inside her, and massaged her G-spot with deliberate strokes. I didn't touch her clit. "Do you feel that?" I asked. "Because it's going to stop if you don't change your attitude."

"No... I want more," she whispered.

I stopped, stood up, and lay down in bed while she stayed bent over the footboard.

"I'm going to sleep now. You can join me in bed—or stay there all night. But your attitude better be fixed."

She eventually crawled into bed, making herself as small as possible. I grabbed her hair gently. "Don't ever treat me like that, or you'll never touch me again."

She collapsed into my arms. I flipped her over, spooned her, and ran one hand over her breasts, the other down between her legs, circling her clit slowly. She moaned and pressed against me.

I didn't let her come. I got up, put on the complete harness and one of the bigger dildos, slicked it with lube, and returned to bed. I had her lift her top leg forward so I could slide into her.

Slowly, I began thrusting. She rocked her hips against mine, the rhythm growing deeper.

"You're going to come hard," I whispered in her ear. "And then we're going to keep going."

"Yes, Belle," she said, breathless and sweet.

I buried deep inside her, reached down to rub her clit, grabbed her breasts, and pressed her down onto me.

When she came, her whole body trembled. I didn't let her off me. I rolled her into reverse cowgirl and held her.

Then I started again. Sliding her up and down that massive dildo, watching her ass bounce, her body dripping with desire. I pulled her back into me, spooned her, fingered her clit again, then grabbed her hair.

"Is this the attention you wanted?" I growled. "You wanted me all to yourself, didn't you?"

"Yes," she gasped. "I don't want you touching anyone else. You are my whore."

"You can't afford me, bitch." I said as I fucked her even harder.

She turned to face me, with a mean look that I found hot, then climbed back on, riding me with that slow, intoxicating grind. She worked her hips perfectly, faster, deeper, slamming it down until it was buried inside her. I came hard, shivering beneath her.

I didn't bother to get her off.

New Year's Day

Rarely had the New Year felt so absolutely, deliciously full of promise.

Still hoping for breakfast in bed, which I didn't get, but I went downstairs in my bathrobe—retrieved from my room—and there was coffee waiting for me. My little date had been busy. She had breakfast laid out: coffee, lox, bagels, and the crossword puzzle folded open. I couldn't have been more thrilled with the arrangement.

We were alone in the kitchen. The others were still asleep or at least behind closed doors, and it felt like a little domestic vignette out of an alternate life. I wanted to make sure we were on the same page. It had been quite an epic night, and I wasn't sure how she was feeling about everything. We talked—honestly, gently, with more openness than I expected. She said she'd never felt so free, so unburdened, like she'd finally stepped into herself for the first time in years. That meant something. It did.

But calling me a whore was not the power move she thought it was. Maybe she really felt that I was her toy for the weekend. Or she was trying to be sexy. I am not sure I really cared that much.

I was planning on driving back early; she was going to stay through the weekend. The morning felt soft around the edges, but the ticking clock made everything feel just a little bit heavier. I kissed her. I grabbed her hair just a little—not for play, but as a small reminder of everything we'd shared. Then I told her to go upstairs, pack my bag neatly, and bring down an outfit for me. She ran upstairs, almost giddy, and returned with care: a denim jacket, a t-shirt, a pair of khakis, sneakers, and fresh underclothes.

I changed in the downstairs bath, brushing my teeth with the quiet concentration of someone trying not to think too hard. My hair was a mess—beyond salvaging with any brush or spray—so I twisted a scarf through it and let it be. I stared at myself for a long moment in the mirror. Then I exhaled. Hard.

At the front door, I looked at her. "I'm not going to get to say goodbye to everyone," I said, low and steady, "but I want you to know—I had a great time. It will be $10k for the weekend."

"You are still mad about that?" she quietly asked.

"Whores get paid. I only take cash."

"Look, I get it. You were offended." She countered.

"And if I am a whore, I am not *your* fucking whore." I said sternly.

I grabbed my bags and left.

A few days later, an attorney called and told me to swing by his office to pick up an envelope, so I went, curious, and inside was twenty thousand dollars in twenties from Chesapeake with a note that read, "Come back and I can set you up. I can take care of you." This is Washington, DC. These sorts of arrangements happen all the time. Influential people like to keep comfort on standby, and sometimes they lock in a longer arrangement because it is easier.

Who the hell did she think she was? I cannot be bought. I am my own woman. I make my own money. I pay my own rent. I have been taking care of myself my entire life. She thought she could buy my ass? Please. If there were ever a price—and there is not—it would be a hell of a lot higher than twenty grand. She could empty every trust fund, pawn off the family jewelry, and auction her Georgetown row house, and she still could not afford me.

26

Summer Session

People from all over DC either have beach houses, summer shares, or stay in hotels along the Delaware and Maryland shores. It does means crossing the Rubicon, the Chesapeake Bay Bridge, the scariest bridge I've ever driven, and then driving two hours through the countryside to reach the beach.

They go to frolic, drink and hook up with other DCists. In my earlier years, I started going to Dewey Beach, which was, at the time, the cheaper option. You could spend about $400 for an entire summer, visiting every other weekend or even weekdays. It was a place to gather with your friends, drink lots of beer, and recover on the beach all day. Some parts of it were just amazing.

If we left work early, we'd arrive around 2:00 pm or 3:00, just in time to drop our bags and head to The Lighthouse for what was promotionally known as the Taco Toss. It's where you find someone to hook up with for the weekend, have dollar tacos, two-dollar beers, and watch the sunset.

After tacos and beer, we'd head back, shower, and take a quick disco power nap before heading out dancing at Bottle n' Cork, a music venue affectionately known as Throttle and Pork.

We were all young, bikini-clad, and wore the trashiest dresses we could find. Every weekend, we danced, flirted mercilessly, and enjoyed desperate hookups on the beach and in dark corners of our sandy beach houses.

This is the story of one such hookup. He was incredibly handsome, tall, with black hair, and stayed in the townhouse next to mine, bay-side at Dewey Beach. He was a historian for one of the armed forces, though I won't say which. He was charming in his own way, loved dancing, and would spin me around the floor with the kind of flair that makes you laugh while you're trying not to fall. And then he took me to bed and kept going all night with the relentless enthusiasm only a man in his twenties can manage, much of it frantic, some of it fun, and not all of it good.

"Let's get some Dewey Devils," he'd say enthusiastically.

"God, those drinks are lethal," I'd laugh.

"That's the whole point," he'd grin. We'd pair them with Old Bay sprinkled baskets of peel-and-eat shrimp served ice-cold.

After a long beach day, sunburnt and salt-streaked, we'd drag ourselves back to the bar, half-dressed and sandy, to order those towering frozen concoctions with umbrellas, fruit slices, and way too much rum. We never learned moderation. We'd drink until the world went pleasantly hazy, until the music started to make sense again, until our skin was cool and sticky from sweat and salt and sugar.

Stumbling home, laughing too loudly, collapsing into the cool dark of the townhouse. We'd nap just long enough to reset, curled around each other in a tangle of limbs and damp towels, then wake up starving and aroused, always both. We made love slowly, lazily at first, then with a sudden urgency that felt like the last time, even though we both knew it wouldn't be.

Afterward, we'd rinse off, get dressed again, and head back out to the bars as if we were starting the night. Dancing until one, somehow still finding the energy. It was reckless. It was excessive. It was unsustainable. It was the perfect way to waste our youth.

We had almost no real responsibilities, though some of us had already bought houses and held incredibly demanding jobs. For the first time in our lives, though, we had flexibility. We had autonomy. We had weekends and evenings that belonged entirely to us, and we were starting to understand what that meant.

In another generation, we would have been married off by now. Tied down. Settling. But instead, we were living in this strange stretch of extended adolescence, drinking and dancing and reveling in the joy of simply being alive. Not trying to prove anything. Not chasing grades or internships or promotions.

We had already done all of that. We had landed the dream job, or at least found ourselves on the path toward it. The scramble of university was behind us. The hustle of our first year in the workforce was over. And now, the work came easily. We were good at what we did. So good, in fact, that we no longer had to push ourselves to the limit.

Yes, it was exciting. Yes, we were doing big things, working with serious people, building careers. But it was no longer about survival or striving. We had arrived at a kind of plateau, where the only thing left was to live for ourselves.

In that space, where ambition stopped being desperate and started feeling like a choice, we found a lightness. A freedom. Anything felt possible. We were surrounded by the kind of people who didn't just talk about ideas. They executed. They got things done.

We were golden, and we knew it.

Back in the city, we'd meet Sunday nights for dinner, maintaining a fascinating double life.

"Funny how we're like a normal couple at the beach," I'd tease him.

"And then we flip the switch," he'd respond eagerly.

Indeed, in the city, we'd slip into a dominant-submissive dynamic, and he was always incredibly eager to please. He had a house with a basement set up for our adventures. Our roles would shift as soon as we started the drive back from the beach.

"Can I call you Mistress now?" he'd ask, visibly aroused as soon as we hit the road.

"Maybe," I'd say coyly, placing my legs provocatively on the dashboard. "if you behave yourself."

"You're killing me," he'd groan, glancing over.

"Good," I'd reply, sliding my hand beneath my skirt, teasing him mercilessly. "Watch closely, but no touching."

"I can't control it," he'd admit breathlessly.

Sometimes we'd stop ostensibly for ice cream or soda, but mostly he'd reach over and get me off in the car.

He was young, feral, very muscular, and extremely tanned. He insisted on wearing board shorts, and his tan contrasted starkly with the bright white skin beneath, highlighting his rather substantial assets.

"You could never wear a Speedo," I'd laugh.

"Probably not," he'd reply, smirking. "As Burt Reynolds said, it'd be like stuffing two bowling balls into a marble sack."

We'd laugh together, entirely at ease, eagerly anticipating our next playful adventure.

He was talented in other ways as well. He was relentless, dedicated, and intense, especially when it came to going down on me. He loved to pick me up, physically lift me, and hold me in vertical positions while he ate me out. I'm talking full-body-lifted-off-the-floor action.

"Hold on to the chin-up bar," he'd say. It was mounted above the door in his room. I would, gripping it while he lifted me effortlessly.

"You like that?" he'd growl, his mouth already between my thighs.

"Don't stop. Don't ever stop," I'd moan.

He was that kind of man, dedicated to his work, but just as dedicated to his partner's pleasure. He adored being told what to do.

We did have a pair of handcuffs that we played with from time to time. Not that I needed to tie him down. If I told him to stay in a position, he'd hold it as long as I wanted, especially if it was anywhere near my body.

When we slept together, he was incredibly protective of me. He always took the side closest to the door, wrapping his arms around me at night. Before I even got into bed, he'd make sure there was a glass of water on my nightstand. It was just easy to be with him. He liked to please me.

His favorite thing in the world?

"Tie me down," he'd beg. "Use the ropes. I want you to ride me." I'd tie him tightly to the bed, climb on top, and ride him until I came, sometimes more than once. I'd leave him there, spent and waiting, until I was ready to do it again. It could go on for hours.

He was always ready. Just walking near him could get him hard. He liked being flat on his back. He liked being flat on his front, too, but that's another story.

He wanted my pleasure first. Always. And that dynamic? I liked it very much. It's not always easy to find.

Indeed, there are numerous service providers available. But he had a way of making it entirely about me. In a way, he was topping from the bottom, but if someone's making me come four or five times a night, I'm okay with that.

He also loved giving me long massages. I'm talking the kind you'd get at a spa. He had a massage table, fresh towels, crisp sheets, and he'd even spray them with lavender because he knew I liked the scent.

"Just lie down," he'd say. "I've got you."

He'd work my shoulders, my back, my thighs, my entire body, for as long as I wanted. And I often wanted.

Of course, I did have to sit through some of his sports obsessions in return. He was a diehard fan of one of the local teams. I didn't mind going to a game or two, but watching televised sports? Torture.

"Do I have to watch this again?" I'd ask, dramatically flopping on the couch.

"Come on," he'd say, laughing. "One inning. I'll give you a massage later."

"Make it an hour massage and I'll stay till the seventh."

"Deal."

He kept his word. Always. I made him promise I'd get a long massage every time I sat through a finale or playoffs.

When we got home from being apart, he'd kneel in front of me.

"May I serve you today?" he'd ask softly.

Sometimes I'd nod. Sometimes I'd say, "Make your case."

He'd rise to his feet and start doing things, massaging my feet, cooking dinner, setting the table. I never had to lift a finger in his house. I haven't even brought over a bag of groceries the entire summer. We weren't living together, but we spent Sunday nights together after the beach. Then we'd go our separate ways, and I'd go home. We'd meet again for drinks midweek, then I'd head back to the beach every other weekend.

Unfortunately, the romance only lasted a summer. But that was okay. It wasn't meant to last. We were a great couple in private, but in public, we were just... fine.

He was looking for a wife.

The wife he wanted was never going to be me. I knew it.

I didn't want to live in the dynamic full-time. I liked it as part of our sex life, not our whole life. There needed to be a separation. A clear line between the bedroom and the rest of the house. Eventually, if you have kids, how does that work? I know couples manage, but I didn't want that to affect my family life.

It's one thing to install trapezes and poles and do whatever you want in your sex life. But it needs to stay separate. He wanted someone who would live in that world with him, all the time.

Plus, he wasn't even sure he wanted kids. He was ambivalent about it, and for me, that was a red flag.

So, no, I didn't end up staying with him. But during that reckless, seashore-soaked summer of youth and possibility, we did the time. I was doing great work, climbing in my career, and so were my friends. We were all on the verge of something. It was such an excellent time to be young, stupid, hot, and brave, extended adolescence at its finest.

There was one time, just one, when the dynamic crept into the daylight. We were on the beach. We weren't in our roles, but it bled through. I gave him an order. Just a small one. Something silly. But I said it with that tone.

He paused, surprised. I paused, too.

"Oh," I said quickly, trying to cover, "that wasn't a-never mind."

But it was too late. He stood still, caught between play and public. He loved commands. He loved facing consequences.

Later that week, back in DC, we talked about it.

"It just slipped out," I told him. "It was a mistake."

He nodded. "But I liked it. I liked that you did it without even thinking."

"That's the problem," I said. "I didn't mean to. And if this starts creeping into the rest of life... I can't live like that."

He understood, but I could see the disappointment in his eyes.

"You need someone who wants to live this full-time," I said gently. "That's not me."

I wasn't the proper Mistress for him. I certainly wasn't the right wife.

I suppose the question is the same one *Sex and the City* posed years ago: can women date like men? Is it ethical? Does it matter if it is? Or are we just finally meeting men where they've always met us, willing to spend six months, a year, sometimes more, dating someone they already know they will never marry. They'll eat up your time, meet your friends, learn your favorite takeout order, sleep in your bed, and all the while know there's no future.

So when I do it, when I date someone I know isn't going to be forever, is that just equality? Or is it cruelty?

Did I lead him on?

He said he wanted marriage. He said he wanted me. But men say a lot of things. They say what they think they're supposed to say, what they think we want to hear. They say things they might even believe in the moment, until the moment passes. And how are you supposed to know what's real and what's performative? If you already assume men lie, and let's be honest, we're not pulling that belief out of thin air, then where's the line between skepticism and self-protection?

Was I supposed to take him at his word? Or was I supposed to clock the warning signs and pace myself accordingly?

It could be a summer thing. A fling. A beautiful body, a few shared routines, and some very good sex. Perhaps he was a somersault, not a soulmate. A little seasoning to make the season more interesting. And maybe that's not wrong. Possibly, he got precisely what he wanted, even if it wasn't forever.

But still, part of me wonders.

If he really did think I was going to be the love of his life, did I owe him more honesty? Or did he owe himself the clarity to ask more complex questions and believe the answers?

There's no universal rulebook. Just the tension between wanting what you want and trying not to hurt anyone in the process. I can tell you this much: whatever else he may have lacked, the man had *incredible* talent.

27

Close Quarters

He once told me there was a Harvard study that said the reason most people hook up in college is due to mathematical proximity—the number of times you run into someone in a hallway, in common areas, or out on the quad. You start seeing each other, flirting in passing, and eventually-proximity does its work.

But when that proximity disappears, does the fire stay? That was the question I turned over in my mind during the month and a half, during which I flirted with a particular neighbor who lived two floors down from me. Somehow, we always ended up in the same elevator.

A few embarrassing mornings stand out: once, he had a date leaving his apartment as I was heading out. Another time, I had a date leaving mine. He walked to the curb, all gentlemanly. I, on the other hand, timed it so the guy had to go.

He was charming—a lawyer, naturally. Not even a showy one. Just a solid, nice Harvard Law guy. Sweet, unassuming, kind. The type of man you'd never expect to do you wrong, though maybe not the type who made your pulse race. Still, over time, we kept seeing each other. We chatted, flirted, and lingered at mailboxes. But we never made actual plans. Until one day, we did.

We were walking into the building together when he turned to me and said, "I'd love to make plans with you."

"Like actual plans?" I asked.

"Like a real grown-up drink," he said.

So, we made them.

That first drink turned into dinner. Dinner turned into rooftop dates. Our building had this stunning deck with a view of all of D.C. monuments lit up, the Capitol dome gleaming. We'd hang out up there, sweaty from the day, sneaking wine into plastic water bottles and laughing too loudly. Sometimes we dipped in the pool. Sometimes we pretended not to.

It was peak D.C. summer rom-com energy.

He wasn't a gym rat or anything. Slim build. Maybe 5'10" or 5'11", I just assumed he lied about his height. But sweet. And funny. And genuinely charming.

One Saturday, we stretched out side-by-side on the pool loungers. I tried to read while he tried to distract me with crossword clues.

"Twelve across. Four-letter word. 'Blunt weapon used in medieval combat.'"

"M-A-C-E," I answered.

"Are you sure?"

"Never doubt me when it comes to words. One day, I will make a miserable living off what I write." I predicted.

"It doesn't fit."

"That is what you said last night, but it worked out fine after you relaxed a bit." I quipped back and gave him a teasing kiss.

He told stories about undergrad antics and law school parties. I teased him mercilessly for being in a frat. Excuse me, fraternity. As he would endlessly correct me. 'You don't call your country a cunt don't call your fraternity a frat.' Ugh. And these are the guys up in arms about pronouns?

"We weren't douchey, I swear."

"You say that, but now I can't unsee you in a comical t-shirt, cargo shorts, and boat shoes." I retorted.

"I'll have you know I only wore cargo shorts ironically," he lied.

"There is no such thing as ironic cargo shorts, Harvard." There I go dropping the H-bomb again. It's really only funny because I attended a low-cost state school, and he attended an Ivy League school, but in D.C., the only thing that matters is your ability to get people to do what you want, and I win that race.

We were tipsy, covered in sunscreen, chlorine, and late-July glow. After two hours of flirting, we were both ready to combust. He offered to carry my things back to my place—it was only a floor down—and I didn't stop him.

"You're coming in, right?" I asked, unlocking the door.

"Only if you promise not to beat me at another crossword."

"I promise to beat you, but only with a safeword and a clear consent path." Yes, I said that.

We made it about four steps before we were kissing and then stumbling toward the bed. Tangled in wet bathing suits and limbs. Everything smelled like wine, sunblock, and sweat.

"Condom?" I asked, already half out of my suit.

"I've got some... in my apartment," he admitted.

I rolled my eyes. "Of course you do."

He bolted—literally bolted—out of my apartment, down the hall, down two floors, and came back with a box of twenty.

"Twenty condoms, huh?"

"Just being optimistic."

"Twenty would be a personal best, but I am game. Bend over so we can get started. Just relax, it won't hurt as much as you think it will. Just bear down a bit." He thought I was joking.

He laughed and kissed me again. "Wait. What?"

He wasn't a natural bottom, which surprised me, being a blue blood from Harvard. All those guys are bottoms when they are with non-marriageable girls. Let me explain that.

The Ralph Lauren set tend to act one way to the girls they marry vs the boys, girls, theys and thems who they think about when they are fucking the ones they will marry. With the girls they marry, it is straight sex, nasty cunnilingus (which is a high crime and should be prosecutable), and unenthusiastic 2.5-minute blow jobs, if it is their birthday or anniversary.

I personally think it being chronically ignored by all those workaholic, cheating with the secretary, dad's who never saw their kids and the moms who never got over the fact that their husband would rather be fucking a farm animal than them. Consequently, they crave praise and attention from those who accept them despite their privileged upbringing and monstrous mounds of generational wealth. We all have our burdens to bear.

With my Ivy, I assumed that he had never ordered off the menu before, except that one time in college at the frat house where he had to give hand jobs to all his brothers through a glory hole. But what privileged boy hasn't? It is a rite of passage or a desperate attempt to gain love and acceptance from men that is the homoerotic core of Greek life.

I did notice that he was deeply service-oriented in our romantic fumblings thus far. I assumed that meant that the only love he got was from the nanny, and probably why, when he does get married to a respectable girl who went to Smith or Vassar, he will have kids that he will fuck the nanny on the washing machine during the spin cycle.

But all that was still years away when, at 35, he would marry a young lady 23-year-old fresh out of school who, for her sorority hazing week, had to go without makeup in public.

"What do you like?" he asked, breathless.

I grinned. "For you to do whatever the fuck I ask. Would you like that? And before you answer, know that your cock has already said yes." It responded enthusiastically. It even gave a little twitch, a hand raise, if you will, at the very thought of seeking servitude. Boys will be toys.

From there, well... proximity did its magic.

He was on a mission to get me off, which he gladly accepted. He was incredibly gifted with his mouth—he found my g-spot right away and worked it with reverence, like it was his life's calling. He'd cover my clit with his mouth, swirling his tongue around it, flicking at it just right, while his hand worked me from the inside. I didn't want him to come up for air. I didn't care if he suffocated down there. He would've died happy, and I wanted that for him. Death by muff diving. It almost sounds like a day trip one might arrange from Positano.

My legs clamped around his head, and I whispered, "Don't stop. Just go."

Clearly, this guy wanted to keep me happy—and that was one very effective way to do it.

After about two months of this cliff-diving-into-my-crotch situation, followed by me getting on top of him and him holding off—like seriously, he wouldn't come until I did at least once or twice—I started to wonder if he was even human. The control he had was superhuman. When I told him, "You can come now," he'd do it within a minute, like a well-trained show dog with stamina. It was incredible.

I told him once, "You would've made the best porn star."

He laughed and nuzzled into my neck. "You think they'd let me in just for eating pussy?"

"Yes," I replied, breathless. "They'd give you your category."

He wasn't even twenty-seven. Usually, guys that age lack control, but not him. He had the energy of a young lion, with the discipline of a tantric monk. I was hooked. We were like a bad French movie—cigarettes and red wine, our plans to go out always ending with us tangled on the couch.

He'd show up with a bottle of something good, which we would drink while he undressed me with his teeth. He'd go down on me until my head caved in. It was decadent.

Eventually, I wanted to introduce some light bondage. He was obliging. Attentive. Curious.

One night, I was on top and told him, "Grab the headboard."

He did.

I used a couple of scarves to tie his hands, straddled him, and just used him. "I don't care if you come," I said. "I'm going to come over and over again until I'm done."

He grinned. "Yes, Belle"

After that, I rented a porn with bondage elements and showed it to him. "Does this look good to you?" I asked.

He studied it. "Do I still get to fuck you?"

"Yes."

"Then tie me up. Let's go."

He was so agreeable. Adventurous. Eventually, I'd blindfold him and walk him into the living room, position him on the coffee table—what I called one of my altars—and tie him to it. Hands on the edge, feet braced, open to anything.

I'd tease him for hours. Kisses, nails, teeth. Flip him, spank him, bring out the riding crop. He adored it.

But what truly got him off was service. Giving. Pleasing. Worshipping.

He wanted to fuck me every which way. On road trips to Middleburg, we'd take country roads, and he'd beg, "Pull over. I want to go down on you. Right now."

I'd laugh. "We're in Virginia. I won't risk that."

"But it's for lovers!"

"Virginia is for straight, married lovers," I corrected.

Still, we did it. In the car, on the hood, under a long skirt. He'd crawl up into it like it was a portal to heaven.

He was the best oral I'd ever had—outside of women, of course—but among men? Unmatched. We went everywhere together. Dances. Balls. Events for his firm. And the whole time, we were grabbing at each other like teenagers, like our skin was the only oxygen.

I know some crazed newlyweds who just discovered what sex was, and we were definitely in that stage. One time I spilled champagne down my leg at a party—no tights, of course—and before I could react, he dropped to his knees and licked it up, slowly, all the way to the hem of my panties.

"Are you out of your mind?" I whispered, eyes darting around the crowded room.

"Completely," he said, his voice low and delicious. "But your legs taste like Moët."

I don't think anyone saw, but I wouldn't have cared. That night was wild.

He was a fantastic dancer, too. He'd spin me around like we were in a musical. So commanding. So confident.

"You look like trouble," he'd whisper in my ear mid-twirl.

"I *am* trouble," I'd whisper back.

We dated for about a year. Still kept our separate apartments. He was serious—or at least, he thought he was. He bought a condo four blocks away and asked me to move in with him.

"I love where we are," I told him. "But are we heading somewhere... specific?"

He blinked. "Like what?"

"Like a ring. A wedding date. A marriage license."

He smiled nervously. "I was thinking... maybe when I'm 31 or 32."

"What's magical about that age? Do you suddenly wake up husband-shaped at 31?"

He laughed but didn't answer. And I had to be blunt. "If you want to get married someday, maybe make me an offer *before* I move in."

He said he wasn't ready. I was. I didn't want to be the girl who got strung along. The one that is with him for years, and finally he begrudgingly says ok, gets her a shut-up ring, and then they break up, only to be engaged in a month to someone half her age.

So I ended it. Despite living four blocks apart, we somehow never saw each other again.

It was a shame. We had something real—hot, sweet, compatible. But he had this mental block, like he was always looking for the next phase instead of enjoying the one we were in. I hoped he found what he was looking for. I never checked.

Sometimes I wonder if I'm his "one that got away," or just the one who said no before things got too convenient. I can't prove this, but I am sure that while he is fucking the nanny, he thinks of me.

We saw each other daily for a year, slept in each other's beds more often than not, and shared our lives like it meant something. And maybe it did. But the course of true love doesn't always run smoothly. Sometimes, you meet the right person at the wrong time. Or he wasn't the right person at all.

Even now, I remember the sight of him between my thighs, champagne on his lips, and that look in his eyes like I was the only woman in the world. And honestly?

That memory alone might've been worth the heartbreak.

28

Epilogue

Now you know who I am. I have told you my stories. You have seen me naked in every way that matters, my heart and my body both laid bare. You know what I have done, what I have wanted, who I have wanted, and how I went after it.

You might admire me, or you might be clutching your pearls. Maybe you're somewhere in between, fascinated but unwilling to admit it. I am fine with any of it. The truth is, I have been called every name you can imagine, and the ones that were supposed to sting have never kept me awake at night. Whore. Slut. Loose. Fast. Promiscuous. Too much. Too experienced. Too picky. Too confident. Too old. Too young. Too everything. Men never get this list. Men are not told they have too many lovers; they are congratulated for it. They are "studs," "players," "ladies' men." Women are expected to sit on their hands and keep their knees together, and if they do not, they are told their worth has diminished with every kiss, every fuck, every adventure. I say the opposite is true.

Experience does not diminish you. It makes you incandescent. The more you have seen, felt, tasted, and risked, the more you understand what your body can do, what your heart can survive, and how both can still surprise you. That is what this book has been about—not a catalogue of conquests for the sake of bragging, but a map of my own education in desire. I have never believed in the myth of one perfect love, one perfect person, one soulmate ordained by fate and held onto until death do us part. That is a fairy tale written for the purpose of keeping people in line. Men are allowed to look, to sample, to fuck their way across their twenties and thirties and forties, and when they finally choose someone to marry, no one asks them for their "body count." They are assumed to have lived, and the living is considered an asset. They are worldly, experienced, charming, and dangerous. When is a woman experienced? We make up words to punish her. We make up rules to control her.

I have never followed those rules. That is what makes some people uncomfortable. And that is why I wrote this—to put the stories out where they cannot be taken back, to make sure another woman somewhere reads them and realizes she is not strange or wrong for wanting. Desire is not a crime. Curiosity is not a sin. And there is nothing wrong with being hungry for more.

Sex is a buffet, not a ration pack. No one says you must take everything, but why not at least look at what is on offer? You might discover something you never knew existed. I have stood at that buffet table and sampled widely—tastes I thought I would love but didn't, dishes I was certain would not be to my liking but surprised me. A sharp-tongued man who only melted when I had him tied to the headboard, begging. A young woman whose trembling stopped the second I slid my hand into her hair and told her exactly what to do. A non-binary lover who wanted to be worshipped until their voice broke. Men who wanted to be pegged until they were moaning into the pillow. Women who wanted to be punished until they cried. Lovers of every gender who had never been kissed slowly, as if their mouths were worth lingering over. People who wanted both worship and punishment in the same night. It does not make me less. It makes me fluent.

Let us be honest—most people have wants they will never confess to a spouse or a long-term partner. They will only tell a lover or someone who will not judge them. They are afraid. Afraid of rejection, terrified of being laughed at, afraid of being told they are somehow less.

But I will tell you something—there is not a person alive who does not want to feel truly desired. You can tie them up, ride them, whisper in their ear exactly what you plan to do. You can make them beg. You can make them earn it. You can tease them for hours, or take them fast and hard. If they do not light up at the thought, check them for a pulse.

If you have someone tonight, here is what I want you to do. Pour them a drink. Look them in the eye and say, low and certain, "I am going to have you." Touch their throat lightly with your fingers. Undo their belt, but do not take their pants off yet. Make them ask. And when they ask, make them repeat it. Then decide whether to give them what they want or make them wait until tomorrow. You will be shocked at how much control you have been sitting on all this time. Desire, freely given and freely taken, is the most intoxicating thing in the world. And when you match desire with desire, when you stop worrying about whether you will be judged for wanting, the game changes.

So, here is my advice: stop apologizing for your body, for your appetite, for your number. Your number is your history. It is your education. It is the proof that you have lived in your skin and claimed your joy. If you want more, go get more. If you have had enough, stop. If you want someone to kneel, tell them. If you want someone to tie you to the bed, ask for it. And if someone calls you a slut? Smile. You have just been recognized by a member of the Church of the Sexually Repressed, and their opinion is worth exactly nothing.

I will tell you one last secret before I go. I did find a love that lasted. I got married. We built a life together. Slowly, over time, the kind of love that grows deeper every day took root. It was not the first love I ever felt, and it will not be the last. That is another lie they tell women—that love comes only once, and if you miss it, you are doomed. I have fallen in love more times than I can count, and every single one of those loves mattered. They taught me how to live, how to want, how to stay, and sometimes, how to leave. So yes, I settled down. But settling down is not the same as settling for less.

I am still the person who walked through the marble corridors of Washington, D.C., in stilettos, with a flogger in my bag and a plan in my head. I am still the person who said yes when yes was right, and no when no was necessary. And I am still the person who will tell you, without shame, precisely what I want—and who I want it from. If you take anything from these pages, take this: love is too precious to be locked in one box and handed to one person for life. It is everywhere. It can be found in a stranger's gaze across a room, in a kiss that leaves you dizzy, in a night that you still think about years later. It can be found in a marriage, too—but it does not erase the loves that came before. Those are yours. Keep them. Cherish them. They are part of the whole.

The marble facades of this city hide more doors than you would ever guess. Behind them, people are waiting. Parties you cannot imagine. Rooms you will never forget. If you are fortunate, one night you will find yourself inside, and you will understand precisely what I mean.

Goodnight from Washington. I hope you make your own tales. And if you do... write to me. I want to hear everything.

www.ingramcontent.com/pod-product-compliance
Lightning Source LLC
Chambersburg PA
CBHW070645310726
48982CB00001B/422

* 9 7 9 8 9 8 9 1 2 6 4 7 7 *